Praise for

Bear with Me Now

"A funny, poignant, romantic exploration of mental health and of the way love can help us heal. Katie Shepard has a unique talent for mixing gentle humor, weighty topics, and swoony moments. You will fall in love with Darcy and Teagan on page one, and you will laugh and cry and cheer as they discover themselves and each other. A perfect, dazzling debut, and the start of my new favorite series! (And let's not forget the bear, the wolves, and all the otters. . . .)"

— Ali Hazelwood, *New York Times* bestselling author
of *Love, Theoretically*

"I didn't even have to play dead, because this book already killed me. Shepard's nuanced wit and vibrant prose sparkle off the page. Readers will go wild for this sexy and heartfelt romance between two unforgettable characters as they help each other make it out of the woods of life."

— Thea Guanzon, author of the Hurricane Wars trilogy

"Angsty, swoony, sharply written, and full of heart, *Bear with Me Now* is a deeply compassionate romance about finding love in the midst of profound struggles and vulnerabilities [and] discovering the gift of entrusting all of yourself to a worthy someone to love and be loved by in return."

— Chloe Liese, author of *Better Hate than Never*

T0005861

BERKLEY TITLES BY KATIE SHEPARD

Sweeten the Deal

Bear with Me Now

Sweeten the Deal

Katie Shepard

Berkley Romance

NEW YORK

BERKLEY ROMANCE
Published by Berkley
An imprint of Penguin Random House LLC
penguinrandomhouse.com

Library of Congress Cataloging-in-Publication Data

Names: Shepard, Katie, author.
Title: Sweeten the deal / Katie Shepard.
Description: First Edition. | New York : Berkley Romance, 2023.
Identifiers: LCCN 2023007760 (print) | LCCN 2023007761 (ebook) |
ISBN 9780593549315 (trade paperback) | ISBN 9780593549322 (ebook)
Subjects: LCGFT: Novels. | Romance fiction.
Classification: LCC PS3619.H45425 S94 2023 (print) |
LCC PS3619.H45425 (ebook) |
DDC 813/.6—dc23/eng/20220921
LC record available at https://lccn.loc.gov/2023007760
LC ebook record available at https://lccn.loc.gov/2023007761

First Edition: October 2023

Printed in the United States of America
1st Printing

Book design by Shannon Nicole Plunkett

Dedicated to Taylor Swift

AUTHOR'S NOTE

This book includes depictions of ableism, including ableist language, internalized ableism, and ableist emotional abuse by a parent against their child. This book also depicts alcohol and marijuana use, prior death of a grandparent, misogyny, explicit and graphic sexual content, and vulgar language.

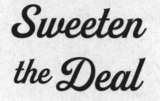

Sweeten
the Deal

Chapter One

CAROLINE NARROWED HER EYES, FOCUSED ON THE LAST red cup on the opposite side of the Ping-Pong table, and exhaled to steady her hand. She lofted the little plastic ball into the air and watched it land in the perfect center of her opponent's cup. She allowed herself only a tiny, fleeting smile of victory when he sighed and chugged the final beer in front of him.

"Good game," she told her business school classmate, hoping he'd respond.

He didn't.

Caroline had attempted to shake hands at the end of the first match, but that was apparently not done in beer pong. She'd thought it was like a tennis match or business deal, but her classmate had stared at her outstretched hand until she pulled it back and pretended to have been stretching.

"Are you still mad that I called your pants pink?" she asked him.

"They're Nantucket reds," he stiffly replied.

"I was trying to give you a compliment," Caroline said, desperate to salvage the single social interaction she'd enjoyed at the party. She'd liked the color of his pants, not to mention how they fit him. She'd liked the idea that he was a little different too, because everyone else was in jeans or chinos. Caroline wore a sundress from an Old Navy outlet she'd passed on the trip into Boston, but she felt overdressed.

"Oh, thanks," he said, putting his hands on his hips and swiveling to scan the yard behind her.

Maybe it wasn't the pants. Maybe he was upset she'd beat him in straight sets. That would usually do it.

It was her first time playing beer pong, but it seemed like she was good at it. It was her third round, and she'd only lost a couple of throws. The hardest part had been figuring out the rules; everyone else seemed to have learned in undergrad, but Caroline's tennis coach had forbidden his players to attend parties where alcohol was served during tennis season. Not that she'd been invited to many.

The rules of beer pong weren't complex, but they were counterintuitive: the person who lost a point had to drink the beer, even though everyone seemed to be at this party just to drink beer. Maybe it was a penalty because the beer had someone's dirty Ping-Pong ball in it? But if that was the case, why didn't the winner get *clean* beer?

These questions remained unanswered, but the action was close enough to tennis that Caroline had figured it out after watching a few matches from the back patio.

"Can someone else take a turn now?" her opponent asked as he reracked and refilled his cups, voice pitched in that fake-nice tone that usually meant Caroline had annoyed someone. He'd given her his name when they met, but she'd immediately forgotten it in her haze of anxiety, and now it seemed awkward to ask.

"I didn't realize anyone was waiting," Caroline said.

The weather was pleasant in Boston's September, and people were sitting in lawn chairs under the string lights crisscrossing the packed-dirt yard, but nobody was especially near the table. She'd thought the rule was that she got to keep playing until she was defeated, but she must have been wrong about that.

"I was going to grab my girlfriend from inside," her classmate said, pointing his chin at the interior of the row house. "See if she wants to play with me."

"You have a girlfriend?" Caroline blurted out, surprised. She'd been certain he was flirting with her before they started playing, but possibly she'd been wrong about that too. Her stomach sank; she'd already started telling herself a story about how she met this cute guy at the beer-pong table and he introduced her to all his friends.

Nantucket Reds hesitated and rubbed the back of his neck as though the existence of his girlfriend was potentially subject to dispute. A contingency that might not make it onto the audited financial statements.

"Yeah, I mean . . . unless you wanted to get out of here?" he suggested, lifting his eyebrows. "You seemed pretty dead set on the game. But we could head back to my place if you wanted to."

Caroline glared at him. She'd toyed with the idea that she might go back to someone's house from the party, but in that fantasy, they'd wanted more from her than five to ten minutes of potentially adulterous sexual contact. If Nantucket Reds had a contingent girlfriend, he probably wasn't going to make brunch plans with Caroline. She shook her head.

Slinking back to the outdoor couch where she'd spent the first hour of the party, she took a longneck from a cooler by the wall. The couch smelled like piss and spilled beer, and most of the tattered surface was taken up by a sleepy Labrador retriever, but the dog obligingly shifted her paws to make some room as Caroline squeezed in at one end.

"I won three games in a row," she told the dog after a few minutes of watching the next match. "Good job, me." She tried and failed to convince herself that this was a significant achievement, and the evening had been a success.

A Friday night in college would have been spent at a budget motel on the way to a tennis tournament, if it was tennis season, or watching TV with her grandmother, if it wasn't, and she would have enjoyed either of those activities more than going to a party and not meeting anyone new. Thinking of her grandmother made Caroline cringe.

I know you haven't been happy, she'd written in the letter attached to her revised will, even though Caroline had never complained. *I'm leaving you everything*, even though Caroline had only asked about the SUV. *Go live a big life*, even though Caroline's stated ambitions had been limited to moving out of her parents' house. However unexpected that last vague command had been, Caroline had initially considered it a natural consequence of getting the hell out of Templeton. Everything else was supposed to follow naturally.

In her headlong dash for freedom, Caroline felt as though she'd run straight into a screen door. Whatever she'd meant by *a big life*, Gam had probably not intended for Caroline to spend her time petting someone else's dog and watching strangers play beer pong.

Caroline's plan had been very modest: she'd save a couple thousand dollars for business school applications, somehow acquire a car, and when she moved away to the other side of the country, she'd get to quit doing exactly what her father told her to do every minute of the day. The kind of life she'd have was very hazy in her mind, but she'd populated it with friends, a boyfriend, even, and she'd imagined all sorts of new experiences. She'd go on dates and ski trips and cosmopolitan adventures. She'd meet interesting new people who were funny and kind. Gam's will shouldn't have changed anything about the plan, but somehow it had.

Caroline couldn't say which had been the bigger shock— the number of digits on her grandmother's brokerage account balance or the furor that erupted when the rest of her family learned that it would all go to Caroline. Two million dollars! That ought to have let her do whatever she wanted. It ought to have convinced her family that there would be plenty left over for them once she was done with business school. But instead, Caroline had managed only a few stilted conversations about classes with the other people here, she'd scarcely left her apartment since arriving in Boston, and most of her family weren't speaking to her. Caroline shredded the last bit of the label on her beer bottle and sighed at the pile of scraps in her lap. Her older sister had once told her that beer was an acquired taste, but Caroline hadn't managed to acquire it yet.

"The guy in the pink pants didn't really have a girlfriend, I bet," she said to the Lab. "He was just insecure about his beer pong skills and weak grasp of color theory." The dog didn't lift her head, but Caroline sensed her agreement with those propositions. Caroline nodded as though the dog had replied. "I should probably go home and let him recover from his defeats."

It was still early, and the party showed no signs of abating, but Caroline had exhausted the few opening gambits she knew for interacting with strangers. She wasn't going to meet anyone else here.

"You have a good night," she began to advise the dog. "But don't take drinks from men you don't know. And don't stay out too late."

The Lab blinked, wetly exhaled, and closed her eyes. Caroline took that as a dismissal.

After patting the dog's head in farewell, Caroline wove through the crowd of much drunker people on her way to the front door, stepping around couples dancing or making out in dark corners. She found her SUV on the street outside and turned off the music to match her mood.

Graduate students mostly lived in the wooden Victorian houses that ringed the university, but Caroline's apartment was in a high-rise a little farther away, down Commonwealth Avenue. Not a lot of the students drove to campus, but she was still not comfortable walking alone at night in the city, if she was supposed to get comfortable with that.

She parked in the underground garage and dragged her feet to the elevator. Some packages were stacked neatly on her doormat in her third-floor hallway; she'd ordered a new cake pan and the dried currants she couldn't get at the grocery store down the block. She tried and failed to get excited about spending Saturday baking. She didn't have anything else on her calendar for the next day. She'd hoped the party would change that.

Caroline gritted her teeth and tossed her keys in the cereal bowl on her countertop, where her keys and sunglasses went. Talking to strangers was a thing she was not good at, unlike beer pong. It was as if everyone else was speaking a different language, one she'd never learned. Her classmates stared at her as though they couldn't understand what she was saying if she tried to have a conversation with them about anything more personal than Excel shortcuts, and she didn't think her Texas accent was at fault. She had nothing to connect with them over.

She was boring, probably, compared to her classmates. Unlike them, she'd never really done anything— except get pretty good at tennis. And nobody wanted to hear about tennis. Even Caroline's college teammates hadn't wanted to talk with her about tennis. And what else was there to her? What else could she say? *Good evening, did you know the fast-food milkshake machines are only broken because nobody wants to spend four hours cleaning out all the fermenting dairy bits from the dispenser nozzles? Hey, stop walking away! I'm fun.*

Caroline hung her dress back up in the closet and changed into sleep clothes. In her favorite tangerine tank top and matching underwear, she flopped onto her bed, not bothering to turn on the overhead lights. She grabbed her laptop where it was charging on her nightstand, then clicked over to a dating website. Caroline had signed up two months ago, upon her arrival in Boston, but without any success so far. While several people in her area were very eager to send her photos of their genitalia, she had yet to field a proposal to meet anyone in person under a scenario more elaborate than *hang out at my place and see where the night takes us.* She knew better than *that,* at least. Even if she didn't already suspect that sex, like beer, was overhyped by advertising agencies, she knew that getting naked with someone was not a viable launch strategy for a friendship or a relationship.

In the six months since her grandmother's passing, Caroline had discovered that some problems could be solved with money. She'd applied to MBA programs and not worried about the tuition. She'd moved into an apartment that her father didn't have a key to, and she had every confidence the doorman wouldn't let him in if he somehow discovered the address and drove up to confront her.

She remembered the wonderful day she'd discovered that she had enough money to order *anything* over the Internet. She'd bought some good stuff. The exact beehive-shaped cake pan used by the Barefoot Contessa. Custom women's size 10–12 socks with Irish setters printed on them. Netflix *and* Disney+. But her life, if anything, felt smaller than it had before. Before, she'd had tennis and her family, at least, and if the limits those two groups put on her had sometimes felt so constricting that Caroline had wanted to scream and kick and flail against them, at least they'd kept her too busy to be lonely.

Caroline grabbed her pillow to her chest and rolled over, staring at the bare walls of her apartment. The unstructured expanse of the weekend loomed ahead of her like a minefield. Every time she screwed something up, even if it was just a baba au rhum cake or the deadline to join a study group, she heard her father's voice in her head: *You can't possibly handle this much money. This is just going to get you into trouble. I don't know what the hell my mother was thinking.*

What *had* her grandmother thought she was going to do with two million dollars? The things Caroline wanted weren't really available for Amazon Prime delivery. It wasn't as though she could go on Etsy to order a sophisticated boyfriend and an exciting social life to be dropshipped to Boston by Ukrainian artisans. Her father's insistence that she spend most waking moments of her previous two decades with a racket in her hand was a much bigger obstacle to her goals than her lack of funds had ever been. While everyone else had figured out how to elegantly segue from the Black-Scholes model to wind-surfing and dinner parties (if that was what her class-mates were doing on the weekends—she didn't actually know), she'd been mastering a backhand smash.

Tucking her fists under her chin, she decided to be rig-orous about it. Perhaps she could Six Sigma her social life and transition from a person who had to sit with the dog at parties to a person with exciting plans on her calendar. So what if she'd made no inroads with her classmates? She couldn't dwell on sunk costs. This was a strategic de-velopment problem at base, and she was enrolled in a prestigious MBA program devoted to teaching her meth-ods of solving it. It was only a matter of applying the prin ciples she'd studied and following the program those rules dictated: if she was keeping too much cash in re-serve to meet her growth targets, the accepted solution was to make capital investments. There was no reason not to start living that big life as soon as possible.

She looked back over at her laptop, a bad idea begin-ning to prickle at the base of her skull.

She had enough money to buy *anything* over the In-ternet.

Chapter Two

ADRIAN DID HIS BEST TO IGNORE TOM'S ANXIOUS SHUFFLE around the kitchen when the other man arrived home before his usual hour on Saturday night. Adrian didn't react. He didn't ask why his roommate was home early. Privacy was only an illusion within the 750 square feet of their poorly insulated Brighton apartment, but it was an illusion Adrian strove to maintain. He could offer Tom that much, at least.

Unlike Adrian, Tom had a regular work schedule and an active romantic life, so Adrian did not comment on Tom's comings and goings. (The latter mostly took place away from the apartment, thank God, because the walls were very thin. Adrian had unintentionally *heard things* in college while sharing a double dorm room with Tom, and he didn't care to review the progression of Tom's technique during the intervening years.)

Adrian kept his gaze focused on *PBS NewsHour* as Tom put the evening's leftovers away in the fridge and paced. Tom was usually a chatty guy, which Adrian might enjoy at the end of a quiet day like this one. But Tom's silence was telling. It was a sign of more bad things to come for Adrian.

Adrian had therefore begun to worry even before Tom

ran a hand through his shaggy black hair and announced, "We need to talk."

These were ominous words. Not least because Adrian had recently uttered the same ones to commence the conversation with his ex-fiancée that had left him single, unemployed, and squatting in Tom's second bedroom. If Tom's typically cheerful expression had turned so serious, Adrian assumed his roommate had an unpleasant piece of news to drop and did not want to discuss, say, whose turn it was to take out the trash: Adrian's turn, always Adrian's turn, because Tom was a slob who expended all of his cleaning energies at the high-end Greek restaurant where he was a waiter.

Adrian flicked off the television and rolled to a seated position on Tom's couch, which had been serving as Adrian's base of operations since his late-night eviction from his home of five years. He schooled his features into an attitude of mild interest as Tom mixed a drink, added half a jar of maraschino cherries to it, and worked himself up to whatever he had to say. Tom rolled up the sleeves of his dress shirt over furry, muscular forearms and leaned back against the peeling linoleum counter.

"So, you know you are welcome to stay here for as long as you like—" Tom began.

Adrian sighed. Of course Tom wanted him gone. Even though Tom's apartment was cleaner than it had ever been, and Adrian made himself scarce whenever Tom had dates over, no self-respecting adult wanted his former college roommate camped out indefinitely in his second bedroom, and it had been two weeks.

Adrian had thought he would have more time though. After all, ten years ago their situations had been reversed, and Tom had been the one sleeping on the couch and pondering how he'd fucked up his life so thoroughly.

"When do you need me out?" Adrian interrupted him.

His friend's thick, straight eyebrows jolted.

"I wasn't going to ask you to move out," Tom said too quickly.

"Okay," Adrian said, nonetheless beginning to calculate how many nights he could afford at a motel before he had to prevail upon friends who owed him fewer favors than Tom.

Tom's shoulders slumped before he consciously straightened them. He mixed a second drink for Adrian and carried it over to the sofa. He set their drinks down amid the tangle of Adrian's printed notes and revisions and sat next to him.

"The restaurant isn't doing well," Tom said softly. "And I need to get a roommate. A *paying* roommate. I'd prefer that still be you—"

Adrian rubbed his face. "I'm broke," he reminded Tom.

The shorter man shifted in discomfort. "Can't you just sell a painting or something?"

Adrian groaned, because if he'd been selling more paintings, he wouldn't be imposing on Tom. He didn't understand why sales were down. His last exhibition had made it into *Artforum*. He'd assumed sales would follow, but he hadn't paid a great deal of attention to his bank account until he was standing on the curb in front of his former home, suitcases at his feet.

"I'm still under contract with Nora's gallery through the end of the year," Adrian muttered. "And inexplicably, my art hasn't sold at all since I left." He hadn't gone by the gallery to check if anything was still on display since their breakup, as all the gallery staff had come down firmly on

Team Nora, but it wasn't like she'd asked for a forwarding address to send checks to.

Tom sighed and screwed up his lower lip. "Well, do you have any other ideas? Could you just go pick up a few shifts at Starbucks or something until things turn around at the restaurant? Have you even been going into your studio?"

"I'm planning a new series," Adrian said, tapping his notes. "Historical scenes from the Anglo-Ottoman War."

"Uh-huh," Tom said, unconvinced that this was a quick route to rent money. "That's, like, another step away from actually painting?"

Adrian thought that was a low blow, so he merely stared at his roommate mulishly.

The other man stared back. "Could you ask one of your parents to help you out for a while?"

"Do you remember that I could have been a doctor instead of an artist? They do."

"Or you could teach? You have an MFA."

"Ha. Do you know what they pay adjunct art professors? I'd make more slinging coffee."

"Then sling some coffee, or we're gonna get evicted," Tom said, tossing his hands in the air.

Adrian appreciated the *we* in that sentence for its suggestion that they were in this situation together, even though the easiest solution would be for Tom to tell Adrian to get out so he could move in someone who had a stable income.

Coffee. Jesus. The idea that he'd work a cash register would have been inconceivable to him just two weeks ago.

Adrian propped his forehead against his fingers. His swift descent from locally prominent artist to deadbeat couch surfer had happened so unexpectedly as to leave him feeling like he'd tumbled down a mountain and hit every boulder on the way.

"I'll . . . apply for something," Adrian unhappily promised. "Some new grants. Or teaching, you're right. I still know a few professors in the area." It sounded pretty thin.

They both looked at the black television screen. Adrian imagined Tom was as disappointed in him as he was with himself. Until recently, he'd been the reliable one—the one whose life had gone according to his expectations. Tom slurped the rest of his drink and tipped his head back against the couch with his eyes closed, stress forming little lines around his mouth.

Adrian clenched his teeth as guilt hit him. It wasn't Tom's job to worry about his failing career and broken engagement. Two weeks was more than enough time to sulk about his breakup and his gallery and his declining sales.

"There's no reason I can't try waiting tables, I guess," Adrian said reluctantly. "Do you know if anyone nearby is hiring?" At least Tom's neighborhood was far enough from Adrian's former one that he wasn't likely to encounter anyone he knew.

Tom didn't open his eyes, but his chest rose in amusement. "You'd suck at waiting tables."

"Why? I think I get the theory of it."

"Sure, *you* are going to hustle for tips." Tom scoffed.

"That's the point, isn't it?"

"Yeah, but the first time someone tried to order their boeuf bourguignon with the sauce on the side, you'd make a face—"

"What face? And how the hell would you do the sauce on the side, it's a *stew*—"

"That face! That one you're making right now. You'd

make that judgy face, and boom, no tip for you. Plus, anywhere nice is going to want you to have experience. You'd have to start at, like, some hole-in-the-wall, and you'll barely clear minimum wage."

Adrian waved a dismissive hand. "You figured it out. You managed to pay for your divorce waiting tables. I can come up with half the rent, at least."

Tom was silent for a moment, his mouth twisted to the side. He looked back over at Adrian, seeming to size him up.

"That's not how I paid for my divorce," he finally said. "Not waiting tables."

"I thought you were barely making a hundred bucks a week in the chorus," Adrian replied. He remembered that year clearly: his apartment in Back Bay, Tom present only long enough to sleep on the couch, shower, and radiate misery between restaurant shifts and rehearsal.

"Yeah. And I definitely wasn't making enough to pay for a lawyer at the first restaurant I worked at."

"Okay, so, what did you do?"

Tom blinked a few times, gave Adrian a guarded look, and then, after a long hesitation, grabbed his laptop off the coffee table.

"I'm not saying it was ideal. But it was fine for a while. And I think, you know, it's not as stigmatized these days—"

"What," Adrian said flatly, worried he was about to hear that his roommate had been selling Adderall to Harvard undergrads.

"For an artist, you are surprisingly conventional, did you know that? Practically bourgeois."

"Tom!" Adrian said, now impatient to hear about it.

"I'm just saying, hear me out." Tom typed something into the search bar, then spun his laptop to show the page to Adrian.

A young woman in a short party dress laughed and displayed her white veneers to a middle-aged, tuxedo-clad man with a chiseled jawline and graying sideburns. *A relationship on your own terms*, the site's slogan promised in lacy white font. The log-in prompt was discreetly tucked at the bottom of the page. Adrian reeled back from the screen, hoping he was vastly mistaken about what the site advertised.

"Jesus Christ," he said automatically.

"You don't know what it is."

"It's an escort site," Adrian said.

"It's not that. It's different."

"Okay, what is it, then?"

"It's, like, a sugar-baby thing—"

Adrian snorted, the noise ripping unwillingly from his throat. "That is the same thing! Jesus, Tom, you were *hooking*? You should have said something."

Tom winced. "Yeah, this reaction? Is why I didn't."

"No, no, no, I'm not— Sorry. I'm not upset at you. *I'm sorry*. I wish I could have—done something else. I thought you were just upset about Rose. If I'd known you had to—"

"I didn't *have* to do anything. And you were doing plenty! You were already feeding me, housing me, listening to me whine about my divorce—"

"I would also have done something to keep you from taking a job that leads to your dismembered body turning up in the Charles River!" Adrian said, catching his voice just before it turned into a shout.

"You've got the wrong idea about it. It's not sex work," Tom insisted, shoving Adrian's shoulder lightly.

Adrian gave him a long, skeptical glower.

"I mean it," Tom said. "Not this site, anyway. Not even all the men I went out with thought they got to sleep with me."

"So it's just a dating site, then?"

"Sort of. I mean, it's dates, yeah, but for money."

"Which is . . . different from sex for money," Adrian repeated, still alarmed.

"Because you don't have to have sex with them! That's not what they're paying for."

"What are they paying for, then?"

Tom relaxed a little. "Well, there are an amazing number of rich people who are divorced, widowed, single, whatever, and they just want someone hot to stand next to them at their fancy rich-person things and impress their friends. You don't have to sleep with anyone. You're not meeting people in hotel rooms. You're getting paid for going to parties and stuff."

"What do you mean, 'you'?" Adrian said, stiffening. "Do you mean 'you' like you or 'you' like me? Because I am not doing this, and I don't think you should either."

"Hmm. So. You can either serve clam chowder to tourists for an entire week, or you can look pretty for just a couple hours. How do you want to earn five hundred bucks?"

Adrian paused. His mind had already illustrated forty hours at a restaurant, and it looked not like Renoir's *Luncheon of the Boating Party*, but like someone throwing iced tea in his face because he didn't bring the drink refills fast enough. Unwillingly, his mind began to sketch an easier job, one that would still leave him time to paint.

"Five hundred dollars? Are you serious?" he said, wishing the words back as soon as he'd uttered them.

"As a heart attack. That's what we'd ask for. You'd only have to go out with someone a couple times, and we'd be clear on rent."

It still sounded dangerous and unlikely to Adrian, even

if toiling in food service was not exactly appealing either. "You were making that much money to go out with people, no expectation that you would . . ." He didn't finish. He wasn't sure he really wanted to know.

"Well, I was making a few hundred dollars a week, but I think you could do better than that," Tom said.

"But why?" Adrian regretted saying that, because that made it sound like he was really considering it, which he wasn't.

"Because you look good!" Tom said. He eyed Adrian, who was dressed in jersey pajama pants and a bleach-spotted Boston Public Radio T-shirt because he hadn't gone outside yet. "I mean, maybe not at this exact moment. But you are, like, the most attractive person I know in real life. You're *hot*—hotter than I was at twenty-three, even. Take advantage of that."

"You sound like you're trying to get me into the back of your van so you can take photographs of me," Adrian deflected, uncomfortable every time his looks were mentioned. Too many of his old reviews had been organized around the theme of "pretty man makes pretty art." Which didn't lend much to his reputation as a serious artist.

"If I owned a van, you could be driving for some rideshare app, and we wouldn't have to have this conversation," Tom said airily. "But, you know, the more I think about this, the better of a solution I think it is. Why should you get a *job* job? Let's just bridge the gap until you can sign with a new gallery or the restaurant can give me more hours."

Adrian closed his eyes tightly and rubbed his forehead with his palm.

"I could get a job," he mumbled.

"You've never *had* a job. But you have spent five years sucking up to a really terrible rich lady—"

"Tom," Adrian warned him, because he didn't want to hear Tom trashing Nora. Or suggesting that they'd been together because of her money. Which wasn't true. Or, at least, hadn't been true to start out with.

"Oh, fine, you know I didn't like her. But you have to admit you get along with those people. Better than you would with the average fast-casual-restaurant diner, anyway. Picture yourself getting paid to stand around and be handsome. Now picture yourself still on your feet, still handsome, but you're in a seafood shack, you're earning four thirty-five an hour, and your table of twelve is yelling at you because they had to wait ten minutes for their lobster rolls. . . ."

It might be the best bad option, put that way.

"What would be involved, exactly?" Adrian said, trying to stress the reluctance in the question.

Tom beamed at him, newly energized by this horrible scheme. "First, we make your profile. You still own a tux, right? Let's dress you up. Like you're going to a silent auction to benefit the Society for the Advancement of Shrimp Cocktail and Prevention of Testicular Cancer."

Adrian did own a tux, even though he had loathed Nora's charity-ball circuit. It always felt like performance art: a dance performed for some of the worst people in the world, who didn't actually care about supporting the arts but liked the idea of rubbing elbows with artists. He supposed putting clothes on for money was marginally better than taking them off though.

"You can do it," Tom urged him. "You're exactly the arm candy a certain kind of woman is looking for. Didn't

Nora always complain about rich people hitting on you at gallery openings?"

"I hate those people."

"Don't be so prissy about this. Come on." Tom groaned. "It's bumming *me* out to see you on the couch all day long. This is depressing, you know? You look like a very depressed person. Let me just set you up a profile. It'll get you out of the house at least."

Adrian demurred.

Tom insisted.

Adrian offered to sell some plasma.

Tom told him he could keep every single bodily fluid to himself.

Eventually, Adrian felt exhausted from the longest conversation he'd had in weeks, and he gave in. At Tom's instructions, Adrian dug his tuxedo out of his luggage, put it on, and stood against the wall. Tom had one of Adrian's old paintings hung over his sofa—a sentimental one, lush florals and bright colors, the sort of thing he hadn't done in years—and it was going to serve as proof of his bona fides as artist arm candy. Adrian uneasily shifted from foot to foot as Tom tried to take a decent picture under the cheap fluorescent track lights.

"Just use an old picture," Adrian complained. "Grab the one off my gallery page."

"Uh, we are not going for pensive and temperamental. No. In this fantasy, you are charming. Look at the camera and smile. Come on, look happy. You're at a cocktail party, you just said something hilariously mean about Jeff Koons, and everyone is laughing."

Adrian suppressed a scowl and tried to fix his features in an expression he could barely remember making naturally. It seemed to satisfy Tom, who uploaded it to his laptop and then turned to filling out Adrian's profile, greatly embroidering Adrian's preferences regarding black-tie galas and long walks on the beach.

"What if someone I know finds my profile?"

"Then you know a bunch of people who pay a hundred bucks a month to check out sugar babies. Nobody ever found out about *me*. Relax."

Adrian did not relax. He gritted his teeth and peered over Tom's shoulder.

"And why *women* and not *any*?" Adrian asked, pointing to the *Seeking* drop-down menu. He imagined there were a lot more men looking for paid companionship than women.

Tom gave him another long look. "You need to pick a struggle, buddy," he said. "If you're gonna start dating men, maybe try it for free first? I wish I had."

"If it's not about sex though—"

"Well, obviously, it's a *little* bit about sex, or at least the *idea* of sex. . . ." Tom's voice delicately trailed off as he pursed his lips.

Adrian groaned and stuck his hands in the air, backing away from the laptop. "I'm not doing this," he said. "I am not! I'll start looking for a job tomorrow."

"I just uploaded your profile," Tom said firmly. "At least take a look at who's on here?"

"Take it down, Tom," Adrian instructed him, going to the kitchen to investigate the leftovers Tom had brought home. The tuxedo felt a little tight, and Adrian didn't know if that was because he'd been in drawstring pants for two weeks or because Tom's leftovers all seemed to contain a great deal of béchamel. Adrian found a paper container of braised chard, which couldn't be too bad for him, and dumped it into a bowl to reheat in the microwave.

"Okay, how about this lady? She's going to the Cape soon, her sister is bringing her ex-husband as a date, and she wants someone to spend the week rubbing suntan lotion onto her shoulders and asking her ex pointed questions about his real estate portfolio. She says there's only one bed at the beach house though. Is that weird?"

"Take it down," Adrian repeated, watching his dinner circle in the microwave. He'd apply at the retail shops on their block, and maybe he could make some extra money teaching those paint-and-sip classes for seniors or something.

Tom clicked again. "This lady is in her eighties, but she's flying to Arizona for the Ring cycle, and I know you like opera. You can lift fifty pounds, right? She has oxygen tanks." He paused. "Oh, and she's into BDSM. Huh."

"Take it *down*, Tom!"

The microwave chirped, and Adrian stirred the greens. He took a bite. Bitter. Just roughage. It tasted like penance. Mentally vowing that he would go to the gym the next day, he opened the fridge and got out a carton of moussaka. He put the food into a new bowl and started the microwave again.

Tom continued clicking on his laptop. When dinner was done, Adrian arranged it on the tiny kitchen table and was sitting down to eat when Tom stood up.

"Look," Tom said triumphantly, turning the screen of his laptop around to show him. "What about her?"

Adrian paused with his fork halfway to his mouth.

Tom had expanded his potential patron's photograph until it filled the entire screen. The blond woman's face was obscured by the shade of a visor, but she was wearing a short white tennis dress and sneakers, her racket held at the ready. The picture had been taken on the court, the sun shining on the woman's long tan legs. She looked way too young to be hiring a sugar baby.

"That picture's probably thirty years old," Adrian said.

"So?" Tom said. "At least you know she used to be hot. Maybe she still is."

Adrian ignored him for a minute as he chewed his reheated dinner, and Tom browsed the rest of the woman's profile.

"What does she want?" Adrian finally asked, unable to immediately discard the concept of going out with the tennis player.

Tom smiled in suppressed triumph. "She's new in Boston, and she wants someone sophisticated to show her around the city."

Adrian waited for him to continue, but he didn't. Instead, Tom began typing. Adrian worried that Tom was now going full Cyrano de Bergerac: Tom did regional theater when he wasn't waiting tables, and he had a large flair for the dramatic.

"What's the catch?" Adrian asked suspiciously. He thought he was broad-minded, but he had some firm lines he was not going to cross, even if Tennis Girl had grown up into a reasonably attractive Tennis Woman.

"Hmm?" Tom said, typing, deleting, typing again.

"What's the weird thing she wants that she can't get for free?" Adrian demanded. With his luck, it was something painful or illegal.

"Nothing weird. It looks like she checked every single 'interest' box. Art, music, theater, *and* fashion, plus everything else under the sun." He peered up at Adrian, a grin tilting the corners of his mouth. "Fortunately, you're a total snob. I'm sure you'll fit right in at whatever bullshit charity events she wants you to impress people at."

Adrian bit down an objection, contemplating the potential arrangement as he finished his dinner. Maybe it wouldn't be worse than his relationship with Nora. She'd paid the bills, handled all the business of selling his paintings, and demanded very little in the way of emotional engagement. In return he'd managed the house, let her dictate their social life, and—until two weeks ago—been so absorbed by his art that he failed to notice her cheating on him. It could have continued indefinitely if she hadn't saved someone else's nudes to their joint photo account.

Tom stopped typing and shut his laptop.

"I'll think about it," Adrian promised him. "Maybe I'll contact her tomorrow."

"Okay," Tom conceded. Too easily.

"What?" Adrian said with deep alarm. He crossed his arms over his chest, feeling his heart rate pick up along with his anxiety.

Tom beamed at him, his dark brown eyes cheerful again.

"You have drinks with her tomorrow at seven to discuss a date to the theater. She's open to paying a thousand a week. Her name's Caroline Sedlacek."

Chapter Three

CAROLINE—IF SHE WAS USING HER REAL NAME; ADRIAN wished he had not—was late. She'd left it to him to choose the place, which made sense if she'd just moved to the city. He'd selected this lounge because it was attached to a hotel, where nobody local could happen to see him meeting someone off a sugar-baby site. He took a seat where he could see the entrance and keep an eye on the crowd at the bar. When Adrian ordered a glass of ice water, his server gave him a dirty look and promptly abandoned him.

As Adrian waited, he caught himself shifting uncomfortably in the plush velvet armchair and willed himself to stillness. He barely remembered this part of dating. He knew he'd been on bad dates in his twenties. He had been stood up. Women had gone to the restroom and not come back. It had been years though. He wasn't used to sitting alone in a freshly ironed shirt in public anymore, feeling painfully on display and a little tawdry.

This wasn't really dating, he reminded himself. This was business. It wasn't terribly different from bringing over a painting to some lonely divorcée's mansion and staying a few hours to praise his patron's interior decor. He'd been willing to do that if it helped close a sale: go socialize with someone buying art, role-play Sandro Botticelli to their Lorenzo de' Medici for the benefit of their ego. Still, he thought, *I hate this, I hate this, I hate this.*

Adrian was about to leave a couple of dollars on the table in compensation for the water and the space he'd occupied when Caroline finally arrived. She entered in a rush, shaking precipitation off hair that looked golden blond rather than platinum in the dim light of the bar. She halted at the host's station, scanning the room and giving him a chance to absorb the fact that, no, her profile picture wasn't old, and neither was she.

She was very tall for a woman, almost as tall as he was—and at six feet, he never felt short—but her shoulders were tight and bunched together. She wore a cheap blue floral sundress over a long-sleeved white T-shirt and black leggings, an outfit that didn't quite work for either the scene or her spare, leggy frame. Caroline turned until her gaze landed on him, and after a visible deep breath, she approached, her big white running shoes squeaking on the polished tile of the floor.

He didn't have to make a decision about standing, kissing her cheek, or shaking her hand, because she dropped into the seat on the other side of the table before he could slide his feet back underneath him.

Up close, he could tell he wasn't mistaken about her age. Her thick straight hair was cut off in a matronly bob just above her shoulders, which did nothing to flatter her round cheeks and pointed chin, but she had to be at least ten years younger than him. Maybe more.

Caroline's large green eyes—vividly lovely, though ringed in too much black pencil—narrowed at Adrian as he realized he had yet to speak. He instinctively sat up straighter. The entire effect of her presence was that of an angry adolescent cheetah: long limbs and natural grace inexpertly deployed. She nearly vibrated with agitation.

She was *pretty*, he belatedly noticed, because nothing

about how she was dressed or the entire situation had prepared him for that. As pretty as any woman he'd ever gone out with on purpose.

I hate this a little bit less.

"Did you have any trouble finding the place?" he asked, not realizing until the words left his mouth that he would sound like he was complaining that she'd been late. Not that it really mattered; she didn't look apologetic, despite her evident nerves.

"There's nowhere to park around here," she said, her voice carrying a thick, syrupy Texas accent he rarely heard outside the movies.

"You drove? To Copley Square?"

She didn't dignify that with a response, looking him over the same way he had appraised her. Adrian hoped that her inner critic was kinder than his own. He should have led with a compliment, because he ought to have been thanking his lucky stars that he found her attractive.

He closed his eyes. This wasn't starting well. He would have been a lot smoother with the fiftysomething social-ite Tom had promised than a woman he might have looked at across a bar under different circumstances.

"Can I get you something to drink?" he asked, dusting off his manners.

"Sure," she said. "Thank you." Her expression was still guarded, and he supposed he couldn't blame her for that.

Without any prompting, she dug into her large yellow shoulder bag. It was nice, but too old for her, something a woman twice her apparent age would carry. She came out with a credit card and passed it over to him. He looked at it uncomprehendingly for a long second, absorbing only that her name actually *was* Caroline.

Oh, right. She was going to pay for things. That was the

reason he was here. Shame prickled along his cheek-bones.

"What would you like?" he managed.

Her lips pursed. She was *very* pretty, just poorly styled, and her mouth was full and heart-shaped. If she was at all impressed with him so far, she wasn't showing it.

"What are you having?" she responded.

"A glass of Tempranillo."

She showed no sign of familiarity.

"Do you like red wine?"

"No, not unless it's really sweet."

"Then you probably won't like it," he said, again recognizing too late that he probably sounded like an ass. "What do you usually drink?"

She tilted her head to the side, considering.

"I'd like a Midori sour," she said, her announcement not even delivered like a confession.

He couldn't help but snort. "I'm not ordering that. Come up to the bar with me if you want something that's mostly food coloring."

A flicker of anger like summer lightning worked through those luminous sea-glass-green eyes.

"What's wrong with it?" she asked flatly.

"Try something off the drink list instead," he said, pushing the cocktail menu across the table to her. If she was hiring him because she wanted more sophistication in her life, she could start by drinking something not marketed chiefly to Jell-O shot enthusiasts.

Caroline took the menu, scanned it briefly, then put it back down.

"I don't know what any of this stuff is," she said. She crossed her arms, which he recalled as a sign that a date was not going well. She stared hard at the menu. "How about a fuzzy navel? Do they make that here?"

She had to be screwing with him. He hadn't ordered something like that since throwing out his fake ID. Nobody drank that crap after they turned—

Adrian sat back in his chair, eyes widening.

"How old are you?"

"What does that matter?" she asked, chin thrust out pugnaciously.

The hot sweep of embarrassment traversed his entire face before continuing its trek down his neck and across his chest. Of course it mattered. Adrian suppressed the urge to swivel and see if anyone was looking at him arguing with his age-inappropriate date. And then something even worse occurred to him.

"Let me see your ID," he blurted out, horrified by the thought that perhaps she was not even eighteen. What did high school girls look like, anyway? He hadn't paid any attention to them *since* high school. Maybe she was even younger than she looked, and she looked a *lot* younger than him.

"No," Caroline said, her own face beginning to pinken to match his own. "I'm twenty-two."

"I'm not taking that for granted," Adrian gritted out. "Or committing any felonies." God, he was going to kill Tom for ever suggesting this plan.

She managed a weak sneer. "You don't have to worry about that. I'm *not* going to have sex with you."

Caroline made that last pronouncement in a voice that crossed the room. Now Adrian was certain that other people were staring at him and the young woman who didn't want to sleep with him.

Hello, good evening, friends, I will not be getting laid to-night. He probably looked like he was trying to coerce her into it, though he'd come to this bar dreading the idea.

He took an agitated breath and gathered himself. He ought to be relieved. He didn't want to do sex work, even for beautiful women who were inexplicably angry at him, which increasing evidence showed to be his exclusive type.

"Do you want me to leave, then?" he offered.

Caroline hesitated, obviously thinking about being the first one to walk. Her lower lip curled inward, but she ultimately opted to fish for her wallet, cursing not quite under her breath. She tossed a driver's license across the table at him. He fumbled and nearly dropped it. When he got it under control, he had to lean close to read it, because it was dark in the lounge.

His mental math told him she hadn't lied about her age. That was more reassuring than it ought to have been, considering their relationship was going to be a clothed one. The driver's license was out of state, listing an address in Templeton, Texas, wherever that was. But of course this whole ridiculous setup was on account of her being new in town.

He handed it back to her, and she shoved it loosely into her purse.

"Where's Templeton?" he asked.

"Nowhere," she snapped.

Adrian held up his hands in exasperation. "We don't have to do this. We can just go."

She glanced off to the side, struggling with her annoyance. "It's literally nowhere. An exit on I-35. Nothing but outlet malls and frontage roads."

That hung in the air for a while as Adrian processed everything he now knew about her. None of it added up to a woman who had to spend a thousand dollars on a date to the theater. Or even one who wanted to spend a thousand dollars on a date to the theater, a little light conversation about the arts, and then sex. A woman who looked like Caroline could find sex in any bar in town. If she was willing to be discerning, odds were she'd find at least one guy in the crowd who wanted to see *Hadestown* with her before or after the sex. Where Adrian fell into this sequence was not at all apparent, given her pronouncement that they were not going to be having any sex—

"Is this for television?" Adrian asked.

Her blond eyebrows drew together. "What?"

"If it's not *To Catch a Predator*, is this a different reality show?" he guessed.

Her expression was silently hostile.

"If nobody's going to jump out with a camera, I don't get it. Are you trying to recruit me as a drug mule? Or steal my kidneys? Is this a con?" He had uploaded an uncomfortable amount of personal information on the website, theoretically for a background check. "Identity theft?"

That last pissed her off enough that she leaned across the table on her elbows.

"If I wanted a new identity," Caroline said, beautiful eyes heavy-lidded, words dripping with the sugar of her accent, "I could probably get a better one than *middle-aged hooker*."

Adrian choked. It was a good thing he didn't have a drink yet, because he would have spat it out. He closed his eyes and drew in deep breaths through his nose, willing his breathing to normalize and his fists to unclench. God, did she ever have his number. That was what he was doing here, and he was just as bad at it as circumstances suggested he was at anything else. Abruptly, he started to laugh, the chuckle emerging from deep in his chest and then finally working its way out through his throat.

He opened his eyes to see Caroline stiff and tense, her face gradually shifting from angry to mortified as he laughed at himself. He probably was middle-aged, from her perspective. And sure, a prostitute too, because wasn't that the point of the sugar-baby site, no matter what Tom tried to say about it?

"I suppose I deserved that," he said. "But I'm only thirty-three. And since you just said we're not having sex, I'm not sure I qualify as a prostitute just yet."

She squirmed in her seat, chewing on the inside of her cheek.

"I don't think you're a prostitute," she amended. A flash of guilt crossed her face. "Or, really, I don't care if you are or you aren't. I'm just not trying to hire you for—" She closed her mouth, distressed.

Adrian huffed out an exhale, shaking his head to clear his mind. "It's all right. I'll take you at your word that no sex will be had. That is really"—he took a deep breath—"really acceptable to me." He couldn't feel anything but relief, in fact, that he was not going to be crossing that particular bridge for money.

He tried to meet her eyes. "But if not—that, what do you need me for?"

Caroline looked at a spot just over his shoulder with a fierce mix of uncertainty and bluster. She'd picked up the cocktail napkin under her water glass and was twisting it in her lap.

"I thought—I thought this was going to be a date?" she said, her tone making it a question halfway through.

Adrian blinked, because of all the reasons that someone might want to hire him, he had not really believed that one of them might be his company. Not that she was likely interested in it at this point. It had been a long time since he'd cared what anyone thought of anything about him except his artistic abilities, and yet he found himself wishing this had gone even a little better.

However bad it was for him to sit on display, waiting for his bad date, it had probably been scarier to be her, when she did not seem like she'd been on many dates at all. And she'd probably expected someone more charming than him. It wasn't her fault he was in this situation; he should have been kinder to her, no matter her reasons for meeting him.

Adrian propped an elbow on the table and stuck out his hand for her. "I think we got off to a poor start. Can we try again?"

She looked at his palm with suspicion, but she eventually took his hand, shaking it gently.

"Adrian Landry," he introduced himself, taking her slim, firm fingers in his own. "Starving artist. Not a prostitute."

That finally got a hint of a smile out of her, absurdly gratifying for him.

"Caroline Sedlacek," she replied. "MBA student. Not a john."

CAROLINE EYED HER DATE OVER THE RIM OF HER HIGHBALL glass, glad to have something to do with her shaky hands. Adrian had finally gone up to get their drinks, returning with two glasses of red wine (he was right; she didn't like it) and her Midori sour, which she supposed was meant to be an apology.

They'd talked about the bar, the neighborhood. Some restaurants he knew nearby. He'd kept up the conversation smoothly enough that she was convinced he could manage that any time he wanted to, even with someone as awkward as she was. Whether he wanted to keep up a conversation was the question.

Caroline was admittedly very new to this, but her understanding of the supply-and-demand dynamics in the sugar-baby/sugar-daddy market had been that he was going to suck up to her because he wanted her to pay him large sums of money. And yet she got the impression that he was the one auditioning her, not the other way around. His skepticism—and that heated, assessing stare—had thrown her.

Maybe she didn't understand the forces affecting spot availability of hired dates? Maybe there were a lot of people who, like her, couldn't manage a social life without going to the market? Or maybe there was a deficit of broke artists? Could Adrian really set the transaction terms from the supply side?

He was obviously intelligent, moving easily between topics whenever Caroline drew a blank. He had a lovely silky voice. And he smelled nice, like Lava soap instead of abrasive men's cologne. This much she'd expected for someone who thought their company could command a thousand dollars a week. She was sure he did very well for himself when dating recreationally; he probably had significant boyfriend experience. Standard sugar-baby qualifications, she assumed. But perhaps she'd stumbled on some kind of exclusive, high-quality sugar baby only available to VIPs?

He was *so* handsome, in a way she'd only ever seen in advertisements for expensive wristwatches. He looked like an old-fashioned movie star with his square chin and thick auburn hair combed back behind his ears. Even better-looking in person than in his profile photo, though when she received his message, she'd given more consideration to the beautiful painting behind him than the tall unsmiling man in a tux, looking down his Roman nose at whoever had taken the photograph.

Nobody looked that good in real life, she'd thought. His

face was a product of AI. A computer-generated fantasy of sculpted lips and piercing blue eyes. That was fine; she knew about marketing. She wouldn't have blamed Adrian for using a filter on his profile even if he'd arrived looking very little like his picture. She hadn't been prepared for the reality of him: speaking, breathing, absently tracing the coppery stubble on the edge of his jaw with one angular hand. Her own trembled on her highball glass when he leaned back in his chair to think about something and his shirt stretched tight across his chest. Jesus.

Was he *too* good-looking for what she had in mind? Movie-star looks were what her supply-chain management professor might call *overly specified for the projected use*. There were probably cheaper sugar babies who looked more in her league. She wouldn't be able to attract someone whose cheekbones looked like they could carve diamonds on the traditional dating market. She couldn't afford to get used to men who looked like this.

Caroline took a deep breath, frowned, and purposefully shoved that last thought out of her mind. Her grandmother wouldn't have expected her to economize on *this* transaction. She might as well enjoy the upgrade to first class as long as she was flying. If she was paying for a boyfriend, why not get a *hot* boyfriend?

"So, what did you have in mind for this arrangement?" Adrian asked when he'd decided it was time for a segue to the reason for their meeting. He lounged in the velvet armchair, knees spread and ankles crossed. His dusty-blue eyes studied her, surrounded by long, thick eyelashes the color of fox fur.

Caroline nodded and refocused, taking her phone out of her purse. She'd written down some bullet points in her Notes app. She pulled them up.

"I'm basically contracting out the position of my boy-friend," she said.

Adrian gave her a slow blink. That usually meant confusion. But how could she have been clearer? Oh.

"I guess technically it's employment, not independent contractor status," she rushed to explain. "I can withhold taxes and everything if you want me to."

"Okay," he said. "Don't worry about that. I'll do my own taxes. I meant what you wanted me to do as your . . . boyfriend."

Right. Job duties. It was important to get those straight.

"So, you don't have to do, you know, the sex part. Or text me about my day or anything like that. I meant you would be my boyfriend in terms of the amount of time involved. I was going to propose we go out Friday and Saturday evenings, maybe once during the week, and either of the weekend days."

"That's a lot of time," he said.

"A thousand bucks a week is a full-time job," she reminded him. It was a lot more than she'd earned flipping burgers during college for roughly the same hours. "You'd even have time for a second job during the week, while I'm in class, if you wanted one."

"I meant for you," he said, shifting his weight in apparent discomfort.

"What do you mean?"

"You want to spend that much time with me? You don't even know me."

"I just moved here," she said defensively. "I don't know anyone."

That was a little white lie of omission that suggested that she'd have people to go out with somewhere that wasn't Boston, and it made her nervous that he'd somehow know and call her out on it. Adrian's sculpted mouth twitched as he seemed to ponder whether he could handle so much time with her. It wouldn't be too bad for him, would it? About fifteen hours? Her stomach clenched with the fear he'd decline. She didn't want to have to audition someone else—it had taken her fifteen minutes of breathing exercises to get out the door for *this* date.

"Got it," he said. "And what specifically did you want to spend that time doing?"

On firmer ground, Caroline slid through her bullet points.

Adrian was an artist. That hadn't been the only good option from the website she found him on. There had been a slightly older man who owned a little boat and liked sailing, and a girl her own age who liked yoga and community gardens, and a guy with a lot of interesting tattoos who played the bass guitar in a cover band. All of those lives had sounded vastly bigger and more important than the one she'd been living. But Caroline had liked the idea of an artist, and patronizing the theater and the symphony and museums had sounded like an appropriately important thing she could do with her grandmother's money.

She'd picked up the Sunday edition of the *Boston Globe* the previous weekend and looked through the arts section before getting overwhelmed. There had been a lot of ads for different performances and exhibitions, and she had no metrics for evaluating which she ought to prioritize.

Delegate, that was what good managers did when subject matter specialists were better equipped to make decisions within their area of expertise. Adrian's credentials looked good. She'd leave it up to him to decide which of the dizzying array of artistic experiences she ought to explore first.

"I want to go to the theater. Museums. Concerts. And

have dinner after or brunch before. Whatever you usually do. You pick."

"And that's it?"

"Can you not do that?" she asked, confused. His profile had included a collection of candid photographs at places like that, apparently taken across a number of years, and in every one, he'd been with other people in party clothes, talking and laughing. It looked like a nice life, one she was eager to figure out.

"No—I can. Or rather, I would, but I'm broke," he said.

"Yes, see, that's why I'm offering you money," Caroline said, beginning to get frustrated. She'd thought the basis of this exchange was pretty well understood.

Adrian leaned onto his palm, pinkie finger pressed along the bridge of his aristocratic nose. He looked at her through his fingers. "You really want to pay me a thousand dollars a week just to go with you to the theater?"

"It doesn't have to be the theater, specifically," she said. "It's whatever you think I'll enjoy."

One corner of Adrian's mouth pulled up and to the side, making an interesting dimple flex in his cheek. "That's never guaranteed. I could have terrible taste."

"Do you?" she asked, concerned. She'd liked his painting. She'd assumed an artist would have good taste.

"No, but taste in art is personal."

"You mean, it's all good art for someone?"

"Well—" He hesitated. "I wouldn't go that far. I usually know whether *I'll* like something, but . . ."

"Because you know a lot about it."

"I do," he said, still seeming cautious.

"If you had all the money in the world, you'd go out every week to the theater and museums and all the rest, wouldn't you?"

"Of course, yes."

"Because you already know what you want to see."

"Yes, I suppose—"

"And after it was over, you'd know if it was, you know, a good or a bad show. You'd talk about it with your friends. Or your girlfriend, if you had one—" She froze, that unpleasant possibility occurring to her for the first time.

"I don't," he quickly answered the question she hadn't wanted to ask.

Caroline exhaled, slightly reassured. "So that's what I want. Show me how to do that. Just make me the person you go to the theater with, for a while."

That's what she thought her boyfriend would do, if she had one. He probably wouldn't be as handsome or accomplished as Adrian, if she somehow, someday acquired an artist boyfriend through nonmonetary means. (Though he'd hopefully be a lot more excited about spending time with her than Adrian seemed to be.) He'd talk to her about all the music and art and shows they'd go see together. He'd *want* to. But like the Barefoot Contessa always said, if you didn't have homemade, store-bought was fine.

Adrian still looked skeptical, but his reluctance only focused her. She felt that adrenaline rush she got when it was time to close a mock negotiation or call match point. She reminded herself that Adrian was there primarily because he needed money, and she had it. She just had to convince him the time commitment was worth it.

"My opinion is available for free," Adrian said slowly. "But historically, I have a hard time giving it away."

"Are you a jerk?" she asked, mostly curious. He didn't seem like one, but sometimes she didn't catch that kind of thing right away.

He snorted. "No. Maybe. I don't think so? I've just been told I'm best enjoyed in silence." He gestured at his face.

Caroline settled her shoulders like she was ready to return a serve.

"Okay," she said. "Lay it on me. Let's see."

"See what?"

"One of your opinions."

"About what?"

"Like, what was the last book you read?" she asked.

He blinked his blue eyes at her and thought about it.

"*Hard Like Water*," he said.

She made an encouraging noise, although she hadn't heard of the book. "What's it about?"

He checked her interest, then continued: "It's a novel set during the Chinese Cultural Revolution."

"Okay," Caroline said. She gestured for him to keep talking.

"It was in translation, unfortunately, so I'm afraid it lost a great deal of the cultural nuance, and I'm certain I caught less than half of what was still there. The *New York Times* Book Review thought it was an homage to *Anna Karenina*, but I think that's a very facile connection to draw out of train stations and affairs as mere plot points. If you have to assume any reference to Russian literature at all—and there's no reason to believe a Chinese author was inspired by Russian literature, it's far more likely that he's referring to Chinese literature that the critic was unfamiliar with—compare it to Bulgakov, since he was at least exploring the inherent inapplicability of revolutionary economic theory to sexual morality. . . . This can't possibly be interesting to you."

His voice, which had gone unaffected and impassioned when he started talking about the book, turned confrontational when he noticed her head tilted toward her lap.

"No," Caroline said, looking up from her phone. "I was listening. I bought the book." She turned her phone so that he could see the electronic receipt.

"See?" she said, holding the screen out to him. "You can keep talking."

Adrian developed a small wrinkle between his eyebrows. He didn't continue, even though she wished he would. The book did sound interesting if it featured trains, an affair, and a revolution. More interesting than anything else she had read recently—the *Harvard Business Review*, mostly, though she had no one else to blame for that, since she could now afford any books she wanted to read. If he wanted to talk about books, she could read some more books.

"I'll read it," Caroline promised. "And then we can talk about it next week."

Adrian pursed his lips, deep in thought, and Caroline found herself holding her breath, half-convinced that he was going to stand, thank her for her time, and tell her that he wasn't interested in any kind of arrangement with her after all.

"Let me see if there's anything at the symphony right now," he said, pulling out his own phone.

After a few minutes of scrolling, he told her to buy tickets for next Tuesday night.

A small effervescent flower of anticipation bloomed in Caroline's chest. She barely contained her rising glee. Done. This was huge progress.

"Can you make dinner reservations for afterward?" she asked.

"Yes, I can," he said, slowly nodding.

"And send me calendar invites for whatever you decide on for the next weekend?" she followed up.

He made her wait for a bit before he nodded, agreeing

to that too. Caroline's face split into a grin. Now she had plans. A whole week's worth of plans.

"Okay, what do I wear to the symphony?" she asked. "I've never been."

"A cocktail dress," he replied with a minute shrug.

Caroline tried to summon the parameters of a cocktail dress and failed.

"You're going to have to be more specific," she told Adrian.

He'd relaxed after agreeing to spend at least a week taking her around town, but now he began to frown again.

"You can wear whatever you want."

"I want to wear what I'm supposed to wear."

"The same thing you'd wear to the theater or an evening charity event," he said. "I'll be in a suit, if that helps."

"Well, I still have the dress I wore to my sister's wedding. It was kind of a peachy yellow, and there were sequins across here—" She sketched a hand across her neckline. "I was sixteen." That was just before her father had pulled her out of high school to focus on tennis, and she hadn't been to a formal event since.

Adrian looked at her. Caroline could recognize *judgment* as an expression pretty well.

Caroline sighed. "Please explain it to me like I'm from Mars," she said.

After another silent evaluation of her motives, Adrian held out his hand for her phone. When she obliged, he pecked at it for a minute or two, then looked at her.

He'd looked at her when she first arrived, but after they began speaking, she'd gotten the impression that he was trying to avoid it. But now his gaze roamed over her body in an assessing way, and she had to cross her ankles to avoid squirming under the force of his scrutiny, because he was transparently thinking about her shoulders, her waist, her breasts, even. She held her breath and willed her heart rate to slow.

After a minute, Adrian handed the phone back to her, browser showing a short formfitting black dress with long sleeves and a low asymmetric neckline. It was like nothing she'd ever owned.

"Why this one?" she asked.

Adrian had a few freckles across his cheekbones. They were more prominent as a bit of color rose in his cheeks.

"You don't have to get that one," he said.

"No, I mean, I'm trying to understand what makes this a cocktail dress."

His lower lip tightened again. "I just thought it would suit you." Clearly uncomfortable with the topic, he buttoned his jacket in a smooth motion as he moved to stand. "Tuesday, then?"

"Wait," she said, even though Adrian looked ready to leave.

He turned back, and Caroline suddenly appreciated that he was as tall as her, which was never a guarantee, and his shoulders were set with a physical confidence missing from most of the guys she encountered at school. She couldn't think of him as a guy, really; he was a man, and that label seemed ridiculous to apply even to the students a few years older than her.

Caroline swallowed hard over her dry throat, because she was going on a real date with a *man* she didn't know, and she'd never even figured out dating *guys*.

She handed her phone back to Adrian, playing through the moment of apprehension.

"Could you pick out some shoes too?"

Chapter Four

ADRIAN USED THE MOMENTUM OF PUTTING ON REAL CLOTHES and leaving the apartment to carry him over to a visit to his studio space the next day. He hadn't gone in since splitting with Nora. As he rode to his stop on the edge of Fort Point, he wondered whether Tom had wanted him out of the apartment as much as he'd needed additional rent funds.

In either event, it was energizing to walk to the former factory the city had converted to studio spaces, wave hello to familiar faces as he transited the long hallway bisecting the building, and unlock the plywood door to the room where he worked. The space was long and narrow, with a large window at the north end of the room and a share of skylights above. The walls were only plaster and drywall, so the sounds of other artists moving in their own studios reverberated around the room. The air was redolent of linseed oil and turpentine, and for the first time in months, the day felt promising. Adrian put on headphones and pulled a playlist up from his phone as he took stock of his works in progress. He queued up a little Brahms, *Allegro non troppo*, to blur out the background noise.

He had a few pieces in various stages of development. He'd always worked primarily in oil on canvas, but the last thing he'd touched before decamping to Tom's couch was nothing but pencil marks and some grisaille he'd started laying down. He frowned at the reference images he'd taped to the wall behind his easel; his most recent series had drawn from historical battles and depicted conflicts coincidental with the rise of Postimpressionism with those famous *effets de soir* techniques. His research had taken him to the Boston College library, where he still had alumni access. There he'd gotten distracted by some medical texts with useful reference images for the bodies, which had made him question whether he really had the skill to execute this composition without live models, which had led him to—

Not paint for more than a month.

As Adrian squinted at a blurry image of Ottoman soldiers, his phone beeped from his pocket.

Texts from an unknown number with an unfamiliar area code:

Unknown: Good morning!
Unknown: What's your Venmo?

It took him a moment to realize the text had to be from Caroline and Venmo had to be a payment mechanism. He saved her to his contacts, the action of putting her name into his phone feeling uncomfortably intimate. He guiltily insisted to nobody in particular that his intentions were very pure with respect to the twenty-two-year-old blond girl trying to send him money for a date.

Adrian: I don't use Venmo.

He returned the phone to his pocket. He tried to muster enthusiasm for the Ilinden-Preobrazhenie project but let his hands fall before he reached for one of his smocks.

His phone immediately beeped again.

Caroline: PayPal then?

Adrian: I don't use PayPal either.

Wasn't he very appropriate? So appropriate.

His gaze turned to the pile of lumber he'd acquired for canvas frames. If he didn't feel like painting, he could still spend the day productively assembling a few new canvases, he decided. He set the phone on a stool and squatted to sort the pine boards.

He kept the phone in the corner of his vision as he selected pieces for a couple of forty-by-sixty canvases. *Couch art*, a judgmental inner voice told him, because his work always sold best in that size, and it inevitably ended up in someone's formal living room, tucked away behind their least comfortable settee. He sternly instructed his artistic conscience that he would be making no art at all if he didn't start selling more paintings soon.

The next message took longer to arrive. He determined how many canvases he could make out of the materials he had on hand—not a lot.

Caroline: Do you still want to be paid?

Adrian eyed the screen indecisively. He supposed the decent thing to do would be to go out with her a few times, chat with her about books and art, wait until she'd attracted a crowd of friends her own age, and then refuse her money. It was hardly labor to spend an evening out with a pretty woman—girl—Caroline. He'd probably feel better about himself if he forfeited payment, and nothing about Caroline suggested that she had thousands of dollars to throw around.

I thought this was going to be a date, she'd said, the sweet line of her mouth vulnerable.

Keeping this transaction brusque and financial would remind him to keep up important boundaries. He could handle this in a businesslike fashion.

And he was almost out of archival-quality linen.

Adrian: Yes, very much so.

Once he'd found sufficient pieces for two stretcher frames, Adrian took the wood to the shared workshop space to use the communal miter saw to cut the board at forty-five-degree angles. He ignored his phone until after he'd hunted down the nail gun and secured the frame pieces with brad nails and a dab of wood glue.

Caroline: ??

He rolled his eyes, wishing she could see it.

Adrian: Just give me a check on Tuesday.

He hoped that would conclude the matter and let him focus on making canvases, which was industrious and necessary and forward-moving. When inspiration returned, he would be prepared to lock himself in his studio for days and be really productive. He went down the hall to fill his mister with water from the big stainless wash sink. It was always disgusting, splattered with paint where other artists had cleaned brushes and half-clogged with sediment from pottery and sculpture and God knew what else. Artists were, in his experience, uniformly terrible, self-centered people. Granted, he could hardly exclude himself from that assessment, though he wiped down the faucets and knobs when he was done.

He looked at his phone again as soon as he returned with his full mister.

Caroline: Gold prices on the London fix are $1933.00/oz as of last hour. I can buy one bar. Do you have a jeweler's saw?

Brat, he nearly replied. He had to stop himself and delete it, because that sounded like a sex thing. He absolutely could not hit on the bratty twenty-two-year-old who'd already announced that they were never having sex. So he chose not to reply while he measured linen for his new frames. The corners of his mouth were twitching despite his best efforts. She was funny, at least. It helped with how bizarre the situation was.

He was ready to cut the fabric when his phone beeped.

Caroline: I don't have checks??

He sighed and put the utility knife aside. He hit the phone icon on her contact.

Caroline didn't bother to greet him again when she picked up the call.

"So I could just withdraw the cash," she said in a rush. Pop music blared in the background. "But I'd feel like a drug dealer carrying all that to the symphony. Or like someone about to give someone else a really good night at the strip club. Even if you wear a suit, I'll have a hard time finding somewhere to tuck a thousand bucks."

He ignored that.

"Your bank probably gave you some checks when you opened your account," he said, performing genial, elderly patience.

Cabinets clattered over the line, and a mysterious set of whirs and thuds followed. He hesitated.

"What are you doing?"

"I'm making goat cheese tarts," Caroline proudly declared. "They showed how do to it on *The View* last week. They're *French*. One sec, the pan's about to go in the oven."

He heard the oven door close, and then the noise of music receded. He sat there listening to her moving around her apartment, his impatience warring with the mental image the sounds were conjuring. At twenty-two, in his last year of college, he'd shared a big house in Somerville with Tom and Rose and three other BC students. The women among them had wandered around in tank tops and tiny pajama shorts that showed their legs, they'd all learned how to cook, Adrian had sold out his first show, and, in retrospect, it had been the best year of his life.

After a rustle of shuffling paper, his phone chirped with the sound of another incoming text.

He pulled his phone away from his ear to see the picture of a blank check with the number 1001 in the upper right-hand corner. It rested atop a faded floral duvet sprigged with little yellow tulips. Something made of orange lace, potentially lingerie, showed in the corner of the image frame. He would have pegged her for more of a white cotton kind of woman than orange lace, he thought, turning the phone to take a closer look.

Stop it.

"Yes, well done," he said, reaching again for appropriate social distance. "You have correctly identified the checkbook."

"You're going to have to walk me through the rest of it too," Caroline said, the distance of her voice indicating that she'd put him on speaker. "I found this thing with my vacuum tubes and rotary phones. Who is this *to the order of*?"

"Me." Adrian paused. "My full name."

"Gotcha," she said. "Anything else?"

Rolling his eyes so hard they nearly hurt, Adrian instructed her to write the amount on the two separate lines.

"Is it okay if it's not in cursive? They don't teach it in school now, you know."

"That's fine," he said impatiently. His stomach was beginning to rumble. Maybe it was the thought of goat cheese tarts. He'd forgotten to pack lunch.

"And date, which date is that?"

"Today's date, Caroline." He sighed.

"Signature—that's my signature you want?" she asked very sweetly.

He squinted at his phone, beginning to feel suspicious. "Yes, the same one you signed up at the bank with."

"Okay, almost done. The memo line. Should I put *nothing illegal*, or do you think that's a red flag for the bank?"

Adrian put down the phone. Looked at the ceiling. Wished for strength. When he found some, he picked up the phone again.

"Did you already know how to write a check?" he managed to ask in a civil tone of voice.

A strangled giggle slipped out of Caroline's throat. Possibly there was a snort as well.

"Yeah, but you were being kind of a dick about it." She laughed at him.

Adrian popped his jaw to the side, contemplating an appropriate rejoinder for a long minute as Caroline's chuckles faded into more sounds from her kitchen. It would be so much easier just to flirt with her. *Would you like me to be nice to you? I can be nice*, he'd purr, imagining her blush like she had last night. His stomach rumbled again.

"I'm sorry, I'm probably just hungry," he finally admitted.

"Oh! Do you want one of these tarts? I could bring you one in a ziplock baggie. The recipe makes four."

"To the symphony? No, thank you," he said, imagining the usher's expression if Caroline tried to smuggle a savory pastry into the mezzanine.

"Are you at your studio? I could drop it off. I'm already done with class today. I'd love to see your paintings."

Adrian winced, looking around a studio cluttered with much fabric and zero finished works. It wasn't like she couldn't already guess the art wasn't doing well right now—given the potential sex work and all—but maybe she didn't care to see him metaphorically naked either.

"No, thank you," he said again. "I'm busy the rest of the day." He'd get lunch and come back to finish the canvases, he decided. There was usually an Italian food truck roaming the neighborhood. Or maybe he could go to the library afterward. The problem was likely that his reference images were uninspiring. He'd want to paint if he found better images of the Thracian soldiers.

"Oh, yeah, of course," Caroline said, now sounding subdued, which made him feel even more like a dick. "Um. Are we still on for tomorrow night?"

"Yes, I'll see you tomorrow," Adrian said, trying to make his tone gentler this time. He hesitated, then decided to be honest. "I'm looking forward to it."

THEY MET IN FRONT OF BOSTON'S SQUAT BRICK SYMPHONY hall, like hundreds of other concertgoers trickling in from the early September twilight. The largest contingent of the audience were elderly ladies with beaded bodices and sensible shoes, though there were also girls in their twenties with glossy hair and structured dresses. Caroline was glad she'd asked Adrian what to wear. There were some people dressed down in jeans and sweaters, but the black dress she wore straddled the line between the two camps. Nobody could tell, probably, that she'd never set foot in a concert hall in her life. Especially since she was with Adrian, who looked as native to the scene as she did buying chips at the gas station.

"When was the last time you were here?" she asked him after they were seated, trying to imagine a life where she came to the symphony often. In this hazy future, she was dating a T.J.Maxx version of Adrian, and maybe his face didn't stop traffic, but he was impressed by Caroline's taste in entertainment, and he had his hand on her knee.

Oh, I've followed Bach for years, she'd tell him.

Adrian tilted his head back to think. "My ex was a season subscriber. So we used to come about once a month. If she was busy, I came alone."

Caroline tucked that mention of an ex away for future consideration, quashing the instinctive prickle of affront. The ex must not have been a very good girlfriend if she had more important things to do than taking Adrian to see his favorite music.

The full hall went quiet and still as the conductor walked out to his podium. Hundreds of voices hushed, hundreds of bodies took deep breaths as the performers raised instruments. Caroline froze, trying to fix the order of the ceremony in her mind.

The first half of the program was a Bach concerto, performed by a full orchestra. She had heard of Bach, could have identified him as an important classical composer. Listening to Bach at the Boston Symphony Orchestra was for sure a thing she would have said she ought to try. She could have imagined a future that involved a lot of Bach.

But sitting here now, she didn't think she liked it.

The concert hall had a high coffered ceiling and elaborate crystal chandeliers. The orchestra of formally dressed musicians with their interesting array of instruments was nice to look at, she guessed, and Adrian's face had been nothing but respectfully intent from the moment the orchestra began to play, an attitude matched by most of the other people in the audience. He actually closed his eyes and sighed at one point as though overcome with emotion, like he'd just watched the series finale of something on the CW and his favorite character hadn't died after all. He was having an *experience*.

Caroline felt like she had the first time she hooked up with a guy. Nervous, uncertain, a little uncomfortable. Waiting patiently for an orgasm that had never come. What was the point of this? Was the Bach supposed to transport her? Was she supposed to feel different after having listened to it? Was she supposed to be counting the time, or noticing something about the musicians, or translating the melody into a story? Was it supposed to sound a lot different from when she was put on hold with the bank?

She'd have to read up on it later. Maybe she hadn't prepared enough.

At the intermission, she wobbled out of the hall, braced gingerly with her hand on Adrian's shoulder until they reached the lobby. She wasn't used to wearing heels. Even though her new snakeskin-print slingbacks had a solid block heel and no platform, they were still three inches more of a heel than she'd worn since her last growth spurt. It put her a couple of inches over Adrian's height, and she felt conspicuously oversize, awkward next to Adrian's polished elegance. The shoes were giving her a blister on the back of her left foot too.

"You could have worn flats," Adrian murmured without looking at her, crushing her hope that he somehow hadn't noticed that she was balancing against him. He hadn't flinched, but he was carefully looking elsewhere.

"I'll get the hang of it soon," Caroline said. "Just like learning to ride a bike."

"There's no reason not to be comfortable. You're here for the music," he said, even though she doubted he lounged around his apartment in a sharp navy suit and oxfords. Maybe he did though?

"I'm sure there are good and important reasons to wear high heels," she said, dolefully eyeing the line for the ladies' room and deciding to wait.

It had been a rhetorical statement at best, but Adrian answered anyway.

"It creates an optical illusion. Lengthens your legs."

If her legs were in question, they were very much on display in the dress he'd picked out, and she'd thought they were one of her better features. Caroline gave Adrian a stern look, caught his eye when he glanced her way, and enjoyed the way his ears turned pink.

"Not that you need any help with that," he said.

"Nice save," she said dryly. "I thought you were supposed to be nice to me?"

They took another two steps.

"You look . . . pretty tonight," he said, the words slowly shuffling out of his mouth. He closed his eyes and scrunched up his face as he realized how poorly he'd delivered that line.

Caroline laughed at his pained expression. "Wow, not that I'm some kind of connoisseur or anything, but you are really, hilariously bad at this line of work, did you know that?"

She thought she'd managed better customer service when delivering cherry limeades to cars full of surly soccer moms and their soccer spawn than Adrian was doling out at the symphony. She'd hired him to act like her boyfriend! It was a good thing she hadn't hired him to stroke her ego—or anything else—because he was so obviously embarrassed to be out with her. His incompetence at his job was only making her feel better about her reaction to the music though.

She couldn't hear Adrian's answer because he turned his head away.

"Sorry, what was that?" she said, tugging on his arm.

He looked back at her, mouth twisting ruefully.

"I'll get the hang of it soon," he repeated her words. "I'm new to professional dating." His gaze dipped down to her legs again, lingered for a moment, then flicked away. "You do look beautiful, really. I had to try not to stare. I just wasn't sure you wanted to hear that from me."

Caroline smirked at him in triumph, because even if he didn't mean it, he sounded like he did.

Caroline had never been good at anything the first

time she tried it. Some people had natural gifts, she appreciated that, but she had to work for everything. She wasn't even sure she'd been any better at tennis than her sisters when she started playing, but she'd spent hours on the concrete court down the block—mostly for want of anything better to do—until people began to say she was very talented. Every time she noticed someone else struggling to learn something, the way Adrian was struggling to be nice to her, it made her feel better about all the things she didn't yet know how to do.

They'd both get better at this. Soon she'd have appropriate reactions to the music, and he'd tell her she was pretty in a more believable way.

It was a relief to be standing up, even in the painful shoes. Caroline had bought the most expensive tickets, assuming they were the best ones, but that put them right in the middle of the center orchestra, four rows back from the stage. People were sitting all around her, and she'd felt claustrophobic even before the music started playing. It wasn't *so* loud that she couldn't stand it, but the combination of strangers pressed around her, loud noise, and unfamiliar circumstances had made her close her eyes and press her teeth together in discomfort for the last movement of the first half. She didn't know Adrian well, but he was the most familiar thing there, and she'd ended up crowded against him, breathing in the faint, warm scent of Lava soap every time he moved.

"What are they serving?" Caroline asked, eyeing the crowd of people around the refreshment stand.

"Champagne, usually," Adrian said. "It's not bad here."

As that sounded like high praise in his mouth, she assumed he wanted some. It would probably help her relax too. She got in line.

When the refreshment queue didn't seem to get any shorter, Caroline got her credit card out and handed it to Adrian, asking him to get their drinks while she went to the ladies' room. The look he gave her in return was confused, like maybe he'd forgotten again that she was there to pay for things. The thought made her smile, because if he could stop looking mildly appalled at the need to stand next to her, it would be a lot more fun to be with him.

Caroline headed to the line for the restroom. After a few minutes of waiting, she pulled out her phone, intending more to mindlessly scroll Instagram than to check her messages, because she almost never had any. But she had two missed calls. She nearly pressed the icon to check the names, see whether they'd left any messages, but pulled her hand away at the last minute. It was probably spam, she told herself. And if it wasn't spam, she couldn't handle it just then anyway. If it was her family, she'd need to schedule a few hours to feel really terrible about herself after the call. She put the phone back in her purse.

Adrian was waiting impatiently for her when she returned, credit card in one hand and a flute of champagne in the other. People were filing past them back to their seats, heads turning as they caught sight of Adrian.

Caroline understood their reaction. He was so pretty it was jarring to see him in a crowd of normal people, like a bird stuck in an underground parking garage. He probably didn't like it, she mused, any more than she'd liked it when she hit five foot eleven in seventh grade and ended up taller than most of her teachers.

"The bell just rang," he told her.

She took the champagne from him and sipped it. It seemed warm and flat, but she didn't care. She wanted a little buzz to blur her perceptions when she sat back down.

He shifted his weight when she took another sip.

"We should be in our seats when it starts again," Adrian said, looking at the door to the orchestra floor.

"Or we won't be able to follow the plot in the second half?" she teased him.

He stuck his hands in his pockets. "It's so full tonight because of the soloist who's about to come on and do a Paganini caprice. A violin prodigy, only twenty-one. It's his first American tour. They've been promoting this performance for months. You don't want to miss it."

She didn't know how he could be so confident about that after the Bach, and nearly told him as much, but then a different thought occurred to her.

"You mean *you* don't want to miss it?" she asked.

Adrian rocked back on his heels without taking his hands from his pockets, gaze on his feet. The small smile that tugged up the corners of his mouth was unexpectedly boyish. It transformed his face, made him look younger and less remote. It was the first sign she'd gotten of the person he was when he was off duty, and her breath caught at the loveliness of it.

"I was looking forward to it," he admitted. "And I didn't think I'd get to go."

"Okay," she said, chest filling with pleasure at the idea that she was the only reason he got to see this performance. She was a good sugar daddy. Someday she'd be a good girlfriend. She tipped her glass back and chugged the rest of the champagne. "I'm ready, then."

Caroline followed him back to their seats, a few rows away from the stage. The big ring of chairs where the orchestra sat had been cleared, and the lights were dimmed save for a spotlight in the center. The energy level in the audience had risen; the younger people in the crowd were giggling with one another.

When the performer walked onto the stage, Caroline saw at least one reason that the crowd was full of anticipation: he was cute, his long hair framing his face and his muscular shoulders filling out his snappy tuxedo.

Applause broke out as he gave a small, stiff bow to the audience. There were even a few muted whistles. Adrian made a minute expression of displeasure at the level of noise.

"Is this the symphony equivalent of rioting and throwing panties on the stage?" Caroline whispered to him.

His nose wrinkled as he looked at the other patrons. "Yes."

The soloist launched into his performance without addressing the audience, his serious face growing passionate and rapt as his bow moved over the violin strings. Caroline had never heard the song before, but it was obviously very difficult, with lots of fast little notes requiring the violinist to saw his arm back and forth rapidly across the strings.

As soon as the music began, Adrian looked enthralled again. Caroline studied him out of the corner of her eye. What was he so interested in? The soloist's expression gave emotion to the work that Caroline had been unable to feel from the larger symphony, but it was borrowed. She couldn't relate, to either the soloist or Adrian. Whatever everyone else in the crowd was getting, Caroline was not. She didn't feel any different. She must not be doing this right. She closed her eyes and let her mind drift.

When the performance was over, the crowd jumped to their feet, applauding with gusto. Adrian smoothly followed them, clapping enthusiastically.

"So, it was really good?" Caroline asked him, taking in the rapturous expressions of the people around them.

Adrian turned his head to look at her, one eyebrow lifted. "Well, what did you think?"

Caroline twisted her ankle in a small circle, considering it.

"I liked the solo better," she said, which was an honest thing she could say without admitting she hadn't enjoyed it. She picked up her purse, still looking forward to their dinner, at least. It had been two months since she'd eaten at a restaurant, because she hadn't had anyone to go out with. Now she had a date.

Adrian sighed.

"Of course you liked the soloist better," he said ruefully. "Everyone loves a prodigy."

Chapter Five

THE SECOND TIME CAROLINE STUMBLED IN THE SPACE OF A
block, Adrian called to cancel their dinner reservation. In
lieu of his favorite little French bistro, which was nearly a
mile away, he steered Caroline into a small sushi restaurant across the street from the looming brick shoebox of
the symphony hall.

"Sorry you have to play zookeeper to my baby giraffe,"
Caroline said, digging her nails into his sleeve and wobbling to the nondescript entrance of Symphony Sushi.
He'd eaten there before, so he knew it was reliably good
and not too busy. It wasn't Masa or Nobu, but they'd be
able to hear each other talk.

"Don't worry about the restaurant," Adrian said, ignoring the inconvenient rush of protectiveness he felt as he
held out his arm for her to hold while they crossed the
street. Guilty, that was how he ought to feel; he'd picked
out the shoes in the first place.

"Is sushi all right?" he asked belatedly, once Caroline
had already taken off her pink sleeping-bag-shaped parka.
It ruined the line of her dress. He wondered if she knew,
or cared. It was probably for the best that he spent less
time looking at her legs.

"Yes," she said, but she looked a little uncertain as the

hostess led them to a table against the banquettes in the back and handed them order cards.

Caroline took the seat on the upholstered bench and removed one strappy shoe, prodding at a red spot on her ankle.

Adrian automatically reached out to take her heel in his hand and examine it himself. He'd been premed for a single miserable year, but he didn't realize until her foot was in his lap that, first, he wasn't exactly going to perform surgery in the middle of the sushi restaurant, and second, he needed to scoot his chair back so that he couldn't see up her dress. He felt his cheeks heating as he brushed his thumb along the little blister.

Caroline smiled at him, expression innocent of both conclusions, and said, "Probably not a fatal injury."

"No," he agreed. "I think you'll live." He wasn't an EMT; he needed to keep his hands to himself. He gingerly put her foot down and moved back to the other side of the table, now uncomfortably burdened with knowledge of the extent of Caroline's tan and the color of her underwear. He willed his libido to go home early.

The server came to get their drink orders.

Caroline stared up at the server for a minute, then turned her head to Adrian. "What do people drink with sushi?" she asked.

"Rice wine," he told her. "Sake."

Her furrowed brow was skeptical, and she must have decided that was a bridge too far, because she stuck to water. She picked up the long white order card, her expression guarded as she scanned the options.

"I'm going to put some paper towels or something in my shoe," Caroline said when she set the card down. She looked from the restroom to the front entrance. "Or would that not be classy?"

Adrian shrugged. The restaurant had a white tile floor and big-screen TVs showing satellite soccer games. The vibe was casual. "I don't think we'll be asked to leave. What should I order for you if the server comes?"

"Whatever you're having," Caroline said, pushing up from the table and limping on her blistered foot.

She left her purse on the table and wobbled off. Adrian checked off the same sashimi platter and unagi rolls he'd ordered the last time he'd eaten there, then took her card. Did they have sushi restaurants in Templeton? Just in case they didn't, he ordered her a sampler so that she could figure out what she liked.

When the server came back to collect their cards, Caroline's phone vibrated in her purse. Adrian ignored it, but after fifteen seconds of silence, it started vibrating again. He looked awkwardly at the restroom until Caroline emerged, wet paper towels rolled around the buckles on the ankle straps of her shoes.

As she was making her painful way back to the table but before he could tell her that her phone had been ringing, the restaurant door opened again, admitting a blast of cool evening air and a middle-aged couple in tailored charcoal wool, both of them dressed for the theater. Unfortunately, Adrian recognized their faces, even if he couldn't quite summon their names.

The wife elbowed her husband sharply in the ribs when she saw Adrian, and a wide smile spread across the man's face when he saw who his wife was pointing at. Adrian had sold them a painting the previous year . . . and maybe another one a couple of years before that? He remembered their poorly trained Lhasa apso. Jan, that was the husband's name. Jan Mayer the hedge fund guy, who had bragged about his bonus and tried to pass Adrian stock tips. Jan lumbered across the restaurant so quickly that he beat Caroline to the table, his wife following more slowly behind him, hobbled by her tall spike heels.

"Adrian Landry!" Jan exclaimed. "Small town, huh?"

His wife cackled as though Jan had said something supremely hilarious.

Caroline hesitated on the outskirts of the conversation as Adrian's hand was seized and pumped.

Jan drew away from the space between the tables, but not very far; Caroline had to brush past him to make her way to her seat. Jan and his wife looked back and forth between Adrian and Caroline, evidently impressed by his pretty, too-young companion. Adrian took a deep breath, wishing he could have avoided the entire interaction.

"Jan, this is my friend Caroline," Adrian told the collector, and Caroline startled with pleasure, as though not expecting to be introduced. Adrian couldn't remember whether Jan and his wife had been friends with Nora or just frequent gallery customers. The very interested gleam in Jan's eyes as he raked them over Caroline suggested the former, in which case Adrian needed to brace for the fallout of being caught having dinner with a pretty woman almost two decades younger than Nora. Or maybe Jan was trying to see whether he could look down Caroline's dress; he was looming over her, well positioned to ogle Caroline's exposed collarbones. Adrian gritted his teeth at the man's sleaze.

"Very nice to meet you. Never would have thought to run into our favorite artist right here at the symphony, huh? Small world," Jan proclaimed.

Caroline was oblivious to Jan's wandering gaze. She smiled up at him as he chattered about how he knew Adrian, bringing his phone out to show Caroline pictures of the couches he'd decorated by hanging Adrian's art behind them.

"Samantha," Jan said to his wife, "didn't we just get asked about the one with the nurses at the Battle of Passchendaele?" He mispronounced it *passion-dilly*.

"Oh, yes!" Samantha said. "We gave away all the gallery cards you left." She put her clawlike hand on Adrian's shoulder, squeezing him through his suit jacket, then resting her hand familiarly on the back of his neck.

Now he remembered them better. Samantha had called to ask him to come back a week after hanging the last painting to "look at matching fabric swatches," which he'd worried was code for her clothes on the bedroom floor, given the amount of casual groping she'd subjected him to already. He hadn't gone; that was when he could afford boundaries.

"Do you have more?" Samantha asked.

"I'm afraid I may be moving my collection soon," Adrian said.

Both Jan and Samantha made faces of disappointment.

"Take my card," Jan said, pulling one from his wallet and handing it to Adrian. "Next time you have a show, give us a call and we'll come." He looked at Caroline. "Are you an artist too?"

"No," said Caroline. "I'm a business student."

Jan gave her a card anyway before leading his reluctant wife to a table on the other side of the restaurant. They were still in line of sight. Adrian didn't immediately speak after they left, feeling drained by the brief interaction. He probably should have tried harder to impress the

Mayers. Told them about his works in progress, performed a little salesmanship. Nora had always complained that he didn't engage enough with the potential customers. *What, like you're shy?*

Caroline, though, had perked up, energized by her brush with the bloody commerce of professional art. She'd been so stiff and nervous throughout the entire symphony, and he'd worried that she was not enjoying herself, but now she was bright-eyed.

"So," she said. "You really are an artist."

"You didn't look me up before we met?" Adrian asked. He hadn't looked her up, but he supposed she was much less likely to kidnap him than the other way around.

"I saw your gallery page, but anyone can put anything on the Internet," she said. "Those people put your art in their living room!" Her tone made it into a career-capping achievement that he had styled the Natick bungalow of a hedge fund vice president.

He couldn't respond without either rejecting her praise or agreeing with her premise, so he sat there and squirmed instead.

"Can we go see your art at your gallery?" she asked.

"I don't know if any of it is up right now," he evaded, imagining the scene if he brought Caroline into Nora's workplace.

Caroline pressed her lips together speculatively as she followed up: "Or at the museum?"

That was enough to startle him out of his funk and make him laugh. "I'm not in any museums. Yet."

She cocked her head, undeterred. "How do you get your work into museums, then?"

"Die young—or in an interesting way," he suggested.

Caroline wrinkled her tip-tilted nose. "Well, don't do

that, even if it's interesting. I liked the painting in your profile picture. Where are the other ones like that?"

Adrian shrugged. "That was a long time ago—it's in my friend's apartment. An engagement gift to him and his ex-wife. The pictures on my gallery page are more representative of my current practice."

"Oh," she said, thinking about that. "I liked the old one better."

Of course she did. It was pretty and sentimental and full of color. Adrian sighed. "For future reference, painters aren't like rock bands. You don't win any points for saying you liked their old stuff better."

Caroline grinned unrepentantly at him. "As if you know anything about rock bands," she said.

"I like all kinds of music," he objected. "Not just classical."

She got a teasing look on her face. "Okay, Renaissance man, what's your favorite band?"

"I only get one?"

"Yes," she said, beaming at him. "This is a test." She brushed her hair back from soft, round cheeks, unselfconsciously lovely again.

Smiling despite himself, he said, "The Beatles."

"The Beatles is cheating," she retorted, leaning in. "That's what you say if you just want to make sure nobody can say anything bad about your fave. *Cheater.* You're supposed to fess up to the sappy, embarrassing one with bad hair and vague lyrics that you're embarrassed to have the T-shirt for. My oldest sister says she likes the Beatles. What she *actually* likes is Dave Matthews Band."

"I still like the Beatles," Adrian said, something tugging in his chest at the challenging glint in her eye, because this part was dimly familiar: elbows on the table at a cheap restaurant, talking about music, laughing even if you weren't sure it was a joke. "Does it help that 'Rocky Raccoon' is the only song I can play on the guitar?"

Caroline stroked her chin, pretending to consider his answer. "A little. I'll allow the Beatles. I guess we all like the stuff that was popular while we were in high school."

Adrian gave a coughing laugh. "Wait, how old do you think I am, exactly?"

Caroline's teeth showed between her pink lips. She looked delighted with his question. "Contemporary with Bach, maybe?"

Before he could come up with a sufficiently powerful response to her brattiness, the server came over with their dinner.

The restaurant did a nice presentation: his fish was garnished with vegetables and roe formed to suggest exotic flowers. Microgreens and orchids dotted Caroline's sushi rolls.

Adrian made the requisite noise of pleasure and nodded at the server. Caroline's eyes were wide as she stared at her dinner.

"Please enjoy," said the server.

CAROLINE KNEW ABOUT SUSHI. PEOPLE IN BOOKS AND TELE-vision shows ordered sushi. She'd seen sushi restaurants before, tucked into strip malls or spilling out of shopping mall food courts. They just didn't have any sushi restaurants in Templeton, and the only fish her family ate was of the stick or Filet-O varieties. So she knew what sushi was, but she'd never eaten any before.

Adrian took the lime-green paste off his tray with his chopsticks (another hurdle—she'd only handled those a couple of times, and she wasn't good with them), moved the paste to a small dish, and poured soy sauce over it. Slowly copying him gave her something to do while she convinced herself that she was going to eat all this fish and like it.

"Looks good," Caroline said, based on nothing more than hope.

Adrian dipped a translucent pink diamond of food—raw fish, it had to be, because Caroline couldn't identify it as anything else—in his soy sauce, then popped it into his mouth with evident enjoyment.

"Yeah," he agreed. "I've been eating nothing but the leftovers my roommate brings home for almost a month. This is a perfect change of pace."

"Is he a chef?" Caroline asked.

"A waiter." He waved off that line of inquiry, refocusing on Caroline as she tentatively tapped her chopsticks together. "What did you think of the Bach concerto?"

Caroline didn't particularly want to answer that. She busied herself mixing her green paste and her soy sauce. The white part of the sushi rolls was rice, no problem with that. The dark green was seaweed, probably, and that was just ocean lettuce. That left everything else on her tray to be positively identified before she put it in her mouth.

"They all seemed very talented at their instruments." She tried to be rigorously fair. "It was a very complicated piece of music, but I don't think they made any mistakes."

One of the rolls had orange-pink meat in the center. She thought it was probably salmon, because she'd been at awards banquets where salmon was served. People seemed to like it. So she took a deep breath, tried to turn off the voice in her head that was highly skeptical of eating meat without cooking it properly first, and picked up the roll with her chopsticks.

"But did *you* enjoy it?" Adrian asked, not misled by her faint praise. His expression was too interested in the answer.

Caroline tried to dunk the roll in the soy sauce, the way she'd seen him do, but she fumbled her chopsticks, dropping the sushi into the soy sauce, where it fell apart.

"Here," Adrian said, closing his hands over hers and trying to arrange them appropriately around the chopsticks. His fingers were warmer than hers and had a couple of calluses that brushed against the ones that were starting to peel off her own fingers from lack of tennis practice.

Caroline blushed and pulled away, setting the chopsticks aside.

"Maybe next time," she deflected. She grabbed her fork, using it to pry the various components out of the soy sauce and onto a side plate. She got a few drops on the table, and her hand shook when she took the napkin out of her lap to blot them up.

She swallowed hard and admitted the truth before trying to eat again. "I didn't understand the point of it. There's no lyrics. There's no story. And I couldn't figure out whether it was supposed to be happy or sad or . . . if it even was supposed to be anything? What was it supposed to mean?"

Adrian ate a few more slices of fish while he thought about that, and the seriousness with which he was taking her thoughts made her nervous. She supposed she could have read up on it before they went to the concert, but she'd had a midterm that day. She probably sounded really ignorant. And Adrian was treating her opinion like the *Boston Globe* review.

"That's fair," Adrian said, handsome face creased with

internal deliberation. "About Bach. It's music for music's sake, not to tell a story."

She grabbed another roll at random, forwent the soy sauce that had caused disaster before, and stuffed the roll in her mouth. Her mind was still fighting hard against the idea of raw fish, so she barely chewed before swallowing it, getting only the sweetness of the rice and the saltiness of the seaweed.

There. It was done. Fish was in her.

There were nearly two dozen more pieces to go. So many different colors and textures, from God-only-knew-what creatures. Caroline quailed at the thought. She'd been raised to clean her plate, especially at restaurants. She opened her mouth to take a breath, then picked up a second piece. Adrian was no longer watching her eat, at least, while he tried to convince himself that her opinion on Bach was a reasonable one.

"You didn't study any instruments?" he asked.

"No. You did?"

"Seven years of piano lessons."

"That's impressive," Caroline told him before popping the second roll into her mouth. She swallowed quickly, then reached for her water glass to wash it down. There had been big clumps of the green stuff stuck on it, and now her sinuses were burning.

Adrian shook his head in disagreement. "Not at all. I had no talent, and I hated to practice."

"But you learned to like the music?" Caroline asked. She hoped it didn't take seven years of lessons, because she didn't want to wait that long.

"I can't remember not liking it. My parents always had the classical station playing in the car, and my school took us at least twice a year to the symphony for *Peter and the Wolf* or *The Nutcracker Suite.* . . . I suppose it was just around me." His gaze refocused on her. "Why were you interested in the symphony if you don't listen to classical music?"

Caroline's stomach sank. "I'd never been, and it seemed like something people liked in—" She didn't want to admit that it seemed like something people liked in the movies, because that made her sound hopelessly naive. Wasn't never having done something enough of a reason to try it?

Scanning her dinner for her next bite, she saw a yellow piece of something on rice. In her brief review of the order card, she'd noticed egg as one of the choices. It had to be scrambled egg on rice, which was probably the most familiar option. So she shoved it into her mouth to cut off her answer, chewing under the assumption it was egg. But the texture was too soft and creamy, and the taste was sweet and sour. Like seafood yogurt. Caroline's throat closed as she panicked, but she forced it down. Her stomach jumped up in protest, threatening to launch a full-scale revolt, and she grabbed her water to wash it all down over the strong objections of her digestive tract.

Unfortunately, Adrian had seen the whole sequence, and he was watching her with concern.

"What was that one?" she managed to ask him as her throat opened and closed.

"Uni," he said.

Caroline stared at him blankly.

"It's sea urchin," he explained.

"Oh," she muttered, mind summoning pictures of the spiky little critters at the bottom of her dentist's aquarium. Now bobbing uneasily in her gut.

Her head swam despite every effort to sternly instruct

her body that she would keep it together, finish the dinner, and pretend to be a sophisticated person. She tried to pick up another piece, but her gag reflex triggered at the mere thought of more seafood. She put the sushi back down.

"Are you all right?" Adrian quietly asked, killing her hopes that he simply hadn't noticed. For the last few minutes, he'd seemed to relax, but now he was looking at her like he needed to render emergency aid again.

"I'm fine," she snapped, which he didn't deserve. Hot tears of embarrassment started to prickle at the corners of her eyes, and being horrified by that was only going to make them spill over.

"I can order something else—" Adrian began to say, but Caroline's purse vibrated at her elbow, cutting him off.

"I forgot to mention," he said when Caroline didn't immediately move to get her phone out, "it rang a few times while you were away from the table earlier."

That gave her the rationale she needed to grab her purse and trek back to the bathroom, saying weakly that she'd be right back. That couple from earlier was also watching her as she crossed the restaurant, clutching her purse and cursing as her blisters rubbed against the paper towels she'd shoved in her shoes.

It was probably weird that she was going to the bathroom to look at her phone. That wasn't a normal thing to do. But Caroline had to go to the sink and run cold water from the tap over the insides of her wrists before she could even look at her face in the mirror.

This was ridiculous. She'd played through tendinitis, through tennis toe, played with blood running down her knee after a fall. Now she was pale and sick-looking just because she was trying to eat a new food. She made eye contact with herself just to silently yell at mirror-Caroline to get back in the game. This wasn't supposed to be hard.

When sufficient color had returned to her cheeks, Caroline took her phone out of her purse to see four missed calls. The first two from her uncle. The third from her father. The last from her mother. Nobody had left a message.

Her mom had sworn she wasn't taking sides, but she'd also stopped calling Caroline six months ago, which kind of suggested the opposite. This was the first time she'd been the one to pick up the phone since Caroline moved out.

Casting a wary eye over the unused stalls in the bathroom, Caroline called her mother back.

She picked up immediately. Caroline heard one of her nephews squalling in the background, as well as the TV, but not any of her other family members, so she fractionally relaxed.

"Hi, honeybun," her mom said. "Thanks for calling back."

She seemed sincere, but Caroline wasn't sure.

"Of course. Though I'm on a date, so . . ." She trailed off, not wanting to say anything else about it.

Her mother's hand adjusted on the receiver, and Caroline heard background noise recede further.

"Oh, honey, really? How did you meet him?"

Caroline chewed on the side of her cheek. "Online."

"That's what I was worried about," her mother sighed. "That's not safe, sweetie. I wish you'd talked with me about this first—"

"It's fine," Caroline interrupted her. "We're in public. I got a background check on him."

"That's—okay. But let's talk about this before you start dating. You've just barely started living on your own—"

And whose fault is that? Caroline wanted to demand. She could have lived in the dorms on her tennis scholarship, but it was her parents who hadn't thought she could handle that, or couldn't handle that and as much tennis as they wanted her to play.

"Is everything okay? Dad called, and Uncle Jay—" Maybe there was an actual emergency. At a minimum, she wanted to change the subject.

"We wanted to know if you were coming home for Thanksgiving," her mom said after a pause.

"Probably not," Caroline replied, because she hadn't planned on it. "I think I have classes through that Tuesday." And she wasn't sure she was *ever* going back to Texas.

Her mother waited another beat. "Okay, I'll tell them. Your uncle was thinking it would be fun for the entire family to go on a cruise or something."

Well, there it was.

"Oh," Caroline said weakly. "Where?"

"There's one leaving out of Galveston on that Wednesday. It goes to the Mexican Riviera. There's still rooms free, even this late. They serve Thanksgiving dinner on the boat."

"That sounds nice," Caroline lied. It would probably be nice for everyone else. *She* imagined jumping over the rail and swimming for land if she was trapped in the middle of the ocean with her family.

"Do you think you might make it in Tuesday night? We could meet you in Houston."

"I . . . I think I'll need to study for exams. They'll be coming up," she said, knowing she wouldn't fool her mother.

"Oh, okay."

"But, you know, you should still go. Mexico sounds great."

"I don't know about that. Your dad was on the fence about it," her mother said wistfully.

As far as her father was concerned, school breaks were an opportunity for tennis clinics, tennis tournaments, or, failing that, extra tennis practice. Her oldest niece was turning four—she wondered whether her father would start the whole program over again, or whether he'd gotten everything out of Caroline's career he needed.

"No, I mean it. How much is it? Let me just send you a check," Caroline said.

"You don't need to do that, sweetie," her mom said, and for a moment Caroline thought maybe her mother was going to get serious about not taking sides. But then she said, "It's hard, you know. For your father. The idea of taking money from you."

Really? Caroline nearly snapped. It didn't seem like it was going to be that hard for him.

"He wanted to pay for the cruise?" she asked, incredulous. Her father barely believed in vacations in the first place and would never spend money to send his brother or adult daughters on one.

"Well. It would be different. If he didn't have to ask for it. If it was his money."

Caroline leaned forward and supported herself by her elbows on the bathroom counter. She shouldn't have answered the call. She didn't have several hours available right now for feeling terrible.

She'd tried to calculate it. The net present value of two years of tuition and living expenses, plus a little cushion if she couldn't get a good job right away. Made a budget for everything her grandmother might have expected her to do. It didn't have to be exact. She could get a part-time job, if worse came to worst. But there were just too many unknowns. She didn't know how much everything cost in Boston. She didn't know what she had to pay for that different life yet. She didn't know what she could afford to sign away. She didn't know what she was supposed to do.

"I can't yet," she told her mother miserably. "It's not even two years of school. Can he just be patient?"

There was a noise like her mother had walked to a different room and shut the door.

"I didn't want to get into it, I just—" her mother said.

"No, no, I know, I know," Caroline said. "You wanted to go."

She could hear her father distantly calling her mother's name.

"I need to make lunches for tomorrow," her mother said in a rush.

"Okay. Love you. Talk to you Sunday," Caroline said. She hung up. She'd forgotten where she was for a moment. In the bathroom of the sushi restaurant, Adrian left behind at the table. Familiar guilt erased the rest of her embarrassment about the sushi.

Okay, Caroline, focus, she told herself in the same way she would if she were ad-in at a set point. *It's just some stupid fish. You can handle some stupid fish. Other people think it's delicious.*

She put away her phone and rubbed her cheeks until she felt like her face was in a normal configuration again.

When she wobbled back out of the bathroom, Adrian wasn't in his seat. She had a brief moment of concern that he had taken the opportunity to leave, but then she spotted him in the corner of the restaurant farthest from both their table and the table of his . . . clients? Customers? The other couple was watching avidly as Adrian spoke in a low, angry tone into his phone.

Caroline took her seat, feeling as though the evening had gone hopelessly sideways. As soon as she was seated, the server came over with a large plate to set in front of Caroline's sushi.

"Chicken teriyaki," she said in a low, sympathetic voice.

"Oh, I didn't order—"

"Your boyfriend ordered for you," the server said, nodding at Adrian where he stood across the restaurant, shoulders hunched and face tilted to the front window.

Caroline winced as she looked at the plain grilled chicken on white rice before her. It was probably the sushi restaurant equivalent of buttered noodles: food for picky toddlers.

"Thanks," Caroline managed, unable to reject the dish. At least a single person thought it was plausible Adrian was her boyfriend.

She curled her hands into fists, then resolutely speared a sushi roll with her fork. She was going to learn to love this fish if it killed her. She'd come too far to be beaten by lesser vertebrates.

Adrian had begun to pace, and when he drifted closer, Caroline made out the last of his conversation.

"—more than a couple days!" His voice was furious.

Caroline got down three more pieces of sushi, drenched in enough soy sauce to pickle a cow, as Adrian finished his phone call and shoved his phone into his trouser pocket. He wiped a palm over his forehead, looking out the window as he gathered himself. When he turned to Caroline, his face was barely on the grim side of neutral.

Caroline didn't pretend not to have noticed when he

sat back down and stared at his remaining dinner. In a way, it was freeing, not being the only one with problems.

"Sorry," Adrian said, but didn't offer any other explanation.

"Is everything okay?" Caroline asked for the second time in ten minutes.

His cheek pulled to the side in dismay.

"Yes. But I need to reschedule our trip to the Haymarket. I need to move some things Saturday morning, and that's the next time my roommate is off work."

"No worries," she said quietly, wondering if Adrian would prefer she inquire further or not. When he didn't say anything else, she asked, "You're moving to a new apartment?"

He shook his head. "No. I—" His soft blue eyes flicked up at her, as though weighing how much he ought to tell her.

Caroline paused with her fork in another sushi roll, waiting attentively.

Adrian sighed. "I moved out of the house I shared with my ex a few weeks ago. She just told me to take out everything I left behind by Saturday, or she's putting it on the curb."

That sounded pretty bitchy to Caroline, but she didn't want to presume what the circumstances of the breakup had been. Maybe Adrian had done something terrible, though he didn't seem like the kind of guy who did terrible things.

"Do you need any help moving?" she asked.

Adrian waved away the offer, but he took his phone back out of his pocket.

"Please excuse me for being very rude though," he

said, tapping the screen with his thumbs. "I need to reserve a truck. If I can even get one for Saturday."

Caroline wondered again whether she was sticking her nose in where it wasn't wanted, but she didn't believe that Adrian had so much free labor that he wouldn't want more help.

"How much stuff are you moving?"

"Just a desk and a few boxes. I think. But Tom and I can manage."

"Are you sure?" she asked. "I have an SUV. And obviously, I'm not doing anything on Saturday."

He stopped typing. "You're driving around Boston in an SUV?"

She was a little needled by the judgment in his tone. "I didn't buy it for Boston. But it's a Tahoe."

He was obviously reluctant. "Can you parallel park a Tahoe?"

"Well . . . ," she admitted.

Adrian's expression was a portrait of unhappiness. He hesitated, hands still on his phone screen.

"Can you afford to rent a truck?" she pressed. "I'd let you use my SUV for free."

"I can't impose."

"Think about it in economic terms," she insisted. "How many hand jobs do you have to give to break even on a U-Haul?"

Adrian's chest heaved as he put a palm over his face.

"God," he said, eyes cast heavenward. "A lot, I'm sure." He propped his cheek onto his hand, looking across the table at her with resignation. "When you put it like that, I can't say no," he said, sounding as though he really did want to say no. "I mean yes, thank you."

They stared at each other over their mostly untouched

spread of what was now room-temperature fish. Adrian's face said he was back to vaguely mortified to be her sugar baby.

Maybe she'd been too pushy. But wasn't she supposed to financially support him? It had seemed like such a simple transaction—his time for her money. But as with most things, there was some set of unwritten rules that *ought to have been written down and provided to her*, which she'd instead managed to transgress. That thought made her tired, for all that it wasn't even eleven o'clock yet. She felt like she'd hyperextended an underused muscle.

"I'll get the check," Caroline said, waving at the server and then passing her a credit card without waiting for the tab.

Caroline confirmed the time and place for Saturday as they stood up and walked to the street. She'd taken a rideshare to the theater, having learned her lesson about driving downtown from their first meeting.

"Oh," Caroline abruptly remembered as they waited for her car to arrive. "Here."

She took a plain white envelope from her purse and passed it to Adrian. "Sorry that this still feels like a drug deal. I don't know how to make it feel less like a drug deal. You should get Venmo or something."

Adrian hesitantly took the envelope containing a thousand-dollar check from her.

"I really shouldn't," he said, more to himself than to her. His sharp jaw was set in a tense line.

"Why?" Caroline asked, surprised. "You did everything you said you would."

He huffed out a little sound of disagreement. "No, I took you to a concert you didn't like, then a dinner you didn't eat. I think I failed pretty squarely at being a good date."

Caroline looked away. "That's not your fault," she said. Someone who knew more about Bach and fish would have enjoyed the evening. She just wasn't sophisticated enough to appreciate it yet.

Adrian stuck his hands in his pockets, looking like he disagreed with that too.

"We'll get better at this," she reassured him. "We're going to see a movie tomorrow. And we'll still go to the Haymarket sometime, right?"

He looked like he wanted to say more, but her car arrived then.

"Yes, whatever you want," he agreed, opening her door. He hesitated, and Caroline had the fuzzy, ephemeral thought that if he actually had been her boyfriend, this was where he would have kissed her good night. Her gaze dipped to his mouth, and then the column of his throat, which moved as he swallowed. But then he stepped away, hands still in his pockets, and the evening was over.

Chapter Six

SATURDAY DAWNED OVERCAST AND STILL, WITH A FLAT GRAY slab of clouds smothering the horizon. Out on the curb in front of their apartment block in Brighton, Adrian dodged Tom's questions as they waited for Caroline to arrive, burdened with rolls of Bubble Wrap and battered cardboard boxes from the initial move. Despite the leaden sky, the air was still and unseasonably warm. Adrian was already overheating in the battered sweatpants and long-sleeved thermal knit shirt he'd put on for moving the last of his things out of Nora's house.

"Now tell me, what's this girl like?" Tom asked, his expression too interested. Adrian had left most of the details vague, despite Tom's attempts to pry.

"She's twenty-two," Adrian said shortly. That was the most important fact he needed to remember about her.

"That's not a personality trait," Tom protested. "You've been out with her a couple times. Does she actually look like her profile photo?"

"That's not a personality trait either," Adrian groused. It was eight in the morning. He didn't want to be awake, but Tom had to be back at his restaurant by two.

"That's a yes," Tom said smugly. "But is she relatively normal? Do you like her?"

Adrian scowled and looked down the street. He had no

idea what she was trying to accomplish via her relationship with him or where she'd gotten her money from. As best he could tell, she'd been 100 percent honest with him while withholding her most pertinent biographical details. But even if he firmly disregarded her lovely eyes and long bare legs, it was hard not to be charmed by the way Caroline veered from awkward to blissfully unaffected without transition. And even though she'd only known him a week, she was up at eight on a Saturday, helping him move. Of course he *liked* her.

"She's twenty-two," Adrian reminded him yet again. "She's way too young for me."

His roommate laughed. "Twenty-two is fine though. Half your age plus seven, right?"

"How did you pass college math? That would be twenty-three. And still gross."

"Rosie let me cheat off her in math," Tom said proudly. "Also, you were a total slut at twenty-two. I was *there*, Gandalf. Twenty-two is grown-up. What's actually wrong with her? Is she super pretentious? Is that why she's paying someone to take her out to the symphony and stuff?"

"No," Adrian defended Caroline automatically. "She's not."

Tom gave him a lopsided grin. "So she's nice."

Adrian gritted his jaw. "Yes, she's nice," he admitted, even if *nice* didn't quite cover the breadth of her personality.

Tom's face bloomed with triumph.

"And twenty-two," Adrian amended.

They heard Caroline's SUV before they saw it, because a Tahoe made a lot of noise going over the cobblestones of their side street. It was forest green, slightly battered, and at least a decade old. Like many things about Caroline, it made no sense to him: What kind of graduate student had thousands of dollars to spare but spent it exclusively on arts patronage?

She pulled up, nearly scraping the curb, and hopped out to open the custom sliding passenger door. It was clear that she was a morning person from the bounce in her step and smile on her face. Adrian froze in place, suddenly wide awake, heart kicking into gear as he took Caroline in.

Tom received a bright white grin and an enthusiastic handshake before she told him to mind the wheelchair ramp. Adrian got a more subdued nod and a searching look, like she expected him to be emotional about moving the last set of random knickknacks out of his ex's place. Over his objections, she helped stack their packing materials in the rear of the SUV.

"Careful, watch out for the coffee," she chirped. "I picked up some Dunkies. There's cream and lots of sugar, hope that's okay."

Tom climbed through the side door past a collapsed wheelchair ramp and a full gym bag. Adrian took the passenger seat, kicking aside some student detritus: folders, water bottles, a shopping bag full of hair ties and lip balm.

"Sorry it's a mess," Caroline said as she came back around to the driver's seat. She actually did sound sorry.

"No, this is so *nice* of you," Tom said, leaning hard on the adjective as he passed Adrian one of the coffees. "Tom Wilczewski," he introduced himself. "*So* glad to meet you."

When Adrian turned back to accept the drink, Tom gave him a wide-eyed look of intense interest, like a kitten that had just sighted a dangling hair ribbon. It made Adrian immediately wary. Tom inclined his head toward

Caroline where she sat in front of him and lifted his eyebrows even higher.

Are you kidding me? said his expression.

Adrian took his point: Caroline was wearing exercise clothes, which was a perfectly reasonable choice if she thought she was going to help carry a bunch of things, even though Adrian didn't plan to let her. But her exercise clothes consisted of bright yellow running tights, a matching sports bra, and a white hooded windbreaker left unzipped. No shirt. And why would she need one when it was so warm outside?

That was all well and good for her, but she looked like a literal beam of sunshine, bright and blond and happy in the gray morning. Adrian couldn't help but be dazzled. Her leggings left absolutely none of the round shape of her ass to his imagination, and three or four inches of her tanned, muscular stomach were completely exposed, even when she was sitting. If he looked. Which, Jesus, he absolutely should not have looked, and neither should Tom.

"Um, you're welcome to put something else on the radio," she said as Adrian squinted hard at the bricks of the building out the passenger window, willing his mind to get out of her sports bra. "I thought this would be appropriate. She had some bad break-ups too. Did you know that?"

"I love Taylor Swift," Tom said, leaning in between the front seats. "Poet of our generation."

"Yes! Exactly!" Caroline said, pleased, putting the SUV back into drive. "Where to?"

Adrian took a long, bracing gulp of the coffee, even though he usually took his black.

"Go east on Storrow," he muttered.

Caroline stretched, then took an elastic band off her

wrist to tie her hair back into a short half ponytail. The motion did interesting things to her chest. Adrian closed his eyes. Caroline saw his expression but mistook the reason for it.

"This must be hard for you," she said sympathetically.

Adrian nodded without opening his eyes, hoping that his expression suggested a reason other than the beautiful woman in the driver's seat.

BOSTON'S DRIVERS WERE SHOCKING IN THEIR DISREGARD of their city's traffic ordinances, nowhere more so than on Storrow Drive. Caroline silently judged them as they merged without signaling, passed her on the right, and used their horns as communication signals. Adrian was quiet in the passenger seat next to her, hands white-knuckled around his coffee, face tilted resolutely out the window. Maybe he got easily carsick, or maybe he was just upset about putting a pin in his relationship. Either way, she felt for him.

His roommate was as upbeat as Adrian was dour though. Tom looked like he was about Adrian's age, shorter and more muscular, with dark brown eyes beaming at her from under thick black eyebrows. With Adrian silent, Caroline tried to strike up a conversation with Tom as she laboriously made her way east toward Logan Airport.

"Adrian tells me you're a waiter at a Greek restaurant?"

"Is that what he said?" Tom replied, voice full of faux outrage. "I suppose, in a literal sense, I am. But I'm also an actor."

An actor! That was exciting. She'd never met an actor before.

"Oh, what kind?" Caroline asked.

"Stage," Adrian answered for him. "He's been on Broadway."

It took Caroline a few seconds to process that she was meeting an actual *Broadway* actor. This was excellent news. Adrian had been a great choice.

"I was in a Broadway production *once*," Tom said, good-humored about it. "That blessed situation did not recur. Hence the waiting of tables. In Boston."

"Well, I'm still impressed," Caroline told him. "Are you going to be in anything soon?"

"That's entirely at the discretion of our city's casting directors. I have two auditions next week. Are you interested in the theater?"

"Absolutely. I mean, in terms of going to it. Not being in it. Although the only play I've seen in person I was also in—my high school put on *West Side Story* my freshman year. I was one of the girl Jets."

Tom laughed. "That counts! You should try it again."

"Oh, no," Caroline objected, thinking back to that month. She'd been able to try out only because she was recovering from a sprained wrist, and even then her father hadn't liked the distraction from tennis. "I was completely terrible. I can't act. The theater teacher said he bet the show had never had a Jet with such a thick Texas accent before."

"I bet you were an adorable girl Jet," Tom said. "You don't want to go back?"

"Mmm, nothing stopping me but my complete lack of talent," Caroline said, looking to Adrian for her exit as they approached the airport. He gestured at her to turn north toward East Boston.

"You don't need talent to be part of the theater," Tom said. "Adrian doesn't have any talent, and he still helped with most of my shows."

Adrian turned away from the window long enough to glare at his roommate.

Caroline tried to guess in what capacity Adrian had been involved. "Set design?" she guessed.

"I did the art for the promotional posters and the programs," Adrian said, still sounding unamused. His stiff answer kicked Caroline and Tom both into giggles.

"Maybe next semester," Caroline told Tom. "But Adrian and I are going to see a musical soon."

As Tom congratulated her on that, they turned off 1A to a neighborhood of neat colonial houses north of the airport. Adrian directed her to an open stretch of curb long enough for her to drive in, so her parallel parking abilities went untested.

"You can wait with the car, if you'd like," Adrian said when he climbed out and began unloading packing supplies. "This shouldn't take long."

"I don't mind going in to help carry things," Caroline said. "I'm okay at walking when I'm not in heels." She pointed at one of her big white athletic shoes.

Adrian opened his mouth to object again, but Tom beat him to the punch.

"Let the lady work! It'll go much faster with three people," Tom said, draping an arm supportively around Caroline's shoulders. "Besides, she looks like she could pick me up and carry me if it came to that." He waggled his eyebrows at her lasciviously, like he wanted her to try.

Adrian's mouth curved down sharply in response, but he led them to a large gray-shingled house halfway down the block and approached the front door.

"Is your ex here?" Caroline asked, suddenly nervous at the prospect of meeting the woman. She was unlikely to be as welcoming as Adrian's roommate.

"No, she said she's out of town until tomorrow," Adrian replied, pulling a ring of keys out of his pocket. He looked surprised when his key turned easily in the lock.

Caroline followed him into the house, a little curious as to how a starving artist lived, or had lived until two months ago. She halted in the entryway in surprise.

It was the nicest house she'd ever been in. The floors were polished maple, and the walls were painted white, like a church or a museum. There was only a single ivory-colored scarf hung on the coatrack at the entryway. In the living room, all the furniture was upholstered in shades of soft neutral gray. Everything matched, the house was super clean, and all the furniture and rugs were at precise right angles to everything else. The only color in the room came from the paintings hung on the wall. The effect was at once rich and chilly.

Caroline must have had her thoughts on her face, because Tom sidled up next to her and murmured, "It looks like the set for a diarrhea medication commercial, doesn't it?"

She snorted at the painful accuracy of that observation. It didn't look like a place where people actually *lived*. She'd be afraid to sit on one of the stiff little couches for fear that she'd knock a mohair throw pillow out of place and disturb the entire arrangement. She wondered whether Adrian had put it all together or whether the place reflected his ex's tastes instead. Some of the paintings looked like they might be his.

Adrian stomped up the stairs without giving her or Tom any instructions, so she drifted over to a fancy pewter-and-glass console table, where several framed photographs were clustered. All depicted an attractive brunette in her late thirties: at the beach, in an evening gown, in front of a foreign skyline. Adrian wasn't in any of them.

"Were they always just of her?" she whispered to Tom, not sure if even muted criticism was wise.

"I think there used to be *one* of them together." Tom smirked, tapping an open space at the end of the table. "But no, this is the temple of Nora. The only thing Adrian designed is the garden out back."

At that hint of an invitation, Caroline crossed through the kitchen (more white on the cabinets and gray-veined marble on the waterfall island) so she could look out the back window.

"Where's the garden?" she asked, confused.

Tom lifted his head and came to peer out at the muddy pit behind the house. There was a partially assembled aboveground hot tub on the concrete slab leading into the turfless waste of the backyard, but no plants beyond a couple of adventurous weeds clinging to the overturned dirt. It was a mess, a fresh mess.

Tom started to laugh in dismay. "Oh shit," he said. "I wonder if he's seen what happened to his peonies yet."

From upstairs, there came an echoing curse. Caroline supposed that meant he had.

ADRIAN COULD NOT EVEN BOTHER TO BE OUTRAGED AT how Nora had dug up all his flower bushes to install a hot tub. Though that was horrific by itself: What had the Gold-flame spirea ever done to her? When she was done being angry at him, wouldn't she be sorry her backyard looked like Carthage after the Second Punic War?

It got worse though. He knew she was angry at him, but he'd thought throwing him out in the middle of the night was the cruelest move he might expect from his ex-fiancée. Their professional relationship predated their personal one. Nora was a professional. He'd expected her to act like one through the end of the year.

But there was his art on the floor of the guest bedroom. A dozen or more paintings on canvas, all haphazardly tossed together like a discard pile at a garage sale.

He barely dared to move anything for fear that the stack would shift and further damage the paintings, but it looked like Nora had ruthlessly curated everything he'd painted before he met her, then dragged it home in a careless jumble. She'd treated it like trash. Before he met her, he was trash. That was the message.

It had never been displayed at her gallery, but occasionally a collector would come ask after an earlier series, and she'd sell one of Adrian's first works: big scenes of garden parties and crowded rooms, weighty mounds of flowers weaving among the figures of friends who'd modeled for him. People had liked it. Some critics too. Not Nora. *Your technique is decent*, Nora had told him at twenty-six, when he'd begun to eye the international market. *Are you ready to get serious?*

He'd thought so. But wherever Nora had thought he was going with his career or their relationship, he'd never arrived. Now anything that had ever been good or hopeful about the two of them was impossible to remember through the cloudy varnish of years of mutual disappointment.

No doubt drawn by his swearing, Tom and Caroline crept up the stairs to peer into the room after him.

Adrian laced his fingers across the top of his head, counting to ten under his breath. He squatted to gingerly lift the corner of the top painting, recoiling at the dent where an edge had rubbed into the canvas below.

"Fuck," he muttered again. How had it gotten this bad? He was sure he deserved it on some level for getting involved with his gallery director, but how did five years come to this?

Adrian became aware of Caroline squatting next to him, fingers tentatively stroking his shoulder in consolation. The tiny contact was grounding.

"I'm all right," he said roughly. He'd spent half a decade with a woman who could do this for nothing more than spite, which probably said things about his judgment that he needed to examine at length, but he wasn't going to cry about it while Caroline and Tom watched him like he was about to throw himself out the second-floor window.

"Yeah, of course," Caroline said, still managing to disagree. She looked at the pile. "Jesus and Joseph, what did you *do* to her?"

Adrian rubbed his mouth. "I told her I didn't think we should get married."

Caroline screwed up her face, trying to understand the position. "Because you decided you're not a commitment guy?"

"I said I didn't think we were in a position to be making any vows while she was sleeping with her buyer at Sotheby's."

"Ah," Caroline said, eyebrows shooting up. "Not in a sophisticated, post-monogamy kind of way?"

"No, just plain, old-fashioned screwing around," Adrian muttered. He sat back on the floor, staring at the pile helplessly. People he'd worked with for years at the gallery must have helped Nora pull everything out of storage without wrapping the paintings to protect them. Even if he'd been far from the most popular artist at the gallery, this felt like a personal attack.

He'd never do this to someone else. He wouldn't have done *any* of it to someone else.

"Sorry, bud," Tom said.

"Yeah."

Tom came over and lifted the top canvas away from the pile. He was one of the figures in the scene depicted, face in profile and nearly obscured by a spray of dogwood blossoms. Elsewhere in the frame was the silhouette of the guy he'd been dating at the time, the first person Adrian had approved of Tom seeing after Rosie. Tom had moved out by then, but Adrian had talked both men into coming by the studio and modeling for him.

God, maybe it was awful and sentimental, like the critic had said, but the painting represented a year in Adrian's life—everything he'd thought and felt, not just the weeks it had taken to paint.

Tom leaned the wounded painting against the writing desk that had been the original focus of the day's move.

"Can you fix it?" he asked.

"Maybe," Adrian said reluctantly. "I could take them back to my studio and try, at least."

Nora could hardly insist on the exclusive right to sell paintings she'd threatened to throw in the garbage. Maybe Adrian would find a way to sell them.

Caroline jumped to her feet, hands on her yellow-spandex-wrapped hips.

"Right," she said with determination. "So we have a new plan. We are going to take these all out."

Tom shot her an impressed look. "We have a plan?"

She nodded firmly. "You two box up everything else. I'll go buy some more Bubble Wrap and tape for the paintings. We'll get them all wrapped up."

"You don't have to do that," Adrian said automatically,

even though he didn't know what he was going to do otherwise.

"Well, that's what makes sense. Do you have a better plan?"

"This is a lot more work than you thought it would be. You don't have to—"

"I know. I'm just an art enthusiast," Caroline declared with the air of someone who had just decided something about herself.

Tom dramatically swooned. "How *nice* of you," he said, hands pressed over his heart, ignoring Adrian's quick glance of disapproval. "Where did Adrian find you again?"

"Internet sex marketplace. Didn't you set up the profile?" Caroline asked, bright and sincere. She turned and scampered back down the stairs in a flash of citrus-colored activewear, taking all the sunshine and air out of the room with her.

"You goddamn lucky bastard," Tom chuckled as soon as she was gone. Adrian, dispirited and sitting on the floor, felt anything but lucky. "I cannot believe you randomly matched up with the world's most perfect rebound."

Adrian waited until he heard the front door shut to get a few things straight with Tom. His anger was rattling in his body, searching for more targets than just himself. He stood up and crossed the room.

"Stop hitting on her," he growled, lightly socking his roommate in the shoulder.

"Ow," Tom yelped, rubbing the muscle, even though Adrian had barely touched him. "Do you see her? *Someone* should hit on her."

"She's twenty-two!" Adrian repeated, picking up the next canvas in the pile and leaning it next to the first.

"Why does that matter?" Tom demanded.

Adrian glared at him. "Because she *is* nice. Because she's off at this house with two men she doesn't even know, and she had no idea we weren't ax murderers. Because she didn't have anything better to do this morning than clean up my mess. I am *not* going to take advantage of her."

Tom rolled his eyes. "Then don't. Just don't be an asshole. How hard is that? What, are you tempted to be an ax murderer if you start dating again? You won't even admit Nora's a bitch."

They continued stacking canvases on their sides, clearing room to carry out the writing desk.

"Do I look like I'm in a position to date?" Adrian said, gesturing to his broken artworks. "Besides, Caroline wanted someone to talk about the arts with. Not someone trying to get in her pants. She said so herself."

"Uh-huh," Tom said, unconvinced. "Which was why she found you on a sugar-baby app, rather than your gallery page?"

"She doesn't know any better," Adrian said. "And I am trying to be mindful of that."

Tom began wrestling the writing desk away from the wall. "You say that, but there are probably five hundred other guys on that site who *are* going to be assholes to her if you won't do the kinky sex shit she wants, along with the light musical theater talk."

Adrian put down the torn painting he'd been cradling like a sickly child so that he could throw a roll of tape at his roommate. "She said she just wants me to go with her to the theater! What possible reason do you have to think she wants any, quote, *kinky sex shit*?"

Tom ducked and grinned at him. "Well, none, really. I'm just hoping for your sake she does."

IT TOOK A FEW HOURS TO GET ALL THE PAINTINGS WRAPPED to Adrian's satisfaction and his writing desk (a beautiful antique, the exact opposite of all the angular pale furniture in the rest of the house) arranged in the back of the Tahoe. Adrian and Tom went through the kitchen, tossing the odd utensil into a final cardboard box.

Caroline wandered through the upstairs rooms looking for other piles of his belongings they might have missed. She couldn't imagine hating someone enough to destroy their flower garden, much less their art, but maybe making a really pointed Spotify playlist grew less satisfying as people got older.

"What about the art on the walls?" she called downstairs. Adrian's gold-ink signature was in the lower left-hand corner of a painting of women talking amid a flurry of magnolia blossoms. She thought she'd spotted more hung elsewhere about the house.

Adrian came to the bottom of the stairs and looked up at her. He had a smudge of dust across one cheek and a spot of sweat between his chest muscles. It wasn't a bad look for him at all, very *artist at work*.

"Leave them, I guess," he said reluctantly.

Tom called from the kitchen, "Wait, did you ever give them to Nora?"

"No," Adrian admitted.

"You want her to have them?" Tom pressed.

"No, but . . ."

"You can't." Caroline gasped. "You're just going to walk away from them?"

Adrian's face reflected mixed emotions at the idea. Caroline thought she understood his reluctance, since the paintings looked like they belonged where they were hung, but she also thought that the same woman who had trashed his gallery works did not deserve to have his art on the walls of her house.

She put her hands back on her hips and squinted down at Adrian.

"Don't your paintings sell for thousands of dollars?" she demanded.

Adrian rubbed the back of his head. "They don't sell at all, recently, but yes."

Caroline thought that was likely a problem of a less-than-motivated seller, not a fair market valuation. The paintings were lovely. Much better than the ones on his gallery's website, which were gray and uncomfortable and depicted some very unfortunate historical events.

"You can't just abandon your inventory," she informed him.

"My what?" he asked, confused.

"Your assets. Your salable stock. The widgets that your small business uses to generate revenue," Caroline pointed out. Her drawl was less pronounced when she was talking finance, but he'd yet to tease her about it at all.

"I don't have a small business," Adrian said, bemused.

"Not with that attitude you don't," Caroline said, shaking her head in dismay, because this was why he was broke. He needed to get into his personal accounting and gain control of his life. "Anyway, let's get the rest of them. The one in the living room is the prettiest one here!"

Tom shouted an agreement, and Adrian came up to help her get the painting off the wall bracket. He held it in his hands, considering. The swirl of bright colors suggested a party, the background defined by a row of blue asters. Maybe that was what his backyard used to look like before the hot tub.

"You should take one," he said, offering the painting to her. "If you hadn't come, I probably wouldn't have thought to take any of them off the walls."

Caroline snorted. "You can't make money by giving away your inventory either. You should be trying to sell it to me."

His full lower lip twisted in amusement, a little life coming back into his shadowed blue eyes. "And you shouldn't be paying me to help me move."

She looked at the painting in his hands, hesitating because it would be really nice to have in her beige box of an apartment. She didn't have anything up on the walls at all, not even posters. Any of these flowers would remind her of today: the first good day in a long time.

"I can't," she decided. "You can sell this, I'm sure. It's worth more than a morning of packing." She put her hands over his and pushed the painting back toward his own chest.

Adrian didn't budge. "I think I have some old paintings and sketches on paper up in the attic. Do you want one of those instead? You'd have to frame them, but—"

"There's more?" Caroline scolded him, and he held his palms up in resignation.

She spotted the hatch in the ceiling and jumped for the cord, filing away for future reference how Adrian averted his eyes from her chest a little too late for her to avoid noticing.

The attic was dusty and looked like it hadn't been disturbed for years. Adrian followed her up the ladder, sneezing at the stale air. There was the usual clutter of old furniture and boxes of holiday decorations, but also a stack of red rope paper artist's portfolios leaning against the wall. Adrian opened the nearest one, thumbing through it.

"These are really old," he said. "I think from before my MFA."

Caroline grabbed the next portfolio, unlaced the thread catches, and peered inside. There were newsprint sketch pads and a few spiral-bound notebooks with heavier water-color paper. Picking one up at random, she opened it to find it full of beautiful oil studies of flowers and leaves.

She sank down on her heels to gently flip through the little notebook. The cheap paper had never recovered from the moisture of the paint, but the flowers were still vibrant, leaping off the pages in pink and orange and green. She recognized peonies, carnations, spring irises. He must have loved the garden his ex had wrecked. He used to put flowers into all his paintings. She wondered why he'd stopped.

"Oh, Adrian, these are gorgeous." She sighed.

He glanced over his shoulder to see what she was look-ing at. "You can't display those," he dismissed the note-book. "Even if you could cut them out, I didn't bother to prime the paper. They're just studies."

Caroline held the notebook protectively to her chest. "You can't throw it out."

"I don't have the space for everything I've ever painted," he said, lifting his eyebrows at her.

"Don't museums always have the early works too, whenever they do an exhibit on an artist?" she protested.

Adrian laughed. "Museums, sure. And I suppose I also have my biographers to think of."

His smile was self-mocking but not mean, so Caroline

only dug in her point. He obviously had no idea how to go about running his business. He ought to have had a website full of his little flower sketches, like the guy who did the cottage paintings everyone had in their breakfast nooks. Thomas something. Caroline was sure that guy never had to sign up for sugar-baby websites to make rent.

"Well, if you don't have the room right now, I'll put them all in my spare bedroom until you do," she said firmly, packing the portfolios back up. "And then I'll buy one of your paintings when I can get furniture to match it."

Adrian shook his head at her, the corners of his eyes wrinkling up with what Caroline hoped was gratitude. He wiped his hands on the sweatpants hanging off his narrow hips. Dust hung and sparkled in the few beams of light breaking through the wooden shutters covering the only window, gilding the sharp edges of his cheekbones. Caroline wondered if he ever did any self-portraits. *That* would definitely sell.

"If you insist," Adrian said.

"I do," Caroline replied, and that concluded the packing, so they locked up and left. She gave Adrian a moment on the threshold to say goodbye to the house, but he didn't look back.

Chapter Seven

IT WAS ALMOST NOON BY THE TIME CAROLINE'S TAHOE WAS fully loaded, and Adrian's stomach was a hard, complaining ball under his rib cage. He was out of the habit of eating breakfast since moving in with Tom, so he was starving. Though he didn't mention it, Caroline dramatically pressed a hand to her bare midsection and announced that she could eat a horse. It had nothing to do with the loud growl his stomach had just made, he hoped.

"Do we have time to get lunch before I drop you guys off?" Caroline asked. "Or brunch?"

"Love a brunch," Tom said before Adrian could decline on his behalf. He was worried that if he took his eyes off his roommate, the other man might decide he could do Adrian's sugar-baby job for him, only with a lot less respect for Caroline's boundaries.

"How about that IHOP on Soldiers Field?" Caroline asked. "That has parking."

"Love an IHOP," Tom said.

Caroline pulled away from the curb, narrowly missing the bumper of the car in front of her.

Adrian wrapped a hand around the door handle and white-knuckled it as Caroline slowly executed a five-point turn in the road and proceeded west, obeying all traffic laws despite the terrifying rush of cars passing and merging around them from both sides as they got back on 1A.

"What should I put on now? More classic Taylor Swift? Olivia Rodrigo?" Caroline asked, glancing over at Adrian with a teasing expression. "We need a good theme for the drive."

"I'm afraid I am not familiar with the music of Olivia Rodrigo," Adrian replied, wishing she'd keep her eyes on the road. "So I don't know whether it's thematically appropriate."

"Well, did Beethoven ever write something for breakups?" Caroline asked. "I have Apple Music, so we can put on whatever."

"*Christ on the Mount of Olives* is probably as close as he got, but that's too heavy before lunch," Adrian said.

"Love Olivia Rodrigo," Tom said fervently. That worked another bright-white smile out of Caroline.

Adrian clenched his jaw. He didn't think he could take over the lease if he left Tom in the dumpster behind their apartment. At his glare, Tom stuck out his tongue at Adrian.

On a Saturday, it didn't take them long to make their way to the outskirts of the city and the cheerful box of the restaurant facing the river. The parking lot was nearly full though; this IHOP was popular. Adrian couldn't remember when he'd last eaten at a chain restaurant of any kind. Nora wouldn't have been caught dead in one, even if it might have been more appropriate to his budget than the kinds of places they usually ate at. That unhappy thought must have made its way to his face, because Adrian was startled out of his reverie by Caroline's fingers wrapping around the inside of his bicep as they walked to the restaurant. He automatically flexed the muscle, then felt ridiculous.

"Pancakes always make me feel better after a hard day," she told him soothingly. "They're basically salt mixed with butter, and then you pour sugar on top. The perfect recovery food."

Adrian gave a small laugh. "Who'd ever break up with you?"

Caroline's mouth puckered like she was embarrassed. "You'd be surprised. Though I was talking about workouts, not breakups."

She halted as soon as they entered the restaurant. It was crowded, filled mostly with students wearing pajama pants, sweatshirts, and the remnants of the previous night's makeup. They were there in couples and in groups of up to half a dozen, splitting pots of coffee and breakfast combos with an air of cheerful post-dissolution. Caroline scanned the room, her smile fading.

"Do you see someone you know?" Adrian asked her.

"No," she replied, letting go of his arm.

Adrian nearly asked her what was wrong, but Tom had already found a host and a booth. He waved at them from farther inside.

Tom was bouncing on the edge of his red vinyl seat, so Adrian had no choice but to slide in next to Caroline. He tried to slide, anyway—everything was vaguely sticky to the touch, either from cleaning product residue or (more likely) from the bottled corn syrup compotes set out on the table.

"We used to come here after performances when I was at Boston College," Tom said, recollection softening his face. "Seven people crammed into someone's tiny compact. This place smells like *Rent* to me. I think I performed 'Seasons of Love' on top of that booth over there."

Adrian caught Caroline's wistful expression as she followed what Tom was saying, deducing that she probably wished she were there with a carful of friends rather than a couple of men in their thirties. There wasn't any reason why she shouldn't be there with the other students. He embraced another stab of guilt that he'd let Caroline waste half her day with his problems already.

"What about you? Did you ever come here?" Caroline asked Adrian.

"Not that I can recall," he said, picking up the menu. "But it was a long time ago."

He gingerly flipped through the laminated pages of the novella-length menu.

Caroline leaned against him, looking over his shoulder. He ignored the soft press of her breast against his back.

"If you've never eaten here before, the pancakes are very good," she told him.

"Thank you, I'll take that under advisement," he replied, squinting at the picture of the eggs Florentine and wondering whether he dared order them at this place.

She lightly shoved him with her shoulder, tucking her chin and looking up at him through blond eyelashes until he sighed and closed the menu.

"I believe I'll try the pancakes," he said, gesturing at one of the servers to come take their order.

As soon as that was accomplished, Caroline reached into her big yellow purse, pulled out a thin laptop and set it on the table. Adrian had not realized she was carrying around a computer with her, but the bag was large enough that she could have been carrying welding tools or a picnic lunch.

"Okay," she said after a couple of minutes of fiddling with the screen. "You have pancakes. You're halfway there. Now what you need is a business plan."

"Pardon?" Adrian asked once he realized she was talking to him.

"You are going to feel so much better once you have pancakes and a business plan," she said, bringing up a large, complex spreadsheet.

Adrian instinctively recoiled, but Caroline did not pay him any mind.

"This was my final exam one semester," she said. "It's a simple business model. We've got the balance sheet on this tab and the profit and loss on the other one. See? We'll figure out how to get you back in the black."

The spreadsheet was still titled "MegaCorp Widget Factory" and contained about twenty rows for everything from accounting expenses to utilities. Caroline had already changed some of the row titles to things like "Paintings Sold" and, very ambitiously, "Grants Awarded."

Tom stifled a snicker at the look on Adrian's face.

"Um, Adrian can't do math either," Tom said. "I'm not sure he can count that high with his socks on."

"I took calculus. All the freshman premed classes," Adrian objected. "I'm just not a *widget factory*." He'd unthinkingly crossed his arms over his chest. He uncrossed them.

Caroline gave him a long look that disputed that point. "You make paintings and sell them. How is that any different?"

The server arrived with their food before he could

formulate an appropriate answer, dropping stacks of pancakes and piles of eggs and bacon around the table. Caroline slid her computer to the side but did not put it away. Instead, using her fork in her left hand, she quickly and methodically sliced her pancakes into squares and just as neatly shoved them into her mouth. The stack vanished into the girl in less than thirty seconds, and Caroline did not stop fiddling with her keyboard for the entire time.

"So, you have ten large and five small paintings as inventory," she said, tapping two formula cells on the screen with a knuckle. "How much do they sell for?"

Adrian reluctantly told her how they had been priced at Nora's gallery. Caroline dutifully input the numbers.

"And how much did they cost in materials to make?" Caroline asked, clearing out a second set of rows.

Adrian rubbed his chest. "It . . . varies."

"You don't know?"

"No," he said, hoping that was a good off-ramp for the conversation.

"Then how do you know if you're making a profit?" Caroline asked, exasperated.

He gritted his teeth and shook his head.

"I'll figure it out," he said when Caroline didn't look away. "I appreciate the concern, but you don't need to worry about my art career."

"Well, as your sugar daddy, it's my responsibility to set you up for long-term financial stability—" Caroline began.

Adrian had to break off the conversation to kick Tom under the table when he started convulsively laughing at the idea of Caroline pensioning Adrian off like an aging Regency-era mistress.

"What?" Caroline demanded. "I'm sorry, I thought you'd

rather make a living as an artist than an escort." Her mouth spread out in a long flat line.

"'Roxanne,'" Tom crooned. "'You don't have to put on the red light.'" His giggles became nearly hysterical.

Adrian kicked his shin again, promising certain death with his eyes. He inhaled sharply through his nose and then breathed out through his mouth, remembering that he owned every decision that had brought him to this position.

When Tom had shut up and he was reasonably under control, Adrian again tried to decline Caroline's assistance.

"This model doesn't really work for an artist," he said, leaning in and pointing at all the rows for marketing, lease, salary, and other expenses. "My gallery does all of this. I just deliver the paintings and hope they sell."

"You don't, like, market them?"

"No," Adrian said.

"You don't have your own website or mailing list or . . . ?"

"No," he repeated, abruptly wondering if that might have been a small part of the problem.

"So, you need a new gallery," Caroline said.

"Yes."

"And you need to choose one that will do a good job selling your paintings."

"Yes."

"And I bet they're all different in terms of commission, price, and customer base?"

"Yes," Adrian agreed. "That's definitely the next step now that I'm no longer under contract. Then I just have to focus on painting." Presumably, he would someday be in the mood to paint something again. He'd spent hours staring at gray wash on canvas the day before, unable to remember what he was trying to say about the dead bodies oozing in the foreground.

Caroline nodded, satisfied. She saved and closed her draft business plan. Then she went into her file list and pulled up a new spreadsheet. There were just as many columns and formulas already populated in it. "Customer Survey Results" was the title.

"Okay," she said brightly. "So, what you *actually* need, then, is some market analysis."

CAROLINE DROPPED TOM OFF AT HIS RESTAURANT JUST AFter lunch, over Adrian's strong objections.

"He can't be late for work," Caroline said. "There might not be enough time after unloading the car."

"He just doesn't want to help carry anything up," Adrian growled.

"I've got it," Caroline said, rolling her windbreaker up over her forearms and squinting judgmentally at their muscle tone. She'd been swimming and using the weight machines, but it wasn't as intensive as her prior training regimen. Eventually she'd be softer and curvier, like her sisters were now, but she thought she was still fit to carry anything Tom could have managed. "I'm still in pretty decent shape."

Adrian turned his head just long enough to rake his eyes down her body.

"So, you play tennis, don't you?" he said tentatively.

"Yup," she said.

He was waiting for the follow-up for that, but Caroline spotted an open stretch of curb at the end of his block, and she held up a hand for silence as she attempted the approach. It took a couple of tries, but as she maneuvered the Tahoe up the curb, the other cars on his side street were reasonably patient, only honking a few times and questioning her sanity and parentage in more muted tones than usual.

She hopped out of the SUV and went around to the rear hatch. Adrian made efforts to intercept her as she grabbed the side of the writing desk and began to slide it out, but she waved him off.

"I've got it," she said. "Go pick it up from the other side, if you can."

The writing desk was a really nice piece, solid wood and well maintained. Caroline wondered where he'd bought it. She'd looked around a few secondhand stores when stocking her apartment, but the quality had been really hit-or-miss, and she'd ended up just buying stuff from IKEA to fill her bedroom before classes started.

Anyway, the desk wasn't too heavy for her, especially with Adrian standing and holding it from the other side. They lifted it down to the curb, then closed and locked the Tahoe.

Adrian looked up at his apartment building.

"There's no elevator," he said. "And we're on the third floor. If you want to just come back tonight, I'll make Tom help instead."

Caroline picked up one end of the desk again.

"I bet I can deadlift more than you," she said. Adrian was built more lean than muscular, and he didn't seem like someone with the patience for doing reps on the weight machines. She'd like to see him run though. He was probably one of those guys who did five miles without blinking, nothing but sweat and focus.

"I also bet you can," Adrian said, looking at her thighs.

He took the backward position, and they maneuvered

the desk through the lobby of the building and up the stairs.

"You know, Boston College has tennis," Adrian told her as he unlocked his apartment door.

"Oh, really," Caroline deadpanned.

Inside, the apartment fit more comfortably within her experience of human habitations. Most of the walls were painted industrial off-white, except for the exposed brick of the wall containing the windows. The furniture was well-worn and not quite matching, but it all looked comfortable. The en suite kitchen counter was covered with small appliances, and books were stacked against one of the walls in neat piles.

"I doubt there's anything official for the B-school, but there are club and intramural leagues," Adrian told her, not catching her tone.

He picked up his end of the desk again and shuffled backward toward one of the doors at the opposite end of the living room.

"Wow. Where's the tennis at Boston College?" Caroline drawled.

Adrian backed into what had to be his bedroom, breathing audibly from the effort. They set the desk down in the middle of the room, which was cluttered with an iron-frame daybed, more mismatched furniture, and a lot of cardboard boxes. Adrian lifted the hem of his long-sleeved T-shirt to wipe his face, revealing a pale stomach that was flatter and firmer than Caroline might have guessed.

"At the athletic center," Adrian explained. "That's where all the tennis courts are."

"Mmm," said Caroline, beginning to stack cardboard boxes to make room for the desk against the free wall of the bedroom. "How do you sign up to play tennis, then?"

Adrian rubbed the side of his neck, thinking about it. "I think they have sign-ups for the club teams outside the courts. Or there's probably an online tool?"

Caroline rounded her eyes at him, silently asking him to go on and tell her more about the university's tennis options.

"I think they have doubles—" Adrian began to explain before her expression finally sunk in. "Oh. You're fucking with me again, aren't you?"

Caroline gave him a tight-lipped smile. "I did varsity tennis all through undergrad. BC actually offered me a partial scholarship four years ago."

Her father hadn't let her take it, not against the full ride at Central Texas Baptist, where she could live at home besides.

Adrian turned away and scrubbed both hands over his face. "You're welcome to just tell me the next time I'm being an ass instead of waiting for me to catch on."

"I'll take that under advisement," Caroline quoted him, wrestling his desk into place next to his narrow window.

Adrian put his hands on his narrow hips and turned back to her, expression annoyed. "I only thought you might be interested in better ways of spending your weekends than this. Do you not actually like tennis?"

Caroline stared at her feet in consternation. She couldn't remember. It wasn't something she'd chosen for herself—her father and sisters had played, so she'd played, and once she started getting good at it, her family had been so relieved to have something to occupy her that it became all she was *allowed* to do.

Whether she had ever liked tennis was almost beside the point. The point was, she'd done tennis. She couldn't expect it to bring anything new and good into her life when it hadn't in the past.

"We haven't even gone to the theater yet," she pointed out, brushing Adrian's comments away.

"What kind of theater?"

Caroline shrugged. She didn't know what kind was best. That was what Adrian was for. "Whichever you think is the best."

She wandered back into the living room, prepared to go back downstairs and finish unloading the Tahoe.

"Can I get you something to drink?" Adrian said, moving into the kitchen instead.

"Sure, what do you have?"

He opened a few cabinets, then the fridge. He closed the fridge.

"We have St-Germain and tap water. I recommend the tap water."

"I'll have a tap water."

The over-sink cabinet was full of mismatched mason jars and coffee mugs. Adrian grabbed one at random and filled it from the tap. There were dishes in the sink. He glared at them, and she guessed he hadn't left them there.

"You make adulthood look so glamorous," Caroline said.

He exhaled like he was going to agree, but then the corner of his mouth quirked up, his smile crooked and self-deprecating. He wrapped a hand around the back of the mason jar and extended it toward her like he was displaying the label.

"This water is redolent with the distinctive terroir of north Brighton. The forward notes are chemical, with hints of Dawn and chlorine, but the finish is mineral, with a lingering nose of iron, copper, and—troublingly—lead."

Caroline giggled and took the glass from him, taking a long sip like she'd seen people do on TV.

"Mmm," she said, rolling the water over her tongue. "I can taste the chlorine."

At his gesture, she took it to the gray canvas double sofa.

Adrian passed her a remote, nodding at the TV. "I think Tom has Hulu. Or, if you'd like, all my art books are in boxes over—"

"You don't want to finish unloading?"

"I'm going to do that right now. Please. Just sit here. My masculine pride is hanging on by a thread."

"It's really not a big deal," Caroline protested. "I'll help."

"I can't let you pay me to help carry boxes into my apartment," Adrian said firmly. "Let me finish up, and then we'll see what's on the scalper sites for tonight."

Caroline had nearly forgotten that he was supposed to be on the clock all day Saturday, so she didn't respond, passing him her keys instead. It hadn't felt like paying him. It had felt like . . . well, she didn't have a lot to compare it to. But it had felt the way she'd wanted it to. Less than lonely, for once.

Adrian left the apartment, and Caroline turned on the TV. Tom had a Hulu account, but it had expired. She tried to sign in to Netflix, but it seemed he didn't have an account. She signed in to hers, beginning to feel itchy-footed and anxious as she scanned the options. It would go faster if she helped carry boxes.

Her father's paving company had posted a part-time opening in the warehouse during her sophomore year. It paid two dollars more an hour than Sonic, so she'd applied. Her dad had laughed at her, even though she could easily lift the minimum in the posting. *There's nothing open in the office. When you graduate, I'll fire the accounts payable girl and hire you for that*, he'd promised.

At least Caroline had avoided that fate. That was what she would have been doing right now if her grandmother hadn't died: trying to save up for a car and an apartment deposit and still doing everything her father told her to do.

The air was hot and still in the apartment. She tried to open a window but found that they'd been painted shut. Giving up on fixing the temperature, she put on a nature documentary and kicked off her shoes. She curled up on the sofa as Adrian came in and out with his boxed paintings and assorted possessions from his ex's house. It took him nearly an hour to finish by himself, and he was sweaty and red-faced by the end of it. Caroline assumed he'd go take a shower when he was done, but instead he filled another glass from the sink and collapsed on the other end of the sofa.

He glanced at her sideways out of the corner of his eye, then stripped off his shirt with his gaze averted. He wiped his shoulders and used the wadded fabric to buffer the couch from his body. Caroline struggled with the desire to ogle him. He didn't like being stared at in public; she'd already figured that out. But was this part of the sugar-baby package, if she was in his apartment? She decided that it was allowed.

Adrian had muscles in different places than tennis players, ones that had been gained more or less accidentally, just as a result of living in his body. His chest was pale and lean and bare, save for one strip of amber fuzz down the center, which disappeared into his jeans. It was dark and mussed with sweat just above his navel.

Anyone who was *actually* dating him could have reached out and slicked that soft line straight with her fingers.

Caroline probably could have too, she realized; people probably paid for a lot weirder stuff.

She'd told him she wouldn't though, and it wouldn't be appropriate to do something like that without asking him first, she thought. She sat on her hands until the urge passed, her heart pounding like she was the one who'd been carrying too many boxes.

Adrian stared blankly at the screen for a few minutes as his breathing normalized, only seeming to realize what show was playing when the footage changed to the dramatic night-vision death of a large rat under the fangs of an inland taipan.

"God, what are we watching?" Adrian asked.

"A documentary on the ten most deadly snakes in Australia."

"Are you thinking of visiting Australia soon?" he followed up, still confused.

"It seems like a very dangerous place," she replied. "But if I do, at least I'll be prepared."

Adrian grunted in agreement, finishing his glass of water as the narrator breathlessly informed them that the venom of one taipan could kill a hundred men.

"My grandmother used to love nature documentaries," Caroline finally said to fill the silence. "The ones about scary animals, anyway. She said it made her feel better about being stuck in her house all day if I wasn't there to drive her."

It felt at once longer and shorter than six months since Gam had been gone. Ages since she'd done something as simple as watch TV with someone else, and yet it also felt like if she hit the speed dial on her phone, her grandmother might still pick up and ask her whether she could make it for dinner. She had to blink fast at the thought.

"Used to?" Adrian asked gently.

"She died during my senior year," Caroline said.

Adrian tilted his head to show he was listening, but she didn't want to say anything else. If she'd wanted to talk about herself, she would have hired a shrink instead of an escort, and she'd done too much talking that day already. She knew that she wasn't a very interesting person; she needed to change that.

"Let's not talk about me. What do you want to do now?" She tried to move the conversation forward.

Adrian put his elbows on his knees, then his chin in his knit hands. He turned his head to look at her, fingers still wrapped over his lips.

"Caroline," he said, his tone still careful. "If you don't want to talk, why are you even here?"

"It's Saturday," she replied. "We agreed on the whole day Saturday, right?"

He exhaled. "Yes, I know. But this doesn't have anything to do with the arts, which you don't seem that interested in to begin with. If you want to make more friends, go do something with the other B-school students. If you want a boyfriend, go out on a date with one of them. I don't—I don't know what to do for you."

He said it like it was simple. Like she hadn't tried that first.

"You keep trying to put yourself out of a job," Caroline said, narrowing her eyes at the man tensing at the other end of the sofa.

"Yes! Because you were supposed to be sixty years old and *mean* and trying to fill a table at the Homeland Heroes Foundation gala. You don't need to hire me. You're—"

"What?" Caroline said mulishly. "What am I?"

His mouth firmed up. He used one elegant hand to

gesture at himself and the messy apartment both. "Someone with better options than this."

That was easy for him to say. He had a friend who'd show up to help him move on a Saturday. Caroline didn't have a single person in her life who would have done that for her.

"Your position is noted, but I have things under control," Caroline said, tucking her feet back beneath her.

"But you haven't even looked into the other things Boston College has to offer. You should—"

The last word made her teeth ache and her back go ramrod straight.

"If I want you to tell me what I should do, I'll ask you," she snapped.

Adrian leaned away, lips curling in over his teeth. They stared at each other, the moment taut and still.

"I suppose I hardly seem to be an authority on good life choices," he finally said, face shuttered.

Caroline dropped her shoulders, closing her eyes and groaning. "It's not that. I *don't* think you're as much of a mess as you seem to think."

Adrian didn't respond, face still judging himself.

"Come on," Caroline said. "It's not so bad. I liked seeing your paintings this morning. And you just need to get a handle on the numbers behind your business before your life's on track too."

Adrian grunted noncommittally.

Caroline twisted in his direction, trying to be persuasive. "You don't want to still be walking the streets at forty, do you?"

"No," he snorted. "No, I do not." He tipped his head back against the couch as he worked his jaw, deep in thought. Then he looked back over at her through his thick red lashes. "If I fill out one of your spreadsheets, will you at least sign up for *something* over at BC? Something you think you might like on its own merits?"

Adrian had obviously not had the advantage of taking a Principles of Negotiation seminar, or he would have recognized that he did not start from a very good bargaining position.

"Like what?" Caroline said with suspicion.

"Join a theater production," Adrian said, gesturing vaguely. "Just go in and ask for a position on the technical side. They were always desperate for help when I was in undergrad. And the arts and sciences grad students put on a few productions a year."

"I don't see why I would." If the business school students wouldn't talk with her after class, it seemed even less likely that the arts and sciences students would be interested in her.

"The arts— Christ. I'm about to sound like a pretentious asshole. But people make art; they get involved in the arts because they have a passion for it. Because they feel something for it or because they want to communicate something important to someone else. If you want to know about art, or even if you just want to talk about it with someone, do it."

"That's how you feel?" she asked, curious. He hadn't said a thing about his own art to her, not even the painting on the wall that he'd called an engagement present to his friend.

He looked at the floor. "I used to," he said slowly.

She wished he'd explain that, but she wasn't in a position to press him.

The standoff was quiet.

"Student theater though?" she finally asked, very reluctantly.

Adrian shrugged. "You seemed interested. It doesn't have to be that."

"I don't know how to do anything technical," she said, coming up with another objection.

"If you can carry boxes, you can be on the run crew."

Caroline evaluated potential obstacles, planning it out in her mind. It was hard to imagine. She supposed the worst that could happen was that she'd go into the theater and they wouldn't need any help. "I'll do it if you fill out *both* spreadsheets," she bartered.

He exhaled. "Deal."

Caroline nodded, flicking off the television even as the narrator promised more hair-raising facts about the common death adder. She'd watch it the next morning.

"So," she prompted him again. "What are we doing tonight?"

Adrian wiped a hand across his sweaty chest with distaste. Caroline thought he'd be surprised at what people might pay for that privilege. It was her, she was people, even. She sucked on her lip, wondering if she wanted to ask. Maybe a different day when he didn't look so sad.

"I need a shower and a change," he replied. "But I think *Anastasia* is being performed at the opera house right now, if you'd like to see a musical."

"Is it supposed to be good?"

"You'll have to tell me," he said, making it sound like an order. She let it slide.

Chapter Eight

ADRIAN LEANED FORWARD TO PROP HIS CHIN ON HIS FORE-arms, as though the new angle would make the spread-sheet in front of him more encouraging. If he'd been unproductive in Tom's living room over the past few weeks, entering data into spreadsheets from his studio only drove home how little he'd accomplished recently. He was still a man with a spreadsheet, but he was now a man with a spreadsheet surrounded by blank canvases that should have been paintings.

Caroline was right though: the quickest way out of the hole he'd dug for himself was signing on with a new gallery and selling some of his existing work. So he'd spent the morning on the phone with the galleries he admired around the city, slowly realizing that this problem was bigger and more complicated than he'd thought.

He'd never had to apply to work with a gallery before. Exhibitions, juried shows, yes, but Nora had approached *him* with an offer of representation seven years previous. Before that, back when he was an art school wunderkind and an *exciting new talent*, he'd been sought-after and re-cruited by many of the same places he'd called that morn-ing. He discovered that there was now an application process or a portfolio review fee between him and any actual human he might talk to. He tried calling a couple of galleries he'd shown at as a student only to discover that the staff had turned over and didn't know him.

He frowned at the daunting list of requirements he'd copied into a cell in Caroline's market research template— high-resolution photographs, an artist statement, an updated CV—things he'd once possessed but which had vanished from the website of his former gallery. Adrian decided to text a friend from his MFA program and check whether he was really going about this in the right way.

Tamsyn had the kind of solid career he'd assumed he possessed until a few months ago. Now he contacted her because she had the things he'd lost: a girlfriend, a gallery, and a good reputation in the art community.

> *Adrian:* Did you go through the online application process before you signed with Beacon Hill Contemporary?

He winced when he noticed that their last exchange of messages had been nine months ago.

He didn't expect Tamsyn to respond right away, but he hadn't even moved on to another gallery's site before she responded rapid-fire.

> *Tamsyn:* Hi
> *Tamsyn:* Hello
> *Tamsyn:* Good to hear from you
> *Tamsyn:* I was a little worried you might be dead
> *Tamsyn:* Glad you're not dead
> *Tamsyn:* No, I met my gallery director at an after-party for the Whitney Biennial three years ago
> *Tamsyn:* Why do you ask?

Adrian took a deep breath. He hadn't been good at keeping in touch with anyone recently, it seemed.

> *Adrian:* I'm looking for new gallery rep.
> *Adrian:* Why did you think I might be dead?

> *Tamsyn:* Heard Nora dumped you
> *Tamsyn:* Didn't hear from you
> *Tamsyn:* Assumed you were stuffed in the trunk of a burnt-out car down in Southie somewhere
> *Tamsyn:* Surprised she let you live
> *Tamsyn:* That woman scares me
> *Tamsyn:* Guess that explains the need for new gallery rep though

That did, in a nutshell, explain things, he supposed. He pinched the bridge of his nose between his knuckles, at a loss for how to proceed. Just start over. Fecklessly dispatch copies of his art to strangers and hope they liked it. But Tamsyn wasn't done.

> *Tamsyn:* Are you going to Art Basel this December?
> *Tamsyn:* Why don't you just ask around there?

Adrian had been in such a funk that he hadn't even considered his calendar of upcoming events, since they'd all been associated with Nora's gallery. He'd gone to Art Basel twice before, and most of his paintings had sold each time. It drew a crowd much more open to his conceptual work than the walk-in clientele in Boston.

> *Adrian:* I was planning to, but Nora won't show my work now.

Tamsyn: You sure about that? Check the blog.

Feeling a pang of unease, Adrian complied. Just opening Nora's personal gallery page sent a wave of discomfort through him, but he scanned the recent articles until he found what Tamsyn was talking about. Nora had a long post about her most recent application to the art fair, dated only a week ago. There were new photographs of his most recent works. New descriptions. All of it total bullshit.

Adrian Landry reinvents the historiography of Western art, causing the viewer to contemplate the ravages of time and space on our conception of conflict.

Landry's layered use of paint evokes bruises and trauma in the rubble of Kruševo.

Landry's grasp of anatomy makes departures from the figurative more startling in their abstraction.

Word salad. Nora was better than this; it didn't sound like her. She'd probably let one of the new interns run amok. Adrian felt a rush of anger prickle up through his body and inflame his face. If Nora was still selling his paintings, was she just planning to *keep* all the proceeds?

Adrian: Thank you. It appears that I will in some sense at least be going to Art Basel this year

Tamsyn: If you go in real life, take video. I want to see Nora's face if you just show up and stand next to your work.

Adrian liked that mental image. He liked it a lot.

The immediate problem, of course, was money. Nora would have paid for everything. Adrian didn't have enough saved for even flight and hotel expense, and he'd turned over his entire first paycheck to Tom for rent.

Running the numbers in his head, even assuming Caroline kept him on payroll for the next few months, he still wouldn't be able to afford the trip. He could put it on a credit card and assume he'd sell work once he was there, but that sounded like the kind of bet that could leave him permanently indentured to Capital One.

Adrian: Good idea if I can swing it.

Tamsyn: Thanks. All my ideas are good ones
Tamsyn: That's why they pay me the big bucks
Tamsyn: Come to my opening next month?

Adrian: Of course

Adrian put his phone down and rubbed his mouth, considering his options. He supposed he could moonlight with yet another patron off the escort website. Perhaps he'd find some elderly snowbird art lover who'd pay to vacation with him in Miami and rub elbows with the international art set. He could just make that a condition straight up, rather than the weekly stipend Tom had negotiated with Caroline. It wasn't anything like a job to spend time with Caroline; he still had free time to spend on someone unpleasant.

Something told him Caroline wouldn't be impressed by that plan though. She'd probably expect him to ask her first. Which he was reluctant to do.

But if the hypothetical eighty-year-old wanted to go with him, why wouldn't Caroline? He couldn't immediately classify it as a good idea or a bad idea, but his brain began to present him with itineraries. Nora had always wanted to spend most of their time checking out the competition and other galleried works, but Caroline would probably like seeing the installation art best, maybe the moderated panels, if she wanted to learn more about current movements. Adrian could probably secure invitations to some of the bigger parties. He could walk Caroline through the chaos of the satellite fairs. It was the sort of thing she'd hired him for in the first place. New experiences. What was wrong with that?

Before he could talk himself out of it, he texted her.

Adrian: Have you ever heard of Art Basel? Do you have any interest?

If he'd held a piece of charcoal in his hand, Adrian could have sketched the joyous expression his mind rendered on Caroline's face as she gazed up at the rainbow totem of Miami Mountain. Who wouldn't like going to Miami to see contemporary art? And the restaurant scene. Boston was a culinary backwater, but he could show Caroline some real five-star cuisine in Miami.

Maybe they'd even have time to go to the beach.

A warm, glowing tendril of hope skidded through his chest before he even saw her response:

Caroline: I'd love to go!
Caroline: That sounds perfect!
Caroline: When?

Anticipation made him nearly light-headed.

Adrian: The second weekend in December

He pictured Caroline's golden hair reflecting the light off the water. Her first taste of *good* coffee from a Cuban ventanita. Caroline in a swimsuit on the beach. It would be warm, even in December. She was from Texas; she'd probably miss the heat by then. He was getting ahead of himself, but the images were coming to him in a whirlwind, like the inspiration he'd been missing for months.

His phone buzzed again.

Caroline: Not that weekend
Caroline: That's the weekend before finals
Caroline: But any time during winter break I could go
Caroline: I'd also love to go to Paris
Caroline: Or London
Caroline: Mostly Paris
Caroline: Or anywhere, really
Caroline: If Switzerland is where the art shows are, we'll go to Switzerland first, but maybe we could see the other cities too?

The disappointment shouldn't have come on so fierce for a plan that was barely ten minutes old. He mentally shook himself by the scruff of the neck. It couldn't be that easy.

Now that he was no longer a twenty-two-year-old prodigy but rather a known quantity who had been stagnating in Boston for years, there was no reason for galleries to throw themselves at him. He had to get in line with the anonymous masses of starving artists and toss his résumé at impersonal application pages like everyone else. He belatedly realized that he had not responded to Caroline, who, of course, did not know that the December Art Basel show was in Miami, not Switzerland.

It was possible that part of the crushing disappointment was instead guilt that he'd proposed going on vacation with a woman whose finals schedule was the major impediment. Of course she should want to go to Europe, but he was not a necessary part of the trip. And Caroline didn't need or want to go anywhere for an art show; he was just being self-centered.

> *Adrian:* You should definitely go to France if you've never been
> *Adrian:* Boston College used to have alumni trips abroad curated by the art history department
> *Adrian:* They will have at least one to France this year
> *Adrian:* I can tell you about those

The typing icon bounced on his phone for several minutes until Caroline sent him a thumbs-up emoji. Adrian grimaced and put his phone away. There weren't any shortcuts. He just needed to get on with fixing things.

Adrian looked over at the two damaged paintings he'd brought into his studio that morning. He'd perilously transported them on the T, glaring at anyone who approached him and his two unwieldy cardboard boxes. The rest were with Caroline.

If he hadn't been able to paint anything new for months, at least he could fix these. Adrian grabbed his mister bottle and went to work on the battered canvases. He'd spend the rest of the day repairing the dents in his life he could reach.

CAROLINE PRESSED HER PHONE TO HER CHEST, NEARLY DIZZY with delight. France! She could go to France! Going on vacation had been on the list of things that she'd thought she could do with her newfound free time and money, but it had not occurred to her that she could just . . . go. To France.

She wouldn't have wanted to go by herself. So finding someone who wanted to go with her to France—or anywhere, she could go anywhere, any city she'd ever read about or seen as the backdrop to a movie—had been a necessary first step. Which she'd now taken—*Very good job there, Caroline*—even if it hadn't occurred to her that she could ask *Adrian* to go on vacation with her. It had either been a very good decision or very good luck to hire a man who had *go to Europe* in his repertoire of date ideas. Perhaps she was discerning. Perhaps she had just been waiting to meet the kind of people who liked to travel to Europe and visit museums.

Adrian was, of course, the kind of person she wanted to go to France with. He'd know about the museums and the operas, what she ought to wear to them, where they ought to eat and whether snails were actually delicious or just a long con played by the French chefs' union. Adrian probably spoke French. She'd never heard him speak French, but she sensed that he did, that he was the kind of person who impatiently awaited situations where speaking French might be appropriate.

Caroline could go to France over Christmas, even, and completely avoid the question of whether she'd go home to Templeton. No, she couldn't go to her uncle's house to open presents, because she'd be in Paris, eating a baguette in front of the Bastille or something.

The thought was happy enough to give Caroline strength to open her other message string from that morning. Her mother had never texted very often. Presumably she'd texted so that Caroline would have the space to choose her reply with care.

> **Mom:** If you're not coming home at all for Thanksgiving, can your dad and I come up and see you that weekend?
> **Mom:** We could walk the Freedom Trail. Maybe do some Christmas shopping.

It wasn't like she'd planned to never see her father again. But she'd grown more comfortable with *not* seeing him over the past six months. She thought she probably could have happily gone a little longer. But there was always going to be a first time she saw him again, and with just her mom, in Boston, on her own court—or at least off his—was probably the best scenario she could have hoped for.

Making decisions as rapidly as she always did, Caroline wrote back:

> **Caroline:** Sure
> **Caroline:** I'll get you tickets and a hotel room near the university

She put her phone away without waiting for the reply. She didn't know whether her mother had planned to get their tickets, but if Caroline did it, she could schedule her parents' trip over just one night and limit the potential impact if her father decided to yell at her again. He'd have to see that Caroline was managing just fine, that she had her own apartment and a better education and (hope-fully) a lot more sophistication and life experience than the last time he'd seen her, but if he yelled anyway, she'd be able to throw him out.

Personal business concluded, Caroline squinted up at the facade of the building she'd been leaning against. The performing arts building was on the other end of campus from the B-school, surrounded by a cluster of student dormitories she had no reason to visit.

She didn't recognize any of the students going in and out in the early evening. She supposed there was not a ton of overlap between the people she knew from Data Analytics and the grad students involved in the student production of *The Iceman Cometh*.

Her hand tightened on the strap of her backpack. She wasn't sure about the script for this. She'd never gone to a university theater production or even met a theater student. It had seemed very simple when Adrian described it—just go in and ask if they needed help—but what if they asked what kind of help she meant? She wouldn't know what to say. *I thought I could carry things for you* didn't sound very convincing in her head. Perhaps she ought to just go to the student center and take a flyer for the first political organization she saw; she already knew from her time in college that the people in the political clubs wouldn't care how weird she was as long as she'd listen to them talk.

But if Adrian was going to figure out business account-ing this week, she supposed she could at least keep up her end of the deal by actually entering the theater building. She waited for a group of several students to approach the front door and ducked in behind them, following them through the lobby and into a side corridor that ran along the length of the building. Nobody gave her a second glance when the corridor ended in a warren of activity backstage, where people were talking animatedly, carrying bits of scenery back and forth, running lines together, or shouting at other people.

Caroline halted, not knowing a soul among the dozens of people there, and uncertain of her angle of approach or who she ought to talk to. A beefy, red-faced blond guy carrying a roll of sound cable over one arm nearly crashed into her because she was in the middle of things. As he scuttled back in alarm, his eyes narrowed as he tried to place her and failed.

"Are you looking for someone?" he asked, not unkindly.

"Um," said Caroline. Her mind had blanked on the title of the person she needed. Not the director. Not the controller. Not an officer or president. "The person who's in charge of the backstage people."

The big guy's sandy brows drew together in a point as he tried to understand her request.

"You want . . . the stage manager, maybe?"

Yes, that was the one!

Caroline nodded gratefully, and the guy turned and pointed across the room to a tall student with lavender-streaked brown hair to her shoulders.

"Sophia," he said. "She's just about to go to rehearsals, so be quick."

Caroline thanked him and tried to approach Sophia. The stage manager wore a black jersey jumpsuit; flat, pointy-toed black leather boots; and a black nylon messenger bag bulging with binders.

Caroline tapped the stage manager on the shoulder, feeling a little grubby; she was wearing a school sweatshirt over pink running tights.

Sophia must not have felt Caroline's tap, because she gave an order to the student she'd been speaking with and stepped right past her, gaze fixed on the door to the rehearsal rooms.

"Oh, um—" Caroline tried to get her attention, but Sophia was already walking away.

Caroline jogged a couple of steps to catch her at the door.

"Hi, you're the stage manager, right?" she asked, holding the door open.

"Yes, I'm on the way to rehearsal," Sophia said smoothly, not slowing her movement. She shot Caroline an assessing glance out of the corner of her eye.

The other woman was nearly as tall as she was, so Caroline had to scurry to keep up.

"I'm sorry, this will be super quick—I just wanted to ask if you needed any help with the running crew—"

"Run crew."

"The run crew, yeah, or actually, anything else—"

Sophia reached the end of the hall, and Caroline had to turn herself into Sophia's path to gain her attention again.

Sophia gave Caroline a smile that didn't show teeth or use many muscles in her face. "Are you one of the new theater majors?"

"No, I'm an MBA student, but I thought—"

"Run crew positions are reserved for undergrad theater majors fulfilling their practicum requirement," Sophia said, speaking more slowly and enunciating her words.

"Oh," Caroline said, cheeks flushing, because that was probably on a page somewhere that she could have read instead of wasting the stage manager's time. "If you need any other help though, I can, um, I could carry something—"

Sophia's expression was inscrutable as she edged toward the open door to the rehearsal space, but whatever reply she'd prepared to make was cut off by another student popping her head into the doorway.

"Oh my God, Sophia, is that a volunteer?" said the new student, a short, curvy woman whose curly black hair was mostly covered by a coral silk headscarf. "I'm only a third of the way through the props list."

"I can reassign some of the first-years from the set shop if you really need help," Sophia objected, not looking at Caroline.

"I can help," Caroline put in hopefully.

"We haven't asked for volunteers," Sophia objected.

"Well, *I* can put this one to work, at least," the other student said cheerfully, her navy trench coat swishing as she took Caroline by the arm, introducing herself as "Rima, props."

Caroline's mood began to rapidly improve as the girl towed her away from Sophia and down the hall to the props shop. Rima talked very fast, but she seemed friendlier than anyone else Caroline had met on campus. She gave a steady stream of chatter about the production and the schedule and how far behind she was, stopping only to draw breath or for Caroline to grunt her agreement with some proposition.

Caroline managed to gather that Rima's job was to obtain and manage all the objects the actors would manipulate onstage, that Rima was in her second year of her PhD program, and that Rima took it for granted that Caroline knew what she was doing there, although she did not.

One side of the props shop was a fabrication area with woodworking equipment and paints, and the other led into the prop closet, which looked like the world's most eclectic flea market, with floor-to-ceiling shelves cluttered with everything from animal skulls to Greek vases to surfboards. The atmosphere was enchanting. Caroline didn't know where to look, but she wanted to look at everything in the room. She hoped she got the chance.

Rima retrieved her own giant binder off a shelf and flipped through it until she came to a set of old black-and-white photographs of saloon interiors.

"So, if you're in business school, does that mean you're good at buying things?" Rima asked, tapping a close-up shot of old gin bottles with a carefully shaped fingernail. "I need someone to scour secondhand shops for these specific shapes. I can give you a tax-exempt order form—"

Caroline's face spread into a grin. Adrian was right. This part, at least, she *could* do.

"I'll do it. Buying things is becoming, like, a core skill of mine," Caroline said.

IT WAS WELL PAST DINNERTIME WHEN ADRIAN UNLOCKED Tom's front door, but he hadn't eaten all day. He'd forgotten to pack up some leftovers for lunch, and the day's events had made it obvious that he needed to conserve every possible dollar for application fees going forward. His complaining stomach and low blood sugar had combined to give him a sour mood and throbbing headache. He smelled pizza, but that had to be from the neighbors. Tom wouldn't waste money on pizza when he could bring home nearly unlimited food from his restaurant.

Adrian was confronted by an unexpected deluge of sensations and emotions when he stepped into the living room. The television was displaying a grainy, poorly focused video of a student performance of *Into the Woods*. A half-eaten four-cheese pizza was cooling in its delivery box on the stove. Caroline was on the couch, giggling at something Tom had said. Tom was *also* on the couch with what could have been Sour Patch Kids but what Adrian strongly suspected was a bag of edibles.

So, there was an initial positive reaction—*There* is *pizza; oh, hello, Caroline, you're here too*—and the subsequent angry one, because what the hell was Tom doing?

Tom was the one facing the door, so he greeted Adrian first.

"Hey!" he called happily. "You're finally home."

"Did I miss a text?" Adrian gave him the benefit of the doubt.

"Um, no. Forgot to text. But if I'd known you'd be so late, we'd have waited on the pizza. It's still probably hot though. Or you can heat it up. You know. In the oven. Or in the microwave. Or even on the stove, maybe?"

Tom was luminously high, buoyant and serene. Christ.

"I'll do that. But first, can you help me with something?" Adrian said as politely as he could, jerking his head at his bedroom.

"Of course!" Tom chirped, not taking the cue and getting up. "What do you need?"

Caroline swiveled around to see Adrian in the doorway, the slow loll of her head indicating that Tom had been sharing his bag of gummies.

"Guess what," she said proudly, gesturing to the black T-shirt she wore. Black vinyl lettering across her chest proclaimed *Crew*. The shirt was too small for her, and the lines of her lace bra showed clearly through the fabric.

Adrian was getting too familiar with her underwear. He tried to rub out the mental image of the demi cup she was definitely wearing under the T-shirt like a stray pencil mark.

"I'm helping the props master for the fall show. She gave me a T-shirt," Caroline said, fortunately oblivious to his thoughts.

"You're the assistant props master?" Adrian clarified.

Caroline frowned, trying to parse the logic. "I don't think I have a title. But yes. I must be. The assistant props master."

"Well done," Adrian told her as gently as he could manage. He looked at his roommate again. "Tom," he said in a very different tone, "please come talk to me for a minute."

The other man wiggled bonelessly off the couch and into Adrian's bedroom, expression beatific, too high to recognize that he was in trouble. Adrian closed the door, then pushed Tom against it with one firm palm, holding the shorter man against the wall.

"What are you doing?" Adrian growled.

Tom blinked at him in surprise. "Watching my senior performance and eating pizza?"

Adrian's teeth grated. "With Caroline," he clarified.

"Hey, I haven't tried anything," the other man protested. "I wouldn't do that to you."

Now it was Adrian's turn to be confused. "What do you mean 'to me'? You're doing drugs with *her*!"

A bouquet of giggles immediately burst through Tom's throat. "Oh my God. The middle-class respectability police are here to arrest me. 'Doing drugs'? It's not even illegal anymore."

"It technically still is," Adrian said, beginning to feel a little ridiculous.

"What?"

"You know. At the federal level."

"Nerd."

Adrian grunted. "Whatever. But more important, why

did you ask her over here? She's trying to make friends her own age."

Tom gave him a skeptical look. "You sure about that? She came over to tell you about the props thing. She stuck around. We ordered pizza. I put on my old stage videos to show her how the set changes work. Then I took an edible because I don't work tomorrow, and then I shared because *I'm not a jerk*. What's wrong with that?"

Adrian exhaled through his nose, trying to identify the problems with the scenario. He'd be a real hypocrite if he tried to stop Caroline from enjoying her evening along those lines, and Tom probably had photographs somewhere to prove the point. That didn't mean Tom and Adrian ought to be involved.

"We are not supposed to be *corrupting* her," he muttered. "I promised to show her the Boston arts scene. She didn't ask to get high with a couple of men in their thirties."

His roommate groaned, closing his eyes. "What happened to you? We used to have fun. Now it's like you're determined that everything in life has to suck just because *some* of the things in your life suck. Come have some pizza and stop worrying for half a minute. I'm not trying anything with your"—he searched for a word, internally discarding a few—"Caroline. She's fine. She's happy. We'll send her home mildly buzzed and unmolested in a couple of hours."

Adrian was so hungry he could barely think straight, and some part of him wanted to be angry at Tom but was unable to articulate his reasons for it. If he were still twenty-two, he supposed that eating pizza, taking edibles, and watching old theater videos would sound like a good time. If he could do more of that at thirty-three than panicking that he'd never sell another painting, he'd probably be happier.

He opened the door and leaned out to take a good look at Caroline. She had her long legs propped up on the coffee table and her head tipped back to accommodate the floppy slice of pizza she was lowering into her mouth. She looked like she belonged there.

That was the part that was tightening his throat.

Adrian couldn't be expected to be the responsible adult all the time. He didn't have it in him after an entire day of doing just that. He was completely out of willpower to do things he ought to do. So he clenched his jaw and nodded, sweeping past Tom and out the door to the living room. He put a couple of slices of pizza on a paper plate and looked into the fridge on instinct, not really expecting anything beyond condiments and leftovers. Someone (he suspected Caroline) had brought over a large case of flavored coconut water. He took one and looked back to the living room. Caroline caught his eye and scooted to the edge of the sofa, patting a spot in the middle.

If this was what giving up looked like, he wished it didn't look so inviting.

Adrian sat down between Tom and Caroline, his dinner on his lap.

"My solo is coming up now," Tom said, pressing a button on the controller to restart the video. "I wasn't using any props, but I really killed it, so we should watch anyway."

Caroline nodded enthusiastically, curling her body sideways until her head was nearly resting on Adrian's shoulder.

"Did you paint anything today?" she asked him.

"No."

She turned her chin to peer up at him with owlish concern.

"You should. Paint things. You're a painter. Did you do the spreadsheets?"

"I did do the spreadsheets."

Caroline patted his arm approvingly. "You're a good Adrian," she said.

Well, at least there was that.

Caroline settled down again, searching for a comfortable position on Tom's ancient couch. Her thigh pressed alongside Adrian's, warm and absorbing.

"I want to go see *Anastasia* again," she told him, eyes on the screen. "They used a lot of props. I need to watch it for the props."

Adrian swallowed his first bite of pizza and answered, "I'll take you to see *The Barber of Seville* at the Boston Lyric Opera. The run starts next week." He didn't think he could handle another performance of *Anastasia*.

Caroline prized his coconut water out of his hand and took a long swig before handing it back to him.

"We should do both, then," she said, a lock of her sweet-smelling blond hair falling over his shoulder as she nestled closer to him. A dizzy shock of emotion fluttered in his chest like a light bulb coming on.

On his other side, Tom mutely offered him the open bag of gummies. Adrian deliberated for a long moment before popping one in his mouth. It wasn't like anyone would give him an award for staying sober when he was already snuggled up with Caroline and settling in for the duration.

"Okay," he told her. "We'll do both."

Chapter Nine

"SO, THEY ARE BOTH PLAYS WITH PEOPLE SINGING," CARO-line began her analysis, more interested in the way Adrian's pretty lower lip stuck out when he was trying not to sound obnoxious than in the actual, technical differences between musicals and opera. She'd enjoyed her first opera. It was no *Anastasia*, but there was room for both in her life.

She'd liked the big fluffy costumes and the gleaming gilt paint on the sets. The English translation of the libretto had been projected on a screen to the left of the stage, and the story had been a good one, ending with everyone married and happy. It was silly to be proud of herself for liking a thing, but she'd worried that she wouldn't.

The day was one of those clear, chilly October mornings when the sky was piercingly blue and the light reflected white off the pavement and the bricks to make her squint as they moved around the Haymarket, browsing stalls of produce, cheese, and honey. Adrian was not a morning person, she'd noticed. Even though she would have been happy to go when the market opened at dawn, she thought she'd shown great restraint by meeting him there at eight, after her morning workout.

"Most operas are sung all the way through, but most

musicals will have some spoken dialogue," Adrian explained with great patience. He perfectly matched both the weather and the day, wearing a thick cream-colored cable-knit sweater made out of some kind of superior wool that fuzzed instead of pilled. Caroline had covertly touched his arm enough times to fondle the soft fabric that he'd given her an alarmed look, which caused her to stick her thumbs in the waistband of her running tights to restrain herself.

He was painfully handsome. It made her mouth dry to look at him with the breeze ruffling his hair and the sun bringing out the freckles across the bridge of his nose. Other women startled in acknowledgment of his remarkable beauty as he passed, Adrian acting doggedly unaware of the double takes he drew coming and going—the going because the fitted jeans looked nice on his ass too.

You probably can't afford him, ladies, Caroline thought, even though that internal announcement wasn't as satisfying as it ought to have been.

Caroline added half a dozen Granny Smith apples to the large wooden crate Adrian was carrying around. The crate was the first thing she'd purchased at the market; it was one of the few props left to be acquired off Rima's list. She wondered if she could sweet-talk Adrian into painting a turn-of-the-century brand name on the side.

"But not all of them?" Caroline said. She was not really interested but was happy to hear him talk. She bought two grapefruits and added them to the box.

"No. *Les Misérables*, for example, is a musical with no dialogue, but *Beatrice et Benedict* is an opera with spoken dialogue, not a recitative."

Les Misérables was coming up the next week at the Charles Playhouse. Caroline couldn't tell whether Adrian was actually excited to see it with her or just relieved that he would no longer risk watching *Anastasia* a third time.

"So, how will I know, then," Caroline asked, "whether I'm at a musical or the opera?"

Adrian was so obviously bothered by the idea that she might find herself at a performance without due preparation for the experience that he failed to notice her smile as she wound him up on the subject.

"There are exceptions to almost all the rules. Opera used to be entirely unamplified, but the size of modern theaters makes that impractical. You'll rarely see a musical performed in a language other than the local vernacular, but of course there are modern English-language operas. And the musical complexity— Wait, is that a persimmon? You know not to eat it until it's soft, right?"

Adrian broke off his lecture to squint at the latest fruit Caroline had added to the crate.

"I didn't. Good tip," she said. She gave him her most guileless face. "You were saying?"

Adrian opened his mouth and looked at her out of the corner of his eye. He caught her biting the inside of her lip and failed to keep his own expression straight.

"You are such a brat," he said, dimples popping in his cheeks. "If it's performed by an opera company, it's an opera. Otherwise, it's a musical."

"That's a tautology," Caroline teased him.

"You're a tautology." His knees dipped a bit as she added a large melon to the bin. "Do you actually want all this fruit, or is this another joke at my expense?"

"Are you sure it's a fruit?" Caroline asked. She'd heard about melons that were more like vegetables. There was no objective truth outside of Templeton.

"You don't know what it is?"

"No, I'm just buying whatever looks good." Her scruples wouldn't let her impulse-buy very many things. Her grandmother hadn't left her the money just to buy things. But she really did enjoy buying whatever food she wanted without looking at the price first.

"What are you going to do with it, then?" Adrian asked, looking at the big green gourd suspiciously.

"Well, I'll look it up when I get home. If it's a fruit, it'll go into the smoothie rotation. If it's a vegetable, I'll cook it with butter. Turns out I like all vegetables as long as they're cooked with butter."

"A very French philosophy."

"That's where I learned it. I bought a French cookbook a few months ago. I've been working my way through it in the evenings."

"As a hobby?"

"Well, I'm being rigorous about it. I'm cooking every recipe in the book, like the lady did in the movie. Some are not fun. Do you know how hard it is to get the backbone out of a duck? And duck isn't even that great, or maybe I'm not that good a chef yet."

It had looked less like a roast duck than a murdered duck when she was done with it. She'd imagined duck detectives coming around to her kitchen to shake their beaks and speculate that only love or money could drive someone to *this*.

"You spatchcocked a duck—for yourself?"

Caroline laughed. "I don't think you really understand how much free time I had on my hands until I took up with you." How much time she *still* had, because she only saw him three evenings and one day a week. The good news was that rehearsals were coming up soon; she hoped

Rima would ask her to help wrangle the props during the show and not just before it.

Adrian's expression changed to one she didn't enjoy seeing on his face: a mix of pity and confusion.

"You'll make friends at Boston College," he said slowly. "Just give it time."

Caroline shrugged. "Either way, it's just another year and a half." She was keeping her gaze fixed on what happened after graduation, when she'd have a job and a real life instead of just a class schedule and a fitness routine. She'd be caught up on everything by then.

"You must have had friends back in Templeton." Adrian trailed after her as she moved on to a cheese stand.

Cheese was another area that bore investigation. Goat cheese, she'd discovered, was good on just about anything. On the other hand, she could not fool her brain into accepting anything with visible blue mold on it as edible.

"No, not really," she belatedly replied.

"I find that hard to believe."

Caroline dutifully tugged up one corner of her mouth in a partial smile. "Thanks."

She shoved a log of goat cheese wrapped in grape leaves at Adrian, hoping it would distract him from the inquiry at hand. He kept his head tilted at her.

She sighed dramatically. "I didn't," she explained. "Have friends. Or hobbies. Or anything. I lived at home. Played a lot of tennis."

"But why?"

Caroline didn't precisely know that herself. She was sure her dad would have said it was primarily for her athletic scholarship. But she'd always intended to study business. Would it have been so bad to get loans and grants and academic scholarships like anyone else? She would have been okay, even without any of her grandmother's money.

"I was real good at tennis," she said sourly. Nothing else, not yet. "It was basically the only thing I could do without someone yelling at me that I was doing it wrong."

They'd made almost a complete circuit of the market. Now they were near the flower stands, which Caroline had been saving for last.

"But you must have had teammates in Templeton, at least," Adrian said, unwilling to just let things go despite Caroline's curtness on the subject.

"It turns out that being good at tennis is not enough of a common ground to be my friend," Caroline said, because nobody had called after she quit the team. Possibly they were angry at her for quitting in the middle of the season, but if they'd actually cared, wouldn't they have called to at least ask her why?

Adrian's face subtly changed as they reached the florists' stalls, softening as he took in the displays. Even this late in the season, they had a big selection, some of them maybe from greenhouses, others interesting for their spiky seedpods or fall-hued foliage.

"And you think theater or visual arts or the symphony will be different?" he guessed.

After Caroline relieved him of the crate of fruit, he trailed his fingers gently over a bunch of Japanese anemones. There was something satisfying about the look of Adrian's angular artist's hands on the bright petals, an attractive contrast maybe.

"Well, that's what you talk to me about, isn't it?"

Adrian shot her a challenging look, suspicious that she was trying to wind him up again but unable to sustain any annoyance in the face of all the flowers. He looked through the selection with obvious interest, a nearly doting softness spreading across his face.

"Are you buying any flowers?" he asked.

"Yeah, which ones are the best?"

"For?"

She grinned. *For making you smile like that.* "Is there a versatile flower? A team player? Best all around?"

Adrian considered it, then grabbed a sheaf of tiny yellow blossoms.

"Smell," he told her, holding the flowers out.

She took a deep breath. "Oh! Licorice?"

"Yes. These are goldenrod. I used to—" He broke off, probably thinking of his garden that was now a hot tub. "Anyway. These are seasonal. And they do well as a cut flower."

"Perfect," Caroline said, grabbing another couple bunches and piling them into the fruit crate.

After they paid, they made their way to the edge of the square. Adrian took the crate back.

"Should we go put these in your car? What do you want to do next?"

Caroline stretched, flexing her arms behind her as she took in the city center. The aquarium was nearby, and so were the Freedom Trail and the cannoli shop she'd read about. The prospect of a full day of pleasant things ahead of her was like having money in the bank. Better, really— she already had the money. Right now she had Adrian's undivided attention too, her window into the bigger world she wanted. Caroline rolled her shoulders.

"Is your studio nearby?" she asked with studied casualness. She'd asked a few times, and Adrian had been careful not to say no, but he hadn't said yes either.

Adrian winced. "I don't actually have anything in progress there right now. You wouldn't rather go to the Institute of Contemporary Art?"

"No, I want to see what a working artist's studio looks like."

"If you really want to." Adrian sighed, adjusting his grip on the crate. "As long as you don't expect to see any working."

IT WAS RIDICULOUS TO WORRY WHAT SHE'D THINK OF HIS studio. The space itself was nothing to be ashamed of; he was lucky to have the grant that paid for it. But unlike the other dozen or so tenants in the building, Adrian didn't have any finished art Caroline hadn't already seen when she'd moved him out of Nora's house. Perhaps one of his neighbors would be in on a Saturday morning and wouldn't mind showing off what they were working on. There was a radio playing Brazilian ballads somewhere nearby, filtered through layers of drywall and echoing off the metal roof high above them. He put his key in the padlock of his plywood door.

To his relief, Caroline looked nothing but pleased as she followed him into the room and set the crate of fruit and flowers down on his worktable. She took in the toolboxes full of paint, the racks of brushes, the cans of mineral spirits and linseed oil and gesso, the stacks of canvas, and the few rescued paintings under repair.

She peered at the big board of reference images he'd collected for the mostly abandoned Ilinden-Preobrazhenie Uprising project. Wrinkling her nose at the violence of a couple of the scenes, she wiped the expression from her face when she caught him looking at her.

Adrian began moving stacks of books off his paint-splattered futon to clear a space for her to sit, but Caroline remained standing, closely examining every mundane object in the room.

She cleared her throat. "So, this is where you do all the actual painting?"

Theoretically.

"Yes, always in the studio," he said, gesturing between the easels and the stack of canvases. "I'm not one of those artists who can concentrate while working *en plein air.*"

"Even the garden paintings?"

"Once upon a time, in a different studio," he said.

Caroline nodded and pulled the goldenrod out of the crate. "Do you have a vase for these?" she asked.

"Don't you want to wait until you're home?" he replied, looking around his studio anyway. He had a few glasses and cups from years back that he'd scavenged from antiques stores, but most of them were now holding tools or old paintbrushes.

"No, they're for you."

"You bought me flowers?" he asked, confused.

Caroline laughed, the first time his studio had been graced with that sound.

"Yeah," she said. "I thought you could paint them, if you're struggling for inspiration." Her expression was hopeful over the tops of the golden blossoms. It turned a little sly. "Also, aren't I supposed to get flowers for my sugar baby? Maybe shoes too? What else do sugar babies like?"

"Please stop calling me that," Adrian said, striving for dignity. Surely he had some left, albeit a dwindling supply. He reluctantly took the flowers when she thrust them at his chest.

"Come on," she said entreatingly. "Don't you like painting flowers? You didn't forget how to, did you?"

"I didn't forget how, I just moved on in my work," he told her, his tone stiffer than he'd intended.

Caroline's face fell in disappointment, and he mentally kicked himself. He was such an asshole. For everything she'd done for him already, the least he could do was paint some flowers for her. He turned back to his box of bowls and vases, emptying out a tarnished silver julep cup.

"I'll paint them for you," he muttered. "God knows I haven't set brush to canvas for any better reason recently."

"No, no, you don't have to," she said quickly. "I just thought having the fresh flowers in your studio might . . . inspire you. Or the fruit, maybe?"

Adrian tried to rub away the tarnish on the cup with the sleeve of one of his smocks, but it didn't budge. It had been years.

"It wasn't about lack of inspiration," he said absently, setting the cup aside and picking up a glass vase to inspect it for chips. "It's easy to paint flowers."

"What was it, then?"

"People thought my work wasn't progressing. It was time to move on to new subject matter." He'd phrased it more politely than the critics had. *Sentimental and juvenile* had been the message out of that last show. Along with Nora's promise of gallery space contingent on exploring more complex themes with his next series, he'd concluded that the critics were right.

The vase was chipped, and Caroline was looking at him with that pinched expression that he'd come to know meant that she didn't understand what he was saying but didn't want to admit it.

"Can you just hold these for me?" he asked, passing

the bundle of goldenrod back to her. None of his vases were right for the long unstructured shape of the flowers. He nodded at the stool nearest to the window.

"What, like a model?" she asked, sounding surprised but not displeased. She sat obediently on the stool.

"Sure," he said. "Do you mind?" He grabbed a charcoal pencil and put his smallest canvas on his easel. He'd already applied black gesso for the base layer.

With her spare hand, Caroline plucked at the front of her top. She was dressed in neon activewear again, though mercifully her midriff was covered today in deference to the colder weather.

"If I'd known I was going to have my portrait painted, I would have worn something other than spandex," she complained.

Adrian hadn't planned to do a portrait. He opened his mouth to tell her that he'd give her some cloth to drape the flowers with and he'd keep the rest of her out of the frame.

"I'll work around—" he began to say.

But her mouth curved up mischievously. "Should I take my clothes off instead?" she asked. "Would that be better?" She grasped the bottom hem of her shirt as though she was about to rip it off.

Adrian wished he had an immediate, charming quip to respond to that. Nothing came to mind. Picasso had already cornered the market on paintings of beautiful naked women holding flowers. Adrian had worked hard to gain a reputation for unsparing accuracy in his themes, a reputation that would only be squandered if he tried to convince an audience that someone who looked like Caroline had taken her clothes off for him. There was no way he could be expected to paint with all the blood in his head rushing south. No, that last part was obscene as well as not charming.

Instead, he only stared at her with his suddenly dry lips struck still, his mind helpfully suggesting the proportions of alizarin crimson and titanium white he would mix to capture the likely color of her areolas. At which point he discovered that he already possessed firm opinions on what her areolas looked like, as well as the rest of her naked body.

"You can keep your clothes on," he croaked after the moment stretched on, because he really had to say something to counter the obvious implications about why he wasn't saying anything.

"Are you sure?" Caroline asked, eyebrows raised, and he was positive it had to be a trap. "I don't see a lot of Lululemon in museums."

"Maybe that will be my hook. I'll get in with a corporate sponsorship," Adrian said, recovering once he pulled his eyes off her and began rummaging in his sack of clean smocks. He found an oversize men's shirt and handed it off to Caroline, averting his eyes as though she were actually naked, not just wrapped in a few layers of brightly colored performance fabric. He stripped off his own sweater and folded it on his futon, then grabbed a smock for himself.

"We'll just have to work on that," Caroline said inscrutably. She shrugged into the shirt and began to button it up, flowers resting in her lap. The dress shirt swamped her frame, but the fabric was thick enough to drape nicely. She looked down at her now-concealed chest.

"A lot of guys ask for boob shots on dating apps. If you painted me nude, I'd have something to send. Still a boob shot, but, you know, classier."

On more comfortable ground now that he'd assessed

that she was messing with him again, Adrian went over to her stool to turn her to five-eighths profile against the light source and adjust the flowers in her lap. Clothes aside, it wasn't a bad idea for a portrait at all. There was a pillar next to the window that provided an interesting material contrast in the background, and the juxtaposition of golden-haired girl and yellow flowers by the concrete form was a modern enough image to appeal to his sensibilities. He hadn't painted from a live model in years, but he found himself very willing to take on the challenge.

"If you're going to send a nude portrait to someone on the Internet, it doesn't have to be of you," he suggested. "Send one by Jean-Léon Gérôme and say that's you coming out of your well to shame them."

Caroline raised her eyebrows in appreciation of the joke. "But what if he's an educated guy? Then I'm just a *really* old catfisher."

"Maybe you shouldn't be meeting men on Internet dating apps at all," Adrian said. He took a step back to check Caroline's position against the window. "At least half of them are probably serial killers." That proportion sounded about right. "I'm serious. It's not safe." The idea was deeply concerning.

Caroline's head swiveled to follow him. "That's how *we* met." The motion took her out of the pose he'd already envisioned. He swapped out the small canvas for a larger one. He hadn't applied black gesso to it yet, but with Caroline mostly backlit in the frame, he'd want to start with brighter colors on the base to show the light pouring through toward the viewer.

"We didn't meet on a dating app," he protested. He pulled over his side table and got his palette and paints arranged at his left hand. The calm and focus he'd been missing for months began to sweep in as he composed the scene in his head.

"Oh yeah? What was it, then?"

His lips pursed as he strove for the very important differences between himself and whatever dangerous creeps Caroline was dealing with online. His mind was running down well-worn paths of form and shape, the shadows and highlights he planned pushing all other concerns to the background, and he did not want to think about Caroline's extracurricular dating life at all.

"Basically the classified ads," he said absently. "For people."

Caroline snickered. "Now I feel guilty," she said. "*I'm* one of those creeps they warn you about on the Internet." She was nervous for all her bluster earlier. It was probably harder to be the model than the artist, exposed and intimate while he was already withdrawing to the meditative distance he needed when painting.

Adrian was prepared to start his underdrawing, so he took a step closer to Caroline and caught her chin between two fingers. He gently tilted her face back into position. Had he ever touched her before? He couldn't remember. She touched him often, small brushes of her hand on his arm or shoulder. He'd probably remember if he'd touched her before. Her skin was warm, despite the coolness of the day and the temperature inside the studio.

"Can you hold this position?" he asked quietly as she made big eyes up at him. Her throat moved as she swallowed.

"I think so," she said in a tiny voice.

He rubbed a thumb briefly between her eyebrows to soften the expression there, then drew it to the flowers to focus her gaze on them.

He stepped backward to see if she'd comply. She didn't budge.

"Good," he said.

He sat down, picked up a piece of vine charcoal, and lifted it to the canvas. A small, mean voice inside him said that this composition was a cliché and his subject matter saccharine sweet. He hesitated with his hand braced against the unblemished white of the material.

"Is it okay if we listen to music while you work?" Caroline nearly whispered, not moving her head. Whoever had been playing their radio had left, and all Adrian could hear in the studio was Caroline's low breathing and his own heartbeat.

Adrian took his phone out of his pocket and set it on the table next to his paints.

"Of course," he said. "What do you want to hear?"

"The *Les Mis* soundtrack," she said. "Or *Anastasia* again."

Adrian took a deep breath and queued up *Anastasia*.

"Ready?" he said.

"Perfect," Caroline agreed. She relaxed her features as he'd arranged them. There was no reason not to paint her. Even if nobody else liked the work, Caroline probably would, sweetness and all, and then he'd have made *one* person happy in his life. Adrian picked up the vine charcoal again and began to sketch.

Chapter Ten

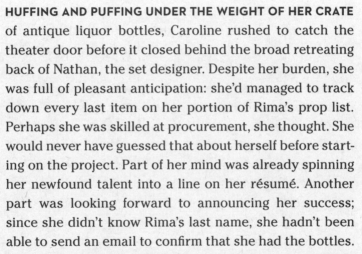

HUFFING AND PUFFING UNDER THE WEIGHT OF HER CRATE of antique liquor bottles, Caroline rushed to catch the theater door before it closed behind the broad retreating back of Nathan, the set designer. Despite her burden, she was full of pleasant anticipation: she'd managed to track down every last item on her portion of Rima's prop list. Perhaps she was skilled at procurement, she thought. She would never have guessed that about herself before starting on the project. Part of her mind was already spinning her newfound talent into a line on her résumé. Another part was looking forward to announcing her success; since she didn't know Rima's last name, she hadn't been able to send an email to confirm that she had the bottles.

Caroline failed to catch the door before it closed. She readjusted her grip and tried to open it with a spare finger, but she was afraid she'd drop her crate. Hefting it higher against her chest, she made a swipe for the large handle of the door with the toe of a sneaker. She had hopped backward on one foot and nearly tumbled onto her ass before Nathan happened to glance back, see her, then rush to push the door open.

"Mother of Jesus, let me help you with that," Nathan said. He made a grab for the crate.

"No, no, no," Caroline yelped. "I've got it. Really. It's a prop. I've got it."

She tried to project serene confidence over the lip of the crate. This was complicated by how the splinters from the rough wood were digging into her fingers. Adrian had deigned to paint a logo along the side of the box, but she still needed to sand and seal it in the props shop if she didn't want the actors to hurt themselves on the edges. That would be a pretty poor showing for her first foray into the world of prop design, she considered.

The set designer trailed after her as she made her way backstage. The deadline for props had been the day before, but several of the bottles Caroline had ordered had only arrived that morning. She found Rima at the props station, taping a grid onto the long folding table and labeling spots for watches, glassware, and cigars. Her long purple wrap dress swished as she reached for a battered pack of cigarettes and placed it in the precise center of its grid square. Sophia was nearby, checking things off her list as Rima did the inventory.

The shorter woman's eyes flew open in delight when she saw Caroline approach.

"Oh, were you able to find one of the black gin bottles?" Rima asked. She hurried to clear a space on the table for Caroline to set the crate down.

"Yes," Caroline said proudly. "I got everything on the list. Look, this one still has the seal on it." She gestured to a black glass flask that had a daub of wax next to the molding cork. She'd found it on a Facebook buy-sell group in Aberdeen, Scotland, and convinced the owner to mail it to her express.

"Oh, that's fantastic—" Rima began to say.

"Props went final yesterday," Sophia interrupted.

Caroline winced. She'd tried to make the deadline.

"We haven't even finished inventory," Rima argued, waving away Sophia's objection. "And these are so much better than what we had. How did you get all of this?"

"Did you bring your receipts?" Sophia interrupted again, eyeing Caroline's purse where it hung mostly empty at her side.

"I—I have them all in my email, but I got most of these bottles off eBay, and—" Caroline stammered, because she hadn't thought about it.

Sophia dramatically pressed her palm to the bridge of her nose. She was wearing an extra large black sweatshirt over leggings, cinched with a tool belt holding rolls of tape and other backstage implements. Her expression was haggard.

"We don't do Internet orders because they're too hard to return. We don't have a budget to keep any of this," Sophia gritted out. Even Rima seemed alarmed at that, looking askance at the crate full of antique liquor bottles.

"Don't worry," Caroline hurriedly explained. "I didn't think I'd get reimbursed. It wasn't very expensive. We can just keep it here, right?"

The bottles themselves hadn't been very expensive, anyway. Some of the shipping had been, but there'd been a deadline, and it wasn't like she couldn't spare the money.

Her reassurances only seemed to take everyone aback.

"Thank you, but we didn't expect you to pay for them yourself," Rima said slowly, her eyes focusing on Caroline's handbag, then her battered athletic shoes. Caroline was familiar with that look by now—it said she wasn't making sense.

Sophia was still torqued about Caroline's purchases.

"I'll need to go check the insurance policy. I don't know if we're set up to accept donations. This isn't how we do things. I'll have to think of how we'll keep track of expenses if we don't link the budget with the props," she said, sounding harassed.

"I'm sorry, I didn't think this would make more work for you two," Caroline said, deflating.

Sophia's pale blue eyes narrowed on the word *think*, as though she agreed that Caroline hadn't thought about this very hard.

Sophia turned and stalked off toward the administrative offices.

Rima blew out a wincing exhale. Caroline's shoulders were stiff and tight together, full of the familiar urge to make herself smaller when she was always one of the tallest people in the room.

"I'm sorry," Caroline said again when Sophia was gone. "I hope I didn't put you even more behind schedule."

Rima lifted her two palms as though to push the thought away.

"Don't worry about Sophia. She's just anxious because we were supposed to be off-book by today, but she spent all morning feeding Pat McGloin his lines."

"Pat?"

"That's one of the lead roles." Rima frowned at her. "Didn't you read the play?"

Caroline had not, in fact, read the play yet. She'd meant to. But she hadn't finished Adrian's book yet, and it hadn't seemed important to read the play when she wasn't in it.

"You know, I'm not really a theater person, and so . . ." Caroline trailed off.

"Of course," Rima said, looking her over again, forehead creased. She hesitated, then went to her binder. She pulled a thick sheaf of paper from the middle. "Here," she said, proffering the pages to Caroline. "Why don't you make a copy of mine? I have my notes on the scene changes in the margins." Her mouth pursed again. "I don't know how Sophia will feel about you running props during production, but maybe—"

Caroline couldn't tell whether Rima's offer was genuine or made out of obligation. Maybe she ought to just leave now and tell Adrian, if he ever asked, that she'd done what she said she would.

"You guys could probably use the help during rehearsal though," Caroline said, not sure if that was actually correct.

"Yes, always," Rima said. She paused. "Was it a lot of money? I'll get it reimbursed for you."

"Oh, um, really it wasn't," Caroline lied, not wanting to make it any more awkward. She squirmed and hefted the play. "I'll make a copy and bring this back." She walked briskly away, leaving the room before she realized that she didn't know where a photocopier was in the theater complex. She could hardly go back and ask Rima though; she'd been weird enough already.

So she left the theater and set off for the business campus at a fast walk, aiming for the document center in the basement of the administration building.

It got dark so early during autumn in the Northeast. She still wasn't used to it. Though it was barely five, the sun was down, and the campus was emptying out as people returned to their apartments and dormitories. Caroline braced her face against the wind. She wished she'd worn her big puffy coat, but she'd been afraid that she'd rip it on the crate. Crap, she hadn't warned Rima about the crate.

She took the stairs to the basement two at a time, mind

still fretting over whether Rima would scrape a hand on the wood. She landed at the base like a vaulter, only then realizing that her phone was buzzing in her purse. The caller was her oldest sister. The screen displayed a picture of Kayla holding Caroline's first niece in the hospital nursery.

Caroline immediately answered, checking as she did that the document center was still open and empty. She perched next to a spiral-binding machine, heart rate rising past the anxious tempo it had already set.

"Hey, what's up?" Kayla asked, as casually as though it had not been over six months since they'd last spoken.

"I— Nothing much," Caroline replied haltingly. She'd assumed that it would take an emergency to get a call from certain members of her family. Kayla especially. Her sister hadn't even come to say goodbye when Caroline left for Boston.

Kayla exhaled, and Caroline heard vague traffic noises in the background. Based on the hour, Kayla was probably on her way home from her job as a receptionist at a Templeton construction firm.

"Yeah, so," Kayla said, pretending that they were in the middle of some long conversation, rather than speaking after months of cold silence, "since you're making Mom and Dad go up to see you for Thanksgiving, does that mean you'll be home for Christmas? Matt was wondering if we could rent a place down by the lake for New Year's."

"I'm not making Mom and Dad come," Caroline protested, attacking the predicate first.

Kayla snorted. "Or you're boycotting Uncle Jay's house, whatever. When are you coming back?"

"I don't know," Caroline said truthfully. She'd thought about *never*. *Never* had been the plan when she climbed out the window to escape her dad and her uncle and the papers they wanted her to sign. But *never* was feeling like an awfully long time recently, because it was hard going days without talking to anyone. "I think I'm going to France or Switzerland over Christmas," she decided to explain. Adrian hadn't mentioned it again, but there was no reason to think he was opposed, and it was still a couple of months off.

"Why Switzerland? What's in Switzerland?"

"That's where they make Swiss chocolate," Caroline said, regretting how snotty she sounded as soon as the words were out. "I mean. Um. Art Basel. It's an art show."

"You're going to Switzerland by yourself?"

Caroline hesitated, wondering if Kayla was concerned or just probing for information.

"No, with a friend," she replied.

There was a moment of silence while Kayla waited for more detail, which Caroline did not provide.

"This isn't the guy you met on the Internet who you told Mom about, is it?"

Caroline scowled. "So what if it is? Why can't I go to Europe with a friend?"

Kayla made a deep noise of discomfort. "You don't know anything about this stuff yet, okay? People can be really terrible, especially strangers you meet on the Internet! Does he know about your money?"

Caroline sucked in a breath to defend Adrian, who'd never asked for a cent more than they'd agreed, but it occurred to her that she was the person Kayla really thought was going to screw things up. "Okay, well, how am I supposed to *learn* about this stuff? How was I supposed to meet anyone at home? Dad didn't even let me go to high school or live in the dorms in college—"

"Do you not *remember* sophomore year? When people were pushing you into lockers and tossing your backpack in the dumpster every day? That's why Dad pulled you out," Kayla insisted. That made their dad sound like such an altruist, as though he hadn't been thrilled that Caroline could put in extra hours of tennis practice once she was just doing classes online.

"Maybe the people at our high school just sucked," Caroline said, even though her eyes had started to prickle at her sister's interrogation.

"And all the people you played tennis with in college just sucked too?" Kayla pressed, probably thinking of the girls who'd pretended to forget Caroline's name every fall for four years, or the guy she'd thought was her boyfriend but hadn't been.

Caroline's chest heaved. "I just didn't know how to handle people yet."

"Oh, hon," Kayla said, her tone so doubtful about Caroline's ability to ever figure this out that it stung.

They let the line hang in silence.

"Your coach called, by the way," Kayla eventually said. "He's worried about you all on your own up in Boston."

Caroline wished she'd been able to take it all with her. Not just her clothes and belongings. Everything her family knew about her because she'd lived at home for all of college. Every disappointment and humiliation that she'd been forced to let them witness. It felt like tar sticking to her sneakers, the knowledge that they still saw her as a helpless child to be protected from any situation where she might be hurt.

"If he's worried, he can call me and I'll tell him I'm doing fine," Caroline gritted out. "You guys don't need to be planning my life behind my back anymore."

"Okay, well, fine, I tried," Kayla stuttered. "I'll just tell him to fuck off if he calls again. That takes care of that. Glad you're doing great. I'll let everyone know."

"Wait," Caroline said, sensing that Kayla was about to hang up. She hadn't wanted their first conversation to go like this. It had taken Kayla a lot to be the first one to call, and Caroline had been angrier than her sister. She searched for some neutral subject matter, something that would let Caroline show Kayla that she was managing despite no natural aptitude for any of this.

"What does Emmie want for her birthday? When's her party?" Caroline asked, naming her older niece.

"Oh, don't worry about it," Kayla said angrily. "She's turning four. She probably doesn't even remember you."

Caroline's phone went to its home screen as Kayla hung up. She stared at the icons for a while, wondering if she ought to call back but unsure what she would say if she did. When the screen faded to black, Caroline put the phone in her purse. The corner of the business center where she stood was dark, and she had the disorienting sensation that she had forgotten what she was doing there. Her ears rang as she fought down the suffocating wash of shame that talking to her family always brought on. She had the sudden, desperate urge to go somewhere else. Do anything else. Speak to anyone else.

She took her phone out. It was a Thursday. She didn't see Adrian on Thursdays. She might have called him on a Tuesday or Wednesday night, when they could get good restaurant reservations, or on a weekend, when they went out to shows and performances, but not on a Thursday.

She didn't know if it was okay to just text him for no reason, for something other than their upcoming plans. She could make up something, but that was pretty pathetic, wasn't it? That would be taking up more of his time than they'd agreed, and she wouldn't do that to him. She'd see him the next day. She'd be fine until then. She had classes on both days, and maybe she'd finish his book and Rima's play with her free time. She'd keep herself busy.

She put her phone away, then bent to turn on the copier.

THE LIGHTS IN THE THEATER WERE DIMMED, BUT CAROline's face was illuminated by the faint glow of her phone screen as she used it to read a translation of the libretto. Adrian would have told her that using her phone was frowned upon during a performance, but she couldn't have failed to notice the scolding looks of the people seated around them, so he saved his breath.

She'd been subdued all evening, even while meeting him at the front door of the Boston Conservatory Theater. She wore the same black dress he'd picked out the night they'd met—she'd worn it to the opera the previous time as well. He wondered whether she thought that a short black dress was the only appropriate attire for a musical performance or if, more likely, she simply didn't care if he saw her in the same dress all the time.

Part of him also wondered if she couldn't actually afford to spend money on clothes. Although she'd never hesitated to buy anything he indicated that she needed, and his checks cleared the bank without fail, Adrian had passed a great deal of time with people who had money, and she didn't act like she had any. The thousands of dollars a week she was spending on theater tickets and restaurant meals and a personal attendant to escort her were the outlier.

Adrian purposefully knit his hands in his lap when he

realized that he was staring at Caroline again, head propped on his fist. He ought to be watching the stage: this was a performance by opera graduate students rather than the opera company, but the soprano was fantastic, better than anyone else he'd ever heard in the part.

Though the stage did not offer a great deal to look at. Perhaps that was the problem. No doubt owing to the brief run, the director had elected to forgo scenery and props. The performers wore street clothes. The entirety of the set consisted of long bolts of white fabric, which the singers held in configurations that suggested the different rooms of the ducal palace. (If he squinted. And used a great deal of his imagination. And thought back to the last time he'd seen this opera performed.)

No wonder Caroline had to keep her eyes on the libretto to figure out what was happening onstage.

Act 1 concluded in the rustling of fabric ladders and Rigoletto's despairing collapse. Caroline looked judgmentally at the bare stage, black and pockmarked under the intermission lights. Adrian stood to stretch his back and shake out some of the cramping muscles in his thighs. Caroline remained seated, slumped in her chair.

"I thought all operas had, like, horned hats and big gilded sets with flower arrangements," she said.

"Some of them do," Adrian admitted, resisting the urge to educate her on the precise performances in which she might expect to see a singer in a Viking helmet. "I believe the concept behind this staging is that without the extraneous visuals, the patrons will focus on the music."

Caroline snorted. "They had an opportunity to wear fun costumes in a pretend Renaissance palace, and they didn't take it? They decided to wear jeans instead? I don't get it."

Adrian scuffed a shoe on a hole in the carpet, secretly in agreement with her.

"If we go to the opening night of one of these operas, you can be the one in the ball gown," he told her. He still hadn't found a reason to wear his tux for her, and that seemed almost like false advertising. Caroline would look beautiful in an evening gown.

She ducked her face to consider that, tilting her chin to the side. She looked back up at him through her eyelashes, big green eyes still shadowed.

"Okay," she said.

With that inducement failing to excite her, Adrian gnawed on the inside of his lip.

"Are you not enjoying this?" he asked.

"I just don't know what's going on half the time at these things," she said, frustration thick in her voice. As she absorbed her own words, she visibly steeled herself. "Probably because I don't speak French," she added, shooting another glance up at him.

Adrian could now recognize her feeble attempt at baiting him into saying that *Rigoletto* was in Italian, so he only pretended to despair.

"Do you want to get out of here?" he asked in a softer tone when her expression returned to its pensive baseline for the evening.

"Yes. No. No, I'm fine," Caroline said, stretching out her long legs in front of her in a carelessly graceful sprawl.

"We can do something else," he offered.

"Like what?"

"Whatever you want. Anything."

That brought a hint of a smile to her face. "Your profile didn't say you'd do *anything*," she said, trying hard to leer but not quite managing the expression.

Adrian's boundaries were well within art-person norms, but he doubted an innocent like Caroline could find his hard limits with a map and a compass. Though now he imagined her trying.

She does not want to sleep with you. She was very clear about that. Do not think about the anythings you could do with her.

"What would you rather be doing?" he rephrased, realizing too late that this question offered the same answer as before. She knew it too and gave him a knowing smile as the heat rose in his cheeks. But her smile faded as she considered his question.

"I don't know," she finally said.

"What would you normally do on a Friday night?" he prompted her when she didn't offer a single suggestion.

She screwed up her face, then took a deep breath. "Tennis," she said.

"Do you want me to find someone to play tennis with you?" he asked.

She gave him a considering look, then inclined her head to indicate that he'd do. Adrian instinctively leaned backward.

"Not me," he said. "I haven't played since high school." He hadn't been particularly good at tennis in high school, even, but she didn't look put off by his disclosure. "I don't have a racket."

"You can use my spare," she said, apparently warming to the idea. When he didn't bite, she sweetened the offer. "You can use my *new* one."

"Caroline. I barely remember the rules," he warned her. Any random yuppie off the streets was likely to be better at tennis than he was.

Her smile broadened. "Well, when I play tennis, I do

like to win," she said, her tone growing much more cheerful. "But I haven't played in six months. You'll probably do just fine."

Adrian rubbed the back of his neck. "I guess we can go tomorrow morning." He'd watch some videos tonight.

"I thought you meant right now?"

"It's eight at night. I'm in a suit," he pointed out.

She gave him pleading eyes. "You can get changed first."

It struck him that playing tennis with her was one of the easier things she might ask of him. Much less likely to send him to hell than *Take me to Europe, Adrian*; *paint me like one of your French girls, Adrian*; *kiss me, Adrian—*

He never used to want things he shouldn't have. He didn't know what was happening to him.

Caroline peered up at him expectantly, arms wrapped around her enormous yellow purse. The conductor began walking back toward the orchestra pit.

"All right," he acquiesced. "I can do a little night tennis."

TWO HOURS LATER, ADRIAN WALKED OUT OF HIS GYM, SCANning the street for Caroline. His gym did not have tennis courts. It was located *next* to a park with public courts. Unsurprisingly, nobody else was on the courts at 10:00 p.m. in the last week of October, though floodlights still illuminated the area. Adrian, in sweatpants, did not look like he had anything worth being mugged over, but he worried about Caroline.

She had suggested they use Boston College's courts. Adrian had in return suggested that he would sooner strip naked and streak through the quad than sign in as her guest at the student gym. Caroline had promptly replied that they could do that instead if he preferred, she would enjoy that just as much as tennis, thank you. Her eventual agreement to change separately and meet at the park seemed likely to be his last win that evening.

She was already there, batting a ball against the back-board. He needed a moment to take in Caroline dressed for tennis: an infinitesimal skirt, white ankle socks, and a ponytail, looking like she'd just stepped out of a college athletics brochure or a daydream whose wholesomeness was subject to immediate change. Her only concession to the temperature was a long-sleeved half-zip shirt. Adrian was wearing a T-shirt under his sweatshirt, and the night air was already sinking in. He wondered whether he ought to offer it to her.

Caroline bounced on her toes when she spotted him. She caught her ball on the flat of her racket, flicked it to the edge, then lofted it over the net at him. He lunged for it and managed to catch the ball in his right hand. She'd left a hot pink racket at the center mark. It looked new; he supposed she'd given him the best one, as promised.

She pulled a knee to her chest, giving him an eyeful of the expanse of her thighs.

He stood there watching her stretch for another min-ute before he realized that he ought to do the same rather than stare at her like a cartoon dog who had spotted a roast chicken on the dinner table. He hastily turned away and bent in some desultory lunges, imagining that there was no amount of stretching that would prepare him for the shellacking that seemed likely to ensue.

He was trying to recall whether it was required to drop the ball before serving it when he felt her palm on his thigh, gently pushing it into a ninety-degree angle. He nearly toppled over. He hadn't realized that she'd crossed the court to him.

"Your legs look pretty tight," she said. "What have you been doing in the gym?"

"Just running," he said, his voice higher and louder than he appreciated.

Her expression was concerned.

"If you lie down, I'll help you stretch out your glutes," she said.

Caroline pressing him down while he worked out the kinks in his ass was a thing that did not need to happen, for his own mental well-being, if not hers. He scrambled to his feet.

"I walked over here from my apartment," he said. "I imagine that's a sufficient warm-up." He put several paces between them.

"Do you want to get right to it?" she asked. "Or practice a bit first?" Caroline nodded at her bag. "I brought a lot of balls if you just want to practice."

"I don't think a few minutes of practice is going to make up for the last fifteen years," Adrian told her wryly, bending to scoop up the racket. He adjusted his hand on the grip. He was the same height as her, but he had larger hands than she did. He wondered whether that made a difference with the rackets; hers felt alien in his hand.

Caroline had left her duffel bag of tennis balls in the middle of the court. She scooped another two out, stuffing one somewhere under her skirt. The second, she lobbed across the net at him. Adrian managed to volley it back with only a minimum of scurrying to reach his position. Caroline caught the ball and bobbled it on her racket again. Adrian felt a moment of optimism. Perhaps it would not be so bad. She approached the baseline on her end of the court and he assumed the same position on his.

"Do you need to move your bag?" he asked.

"No, I don't think so," she said thoughtfully.

Adrian shrugged. She knew whether she was likely to trip over it.

"Let's just play a little baby tennis," she said, giving him an underhand lob.

He hit it squarely into the net.

"It'll come back to you," she encouraged him when he sent her a disappointed glance.

Adrian got the ball over the net with an underhand serve and then managed to send it back when she returned it in a high parabolic curve. They passed the ball back and forth for a few minutes. His confidence grew every time he returned the ball. She'd beat him, but he'd probably win a couple points, he decided. He didn't play tennis or racquetball, but he ran several times a week. He was tall, so he had a good reach. He swung his shoulders to loosen them, smiling back at Caroline as he relaxed into the unaccustomed activity.

"If you're still interested in a match, let's see your serve," he told her.

"Okay!" Caroline called, voice bright and eager. "Ready?"

Adrian bent over as he vaguely recalled tennis players did during matches, holding the racket in both hands.

"Ready," he said.

Caroline tossed the ball into the air, going to her full height as she bounced on her toes and slammed the ball in his direction at the approximate speed of a cruising 747. It hit in the left corner of the service box and then careened off the chain-link fence behind him with such force that the entire structure rang like a bell. Adrian had not even had the opportunity to move in the appropriate direction, let alone intercept it.

Adrian let his racket droop. He gave Caroline a look.

"What?" she asked. "Were you not ready?"

He edged closer to the left side of the court. "No, I was as ready as I get," he said.

"Okay," Caroline said. "Fifteen–love."

The next half hour was rough on his pride. His serves went mostly into the net. Caroline's next serve of the following set hit the right pocket with enough spin on it that it arched out of his reach before he got close. Then the next one startled him by going into his racket. He got the sense that she was not so much trying to keep him on his toes as she was assessing what he could do, but that did not mean he managed to return the ball any more often than she seemed to want him to. She alternated sides with every return, and he was soon panting from the effort of running back and forth across the court. He almost wished she'd just hit the corner with her serves and save him the effort of running before losing every point.

As he stalked past her at the end of a set, she nearly sent him head over feet by smacking his ass with the flat of her racket.

"How are you sweating?" she snickered. "It's forty degrees out here!"

Adrian tossed his sweatshirt off, glaring his scandalized objection at her. His undershirt was sticking to his body.

She seemed to think better of her attitude. Her teeth raked her lower lip as she wet it.

"Good hustle though," she told him, searching for some possible praise in light of his abject subjugation on the court. She returned to the service line.

"Have you not won yet?" he demanded, assuming his position on the opposite side of the court for what felt like the millionth time. He was going to have a heart attack if he kept this up much longer.

"I won, like, two sets ago," she admitted.

Adrian dropped his head back and stared up toward the floodlights above them.

"So, your biggest problem," Caroline said, "is that you should be using your backhand when it comes toward your nondominant side, instead of trying to step around it to get it with your forehand. You're running yourself ragged when you could just extend a little. Play smarter, not harder."

"Oh, is that my biggest problem?" Adrian asked, breathing heavily.

"Well, that and your prereturn leaves a lot to be desired. Let's try to work on it, Mr. Flatfoot," she announced, as though their bodies weren't steaming in the late-night air of a decrepit Brookline tennis court, and they were instead discussing the finer points of form at his father's country club in the New York suburbs on a fine May afternoon, and also he was fifteen.

Caroline sent another serve across the net, the ball passing a couple of feet to his left.

"Backhand," she said.

He watched the ball go.

"Sir, your attitude needs some work," she said firmly, her accent deepening. "Don't you want to win?"

"You are literally paying me to be here," Adrian reminded her.

"I'm not paying you to suck!" she yelled back, a giggle beginning to work its way into her tone. She scooped up another ball from her bag. She sent it over to his left, slightly closer. "Backhand!"

Adrian made one last, abortive lunge for the ball but spun it off the edge of his racket.

"That was better," Caroline chirped. She picked up another ball. "Backhand!"

"I'm done," Adrian growled. "You win."

"Noooo," Caroline mock wailed. "We can make some real improvement on your backhand."

She served another ball to his left, which he ignored. Then a second one that barely missed him. He looked up at her sharply to see if she'd done it on purpose.

"Backhand!" she called.

The next one grazed him. She *was* doing it on purpose.

"Oh, come on!" she yelled. "You're not that old. Are you tired already?"

Adrian squared his shoulders and gave her his sternest look, to no apparent effect. "I'm done," he repeated. He turned to look at all the balls he'd need to pick up, and she hammered a serve directly into his shins. He yelped and swore as he jumped, turning to freeze her with a promise of vengeance. That was going to leave a bruise.

"Backhand?" she said.

He dropped her racket on the hard court.

"Uh-oh," she gasped, quickly bending to scoop up another couple of balls. As she continued to pelt him with tennis balls, he charged across the court, using his last surge of adrenaline to vault the net and barrel right at her. She was in the middle of a final volley when he caught her and wrapped his arms around her, trying to wrestle her racket out of her grip. She squealed and turned so that her back was against his stomach, both of their hands grappling to hold on to her tennis racket.

"Oh, no, no, no, you're covered in sweat!" she yelped, barely able to form words over her desperate, hysterical laughter.

He ground the side of his face into her neck, wiping

sweat into her skin and hair, which still smelled like drug-store shampoo and clean woman, with not even the faint-est hint of exertion.

He should have let go then. She wasn't letting go of the racket, and they were making a scene. If he'd let go first, he wouldn't have had to think about it later. Holding on meant he had to admit that he wanted her, that an animal portion of his brain had noted that this position would do, and that Caroline pressed against the entire length of his body was a very good position indeed. In fact, she was the perfect height for this position, might as well have been designed for him to lean over and wrap around and press his hips into. It felt like sex, like living, like every sharp-edged and vital impulse he'd smothered for years.

You're a disgrace, said a more rational part of his mind. But that part was not in control anymore, and perhaps had not been for the entire length of time he'd known her. So he held on tighter until they stumbled and fell on the court, Caroline sprawled out over his chest, both of them panting.

His chest was on fire as he rolled to his back, ex-hausted, aroused, and bewildered. Every emotion and sensation was centered on the woman laughing on top of him. He couldn't make himself let go. He couldn't see how he ever would.

"I win," she whispered, expression exultant.

Chapter Eleven

CAROLINE HAD BEEN TO BOSTON'S MUSEUM OF FINE ARTS before. Twice. It was located near the university, so she'd gone the weekend she arrived, before all her stuff was even unpacked and put away. In her previous life, she'd been to a couple of museums in Houston on class trips, but *with two hundred other eighth graders* was not anyone's idea of the best way to experience the arts.

On her move-in weekend in August, the museum had been crowded with freshmen and their proud parents. Caroline went alone and felt discouraged from entering the most popular halls. She'd wandered around in the contemporary art wing without much of an idea of what she was looking at.

She'd come back the second time with a plan, a map, and an audio tour, managing to make it all the way through the Dutch masters and halfway through the Japanese wing. She was sure she would have eventually completed the entire enormous neoclassical building in time, had she not given her weekends over to Adrian for scheduling, but she had not known about the monthly young professionals series. He sure knew everything about all the good stuff in life, she thought as they followed the crowd of twentysomethings up the stairs to the entrance of the main gallery, the November breeze frosting her cheeks and ruffling her hair.

This was what she might expect her life to look like once she graduated, she told herself. She'd be one of these people in business clothes tuning in to their social lives after a day spent in tall buildings downtown or along the tech corridor. The mental image steadied her; she was still a little wobbly in her heels but determined to master the things before the snow made any shoes but boots impractical. This was a good way to spend the evening. This was what she'd wanted out of her life in Boston. This was progress. *Good job, Caroline. Nice footwork.*

Satisfaction was not an unfamiliar emotion to Caroline; she'd won a lot of tennis matches, after all. But it had been painfully illusive for the past few months. This group of people queueing for longneck bottles of beer and plastic cups of wine finally fit her expectations for life in Boston. They had alert, intelligent faces and tailored jackets, and they moved through the halls of the museum with purpose and confidence. This was the scene of adult activities she anticipated. Dating. Philanthropy. *Networking.*

Caroline showed her ID to the teller and retrieved their tickets and black-Sharpie name tags as Adrian carried their coats off to the bag check. It was strange, the way he'd stomped off at the end of their tennis match, barely wishing her good night. She'd feared that she had pissed him off, not just injured his pride and possibly his shins. There was a stiff set to his shoulders even though he was guiding her into the American wing for the reception as solicitously as she could hope, looking sleek and handsome in his charcoal button-down and dark green trousers.

The second time she thanked him for suggesting the

event, he told her she should become a member and join a committee if she wanted to come every month.

"Are you a member?" she asked.

"No, this is Young Professionals for the Arts, and I am zero for three, at this point."

When she disputed that, he gulped his red wine and gave a grim chuckle.

"These people are lawyers and accountants and finance types," he explained. "You won't find any actual artists at an event where you have to pay for entry *and* drinks."

"Except you."

"Except me," he begrudgingly admitted.

They followed the mass of gray wool and silk into the main hall, where the museum had set up two more drink stations among a scattering of high-top tables. The entire group shuffled slowly past the paintings comprising the exhibit: a dozen large beige canvases. Caroline and Adrian stopped at the biographical label, where a black-and-white photograph of a serious-looking man in his thirties loomed over a short description of the project and a lengthier recitation of the various awards and honors the artist had received. Adrian impassively crossed his arms over his chest as Caroline read out loud that Jarret Mill had "deconstructed form, color, and image" in his Phoenix series. Adrian tossed back the rest of his wine and went to get another glass.

Caroline picked a beige canvas at random and approached to study it further. There had to be more to the exhibit than met the eye. The individual label read PHOENIX #3. It helpfully informed her that Jarret had painted it beige using acrylics. She leaned in to look at the brushstrokes. They appeared to have been made by a paintbrush. She leaned back to consider the color. It was still beige. At last, she recalled a book from her elementary school classroom that had contained hidden pictures that popped out of seemingly random collections of dots and colors when she crossed her eyes. So she crossed her eyes. That only created additional beige rectangles.

She still had her eyes crossed when the man standing next to her murmured, "So, what do you think of it?"

She was so surprised that someone else had spoken to her that she nearly stumbled in place. The man who had addressed her was very tall, with short blond hair brushed straight up and an attempt at a goatee. The name tag on his navy half-zip sweater read BRANDON.

"I, um, I'm not sure I get it," Caroline confessed once she had recovered her equilibrium.

Brandon frowned, taking a step closer to her as though to align his sight line with hers. Possibly it didn't look like a beige rectangle from a foot to the right? She hadn't tried that yet.

"What do you mean?"

Caroline made a helpless gesture at the painting. "I mean, I don't know what the artist is trying to say with it."

"Does it really matter what the artist is trying to say?" Brandon asked, eyebrows rising over his narrow features. "What does it evoke in you?"

Caroline squinted at him suspiciously, wondering whether he was just trying to hit on her. Being hit on was not necessarily objectionable, though she wasn't sure she wanted it to happen while she was there with Adrian. But if that was Brandon's goal, he'd do better to just announce it straight off, because subtlety usually went over her head.

Where was Adrian, anyway? Another quarter turn of her head and she located him at the next painting over, a few feet away.

"I don't think I'm feeling very evoked by it," Caroline replied to Brandon. "How does the color beige do anything specific for anyone?"

One corner of his mouth pulled out in negation.

"I suppose nonobjective art does ask more of the viewer," Brandon said. "You have to bring an understanding of the history and purpose of art with you to appreciate it. But it's worth it, if you're willing to put in the effort."

Caroline frowned at the implication that she had either not brought the proper knowledge with her to appreciate the art or had not tried hard enough to like it. She was *trying*.

"So what did you bring to the art?" she asked, mildly challenging him.

Brandon gulped his beer before answering.

"The color and formlessness of the canvases suggest the concrete wasteland of American suburbia. It's a critique of the lack of beauty in the visual landscape of the modern suburbanite. But at the same time, the careful arrangement and installation of the works suggests there *is* a kind of beauty in the blankness and promise of the corporate desert. It's a paradox. It leans into the conflict of the presentation," Brandon answered.

It all sounded very convincing, but Caroline hadn't gotten even a hint of that from looking at the paintings.

"You thought up all of that right now?" Caroline asked.

Brandon nodded that he had indeed.

Caroline gazed at the canvas again. Unlike the void, it did not look back. Maybe it was because of all the beige.

"How did you figure all that out from just the painting?" she pressed. Maybe she'd missed a brochure on the way in.

Brandon sidled another half step closer. "It's more

apparent once you've really absorbed the context that the artist is working in. I help plan the lecture series with the Tufts faculty—you should start attending, if you'd like to better appreciate these works." He began fishing in his trouser pocket for a business card.

Caroline wondered whether she was really deficient for not appreciating the painting. Everyone else in the room seemed to be enjoying the art. She hesitated before taking Brandon's card.

"So, you like this stuff?" she asked, wondering how much it would take her to develop the same appreciation for blank rectangles.

The tall man snorted, not really in a nice way. "It doesn't matter if we *like* it," he said derisively. "It's not here to be *liked*."

Caroline's shoulders tightened, and she began to search for a way of extricating herself from the situation. Then she was startled again, this time by the gentle press of Adrian's fingertips on her lower back as he came to stand next to her.

Brandon's eyes tracked the movement, and his face hardened as he took Adrian in.

Adrian didn't say anything. He didn't introduce himself. Possibly because they were all wearing name tags, but Caroline thought the silence was more hostile than it had been a moment before.

"What do you think?" she asked Adrian. *Sweetie*, she nearly added. *Honey*. Because if she'd shown up not knowing anything about nonobjective art, or whatever this was, at least Brandon might come away thinking that she was there with her boyfriend while he was there alone. She didn't add it, because when she relived this conversation in her head while trying to fall asleep later, she'd remember that she actually was single and alone too, which would make her sad. Also, Adrian would probably have an entire litter of kittens if she called him a pet name.

"I think it's boring," Adrian said curtly. His face was implacable.

Brandon laughed. "Another conscientious objector to nonobjective art?"

"No," Adrian said.

Brandon waited for additional exposition, but Adrian did not seem to feel like explaining his answer further. He sipped his wine instead.

"Are you familiar with Mill's work?" Brandon probed for weakness.

"Yes," Adrian said. "I met him a few years ago at the Biennial of the Americas."

Brandon, scowling, didn't like that, but he also didn't back down.

"So, how can you say this is boring?" Brandon pressed. "This is a revolutionary comment on the forms underlying the American visual field."

Adrian didn't even blink as he formulated his retort.

"Kazimir Malevich exhibited his black square in 1915," he began to lecture, his voice cool and precise. "Over a hundred years ago. *That* was revolutionary. The brutalists were making cities out of simple concrete forms in the fifties. That made a statement about our relationship with the blank form of construction. This? This is so derivative of generations of art that came before it that it degenerates into cliché."

Caroline turned her head to watch him as he spoke, feeling a wash of contentment as he articulated what she'd been unable to express. It really *wasn't* very interesting.

Brandon snorted. "Tell me what you really think about it," he said, trying to sneer.

"I just did," Adrian replied, looking dangerously unamused.

"Possibly you have the minority opinion. Mill's paintings sell for tens of thousands of dollars," Brandon defended the artist. "It's not just me who thinks this series is revolutionary."

"These paintings sell because they can add a little texture to the wall behind a thirty-thousand-dollar couch," Adrian said dismissively. "They sell because they're unobjectionable. Because they're nothing more than a mirror for whatever vapid thoughts you had about art when you walked into the room. So, I think it's boring. It barely makes me think at all."

Brandon's mouth was hanging slightly open.

Adrian's fingertips against Caroline's lower back spread until the palm of his hand pressed against her, turning her toward the exit to the room.

"Would you like to look at the John Singer Sargent watercolors?" he asked courteously.

"Yes," Caroline said, finding that she was able to exit the conversation with great dignity now.

Adrian's expression did not shift as he guided her out of the main hall and toward the special-exhibits wing, but he had a faint pink glow over his cheekbones. Caroline leaned into him, brushing his chest with her shoulder, then shoving him with it when he failed to respond.

"That was pretty sexy of you," she teased him, tugging on his arm in glee. "I don't think Brandon even saw the blow that killed him."

Adrian made an amused noise in the back of his throat.

"He can't play Obnoxious Art Guy with me. I originated the role of Obnoxious Art Guy."

"You're not obnoxious," she protested.

"I promise you I was. Though I spoke in fewer clichés than your new friend Brandon."

"I thought you wanted me to make friends," Caroline said, tossing out his business card as they passed a waste bin. Maybe the next time they came here, she would. Not everyone had to be as unfun as Brandon.

The museum was open late for the event, but almost everyone was remaining close to the drink stations by the main hall. They passed into the special-exhibits wing, alone except for a few roaming security guards.

"I bet poor Jarret Mill's ears are burning though," Caroline said. "Did you two not get along?"

"He can take the heat," Adrian said, directing them into a side gallery, a room full of romantic, colorful portraits. This was the room of watercolors. They were lovely, a little reminiscent of Adrian's earlier paintings. He had a not-so-secret soft spot for pretty things, Caroline decided.

"Is he a nice guy, then?"

"He's just as insecure and unhappy as the rest of us. But at least Jarret has an exhibition at the MFA, and I do not." He drifted away to study the first painting in the series, and Caroline's eyes narrowed as she watched him.

"All right," she said, looking around. The nearest security guard was several rooms away. "Let's fix that." The idea had been percolating in the back of her head since the first time he'd mentioned that his work wasn't on display anywhere. She rummaged in her purse, coming up with a spiral notepad and a pen from the Holiday Inn Express she'd stayed at while moving into her apartment.

She tapped Adrian on the shoulder and passed him the ersatz art supplies.

"What do you mean?" he asked.

"Draw something."

"For what?"

"You're going to be in the MFA," Caroline insisted.

Adrian hesitated, holding the notepad and pen.

"You aren't even supposed to have a pen in here," he protested.

"I already met the art police, and I wasn't impressed," Caroline said, rolling her eyes. "Just draw something. Anything." She looked at him expectantly until he braced the notepad against his palm and made a long, fluid movement with the pen, not lifting it from the paper. Perhaps a minute of looping scribbles.

After regarding his work for a second, he proffered it to her.

"Oh, that's me," Caroline said with pleasure. It was a simple minimalist line drawing but readily recognizable as Caroline in profile, holding her little glass of white wine. She'd expected a flower or an architectural detail. But it was cute. She looked cute. Part of her wanted to keep it and hang it up in her room with his little flower drawings. But, no, she was committed to her plan.

She handed the notepad back to him. "Now sign it," she commanded.

He raised an eyebrow but complied, filling the remaining space with his scrawled signature. She retrieved the notepad and carefully folded the paper near the edge of the spiral. She put the fold in her mouth to wet it, then pulled the square of the drawing free of its bindings. Time to be curator. There was a concrete support pillar in the corner, creating a small gap next to the wall.

Using the corners of her name tag as adhesives, she stuck the little line drawing on the pillar where it was not visible from the door. It might go unnoticed for several days, she thought.

Adrian laughed. "The curator is going to have an aneurysm when she finds that," he said.

"I'm sure this happens all the time," Caroline said, defending it. "It will be a temporary exhibit."

"Very temporary."

"Maybe it's performance art too. What's it called?"

Adrian's dimple popped in the corner of his mouth as he replied, "*Caroline Number Two.*"

Caroline stuck the rest of her name tag below the drawing, filling in the numeral before adding, *Ballpoint pen on scrap paper.* That was very official, wasn't it? There wasn't room for biographical details about the artist, but perhaps the illicit nature of the exhibit made it better that his name wasn't really legible.

She regarded the arrangement with satisfaction.

"There," she said firmly. "Now your first work in a museum is out of the way."

Adrian shifted closer to her to look at it, his shoulder pressed against her own. She suddenly worried that he'd think she was making fun of him. But when she peeked at him out of the corner of her eye, his face was suffused with nothing worse than wry amusement.

"There are great expectations in *first,*" Adrian said, eyes half lidded as he looked at her instead of the drawing.

The expression hit Caroline harder than he'd probably intended, catching her low in her stomach with a sensation of spreading warmth.

"I think you can do it," she said, wishing she didn't sound so breathless. "Did you paint anything this week?"

His lower lip flexed a little. "I finished repairing two more paintings."

"Nothing else?"

Adrian hesitated, then pulled out his phone. She'd seen the charcoal underdrawing of the goldenrod picture before leaving his studio. Now there was a wash of nearly transparent paint over the still visible lines, built up in the creases of her shirt and the angles of her face. The effect was dreamy and unfocused. Romantic, even. She curled her body around the phone, pleased.

She tilted her head at his choice of paint color though. "Purple?"

Adrian smiled, then tucked a strand of her hair back, fingertip barely grazing the shell of her ear. Her skin seemed to tingle at the brief touch.

"Blond hair and yellow flowers need dark shadows to bloom against the background," he explained, gaze moving between her face and hair. "I'll build the layers of color bit by bit until it looks like the brighter tones are shining through. You lay the light on last."

Caroline felt more heat suffuse her cheeks at the way he was studying her face, his eyes dipping down to her mouth as he thought about his painting. When he looked right at her, she knew he was thinking about her, the shape of her, at least, and it made it hard to breathe. She was probably turning red. She hoped he'd blame the wine, held loosely in her hand down by her waist. She wished she'd set it aside somewhere.

Adrian was standing very close, so close she could see the rise and fall of his chest and the dark expanse of his pupils. He inhaled, and Caroline went completely still, overaware of every inch of exposed skin. She wondered if she should close her eyes, or if she should wait to do that until she was absolutely, positively certain he was going to kiss her.

Abruptly, Adrian turned away, his breath making an audible sound. He stuffed his hands into his pockets.

The room felt brighter and colder than it had a moment before, the unrelieved white of the walls too sterile and empty even with the watercolors filling the space.

He stepped back, gesturing to the hall.

"I wouldn't mind looking at Singer Sargent's oil paintings too while we're here. It's usually too crowded to spend much time with them. Would you mind?"

Caroline blinked rapidly, wondering what had just happened. Or whether anything had. She'd probably misinterpreted things again. Her throat was very dry and tight.

"No," she said. "I don't mind. Can I get another glass of wine first though? I'm, um. I'd like another drink."

The corners of his mouth barely twitched in response. "Yes. I'd like one too."

ADRIAN WAITED UNTIL CAROLINE HAD SAFELY MADE HER way into the main gallery before he checked his phone. She seemed unsteady on her feet, but he didn't know if that was due to the shoes or the wine, which she was drinking very quickly.

His last messages were still the ones from Tamsyn, a few hours previous:

Tamsyn: Ran into Mike McMurtry last night
Tamsyn: Told him you're looking for new gallery rep
Tamsyn: He said you're a *rat bastard coward*
Tamsyn: And you should call him
Tamsyn: You owe me
Tamsyn: Bring GOOD wine to my opening

Adrian had not yet replied. His initial reaction had been one of dizzying relief, because that was the first solid lead he'd had in months. Mike's gallery had been the first to show his work out of art school. He'd done very well there. The man was fair and reliable and well-connected. Of course, Adrian had thought the same about Nora when she lured him away with the ultimately slim promise of a higher caliber of co-exhibitor, but Mike had never let him down.

Only as he digested the idea of going back to the gallery he'd left at twenty-six did the larger implications begin to swamp him. Getting kicked out by Nora and then slinking back to his prior space was hardly the narrative he wanted for his career. And there was the guilt too, because leaving Mike's gallery for no better financial terms had not been a brilliant move in the first place, which reflected poorly on Adrian. He'd never apologized. He hadn't actually spoken to the gallery owner in years. If Adrian did call Mike, he'd probably need to start by saying he'd been utterly thoughtless to quit without warning at the end of his contract, leaving Mike in the lurch.

Guilt was a familiar emotion these days. He'd spent the past week dividing his time in a very unproductive way: about one quarter thinking of ways to maneuver Caroline into bed, closer to two-thirds feeling bad about the first quarter, and that left . . . well, Tom was correct that Adrian did not do a lot of higher math these days, but that was not a large proportion left for painting.

He'd thought of asking her for a little more distance in their interactions, but what possible reason could he give? She hadn't done anything inappropriate. The problem was entirely inside his own head. What would he say? *Would you mind standing a few feet away and not looking at me? I'm having intrusive thoughts about your thighs and also being between them*. He had most of his life ahead of him in which he'd have to control himself around beautiful young women who were not interested in having sex with him. There was no time like the present to learn how.

Caroline popped her head back into the hall.

"They have a Monet in here!" she advised him. She checked over her shoulder. "*A whole room* full of Monets!"

He unexpectedly grinned at her enthusiasm as he followed her into the small side gallery.

"Is this your first time seeing one?" he asked, accompanying her to a large painting of summer poppy fields.

"Yeah, the European rooms are always super crowded," she said, beaming at the masterpiece.

Adrian couldn't help but tell her about the piece, even as he feared he was slipping into Obnoxious Art Guy territory.

"It's a scene from his estate in Giverny," he told her. "That's where all the water lilies were painted."

"Where's that?"

"Northwest of Paris."

"You've been there?"

He nodded. "Of course. I made the pilgrimage during the summer I spent in France. After my sophomore year."

Caroline sucked in a deep breath, no doubt taken with the idea.

"Can we go see it? Is it nice in the winter?" she asked, turning her face to him. Her green eyes were wide and tentative. It was the first time she'd brought up the subject of going to Europe that winter since he'd misled her about the setting of December's Art Basel fair, and he'd convinced himself that she'd forgotten about it.

"I don't think Normandy is best appreciated in December, no," he stalled, putting his hands back in his pockets.

Spending that much time with Caroline on planes and trains and, God help him, at hotels, was probably not the best plan.

She licked her lips. "So is Switzerland better in December, then? Is it because of the skiing? Because I don't know how to ski—"

He turned away, hiding his expression in his study of the poppies.

"No, not because of the skiing. But, Caroline, what would your family think of you heading off to Europe with me? You could go on a school program, with people closer to your own age."

Her face darkened. "It doesn't matter what they think. And why wouldn't I be safer with you than with a bunch of strangers?"

He clenched his teeth against telling her that he didn't feel very safe for her either.

"The school programs are run by professors in the art history department," he said. "I went on one to the Netherlands."

Caroline brushed that aside and dug in, unwilling to let it go.

"We should probably get plane tickets soon," she said. "Bern? Geneva?"

Adrian sighed. "No, neither. I was thinking of Art Basel *Miami*, but that's during your finals, as you said."

"Oh," she said, absorbing that. Her clever mind turned it around and examined it, even though her eyes were bright and cheeks pink from the wine. "In Florida?"

"Yes, but—"

"And you wanted to go. For professional reasons?"

Adrian didn't answer, but she was only confirming it.

She hooked a hand around his elbow and pulled him back when he would have turned away.

"Why don't you go? I don't mind if you go without me," she said. "I'll be busy studying anyway."

He gave her a tight expression, because it was fairly obvious why he wouldn't go without her.

Caroline frowned, still working through it. "Of course I'd give you the money to go. Why didn't you just ask?"

The discomfort of her question was choking him. He pulled back against her hand until she released him, but she didn't let him back away.

"Caroline. I can't take your money."

She snorted. "Yes, you can. You do! Every week. Isn't that the entire point of this? I'm supposed to get you the things you want."

He struggled to articulate the distinction between taking money for his time (*and letting her pay for everything, and drive you around, and help you move*, an insistent inner voice pointed out) and openly asking her for things he couldn't afford.

"You've probably guessed I didn't earn this money," she said in a more self-deprecating tone when he didn't respond. "So it's not like it's really mine. And giving you money so you can go to an art show is practically like giving to charity. Like building a museum."

Adrian didn't want to be her charity. He didn't even want to be her . . . employee, or whatever he was. It wasn't any better than the slow humiliation of letting Nora pay all of their bills while he was present in that relationship less and less, because he wanted this one to be real. The things Caroline wanted from him ought to have been free. Ought to have come from someone who wasn't him in the first place but should have been free. As Caroline gave him more and more—more of her time, more of her money, more of her care—he was taking advantage of her every day that he accepted it.

"It would cost almost five thousand dollars to fly down and pack all my paintings for shipment," he objected. That was a low estimate, assuming he stayed in a hostel with the international artists rather than the W South Beach, which Nora had preferred.

"Okay?" Caroline said, still not following him.

He settled his shoulders. "Can you even afford to waste five thousand dollars on something like this?"

"Yes, of course I can. I wouldn't have hired you in the first place if I couldn't. Were you worried about that?" she asked, pointed chin turning to the side in confusion.

He vaguely gestured at her outfit. The same black dress she'd worn out to every evening event since the night they met. "I wasn't sure. You always wear the same dress."

Caroline looked down at her body. "Is there something wrong with wearing this here? I get it dry-cleaned after I wear it."

"No," he said, voice halting, because it did look fantastic on her, every time, and the way it clung to her hips had probably taken years off his life already. "I just wondered if you couldn't afford other ones."

Caroline's eyes widened. "You should have told me if I needed to buy more." She took out her phone and typed something into her calendar, presumably a note to herself to go shopping.

"It's fine," he said quickly. "It doesn't matter to me."

She gazed at him with doubt, as though wondering what else he was holding back. Then she rustled around in her big yellow purse again, coming out with her check-book. She was up to number 1008, all written to him. Over his noise of objection, she wrote out a check for five thousand dollars, then tucked it into his resistant palm.

"I want you to be able to depend on me," she said firmly, curling his fingers around the paper. "I can hold up my end of this. We both get to have the things we want. That's how this works."

He swallowed hard, feeling wretched. He shoved the check into his pocket, telling himself he didn't have to deposit it, he just needed the conversation to be over.

Caroline slowly let go of his hand, face still creased with worry. The tip of her tongue wet her lips again.

"If it's not too much travel though," she added slowly, "can we still go somewhere over Christmas?"

He hesitated to make her any promises, because he didn't want to commit to taking her money and going to Art Basel without her, much less going on a second trip overseas. Traveling to Europe on Caroline's money was going to be difficult to erase from his internal hagiography.

"I don't have any other plans," she said in a softer voice.

Adrian pressed his teeth together as it abruptly occurred to him that she'd never said anything about her family except for her grandmother, and there were a lot of bad reasons why she could have a lot of money and no family to speak of. The uncertainty in her expression jolted him out of his self-absorbed paralysis. He found himself wrapping his arms around her for the second time in a week, nose full of the sweet smell of her hair.

"Of course," he said softly, lips against the side of her head. "Anywhere you want to go."

He heard her swallow.

"Okay." She didn't move for a second, and then she wrapped her arms around his waist hard, just short of a painful squeeze. Her heart beat fast against his chest. She squeezed tighter.

God, he was fucked. He was terrible.

He let her go as soon as he thought it wouldn't make him look insincere. Even if he was insincere, even if he wasn't the upright and diligent artist she believed he was, even if he wasn't a good person due to the thoughts rattling in his head, he could act like one for her sake.

"Should we pick an artist to plan a trip around?" he asked, inclining his head further down the European hall, head buzzing with the wine and her presence. "Italy is nice in the winter. So is Spain," he added, aware he sounded completely inane.

Caroline nodded, brushing her hair back behind her ears with both hands. "That's a good idea," she said. "That's a good plan."

They discussed the relative merits of Velázquez and Botticelli until the security guard came to tell them that the museum was closing. Most of the other young professionals had already trickled out in search of better wine and a more intimate atmosphere. When they emerged into the night air, a few white flakes were drifting down from the low, dark sky. Caroline looked up, face softening into delight as they approached the taxi line.

"It's snowing," she said. "It hardly ever snows back home."

Adrian closed his mouth over the automatic rejoinder of born Northeasterners—that it was only pretty in the sky, not on the ground, and she'd be sick of it by February besides.

"I'll have them drop you off first on my way," Caroline

said confidently, her speech a little slurred from all the wine they'd been drinking. "You can't walk home in this."

Adrian should have pointed out that he was better at walking in the snow than their cabbie probably was at driving in it, but he again hesitated to speak, because Caroline had wrapped both hands around his arm and huddled in against him as they waited in line. It was getting colder, he supposed. He ought to tell her to buy a hat and gloves, if she didn't already have them.

They stood there in the snow, watching the thick, wet flakes melt on the street and on the tips of their shoes. Caroline's hair was quickly soaked with it. She bent her head until it rested on his shoulder, cheek pressed trustingly into the lapel of his coat.

"This was a good birthday," she mumbled into the black wool. "Thank you."

Adrian jolted, only stilling himself for fear of dislodging her.

"It's your birthday today?"

"Uh-huh. I'm twenty-three."

Guilt struck him again that he hadn't known. He'd seen her driver's license, hadn't he? But he hadn't taken note of the date, and she hadn't mentioned it again.

"You should have told me. I could have . . . I don't know. Baked a cake."

"You know how to bake?"

It took him a moment to pull the memory up. Tom had turned twenty-three a week after Rose kicked him out. Adrian had baked him a cake using the oven in his Back Bay apartment for the first time. It had been terrible—Adrian thought he'd forgotten the sugar—but Tom had eaten half of it, cried, and then insisted they go out to get very, very drunk.

He could have been a better friend since then, Adrian thought. He could have been a better person. He could have been good for someone, anyone in his life. When had he stopped being the person people came to with their problems and started being the person who needed so much help?

"For you, I would have *tried*," he said.

Caroline huffed in amusement, not letting go of his arm. "You're sweet," she said. "But this is what I wanted to do tonight."

"Do you want me to call Tom? It's not too late for birthday shots in Kendall Square."

Caroline laughed. "That's a cliché, and I have class tomorrow. No, this was perfect."

If she'd seen and heard some clichés that evening, there was probably none worse than him, because after his long run of shoddy life choices, what was more terribly predictable than falling for the pretty young woman he couldn't help but be bad for? He stood breathing in the scent of her wet hair until their taxi arrived, wondering how long he had until she figured that out.

Chapter Twelve

CAROLINE MANAGED TO BE LATE AND WEAR THE WRONG thing twice in one day, which had to be a record, even for her. The first time was probably not her fault: she happened to check her student email on the way to the gym and saw that Rima had apologetically forwarded an invitation for a tech meeting that started in five minutes. The gym was ten minutes away from the theater, so Caroline had to awkwardly jog across campus, only to arrive after Sophia had already started.

There wasn't any space on the risers, so Caroline climbed up the scaffolding and precariously straddled a crossbeam until the set designer spotted her and waved her to a space he created by sliding up against the follow spot.

"Thanks," Caroline whispered to Nathan.

This drew a dirty glance from Sophia, who muttered "weirdo" under her breath. The lavender-haired woman paused long enough for everyone to turn and look at Caroline before she continued with changes to lighting cues.

Maybe Adrian had been wrong about this, after all.

After the meeting, there was a lot of work going on backstage as the various departments sprang into action to incorporate the stage manager's notes. Caroline found that many things needed to be carried to other places—her theatrical specialty, she thought with a little self-deprecation.

She ended up helping Nathan carry the heavy cardboard boxes containing the printed programs from the department van in the faculty parking lot all the way to the front box office. He pulled a bottle opener key chain from the pocket of his faded black denim trousers and used the sharp edge to slice the boxes open.

Caroline began lifting programs out and setting them beneath the desk, then breaking the boxes down for recycling.

"So, uh," Nathan said after a minute, "you like color, I guess?"

Caroline stopped and stared at him in confusion. It took her a minute to figure out that he was referring to her leggings, which were striped in orange and lime green, matching her sports bra and windbreaker. She really hadn't bought much stuff since she'd moved. But she had bought nice workout clothes, and she'd justified it to herself that they'd last much longer than the cotton-blend gear from Walmart she'd owned before.

He was waiting for her answer, as if he'd thrown out an important scientific hypothesis and she needed to either support or rebut. Liking color wasn't a personality trait, was it? Who would take the opposite position? *No, color's no good, actually.*

"Sure, but why do you ask?" she finally said, finishing with the last box.

"No reason," the burly set designer mumbled. "You just see most people in theater wearing black, I guess."

"Should I be wearing black?" Caroline asked, alarmed. She had never been very good at intuiting the unspoken rules that everyone else seemed to live by. She had no problem with *following* the rules. Most rules. But first, she needed to know what the rules *were*.

"Oh, no, you're fine. You don't have to until tech week. Or even until actual performances, really, since there's no audience to see you until then," he said, stammering.

Caroline watched him to see if he was willing to divulge more systematic truths, but he pressed his lips together and opened one of the programs as though he might find the secret of life written within.

Caroline grabbed one for herself and examined it at arm's length. The cover picture was a painting of a wine bottle. She thought Adrian's work had probably been better even when he was a student. Then she flipped to the back to look at the cast and crew list. She scanned for her name and didn't see it. It went straight from Rima to the run crew members.

"Wait, where are you?" Nathan asked. "Aren't you assistant props?"

"Just informally, I guess," Caroline said, stomach sinking down toward her bladder, regardless, in a familiar picked-last-at-recess sensation.

Nathan frowned. "I'll tell Rima," he offered.

"No, no," Caroline said, straightening up. She'd missed her gym window already. She needed to get to class.

"I'm going to say something," Nathan declared. "You've done a lot of work."

"You really don't have to," Caroline said, ducking out the door. "It's not like I need it for my résumé. I'm just doing this for fun."

The fun had been only intermittent so far.

Before she could hear his reply, she took off back toward the business campus, walking at top speed to put distance between herself and the theater. Normally, she would have put jeans and a sweatshirt on to go to class, but plenty of college students went in pajamas and whatever, so as long as she kept her windbreaker zipped, she imagined that her "colorful" attire wasn't a problem for class.

Her mind was tempted to wander; she'd heard the same lecture about organizational behavior back in undergrad. She'd do better to pay attention though. Nothing about management was intuitive to her, and she appreciated that someone had taken the time to distill it down to plans and principles. If only other areas in her life were as susceptible to organization.

For example, with Adrian: it seemed like it was past time for a performance reevaluation. All the articles she'd read for this class stressed that regular feedback was critical to effective management. So they ought to talk about his continued role in her life. Did he have the resources he needed to be successful? (If he needed money for things like the art show in Miami, Caroline could set up an expense reimbursement process.) Did she have any feedback on his performance? (She thought he could stand to act like her boyfriend a little more consistently.) Was he interested in picking up any additional hours? (It was hard not talking to him from Sunday to Tuesday.)

And there was the very basic issue of employment duties. The original job description had been restrictive. But he'd hinted in his profile that he was highly qualified— no, perhaps even available?—to perform a broader range of responsibilities. Ones involving no fraught decisions on appropriate attire. (She could easily be naked.)

She'd been very clear at their initial interview that hands-on personnel management was not required for his particular role. But maybe she'd been too hasty.

(Maybe she'd given him shit about it on too many occasions.) Maybe she needed to adopt a growth mindset.

What if, with Adrian, it was better? If he'd initially assumed that she'd want to sleep with him, she was inclined to trust his judgment. He was so good at finding things to love in his own life, and he just wanted to show her how to love them too. Maybe there was some higher-quality type of sex known only to connoisseurs and enthusiasts. She could imagine his hands on her body, his smooth voice in her ear, *I think you'll like this—*

She had imagined it. A few times now.

Did she risk making things horribly awkward? He looked disappointed every time she didn't enjoy something he'd planned, even if they were hitting more than missing these days. And though Caroline was beginning to suspect that sex would be more fun with someone who knew what he was doing and cared if she had a good time too, what if she still didn't? Would he take that personally? Would it hurt his feelings?

She put a note in her phone to talk to Adrian about it, even as her stomach spun at the thought.

At the end of the hour, the professor reminded them about the career reception directly after class in the main administrative building. Caroline had dutifully put the event on her calendar at the beginning of the semester without knowing much of what it entailed, and she was surprised none of the other students in her class seemed to have any questions about it.

She turned to the guy next to her to ask if he planned to attend. He was the same one who had invited her to his party almost two months ago. Even if they hadn't really spoken since, maybe he'd be willing to walk over with her and tell her what it had been like the previous year.

"I'm not going," he said, shoving his laptop into his backpack. "I think most people are working wherever they did last summer. It's mostly for undergrads."

"Oh, really?" Caroline said, feeling her stomach contract again.

"Yeah, most of the Street firms and consulting shops want to see you for more than one summer before they extend a final offer, you know?"

Caroline didn't know. She'd spent every summer after her freshman year working at Sonic, and the previous summer she'd been busy dealing with the executor on her grandmother's estate. She had no clue what Wall Street firms or consultants expected in terms of summer employment. She hadn't been in a position to make a reasoned decision on whether that was a thing she wanted to do. Panic rose at the idea that it was already too late to pursue these careers she'd never even known to consider.

Her anxiety must have shown on her face, because her classmate hurried to reassure her that, "Tech, you know, or industry, they usually don't hire until they know they need the head count."

"Okay," Caroline mumbled. "I'll go look into that at the career fair."

He scrunched up his face again, hesitating to go, even though he had his backpack on.

"Uh, are you going to wear that?" he asked.

Caroline looked down again at her leggings. She was still dressed for the gym.

"No, I meant to work out this morning," she said. "I'll just run over to my locker and change."

"Yeah, cool, cool," the guy said with a tight smile. "Good luck."

By the time Caroline had run *back* to the gym, changed

into jeans and a sweatshirt, and found the big event space in the basement of the administrative building, she was a little flushed, as well as late for the dean's speech. The configuration of the room meant she was entering via the corner nearest the dean, within full view of the other students standing to listen to him. She plastered herself to the wall, trying to be unobtrusive, but she couldn't help but feel on display as she walked past the other students.

And then she also noticed that everyone else was wearing button-down shirts and black wool trousers, or even sports jackets and pencil skirts. It was immediately obvious, even to her, that there was a dress code for career fairs here. She felt the beginning of a headache to cap off the gut-twisting feeling of being just a little bit off, again, from what everyone else was doing. If there had been a dress code in the event description, she would have added it to her calendar entry. She would have bought the ugly pants and had the hem let out. She would have been ready. She wouldn't have been the only one in jeans and sneakers.

She'd already missed the announcement of half the potential employers present, but she took her phone out and tried to jot down notes on who all was there. A couple of big companies whose names she recognized. She took a deep breath and told herself to get her shit together, because she was only one set down; she could still win the match.

After some polite applause, the dean released the students, and everyone dispersed to mill around the room and collect cups of coffee or diluted iced tea from the drinks station. Some of the adults in the room were professors, and some were employer representatives; Caroline didn't know who she was supposed to approach first.

There were a few booths around the edge of the room where people had set out brochures and business cards—those were probably easier to start with. So she sidled over to the first one she saw, only to attract the dean's attention as she moved.

"Oh, Ms. Sedlacek," the dean said. "Glad you could make it. Are you settling in all right?"

"Yes, thank you," she said automatically, trying to edge by him.

He'd been speaking to a middle-aged man in an expensive-looking suit whose name tag read EDWARD CONWAY, ARCTREE MASTER FUND ADVISERS. He also turned to regard Caroline and took a sip of his ditchwater-colored iced tea as he sized her up, gaze lingering on her sneakers.

"Caroline is the first student we admitted from her undergrad," the dean reported.

"Where from?" Conway asked without much interest.

"Central Texas Baptist. In Texas."

"Hmm. Good move," he said. "Much better opportunities up here, I'm sure."

"Yes," Caroline said, back stiffening, even if that was true.

"What was your major?"

"General management."

"That's what I did," the fund manager replied, meeting her eyes for the first time. "Not as much emphasis on the analytics, but you can pick up the numbers if you're bright. Do you know what you're doing yet for this summer?"

Was she supposed to know? Did everyone else already know? What was the point of this event, if not to find out? Was this her last chance to figure it out? Her head spun.

"No, I . . . thought I'd like to work for a company that makes something though," she said stiffly.

Conway smiled like she'd made a joke.

"We have an internship program during the school year," he said. "You should send me your résumé."

The dean had been standing there listening to the conversation, and he leaned in, hand lightly resting on Caroline's shoulder.

"If she has time," he said. "I'm sure Caroline's still got an extensive tennis schedule. Her team won Division Two her junior year."

"Oh, you were a student athlete?" Conway asked, and it was as though Caroline could observe his attention shift away as he assigned her to a new category of athletic meatheads. His eyes dipped again to her oversize sweatshirt, and he smirked as he mentally connected dots that weren't supposed to go together at Boston College.

"I mean, I'm not anymore," Caroline said, jaw clenching. She shot a dirty look at the dean, who failed to notice.

Pretty good tennis player could have been her career. She hadn't been quite good (or rich) enough to go pro instead of going to college, but she'd been pretty good. Now that she had the money, she could have hired the best coaches in the world and hit the vanity tournaments to build up her ranking. Nobody would have been angry or disappointed with her if she'd done that, not even her dad, probably.

Would that have been a better choice than this? She felt like she'd been training for weeks, and she was still sucking wind.

"Excuse me," she said, because Conway was already trying to make eye contact with one of the guys in sports jackets. She swiped a few brochures and business cards at random from a nearby table and left. She wasn't going to make any headway dressed like she was still trying to win an NCAA tournament, not get a real job.

She stalked out into the quad, slumping on an empty park bench despite the chill of the day. Everything was glazed in a half-frozen slick of precipitation. Her heart was hammering.

She instinctively pulled her phone out and looked at it, wishing it was a day she could call Adrian. Any of her family members would seize the opportunity to tell her they'd told her so and she ought to come running back home to Templeton.

Her mind looped on the awfulness of being unprepared and outplayed. She was tempted to go have a little bit of a cry about it in the gym bathroom, which was never occupied in the middle of the day, but lifelong coping systems immediately rejected that plan. If she wasn't moving, she was losing. She tilted her head and blinked rapidly, sniffling back the gunk in her nose. She had to do something. She wasn't allowed to just sit and feel sorry for herself.

Well, she'd solve some small problems first. *Dress pants* was small enough to fix that day. She could at least buy a lot more black clothes for various occasions while she figured everything else out.

She called Tom—she had his number from the night she joined the tech crew. Theoretically joined the tech crew, anyway. He answered immediately.

"Caroline! To what do I owe the pleasure?" he warbled at her. She had to clench her hands at the thought that he was the first person who'd seemed happy to hear from her in ages.

"Hey, do you want to go shopping? For clothes?" Caroline asked, swallowing past the lump in her throat. *Get it together, Caroline. Wrap it up and get back on the court.*

"Mmm, love to go shopping," Tom said thoughtfully.

There was activity in the background of the call, but she couldn't tell where he was. "When do you want to go?"

"Right now?" she asked.

Tom laughed. "I can't. I'm working today. Why don't you ask Adrian?"

"Oh, he's busy today," she said, trying to sound unbothered about it. She already knew they were going back to the movies the next night to see some documentary about a dead poet, so she couldn't call him about making plans. And he'd been pretty quiet and uncommunicative with her that week. All points to raise on the quarterly review.

"Is he?" Tom said skeptically. "Is he really? Is he *ever*?"

"Yeah, he's getting all his gallery applications in and finishing that battle painting," Caroline said defensively.

Tom's palm covered and uncovered the speaker on his phone as he spoke to someone else.

"Okay, you know what," he said when he returned, "the restaurant's just hosting a rehearsal dinner tonight. If you want to come on over here, we'll do some e-commerce damage while I'm not carrying plates of quail kebabs, all right?"

Caroline agreed and hung up the phone. There, that was minor progress. She'd get new pants. Now all she needed was a real boyfriend, a career, hobbies, and a social life.

ADRIAN GRUNTED AS HE LUGGED HIS HEAVY DUFFEL BAG down the block to Tom's restaurant. His roommate had called to offer him a hundred bucks to touch up the mural in the banquet room, but he'd been vague on what kind of damage and what kind of paint was even involved. Adrian had nearly told him that he wasn't an art restorer, but as the only artistic endeavor he'd completed in the past two months was fixing his own art, he'd agreed. Also, it would be a good thing to earn even a little money he didn't take from Caroline. So he was lugging both acrylics and oil paint with him to the Greek restaurant, even though he hadn't painted with acrylics in years, and his paints were all dried out—

There was a handwritten sign taped to the front door declaring the restaurant closed for a special event. Adrian thought closing on a Thursday night was probably a bigger problem for the restaurant than having a flaking mural of the Temple of Athena Nike in the banquet room, but he was no businessman, no matter what Caroline thought.

He'd spent the day stalking the website for Mike's gallery, trying to decide whether his work still compared favorably with the other artists listed. Not actually calling him, no, because that would be too productive. He still couldn't admit he had no other options besides taking Caroline's money and going to Art Basel. He'd heard exactly nothing from any other gallery he'd contacted.

He pushed past the door and stomped sleet off his boots in the vacant entryway. Directly past the host's stand was the bar, where Tom was mixing drinks. When his roommate spotted him, Tom waved but hastily turned and headed through the back door to the kitchen, where Adrian couldn't follow him. Adrian was confused until he entered the main dining room and spotted Caroline in the back corner. He assumed that was why Tom had run off.

The dining room was freezing; the restaurant saved on the heating bill by relying on ambient heat from patrons and the kitchen to warm the place, even in winter. Caroline was the only person in the room. She was seated with her back to the door, and the contents of her purse were strewn across the table along with some dirty plates and empty glasses. Her hair was piled in a messy half bun on top of her head, barely visible over the back of her down coat. She had one of her spreadsheets up on her laptop, and she didn't notice Adrian until he was standing next to her, looking down over her shoulder.

"Oh, hey," she said, twisting in her chair to peer up at him. "I didn't know you were coming." Her smile was tentative but genuine. The rush of warmth it sent through him was undercut only by his observation that her eyes were puffy. She gestured at the seat next to her, and he dropped his bag and slid into it. He would have taken her hand, but he'd spent the entire week stewing on how he needed to keep his distance if he couldn't keep himself—his head, his heart, any other unruly body parts—under control. He compromised by pressing his knee against hers under the table, as though some observer might assign him points for restraint.

"How was your day?" he asked, hoping that was not too pointed a commentary on how she looked.

"It was fine," she lied.

He gave her a hard look, which she deflected as easily as one of his volleys. She waved it away with a small gesture before pushing her laptop to the side. "Have you had dinner? The kitchen's closed, but Tom's been bringing stuff out from the party in the other room."

"I brought leftovers to the studio," Adrian said, rejecting the implied offer. He spotted a couple of plates of dessert at the far edge of the table and quickly changed his mind. "Are those honey doughnuts?"

"Yes, but those are mine, actually," Caroline said. Her chin was thrust out at him in mock aggression.

Adrian lifted his palms in surrender. He knew all about pretending things were fine. Caroline waited a second to let the taunt land, then rearranged the plates until the desserts were at his seat. When he didn't make a move to take a pastry, she picked one up and held it out in front of his face like she expected him to eat it from her hand.

He gently took it from her fingers and ignored the way she wrinkled her nose in disappointment. He ignored her sucking the honey off her fingers and the implication that he could have done that for her. He caught an explicit image before it could solidify in his mind and resolutely scrubbed it blank. He told himself it was respect and not cowardice dictating his actions, even if that line was blurring further than he could follow.

"Are you doing homework?" Adrian asked once he'd eaten a few bites of pastry. He also wanted to ask what she was doing at Tom's place of employment, but he didn't know how to phrase *Are you just here for dinner, or do I need to have another stern talk with my roommate?*

"No, job applications," Caroline said. "Or, well, making a spreadsheet of job applications, deadlines, materials."

"Oh," he said, unable to keep the surprise out of his voice.

"What?" she asked. She stuck her finger back into the honey on his plate and licked it clean again. He shifted uncomfortably in his seat, thinking about her fingers in her mouth.

"I didn't realize you were going to work after you graduated."

"Why wouldn't I?"

"Some people don't," he said awkwardly. There had been several trust fund babies in his MFA class, because painting was an excellent career for people who didn't need to earn an income. "Especially if they don't need to."

Caroline looked off into the distance, transparently calculating numbers in her head.

"I guess I technically don't need to," she said as she thought through it, apparently for the first time. "But I always thought I would."

Adrian leaned in to read over her shoulder. "You're applying to work at an i-bank?" he asked, barely keeping the horror out of his voice.

She shot him a wounded glance. "Well, I don't know. They were in the employers' list."

Adrian snorted. "I don't think anyone goes to work for an investment bank unless they need the money. Ask Tom. His ex worked at one, and she hated it."

"Is that why they got divorced?" Caroline asked, seeming more interested. "Money issues?"

"No, they got divorced because Tom was a dickhead," Adrian muttered.

Caroline drew back at this slander on someone who now seemed to be their mutual friend, but as Adrian had been the one left to deal with the aftermath, he felt entitled to say it.

Caroline tightened the corner of her mouth and highlighted the name of the firm in red. She propped her chin in her hand and stared disconsolately at the screen.

"I don't know which of these is any better," she mumbled. "Nobody in my family's ever worked outside of Templeton. Maybe these jobs *all* suck."

Scanning the list of names, Adrian thought that was a strong possibility.

"What do you actually *want* to do?"

"I—I wish I had a better idea. I applied to the schools that recruited me for tennis, but I only got a full scholarship at Central Texas Baptist, so I had to go there. And now I'm here, but maybe it's already too late to do the things the other students here are doing? I thought I'd get here and the world would open up for me." She blew a stray lock of hair off her face in a long hiss of annoyance. "Maybe I should just become a pastry chef. I can't get my choux to puff yet, but I'm trying éclairs tomorrow."

"All right . . . ?" Adrian didn't see how a career in French pastry was any less of an option for her than investing other people's money.

"I was joking," Caroline said quickly, but the way she looked at him out of the corner of her eye made him think she'd been waiting for his reaction but didn't know how to process the one he'd given her.

Adrian did his best to keep his tone sympathetic to how stressed she looked.

"Caroline, you're twenty-two—"

"Twenty-three."

"And in your first semester of business school. You don't have to figure it out now. You don't have to figure it out *ever*."

She sighed. "Just because I've got this money, right?"

Yes was not the answer she was looking for, but he didn't want to lie to her. He didn't know anything about career options for business school students beyond what he'd observed during the dissolution of Rose and Tom's marriage. And God only knew he was the last person to offer gauzy reassurances on figuring out her life as she went. But Caroline was always going to have more choices if she didn't have to worry about funding them.

"It can't hurt."

Her chest moved mirthlessly, then she wiped her fingers across her eyelids to rub away the fatigue there.

"This probably sounds obnoxious to you. I mean, poor me."

"You don't need to apologize," Adrian said. "It's your life."

Her lips were still pressed together, like she didn't believe him.

"So, what did you come over here for?" she asked, changing the subject, even though she was the one who wouldn't be expected at his roommate's restaurant.

"I told Tom I'd touch up the mural in the banquet room," he said. He was now very suspicious for having still not seen the man for more than a moment.

"Oh, the party's in there," Caroline said, glancing at the shut door. "I think it was supposed to be over by now, but they're still ordering drinks."

"I suppose they're having a good time."

"I wouldn't really know," Caroline said in a morose tone of voice, wincing at her own words. "Should we wait it out?"

"I'll go check with Tom," Adrian promised. He tapped the top of Caroline's laptop screen. "Maybe work on something else tonight?"

She nodded slowly. "I found a list of Botticellis yesterday," she said, looking up through blond eyelashes, expression still uncertain. "I'll start cross-referencing them with major cities so that we can get tickets soon."

Adrian had still not completely accepted the trip to Europe as a thing that would actually occur in his life, but he patted her shoulder and went off to find his roommate, not caring if he was still skulking in the kitchen. He eventually discovered Tom smoking in the alley out back with a couple of the dishwashers.

Tom braced like he expected Adrian to chew him out

for meeting up with Caroline again, but Adrian did nothing more than lift his hands in mute question.

"She called me," Tom said defensively. "It sounded like she'd had a rough day, so I told her to come over here. I thought we could run lines before auditions this weekend, but those assholes in the banquet room are still ordering drinks every fifteen minutes even though they were supposed to be out by eight."

"Isn't ordering drinks a good thing?" Adrian asked.

"No. They're not tipping."

It was Adrian's turn to shrug. "Sorry," he said, trying to perform grace despite his annoyance. "Does the owner actually want to pay me to restore the mural, or was this some elaborate excuse to get me over here?"

The restaurant owner's most redeeming quality was that she'd kept Tom employed for the past two years despite his lackluster work attendance; she wasn't good at management.

"She does want the mural restored. She *probably* will pay you, except, you know, you could also do it for free because of all the free food you've been eating for the past two months?" Tom said with narrowed eyes. "You can come back on Monday and do it."

"So, you called me tonight . . . why?" Adrian asked, exasperated.

"I called you to come get your jailbait girlfriend and take her home, because it looks like she's had a shitty day, and I'm going to be mixing kamikaze shots until after midnight," Tom snapped.

"You could have just told me that," Adrian insisted.

The two dishwashers stubbed out their cigarettes and headed back to the kitchen, alarmed by their loud voices.

"Yeah, I wasn't sure you'd come," Tom sniffed.

"Of course I'd come."

"Caroline said you've been *busy*," he told Adrian, using air quotes. "That's why she called me."

Inappropriate jealousy squirmed through Adrian's chest. He was relatively certain at this point that Tom had no untoward designs on Caroline, but that didn't make him entirely comfortable with the situation. And he hadn't been busy doing anything important—just putting off the call to Mike and trying not to think about Caroline.

"Why *you* though?" Adrian demanded.

"Because she knows I'm her friend for free, maybe?" Tom said.

Tom wasn't trying to be snotty, but the idea made Adrian's gut lurch like a missed stair.

"She could have called me if something was wrong. I'm not charging her to hear about her day," Adrian insisted.

"You can see how she would think that though. Seeing as she is, in fact, paying you to spend time with her," Tom said without looking at him, finally dropping his own cigarette butt on the ground. Adrian trailed him back into the kitchen.

Adrian clenched his jaw so hard his teeth ached. "Do you think I should quit?"

He thought about it every time he saw Caroline. Or thought about her. So multiple times an hour, he thought, *I should quit.* Of course, he'd wanted to quit before he had even started, but accepting that she'd be a long-term feature in his life regardless of whether she was paying him made the thought even more appealing. Much easier than just walking away and knowing she'd find someone else, probably someone without his scruples. Even Tom thought

Adrian should have had Caroline's ankles around his ears weeks ago, and he was a person of reasonable moral fiber.

"Quit and do what?" Tom asked, looking back over his shoulder as he washed his hands.

Adrian sighed. "I'd still have to do the same thing. It costs money to be an artist. Even if I can't make it to Art Basel this year, I need to start showing again somewhere before I can sell anything, and I can't even afford shipping and application fees right now. And you were right, this is the fastest way for someone with my credentials to make money."

Tom dramatically squished up his face in distaste.

"Do you think Caroline's going to be happy if you can't take her out to the opera on Friday nights because you have to go stick your hand up Melinda Gates's blouse?"

Adrian was vaguely nauseous at the thought. No, he didn't think Caroline would be happy about it, and he wouldn't be either. He covered his face with his hands.

"No," he groaned. He'd always thought that moral choices were obvious, but that didn't mean they were cheap. "I just need to save a few thousand dollars. It'll take me a couple more months. I can quit then." Then he'd be working as an artist again, and if Caroline still wanted his company, he wouldn't have to hang a price tag on it. She'd just be his friend Caroline who he knew from very vague circumstances, and maybe when she was older, someday—

"*Tell* her that. Tell her you like her for free. I wouldn't assume she knows. You know, I think she's neurodivergent?"

"What, did she say something to you?" Adrian asked, wheeling on his roommate, once again stung that Tom seemed to know something about Caroline that he didn't.

"No, she didn't, but she reminds me of one of my cousins, and you know she's from a small town in the South, so—"

"So you don't actually know," Adrian snapped. "I can't treat her differently because of your armchair diagnosis."

"You'd rather just fuck things up by accident?"

"No! I mean, Caroline tells me how she wants me to treat her."

That was one of his favorite things about her, in fact. When he screwed up, she told him about it.

"And this is what she wants," Adrian added.

Tom lifted his eyebrows, unimpressed with that response, and clapped Adrian soundly on the shoulder.

"I'm sure you'll eventually manage to solve the issue of the pretty girl who hangs on your every word and also pays you a lot of money. Which you somehow see as a big problem in your life."

"Thanks for your support," Adrian said dourly.

"Since I'm about to lose my job, I can't help wishing God would send some of these battles *my* way, not just to his handsomest soldier," his roommate said with an exaggerated roll of his eyes.

"Is the restaurant really going to close?"

"Yeah, you see this place?" Tom gestured at the empty kitchen. "It's just a matter of time."

"Ah, shit," Adrian said. He was worried about not only his roommate's financial situation if he lost his job but also his own: that removed any safety net if he did stop taking Caroline's money. He gritted his teeth. It shouldn't be up to Caroline and Tom to salvage his life. This was all on him.

"I'll call my old gallery," he promised. He'd go crawling back. Make whatever apologies were necessary. A wash of relief swept over him as he voiced the decision. Better to make a choice that hurt his pride than one that would slowly erode his claim to integrity. "That's the fastest way out of this. Just do what I was doing at twenty-six. I'll try to get in a position to cover the rent as soon as I can."

Tom let out a deep breath, looking reassured. "Thanks. I mean it, actually."

Adrian grabbed the evening's leftover hors d'oeuvres out of the fridge and went back into the main room. Caroline's head was pillowed on her forearm, and the screen on her laptop had gone black. As Adrian approached, he saw she'd fallen asleep.

As quietly as he could, he cleared the dishes from the table and returned them to the kitchen. He closed her laptop and placed it in her backpack, then slid everything else into her purse. He put a hand between her shoulder blades, barely able to feel her back through the layers of coat and sweatshirt.

"Caroline," he called softly. She didn't stir. "Sweetheart, the restaurant's closing."

She woke up with a sharp intake of breath, blinking at him groggily until she recognized him.

"Did you drive?" he prodded her.

She nodded, yawning and rubbing her face. "Just give me a minute," she slurred. "It was a long day."

"I'll drive you home," he offered. He could walk back.

"D'you know how to drive my car?" she asked with sleepy suspicion.

"I grew up in the suburbs. My mom had a Honda Odyssey."

She gave him a small smile, as though picturing it. "Okay."

Caroline had managed to find a spot on the street outside the restaurant, so she passed him the keys at the door and climbed into the passenger side. She immediately slumped in her seat, mumbling her address for him to put into his phone. He knew the area, but it was farther from the university than he would have thought. He had to clear half an inch of sleet off the windshield, and he was glad Caroline wouldn't have to drive in it. When she'd zipped up her coat to her chin and settled in against the window, he cranked the heater and pulled into the street.

Her radio was off, so there was only the hiss of the sleet and the percussive sounds of the windshield wipers to fill the silence as he drove her home. Caroline didn't speak, but her light breathing suggested she was still awake. He didn't speak either, enjoying the quiet ordinariness of the evening. As he turned through the empty streets, everything else felt very far away. The years and experiences that stood between them seemed like very flimsy barriers.

Adrian stopped at a red light for the trolley to cross. Caroline rolled over in her seat so her knees pointed his direction. Her hands were wrapped around the seat belt as she considered him. He kept his eyes on the stoplight, because he felt her gaze on his profile like a physical touch.

"Adrian, this is okay, isn't it?" she asked unexpectedly.

"What do you mean?"

"This. Tonight. I mean, it's not the opera, or . . . any of the other stuff you like."

"I thought the point was that you thought *you* might like the opera," he pointed out.

"The opera's okay. It's not as good as other kinds of musicals."

Adrian easily dodged that hook and waited.

Caroline took a deep breath before she spoke. "What I

meant to ask is, would it be okay if we do other things, sometimes? Other than we originally talked about."

"Of course," Adrian said. The light changed, and he waited for the customary five seconds to allow the cross traffic to finish running the reds before putting his foot on the accelerator. "Whatever *you* want to do. I meant it when I said we could do anything you want."

That seemed to satisfy her. She reached across the center console to put her hand on his arm, and her eyes closed again for the rest of the drive. Adrian felt the tight painful knot of uselessness that had taken residence in his chest unwind by fractions as he managed to perform the small and necessary service of taking her home.

Caroline's building was a modern high-rise, which he might have expected. At her gesture, he entered the underground parking garage and navigated to her assigned spot. The artificial lights overhead were harsh and glaring as he put the Tahoe in park and unclipped his seat belt. He hesitated to open the door and end the evening.

"Thanks for driving me home on your day off," Caroline said, hand not yet on the door handle.

"Caroline. It's no problem."

"No, really. I know you have your own life. I want to respect that. It's Thursday."

"Caroline," he protested again. He wrapped a hand around her wrist, fingers pressing in despite the layers of down and polyester. "You can always call me. It's not imposing."

"Okay," she said, a little unconvinced.

"There isn't any part of my life you're not welcome to," he insisted. She was the only part of it he liked right now. The only part that worked. "It's just not very exciting."

She swallowed and gave a small nod.

He curled his fingers into hers, interlacing them until she looked happier.

"Do you want to go to an art show next Thursday?" he asked impulsively. "My friend's gallery opening?"

"Your friend?" she asked, perking up a little.

"Yes, from art school. Art openings aren't very good parties, but I said I'd go, and—"

"Yes," Caroline cut him off. "Yes, I want to."

He probably shouldn't have asked her. He would know most of the people there, and half of them hated him now on account of Nora. And it committed him to calling Mike in the next week, before he had a chance to see Tamsyn in person. But then Caroline leaned in and quickly brushed her lips across his cheek, just a quick impression of warm breath and soft skin before it was over. She'd darted out the door before he had a chance to react, not looking back until she was at the elevator.

He found he wasn't able to regret it.

Chapter Thirteen

RIMA HAD BEEN RIGHT TO MAKE CAROLINE READ THE PLAY.
The only other plays she had ever read were Shake-
speare's, which were more of a foreign language project.
The experience of reading the O'Neill play and then watching it gave her a new appreciation for everything that
went into a performance.

She'd caught bits and pieces of scenes over the course of
the week, but when she watched the entire thing from start
to finish at the dress rehearsal, she finally recognized the
art that had emerged from all the different departments.
The costumes, the lights, the set changes—and her own
tiny part in it. It was gratifying to watch the actors drink
apple juice and club soda out of the old bottles she'd tracked
down, even if a couple of the actors were still flubbing their
lines and someone had tripped over the edge of the bar and
chipped the paint where it was visible from the audience.

It was nice to feel part of something again. Most of the
actors knew her name now. The rest of them called her
"Props," which she didn't object to, because it gave her a
reason to be there. The dress rehearsal's energy felt familiar to Caroline, like the night before a big tournament.

Caroline had to rush over to Adrian and Tom's apartment as soon as she and Rima finished prying the props
out of the actors' hands. That was good too, because hav-

ing plans was a good feeling, and "I'm going to a gallery opening" was an excellent thing to be able to say when Nathan asked what she was up to for the rest of the evening.

Adrian opened the door when she knocked. He looked ready to leave right then, even though the opening would go on for hours, but Caroline slipped past him to say hello to Tom, who was crashed on the couch and watching original *Star Trek* reruns on Caroline's Netflix account. He popped his head over the back of the couch like a prairie dog and made a moue of distaste.

"Are you going to wear that?" Tom inquired, slightly scandalized.

"Adrian said I could wear whatever I wanted?" she said, phrasing it as a question and looking more closely at the man himself, who was avoiding eye contact.

He was wearing a nice canvas jacket and the fitted jeans she'd met him in. Caroline frowned at him. She'd asked him for a reason!

"And you wanted to look like a cat burglar?" Tom pressed her.

Caroline had come straight from dress rehearsal, so she was still wearing black leggings, black boots, and a black long-sleeved shirt. She'd bought the shirt and boots just for performances, but she'd figured the art crowd wouldn't mind black. Tom's expression said she'd figured wrong.

"I think I have a dress in my car," Caroline said, turning around over Adrian's mild protest and jogging back down to where she'd parked. The dress she'd worn to the spring athletics banquet was still stuffed in a pocket in her gym bag, she was pretty sure. She'd worn it for only an hour or so, because the banquet had been a week after her grandmother's death, and she'd decided in the middle of the banquet that she was quitting the tennis team.

The dress didn't smell, so she supposed it would pass Tom's judgment. Heels were retrieved from the passenger seat. She returned to the apartment and changed in the bathroom, leaving her old clothes folded on top of the towel rack.

It was a good dress, a yellow-and-white ribbed knit with ruffles where it hit her mid-thigh. She couldn't wear the black bra she'd come in because the top had spaghetti straps, but the fabric was thick enough that she didn't think anyone would notice.

Caroline came out of the bathroom and nearly ran into Adrian, who had that now familiar *We are late, but I'm not going to say anything even if it kills me* expression on his face. His gaze dipped down to her chest, hanging long enough for her to decide that her braless state might be a little more evident than she'd assumed. His eyes bounced back up, met her own, and then moved to focus very intently on a featureless spot ninety degrees to her left. Caroline suppressed a smirk. It *was* a good dress.

"Are you going to be cold? Do you want to borrow a sweater?" Adrian asked with studied casualness.

Caroline looked down at her cleavage. "Do you want me to cover up?" Maybe it was *too* much boob for the art scene.

"I don't think there's a good way I can answer that question," Adrian said, shifting uncomfortably. Caroline tipped her head back to laugh at him, and he stalked off to his room.

"Well, I think you look perfect," said Tom from the couch. "Are you going to wear makeup?"

Crap, she'd forgotten. She'd meant to put some on after rehearsal. She opened her purse and peered within.

"I think I have some lip gloss in here," Caroline muttered, bringing it up to her face.

Tom clicked off the TV and got to his feet.

"I can do it," he said confidently. "Come on." He headed to his room, which Caroline had never been in.

Adrian peered out of his own room long enough to frown at them.

"You don't have to change anything," Adrian told Caroline. "We could go now and be on time."

"I went to every single one of your openings, remember? You can be late," Tom retorted. "At least let the girl get some war paint on before you subject her to all your ex's friends."

Caroline shot Adrian a look of alarm, because that prospect had not occurred to her. His guilty expression confirmed Tom's statement.

"Yeah, let's put on some eyeliner, if you have it," Caroline said to Tom. She tried to think of what she'd say if she did run into Adrian's ex, the flower bush murderer and fine art defacer. She wasn't sure makeup was going to be enough armor for that situation, but it couldn't hurt.

Tom turned on the overhead lights in his bedroom and closed the door behind her. His room was messy and redolent of wet towels and unwashed clothes, in contrast to the rest of the apartment, which was cleaner than her own. Caroline squinted suspiciously at the unmade bed before unearthing a chair beneath a pile of clean laundry and claiming it as her seat. Tom rooted under his bed until he found a large plastic makeup caddy and plopped it on the duvet.

"I haven't noticed you wearing any makeup," Caroline noted as he rummaged in the messy, foundation-splattered interior of the case.

"You should have seen my emo phase. But no, most of this stuff is for the stage. The theaters in Boston generally can't afford a makeup artist, so I do my own these days."

He held up a few different eyeshadow palettes and pencils next to her wrist and set them aside. Then he began hunting for a blush.

"Why do you live in Boston? Is your family here?" she asked curiously.

"No, I came up for school," Tom replied. He sharpened a black pencil and tugged her closer to the bed so that he could begin outlining her upper eyelid. "I worked in New York for a little while after graduation, but then I moved back here."

"Isn't New York a better city for theater than Boston though?" Caroline asked before realizing it might be a sensitive question.

Tom snorted. "It is. But my ex got all our money and most of our friends in the divorce, so I had to live on Adrian's couch for a year while I dug my way out of debt. And then it seemed too hard to just start over, so I stayed."

"I'm sorry," Caroline said automatically.

"Don't be. I made some bad choices."

"I'm sure you didn't deserve to get chased out of an entire city."

"I sort of did. Rosie was working twelve-hour days crunching numbers, and when she got home, I was never there because I would be off watching experimental burlesque in Queens or something."

"That sounds fun though."

"It was. It's much more fun to do Molly at a warehouse performance of *A Midsummer Night's Dream* than to eat microwave dinners on the couch with your exhausted wife, but if you pick one over the other too many times, it turns out that it's impossible to stay married to that wife, so . . ."

Caroline squirmed, because it sounded like Adrian had been correct in his assessment of the reasons for Tom's divorce: he'd been a dickhead. "Maybe you just weren't right for each other."

Tom finished lining her eyes and turned away to grab the eyeshadow.

"I don't know about that," he said. "We met at freshman orientation. Before I even met Adrian—he was across the hall that year—I was crazy about her. Our families were pretty unhappy that we got married right after graduation, but Adrian was thrilled. He thinks I just fucked things up. And maybe he's right. Rosie only worked at that place for a couple of years, and now she's got this nice life in New York. Adrian is still friends with her. Pretty sure she would have gotten him in the divorce too if I hadn't been sleeping on his couch and looking pitiful."

"You didn't try to work things out?" Caroline asked, chin forced to her chest so that Tom could apply eyeshadow.

He gave a small laugh. "I didn't see how things could work out. That's where being so young came in. It was really embarrassing that my friends knew my wife had kicked me out. It seemed like a big deal that she worked in the qualified dividend mines, and I was trying to break into musical theater. I lost sight of me and her in all that other junk that didn't ultimately matter."

Caroline wasn't one for platitudes, so she just drew out the corner of her mouth and gave him a sympathetic grimace.

"Do you think you'll ever go back? Or does she have, like, dibs on the whole city?"

"Her lawyer was good, but not *that* good. Maybe. I don't know. If the restaurant closes, I might start thinking about it."

Tom finished his work, bopped her on the end of the nose with a fluffy brush, and told her to put on some lip gloss.

"Take care of yourself tonight, okay?" he said. "You look great. Text me if you want me to not be here when you guys get home."

Caroline snorted. She wasn't planning on sleeping with Adrian that night. It seemed like the kind of thing she'd want to read the libretto for first. Also, excellent capitalist education aside, she had a few lingering doubts about the morality of sleeping with someone who would be doing it for money. But Tom did not seem to expect such hesitation, even though he knew the score between her and Adrian.

"Oh good, because I'm really loud," she said, rolling her eyes and pretending to knock the back of her fist against the wall.

Tom's grin was openly delighted. "God, he's such a stupid, lucky bastard," he said.

AFTER A WEEK TO THINK ON IT, ADRIAN WAS EVEN LESS CON-vinced that bringing Caroline to the art opening had been a good idea. Tamsyn and her girlfriend were good people, but the art scene could be cutthroat and insular at the best of times. The same people who'd resented him for his early success might be looking to get a little of their own back now that his circumstances had changed. Not that he was primarily worried about his own reception. He'd earned whatever potshots he drew. It was Caroline who was not prepared to navigate the petty rivalries of the small world of Boston gallery artists or even the occasional sleaze of the art collectors and journalists who would also be in attendance.

"Are there any rules for this?" Caroline asked him as their Uber driver wound his way east to the gallery in SoWa.

"Rules?"

"You know. Stuff I wouldn't know to do. Or not do. Instructions for Martians at a gallery opening."

Adrian felt another knot of anxiety form. Her tone was light, but he knew she worried too much about breaking the bullshit unwritten laws of these unfamiliar tribes. He thought hard about it.

"I don't know anything about Tamsyn's new series, but only say positive things if anyone else is around."

"Of course. The artist's your friend," Caroline said, nose pressed to the window to take in the unfamiliar neighborhoods.

"Tamsyn will spend the first part of the event talking to potential customers and any journalists who show up. We're there mostly to help her sell her work."

"Okay," Caroline said seriously. "I'll act very impressed."

"She'll come talk to us later in the evening. If you have questions about the art, you can ask then."

"Okay."

"You don't have to talk to anyone else though. Or stay very long, if you get bored."

Caroline turned and blinked big green eyes at him. "I won't do anything to ruin your friend's opening," she promised.

"I know, I know, it's not that. I just—"

I am just terrified that now you are going to meet most of the people I know in Boston, and you are going to think I'm just like them.

That worry didn't reflect well on him already. And beneath it was the smaller, meaner worry about how he was going to look arriving at a big art event three months after his very public breakup. Arriving at the event with a young blond ingenue on his arm. He'd look like he was trying very hard, when the absolute worst thing to be seen doing, by the standards of the scene, was *trying*.

It didn't help that Tom had rubbed some mousse into Caroline's straight bob and smudgy black eyeshadow into her long, thick eyelashes, and the combined effect suggested that Caroline had tumbled straight out of bed to come to this event—Adrian's bed in particular, since he was the one bringing her. Caroline radiated sex, and Adrian would need to be entire states away from her not to think about it. But anyone else who saw her would think the same thing, which was an even less appealing thought. Jesus, what had he been thinking? He was about to throw her in the deep end. He ought to fake an illness and take her home to watch PBS documentaries on the couch.

The image of curling up on the couch with Caroline— she didn't even need to change—was far too seductive. He resolutely quashed it. This was what she'd asked him for. He grabbed her hand and gave it a hard squeeze, hoping his palms weren't sweating.

They pulled up to the curb in front of the gallery's unassuming facade, and Adrian was glad for Tamsyn's sake that there looked to be a good amount of traffic going inside for the month and the hour.

Caroline clutched her big coat around her for the dash to the door. Adrian hurried after her as best he could while holding the bottle of wine that he couldn't really afford but owed Tamsyn for breaking the ice with his former gallerist.

Adrian took Caroline's coat and his own to toss in a pile beneath a nearby counter, seizing the moment to identify the other people in attendance. Tamsyn, chatting near the entrance with an elderly couple he recognized as serious collectors. A few wealthy people better categorized as art groupies. A couple of men from his art school cohort. Also David and Vanessa, two of the remaining artists at Nora's gallery, along with Vanessa's wife, Jillian. His stomach plummeted, because these were the people he'd least wanted to see that evening.

Caroline had already drifted over to the painting nearest the front door. Adrian moved to stand next to her, catching Tamsyn's attention as he went. She was a tall, Rubenesque woman with a careless fall of shoulder-length brown hair and rugged features. She stuck her head out of the edge of the group she was in and called his name.

"Did you bring my wine?" she demanded, hands on her hips. Adrian had truthfully told Caroline that she could wear whatever she wanted to an opening, because Tamsyn was in paint-splattered denim overalls over a chambray shirt with a red bow tie, her version of formalwear.

Adrian dutifully hefted the bottle of Bordeaux in the air as proof, then tapped Caroline on the back of the elbow to turn her around for introductions.

Tamsyn's eyes widened as she took in his date and retrieved the wine bottle, tucking it protectively against her stomach. Tamsyn didn't look great, now that Adrian saw her up close. It had been a while—Christ, a year, maybe?—but her face was drawn, with a couple of new lines around the corners of her eyes. She and Nora hadn't gotten along, which was probably to Tamsyn's credit, but that had cut down on the double-date opportunities.

Still, she was the only one who hadn't been pretending to be happy for him when he was nominated for the Marcel Duchamp Prize at twenty-five, so he leaned in and kissed her cheek and told her how glad he was that she'd invited him, and that he'd brought his friend Caroline, who had also been looking forward to the opening.

"You and your pretty face and your pretty women," Tamsyn said, shaking her head. "If I looked like you, I'd be in the Met by now, you know. And dating supermodels, apparently."

Caroline grinned and blushed. "I just got a professional stylist for tonight," she protested. "But you're right, I should put a paper bag on him so that people can focus on his art."

"Focus on my art, you mean," Tamsyn said facetiously. "At least for tonight. Not all of us can rely on our looks to impress people."

"You do just fine on both fronts," Adrian said, taking it in the spirit it had been meant. "Where's that travel-size supermodel of yours?" He'd always liked Camila, Tamsyn's girlfriend, who barely came up to his chest but made big abstract sculptures out of construction debris.

Tamsyn tilted her head and gave him a pained look, and Adrian realized that he had stepped in it.

"Camila and I broke up six months ago."

"I'm sorry," he immediately blurted out, and he truly was very sorry to have brought it up. But then he repeated it, because he was sorrier that he hadn't known, because he'd been absorbed by his own problems. And then he was sorrier still that it had happened at all, because the two of them had been together since before art school, and they had seemed very good together.

That made exactly zero relationships that he had personally seen last, including his own parents' marriage. Of course, watching Tom and Rose get divorced had been like seeing the laws of physics rewritten, but it really did seem like nobody ever managed to stay together unless religion or economics forced them to.

"Don't worry about it," Tamsyn said, forced cheer covering the underlying weariness. "It's not like we sent around notices. And, you know, she said she might stop by for this. We're still friends."

Her tone said that last statement was a lie, but Adrian was drafted into the deception, so he nodded and tried to look pleasant.

"Do you want me to go open that wine for you?"

"Jesus, if there was ever going to be a man for me, it would be you," Tamsyn said gratefully. "Don't leave it with the other stuff at the bar—I bought box wine from Target and poured it into the bottles so I'd look fancy." She stepped away and, braced to perform again, waved at a new group of potential customers who were arriving out of the cold.

Caroline followed Adrian to the bar, picking up a paper cup of the cheap stuff while he hunted down a corkscrew. She took a sip that managed to hide how bad the wine had to taste. Her expression was bright as she took in the scene. She was so beautiful and sincere in her interest that the entire room seemed to dim around her.

"Are you okay?" she asked.

He paused his wrestling with the cork. "Why wouldn't I be?"

"I don't know. You just seem stressed."

"Like I said, these aren't very good parties."

"It looks pretty good in comparison to the couple I've been to. Nobody at all is puking in the corner, and I haven't stepped in any beer."

Adrian got the cork out of the wine, poured a generous amount into a paper cup, and hid the bottle below the bar. He'd pass it off to Tamsyn the next time he was near her. Then he got his own cup of cheap wine to hold and pretend to drink.

He steeled himself to make earnest conversation about

art with strangers, although he already wanted to leave. He'd said hello to Tamsyn, dropped off the wine, and he ought to get Caroline out of there before someone taught her it was gauche to admit she liked anything.

"Hey," she said, squaring her shoulders to face him. "You'll have one of these again, okay?"

She'd guessed wrong at the immediate source of his unhappiness, but his heart ached at her unwarranted concern.

"You're the first person I'd invite," he told her.

"I'd better be. I'll bring an entire case of Midori for the bar, plus that terrible red stuff you like, and you *know* I'll buy something even if your show sucks, which it won't," she said confidently.

I love you, he thought, and the words in his mind were like the dot of pigment that changed the entire tone of the piece. Nothing looked the same to him. He saw everything differently since he'd known her.

"Thanks," he said. He pulled his shoulders back, his mind reeling. Oh God, what was he going to do?

Caroline hesitated for another second, then leaned up to press another one of those featherlight kisses on his cheek.

Adrian took a deep breath, still tempted to beg her to go home with him instead of socializing with some of the people he least wanted to see in the world. "Let's go gin up some interest in Tamsyn's paintings."

"Well, that shouldn't be too hard," Caroline said, putting a hand on his arm to return to the beginning of the exhibit. "I think the paintings are *wonderful*."

CAROLINE DIDN'T KNOW WHY ADRIAN HAD SAID THE GAL-lery opening wouldn't be a good party. This was the first party she'd ever attended not to prominently feature birthday cake or a keg, and it was soothingly free of loud noises or oppressive odors. The white-walled space contained smiling people from her own age up to tiny old ladies in moth-eaten fur coats. Adrian had said the wine was bad, but all red wine tasted like someone had left a Juicy Juice out in the sun for too long as far as Caroline was concerned. Soft R&B standards played from an iPhone plugged into a speaker in the corner. They were going to spend the rest of the evening looking at art. If this wasn't a good party, Caroline was going to be extremely impressed if Adrian ever did invite her to one.

Tamsyn's new series—Chicks, Man—was all birds. Each painting was like a boudoir portrait of a different bird, rendered at life size or greater in loving, romantic detail. The brushstrokes were so tiny as to be almost invisible, and the colors were pale and old-fashioned, like in a pinup photo. There were stickers on the labels to show which ones had sold, and it appeared that about half had at that point in the evening.

Caroline enthusiastically marveled over the tiny details of feather and beak with whoever wandered nearby, and that was productive of new stickers on the labels.

It wasn't hard to talk to people at the party. There was an intuitive script to follow. *Hello, look at this bird. Isn't it great to see so many people here?* She could do this all night.

She wondered whether her efforts were better classified as sales or marketing as she drifted into a conversation with a group of other artists who seemed to know Adrian very well from the way the women kissed his cheeks and the man wrapped an arm around his shoulders and patted the back of his head. Adrian held very still for all of it, suffering like a cat whose fur was being rubbed in the wrong direction.

Adrian briefly ran his hand down Caroline's lower back when he was done with introductions. Vanessa. Her wife, Jillian. David. All of them friends. Caroline would normally have taken Adrian's touch as an attempt to reassure her, but he looked like the one who needed reassurance as the trio briefly demanded Caroline's credentials—*an MBA student*, they didn't ask where—before tearing into Tamsyn's paintings.

"Did Tamsyn start working on this before or after the breakup?" asked Vanessa, the tallest and most commanding in presence. She wore a cropped leather jacket over high-waisted red silk trousers, accessorized with chunky gold jewelry. Caroline didn't even know where you bought clothes like that, or how you knew they'd look good on you. Vanessa looked like a creature from an entirely different world from the one Caroline inhabited.

"After. This is the artistic equivalent of eating ice cream in your fuzzy socks," declared David, whose small, unsettling blue eyes had latched on to Caroline's cleavage upon their introduction and never strayed.

"She should have put these on her mom's refrigerator instead of throwing a show though," said Jillian, who was intimidatingly pretty, with hair bleached to a faint, fairy-like shade of platinum. She wore an antique lace dress over dark brown stockings and over-the-knee boots. She wrote for an online magazine Caroline had never heard of, while the other two were artists. "Don't invite the world into your therapy session. I can't imagine what the critics are going to say."

Adrian flexed his jaw, appearing to scan the room for some other errand they could pretend to be on. "I can imagine," he said. "But that doesn't mean they're right. I think this is good work, and it doesn't have anything to do with Camila."

"Maybe she'll take her cash from this show and leave the country for a while," Vanessa said. "That's what I'd do. Lie low. Work my shit out."

"I don't see what's wrong with the paintings," Caroline said, prepared to unite with Adrian in a defense of the birds. "They're gorgeous."

"Oh, sure," said David. "Nice draftsmanship. Very pretty." Somehow it wasn't a compliment in his mouth.

"Like furry art," Vanessa snickered, and the others joined in.

Caroline didn't know what that was, but it also did not seem to be a compliment.

"I don't think it's easy to make something that people want to look at," Caroline insisted. "It's a lot easier to paint a canvas beige and claim it's a conceptual piece. That makes the audience do all the work."

Adrian's knuckles brushed her back again, and this time it felt like a warning, but hadn't he said to be nice about Tamsyn's art? And it actually was lovely.

"It's easier than you think," Vanessa said, chin tilted in with languid condescension. "What's difficult is balancing that with a more interesting idea than beauty."

"You don't think there's an idea behind these?" Caroline asked, surprised. The birds were a lot more compelling to her than the beige rectangles, and not just because she liked the arrangement and colors.

Vanessa sniffed. "If there's an idea, it's so obvious and textual that you can read it off a greeting card. 'Look at these pretty birds.' If you're going to paint imaginary gardens, like Marianne Moore said, you have to put some real toads in them. There's nothing to anchor this. My generation killed irony, and I want it back."

"There's a little irony in the paintings," Caroline insisted.

Adrian now had his hip pressed against hers, trying to indicate that they should step away and go back to the drink station. Caroline dug in her heels.

"Oh, you found the irony?" David drawled.

"They're painted in egg tempera, aren't they?" Caroline said, pointing at the label.

Adrian stopped trying to tug her away, giving her a quick appreciative look out of the corner of his eye. He dropped his head back and laughed at the sour look on the trio's faces.

"She's got you there, David," he said.

He sounded relieved, and that tone sent far more reassurance through Caroline than his hand on her back. *Set point, Caroline and Adrian.* How often did Adrian have to face off against Obnoxious Art Guys? The species seemed pervasive in Boston.

Vanessa snorted, sliding a half step to the left to block Adrian from moving away. "How did you even manage to meet someone new so quickly? I thought Nora kept you on a pretty short leash."

Adrian's eyes narrowed, but he answered "Through friends" at the same time as Caroline said "Internet." His next look at her was distressed, but if they were supposed to be lying about it, he could have told her what the cover story was ahead of time. It wasn't like she'd said she was paying him. She pursed her lips in frustration.

"I read that women look on dating apps for men who are within five years of their own age, but men always want twenty-year-olds," Jillian said to David. "Do you think that's true?"

David held up his hands in mock apology. "There's something so reassuring about twenty-year-olds. Everything's brand-new to them."

"You are such a pig," Vanessa said, shoving his shoulder, though not as though she really meant it. "Also, it's mathematically impossible for that to work, since the twenty-year-olds are looking for twenty-five-year-olds."

"Unless you lie about your age," Jillian said. She gave Adrian a speculative look.

"Everyone does, online," David said.

"Can I get you another glass of wine?" Adrian asked Caroline as though nobody were speaking about them.

"They actually didn't have age ranges on the one we used," Caroline told the group. "I was just filtering for someone with the leatherworking skills to help me repair my riding crop collection. I'm lucky that I got Adrian and not an eighty-year-old saddlery enthusiast."

Adrian choked. Jillian and David stared at her in confusion. Vanessa openly scowled, even though Caroline thought she'd been objectively funny. But she took those reactions as enough of a win to let Adrian lead her away and back to the bar.

"I'm sorry about that," he muttered once they were out of earshot.

"Did you beat them in some kind of artist duel?" Caroline demanded. "Accidentally drop paint on their stuff?" They reminded her of the other women on her tennis team, who had theoretically been on her side as teammates, except for the public ranking of who was the best at the only thing they had in common. She bristled, imagining Adrian having to deal with these people at all of his art events.

"No, I—actually, they're friends of mine. I was on vacation with them in Quebec six months ago. We used to . . .

It doesn't matter. I used to see them a couple of times a week. Not recently though."

Caroline halted. "Really?" She would never have guessed that. She was always getting the wrong read on situations, but she would have sworn he didn't like them from the way he acted. "You guys are close?"

He sighed, rubbing the side of his face. "I don't know. I've known them for a long time. We were at all the same shows, went to the same kinds of places. I went to art school with Vanessa, and she and David were at—" He dropped his shoulders. "So, Vanessa and David were also at my ex's gallery. Are still there, I assume."

What she supposed he meant was, they were all friends with his ex. These were the people Tom had worried about. How he'd thought makeup was going to be enough armor to deal with these people confounded her. People who had spent the last ten years acquiring art and so-phistication were not going to be impressed by a good smoky eye.

Well, Caroline understood loyalty. They probably felt obligated to be awful to Adrian for a while, especially if Adrian hadn't shared his side of the story. His expression was bruised as he took another gulp of the wine he'd dis-paraged.

She ought to go speak with them again. If they were angry because they thought he was dating someone new, Caroline could at least put in a little effort to show that she was not trying to come between Adrian and his mu-tual friends with his ex. And she hadn't been very open to their thoughts on the paintings. Their reactions served her right for making assumptions about them.

Adrian turned his head and swore under his breath as he spotted the two newest people at the party.

"Jan and Samantha," he muttered. "This evening is going to get even better."

Caroline followed his gaze and spotted the couple of middle-aged art patrons she'd met back at the sushi restaurant near the symphony. She didn't know why he was cursing though—she remembered them as friendly.

"Should we go say hi?" she asked.

"No, no, save yourself. I do need to say hello to them though, just in case they're interested in buying another painting someday."

"Of course."

"I'll be right back."

"I'm fine," Caroline insisted, pushing at his elbow and shaking her still mostly full cup of wine.

She scanned the room as Adrian slowly walked away, looking back over his shoulder at her as though she might be not fine in the middle of a well-lit art gallery. His friends had moved to the opposite end of the room and were discussing a large painting of a horned owl voguing on a red velvet sofa.

Caroline took a deep sip of wine and squared her shoulders. She'd try again. This time she'd be charming. And submissive. She'd show her throat and vulnerable belly, and even if they didn't like her, they wouldn't think she was trying to keep her presumed new boyfriend away from his friends.

Approaching people at parties was not a skill she'd attained, but she positioned herself at the next painting over from the owl and pointed her feet at them, hoping the knot of their group would expand to include her. She hoped they weren't still disparaging the art, even though she supposed she ought to hear out what their exact objections were. They were talking with animation, which she could hear even over the background hum of the room.

"—owe me twenty bucks and a bottle of Scotch."

"Like hell I do. I said six months. It hasn't been six months yet."

"He's not going to beg her to take him back while he's still fucking Truck Stop Nooner Barbie. Pay up."

"As if she would care. Plus he's got to be broke by now. He hasn't sold a painting without the gallery's help in years. I'm still going to win the bet."

Without names, it took Caroline a moment to realize they were talking about her. And Adrian. And his ex. She couldn't help a startled inhale, and Vanessa, at the edge of the group, turned and smirked at her.

Caroline dug her fingernails into her palms and reminded herself that they didn't know anything about her.

"I, uh, I don't think we got off on the right foot," Caroline said. She'd just play through it. Rub some dirt on it. Adrian hadn't exactly been easy to get to know either.

"Oh, you think?" Vanessa said with poisonous sweetness, emphasizing the last word of the question.

"You must have been surprised to see your friends break up after so long, but I didn't have anything to do with it," Caroline continued on doggedly.

"That didn't surprise me. Meeting his midlife crisis in person is what's surprising. It's so fucking tacky! I didn't think he had it in him."

David leaned in. "Let it go, Vee. Sometimes a guy just has to clean his paintbrush off, if you know what I mean."

Vanessa scowled at David, wide mouth condensing into a hard point. "No, I don't know what you mean. I don't know why men do the most boring thing possible when they go looking for variety."

"I don't think having athletic sex with girls who still have all their original parts is ever going to get boring."

"You have the wrong idea about my relationship with Adrian," Caroline tried. A hot, shaky feeling was climbing up her back and wrapping around her throat, but they really couldn't be this awful. She'd done something to set them off. "It's really not about that."

"What's it about, then?" Jillian asked, layers of delicate rose-gold bracelets clattering on her wrists as she crossed her arms.

Adrian wouldn't want her to tell them the whole truth. That would be more humiliating for him than showing up with her, which his friends thought was embarrassing enough. Her mouth was as dry as though she'd swallowed gravel. "We—we went to the symphony for our second date, and I wanted to learn more about the opera—"

Vanessa snorted. "Right, I'm sure he broke up with the age-appropriate fiancée with the art history degree and started dating a teenager with her tits hanging out of a cheap dress because he wanted to talk more about the *opera*."

All three of them laughed at that.

It was so *mean* and so *wrong* but so ultimately *true* that the entire room seemed to darken in Caroline's peripheral vision. Adrian wasn't with her because he wanted to talk about the opera with her. He wasn't even with her because he wanted to sleep with her, which would have at least said that there was something he found desirable about her. He was with her because of money, which his awful friends thought would send him back to his awful ex soon enough, so Caroline didn't even have to be very nice to earn the privilege of paying for his time.

Running away was an unfortunate habit. She'd relive

this later and think of clever rejoinders. She'd wish she'd stood her ground and told them off. But instead, she mumbled "Excuse me", and darted for the first door she saw, hoping it was a bathroom. She was through it and closing the door behind her as quickly as she registered that there was a light on inside. Sobs threatened to crawl out of her throat, choked off only by the hot, swelling burn in her cheeks. She couldn't have deserved them saying all *that*, could she? What did she even *do*?

After she blinked enough to clear her eyes, she realized that her hidey-hole was not a bathroom. It was more of a utility closet, crowded with shelves of cleaning supplies and office materials, with a tiny desk wedged into one corner for some miserable administrative assistant. And it was already occupied.

Tamsyn slouched against the shelving unit on the far wall, the neck of her bottle of wine dangling from one fist. As Caroline stiffened and backed up to the doorway with another apology on her lips, the other woman took a lengthy drink straight out of the bottle. Her face was tight and pinched.

"I'm not sure this closet is big enough for two people to have a breakdown in at the same time, and I was here first," Tamsyn said. "So I call dibs."

"I'm so sorry, I was trying to cry in the bathroom like a normal human being, but I couldn't even manage—" Caroline took a deep gulp of air. *Say less, Caroline.* "I'm sorry. I'll go."

Tamsyn tipped her bottle at her in farewell. "Don't mention it."

"I'm sorry," Caroline said again. "I won't say anything."

"Thanks," Tamsyn muttered.

Caroline paused with her hand on the doorknob. Her

mind had already grabbed on to the distraction of someone else who wasn't having a good time at the party anymore.

"Um, why are you upset, if you don't mind me asking? Your show seems to be going really well."

If someone had been rude to the artist at her own opening, perhaps Caroline could exit the party by way of dragging someone into the street to brawl. She hadn't ever been in a real fight, but her serves clocked over one hundred miles per hour, so she thought she could do some damage if it were called for. She felt like hitting something. Preferably Vanessa, but that was unlikely to change the woman's ideas about her.

"As if those three hyenas your boyfriend hangs out with aren't right outside this door, ripping apart my opening," Tamsyn scoffed.

Caroline firmed her jaw. "They don't seem very friendly." It was the strongest statement she felt comfortable making about Adrian's friends.

"They get to you too?"

Caroline nodded.

Tamsyn silently offered the wine bottle to Caroline. The unexpectedly kind gesture made the tears in her eyes well up again. Crap, she was going to undo all Tom's hard work at making her pretty. Caroline took a swig from the bottle, winced, and passed it back.

"Should we go, like, fight?" she asked, trying again to focus on someone else's predicament. Adrian had to like Tamsyn more than the three other artists. Maybe they were fair game. "I really like your paintings. I'll do it. I bet I can take Jillian, at least."

Tamsyn barked out a short laugh. "David's the ripe target. Get him in the nuts just once and he'd shit his nepo baby diaper."

"What did they say to you?" Caroline demanded.

"Nothing directly. And I don't fucking care what they think. Vanessa inherited half a food-additives company, and David's grandpa is in the fucking MoMA. They don't even have to worry about selling paintings, but it still pisses them off that I'm going to sell out this show? Maybe I'd turn out a bunch of unmarketable, masturbatory odes to existential anguish if I didn't have to worry about rent, but we'll never know, will we?"

"Want me to throw them out?"

Tamsyn chuckled grimly. "No. I'm actually just hiding here because my ex showed up with a date."

"Oh," Caroline said sympathetically. The way the other woman had described her breakup, it still seemed pretty raw. Tamsyn twisted the corner of her mouth and tipped the bottle back again.

Caroline considered the other woman's unhappy posture. "Did you talk to her? Maybe it's not what you think. I mean, I'm the date with someone's ex, and it's really not . . ." She wasn't making sense. "You should talk to her."

"It ought to be what I think. We'd been together since we were seventeen. We broke up to try dating other people."

"Oh," Caroline said again. That didn't seem like a good reason to break up with someone she really liked, but what did Caroline know, since she had never dated anyone she really liked besides Adrian? "Are you? Dating other people?"

"No, I'm fucking not. Turns out I don't really know how to." Tamsyn gripped her hair in her hands, looking skyward.

"I get that," Caroline said glumly, retrieving the bottle and having another swig. Red wine was growing on her. "I don't know how to either." She'd been broken up with by guys she hadn't even realized she was supposedly dating, which was a lot easier to handle than the time she found out she *wasn't* dating someone she thought was her boyfriend. In that respect, paying Adrian to go on a specified number of dates with her a week was much easier to manage.

"You seem to be doing just fine."

"I'm not. That's what they got wrong. I'm not really dating Adrian."

Tamsyn made a surprised noise. "You could have fooled me. You're here with him. Your tits look great in that dress. It's not a date?"

"What's wrong with my dress?" Caroline demanded, looking down at herself. "Vanessa said the same thing."

"Nothing's wrong with your dress," Tamsyn said appreciatively. "And don't worry about Vanessa. I've been watching her make a series of increasingly desperate passes at Adrian ever since they met. She's just salty that he didn't come weep in her bony bosom when he broke up with Nora."

"Isn't she *married*?" Caroline understood these people less and less.

"Pretty sure she'd throw in Jill as part of the package if she thought it would help her seal the deal."

Caroline grunted in dismay even as part of her worried that open-marriage threesomes were part of the standard landscape of Adrian's sex life. She'd have to do a *lot* of reading if that were the case. Tamsyn waved the concern away.

"Don't worry. Your boyfriend seems to have an allergy to infidelity, which is one of his more charming traits."

"He's not really my boyfriend. There's nothing to be jealous about."

Tamsyn laughed again and pretended to simper at her. "So, you're single?"

Caroline gave her a long look. "Shouldn't you go talk to your ex?"

"Shouldn't you go take your boyfriend home?"

"It's really not like that. He's—"

Her employee.

"It's not like that," Caroline revised.

"But you want it to be?"

Caroline rubbed her knuckles against her cheek. "I don't know. Not if he's not interested." If he had a full suite of choices, he wouldn't be dating her. He'd be dating some other beautiful, brilliant woman his own age, though hopefully one who wasn't as mean as his ex. Having her nose rubbed in that fact was giving her some doubts about expanding the range of services Adrian provided as her part-time boyfriend for hire.

Tamsyn sniffed loudly. "Well, he called off his wedding with Nora. He keeps turning Vanessa down. I don't see that saying no is a problem he has, so there's no harm in finding out." She tipped the bottle all the way back and drained the rest of it. "Just drag him home and ask if he wants to have interesting, bendy, tall-person sex. I'm going to chase everyone who isn't buying paintings out in a few minutes anyway."

Caroline worried at her lower lip, still feeling shaky and beaten up. She didn't think she was up for any sex that night, interesting or otherwise. But she did want to go. And as long as she did have Adrian, or his time, at least, maybe she ought to take advantage of everything he had to offer. She'd probably always wonder what it would have been like otherwise.

She took a deep breath. "Okay, I'll do it."

"Attagirl," Tamsyn said, hiding the empty wine bottle in a bucket. "Do you want to give me your number in case things don't work out?"

"That was a pretty good line," Caroline said, eyes widening. "It was really smooth! Maybe you're better at dating than you think. But do you want to talk to your ex first?"

Tamsyn winced, a brief flicker of vulnerability crossing her face for the first time. "Do you really think so?"

"It's probably easier than finding someone new," Caroline pointed out, privately thinking that Tamsyn seemed very uninterested in actually dating other people if the only person she'd managed to hit on was Caroline.

"All right. When we leave this broom closet though, can we look like we were making out instead of drinking and whimpering?"

Caroline shrugged, impressed with Tamsyn's gambit. "Sure."

They startled a few people when they opened the door, including a petite woman Caroline tentatively marked as Tamsyn's ex, and the taller woman standing next to her, who Caroline assumed was going on her last date with Tamsyn's ex. Both made appalled faces when Tamsyn copped a theatrical feel on Caroline's rear before swaggering over to insert herself in her ex's conversation.

Adrian was on the opposite side of the room, his back to Caroline. He was arguing with David and Vanessa, his arms waving as he bore down on some point.

Caroline narrowed her eyes, rolled her shoulders, and stalked toward him as though she were heading into the semifinal match of a knockout tournament. She leaned up against him when she reached his side, and he paused briefly to smile at her reappearance. Then he continued with what appeared to be his defense of Tamsyn's show.

"She's referencing the work of Helen Beard, but this is more of a comment on the masculine gaze. You're uncomfortable with the sexualization of the birds because the art asks you to examine the paradigm you apply to pictures of *women*."

Caroline pushed her hip against his in a silent demand, and his arm came almost automatically around her, hand resting in the dip of her waist. Vanessa's face took on an ugly flush, and that and Adrian's arm were both good, but Caroline was ready to leave.

She leaned over to whisper that in Adrian's ear, and he nodded.

"Just one more minute. David's embarrassing himself," he told her in a low voice. He looked back at the other man. "The initial attraction of the birds is the point. You can't engage with a work that gives you no point of entry."

Caroline appreciated what he was doing. She did. But she couldn't take one more minute of this. Adrian had *said* they could leave when she was ready.

She turned to face him, reached up to put a hand on his opposite cheek, and pulled his attention back to her for just long enough to meet his eyes. Then she kissed him square on the mouth.

She'd never kissed anyone in front of an audience before, but she really put her back into it. She curved her hand along the sharp edge of his jaw and parted her lips as soon as he did. His mouth was full and soft, probably with surprise, but she took advantage of that to slide her tongue along his, fragrant with even worse wine than she'd been drinking. Kissing him was easier than she'd thought. It was sweet and effortless. She hummed into his mouth, letting her hand trail down across his chest as she pulled back. Yes, she could do this easily. She already knew how.

Adrian's expression was very pleasing. Of course he looked a little like she'd hit him in the face with a board, but his wide-eyed, open expression of shock was not opposed to kissing her. She didn't think so, anyway, even though he was hard to read sometimes. He still had his arm around her, fingertips curling into the fabric of her dress now. His tongue minutely wet the seam of his lips.

Caroline exhaled and settled her shoulders. She could rescue this evening.

"I want to buy a bird painting," she said firmly. "And then I want to go home."

Adrian had to close his mouth to swallow, and the movement seemed to take a very long time.

"All right," he said faintly.

He didn't move. So Caroline leaned up and brushed her mouth across his slack lower lip again.

"Adrian?" she prompted him, hands pressed possessively against the muscles of his upper arms. She resisted the urge to glare over at Vanessa like a toddler who'd just fought her way to the top of the sandpile.

Adrian swallowed again. "I'll go find the gallerist," he said, edging away with his eyes still fixed on her. She'd never seen him so taken aback.

Caroline gave the other two artists a regal, satisfied nod and spun on her heel to go collect their coats.

Fifteen minutes later, they were in the back seat of a muddy taxi, speeding toward Adrian's apartment. Caroline held the receipt for a pair of mourning doves cuddling in pink satin. Adrian's gaze was still locked on her, eyes narrowed as though he could see into her head if he looked long enough. She didn't know why he seemed so surprised that she wanted to kiss him when it seemed like so many other women did. Just because she hadn't wanted to as soon as they met? Before she knew anything about him but his looks and willingness to go out with strangers for pay? Now that she knew he was loyal to a fault, kind when it would be easier to just be nice—and, okay, still really good-looking—she'd decided that she *would* like some sex with the art and the theater, actually, if that was still on offer.

As for that night, however, she wasn't drunk, but she was emotionally wiped out. That meant she'd get in her car as soon as they reached Adrian's apartment rather than explore whatever Tamsyn had meant by *bendy*. Still, she took Adrian's hand and intertwined her fingers with his over her lap. He didn't object, though his jaw worked as though he was trying to say something and couldn't find the words.

Eventually, he leaned closer to her and pressed his lips to the corner of her mouth, the movement a slow question. *Is this a thing we are going to do?* Caroline turned her head just enough to catch his kiss and return it. His mouth was soft and warm and undemanding. His breath on her face felt like a promise. Adrian glanced at the taxi driver and slowly sat back. His knuckles skated over the hem of her dress and brushed against her knee where their hands were still entwined together.

Caroline closed her eyes and dropped her head onto his shoulder, relishing the little thrill his fingers against her knee sent up her spine. The evening had been a tough match, and she'd been down a set there, but she'd rallied for the win. His friends probably hated her now, but she'd managed to leave with some dignity—and Adrian.

And now she knew he didn't mind kissing her.

They got out of the taxi in front of his building. He looked at the doorway, then looked at her. Stuck his hands in his pockets.

"Caroline—" he started, voice uncertain.

She shook her head. "We don't have to talk about it tonight. I'm going home."

He nodded, but his eyes tightened. "If this is just . . .

because of something Vanessa said, or something I said, and this is another long-form joke at my expense . . . It's not that I don't deserve it. But, Caroline, please don't. Don't mess around with me like—"

"Like this?" Caroline asked. She pressed a palm against his flat stomach and leaned in to kiss him again. Leisurely, this time, because nobody was watching them, pressing her lips against his and asking him to open for her. Adrian was still for only a second, and then his arms came around her, and he was kissing her back, like she'd gotten only the charcoal underdrawing before, and now there was color and texture and light. His fingers caught in the ends of her hair and the hem of her dress, pressing her body against him, soft breasts up against the firm plane of his chest. His mouth moved gently against hers, still more tentative than she thought he ought to be when she'd draped herself around him, but deepening after a few seconds when she tightened her arms around his neck.

He was wonderful at kissing. Fantastic. She should have asked for this weeks ago. She'd wanted to see Boston, she'd wanted to see what her life could look like once she acquired a little more polish and experience, she'd wanted not to be so damn *lonely* all the time—but this was really it. The feeling she'd wanted. Warm and cared for. Kissing him felt more right than anything she'd done since climbing out the window of her father's house.

Caroline broke away only when oxygen became a really pressing concern. Adrian's arms were still around her, fingertips reflexively stroking over her hips.

"Yes," he said, voice a little ragged. "Like that." His expression was still uncertain and guarded. "Don't do that unless—unless you're serious."

Caroline couldn't immediately identify his concern.

She supposed it was rude to ask for the dessert menu if she didn't intend on ordering something, but she did, she really did. She was *definitely* going to sleep with him. She wanted to try everything with him.

"I am," she reassured him. "I'm very serious."

Adrian set his jaw and nodded slowly.

"All right," he murmured. "So am I."

Caroline exhaled, relief surging through her body.

"But you know this has to change things," he said, dusty-blue eyes intent on hers.

"I know," she said. This wasn't what they'd initially agreed to, after all. They had to renegotiate terms and conditions of employment. She'd assumed he'd want more money, or different hours, or maybe a retirement account or something like that. He had to realize she'd give it to him, anything he asked for. "I have performances till Sunday, but maybe we can talk about it then?"

His face softened at that promise, and he lifted his arms to squeeze her shoulders in farewell. He told her to drive safely. Part of her wanted to ask him to come home with her, just to hold her and explain what he'd been saying about Helen Beard and the masculine gaze until she fell asleep. But that wasn't a fair request when she wasn't prepared to negotiate.

So Caroline just pressed one last kiss to his cheek and wiggled in the glow of his smile as he watched her go.

Chapter Fourteen

TOM TOLD HIM THAT HE SEEMED PRETTY SMUG FOR A GUY who came home alone before midnight, though Adrian was duty bound to ignore attempts at fishing and told him nothing. *Smug* wasn't the right term, anyway. *Smug* would have implied some kind of achievement. It wasn't that he'd ever set out to have a relationship with Caroline. Being in a relationship with her was mostly a matter of accepting that it had happened despite their best intentions. But the acceptance was easier than he could have imagined.

Adrian woke up the next day feeling at peace with himself. He was unemployed again, but that was temporary; he would meet with Mike McMurtry on Sunday and negotiate a deal with his old gallery. He was dating a student, but that was all right. He'd managed to be a generally positive influence on Caroline's life, he thought, and he was prepared to take things as slow as she wanted, in light of an age difference that would gradually fade in significance. It was only a year and a half until she'd have some air-conditioned office job creating spreadsheets, and then nobody would think it was too bad that she had an older boyfriend who was a gallery artist.

He was in love. He wanted to paint again. Abruptly, his future looked appealing.

He spent the weekend in his studio finishing the Ilinden-Preobrazhenie painting and organizing his digital portfolio of works still with Nora. Late on Sunday afternoon, he got a selfie from Caroline—fingers in a peace sign, black watch cap over blond hair, drawn theater curtains behind her—with a pink heart emoji attached. His chest ached with emotions that hadn't filled it in years.

Break a leg, he wrote back.

He printed a final copy of his CV and artist's statement, checked his prints for smears or wrinkles, and tucked his portfolio into his battered leather messenger bag. Most artists had to market themselves to galleries, he told himself. True, they mostly did this at ten years younger than he was, but he'd skipped the portfolio review stage the first time around. Dating a twenty-three-year-old meant that he was likely to be reliving a number of other experiences most frequently enjoyed by that age group, many of which he was even looking forward to.

It was easier than he'd thought to find his old gallery, as though he'd been absent for only a few weeks, rather than seven years. The building, set on a quiet street in Chestnut Hill instead of one of the trendier downtown art districts, was exactly as he remembered it: he entered through a small retail area where Mike sold art books and matted prints, then wandered through a warren of gallery spaces to the cluttered office in the rear.

The man stood up when Adrian knocked on the half-open door. Mike was a big guy, a Boston-Irish bruiser who looked like he might be unloading cargo down on the docks as well as selling fine art, but he had shrewd, wide-set hazel eyes in his pink face, and he moved with purposeful restraint. Adrian had somehow expected him to be exactly the same too, but it had been seven years, and

Mike was broader and grayer than he'd been. Adrian abruptly felt those years looming over him. Seven years with little to show for it.

"The prodigal son returns!" Mike announced grandly, thwacking him on the back. "How are you doing, kid?"

Adrian was past the age when he might have been plausibly called *kid*, but he accepted it as the reminder of who he'd been when he first signed up with Mike versus where he was today.

"Glad to be here," he eventually responded, thinking that struck the appropriately contrite note.

They spent a few minutes talking about mutual acquaintances, their health, their living arrangements, and Tamsyn's new show, which Mike had seen in preview. It was less awkward than Adrian had feared. Certainly less fraught than negotiating with Nora over marketing for a new show when he was simultaneously pissed that she'd made joint vacation plans with people he didn't even like without consulting him.

"So things are really done with Nora?" Mike asked.

"Very done."

"You know, I thought it was a bad idea when you two got together. It's a little incestuous, dating an artist at your own gallery."

"Yes," Adrian couldn't help but agree. Of course, even if he hadn't agreed, what else could he say?

"You still have anything up over at her gallery?"

"I've heard she's showing a few of my most recent works at Art Basel, but I'm not sure that's . . . intended for my benefit."

Adrian thought he could afford to be big about it at this point.

"Gotcha," Mike said, eyebrows raised.

Adrian smiled uncomfortably, hoping he didn't need to explain more about the collapse of his personal and professional relationships with Nora.

"So, what else have you been up to?" Mike finally asked, moving back around his desk to settle in his big leather armchair.

Adrian took one of the matching chairs on the other side, gingerly laying his portfolio across several piles of paperwork.

"Do you mean in terms of awards and shows, or . . ." He trailed off. There had been plenty of those, if not in the past couple of years, and he had dutifully updated his CV with every snippet of recognition. If you looked at him on paper, you would think he was an accomplished artist. But Mike had never much cared for the juried shows and expensive biennials before, which was a point Nora had made in convincing Adrian to switch galleries.

Mike waved a hand in the air. "Nah, I don't care about any of that glossy art magazine circle-jerk bullshit. Show me your work."

Adrian nodded and began to open his portfolio, but Mike waved him off again and pointed to a digital projector aimed at a bare wall on the other side of the office.

"Do you have good digital copies?"

With some technological fumbling, Adrian plugged his phone in to the projector and managed to get a painting displayed on the wall, more or less life-size and with good detail.

"Thanks," Mike said. "When the new kids are applying through the website, I usually do this myself. Thought I'd have you over in person though, see if you got ugly."

"I think I found a gray hair yesterday?" Adrian offered.

"That's just because you're twitchy," Mike sniffed. He

got the first of Adrian's paintings up and settled back in his chair. "This the current series?"

"Yes," Adrian said, even though he wasn't really anticipating anything new now that he'd finished the Ilinden-Preobrazhenie Uprising. There were more than a dozen works in the series though, more than enough to fill out a reasonable space. Most of them were still in Nora's possession, but Mike wasn't afraid of Nora, and Adrian would be happy to outsource that transition to his new gallery.

"Got it."

Mike clicked through to the next painting without saying anything else. Then the next. He got up at one point to check out the detail closer to the wall, then sat back down. He clicked to the next.

Adrian began to sweat. It wasn't like Mike to torture him, and Mike had been full of effusive praise back in the day when he'd been the one selling Adrian's paintings. Every minute of his silence seemed to make the room ten degrees hotter.

It couldn't be the pictures; the quality was as good as the images on Mike's website. The brushwork was still visible. The colors were true.

They got eight paintings in, and Mike put his chin in his hand, braced against the table.

A twist in Adrian's stomach made him want to stand, leave the room, and avoid the discussion entirely.

Mike didn't speak, but his expression was eloquent as he gazed across the table at Adrian.

"You hate it," Adrian said, his voice sounding too dry.

"No, I don't hate it."

"But you don't like it either."

"Honestly, I'm not sure I *understand* it. You know I'm just a second-rate art dealer in a second-tier art city—"

"Mike, don't give me that. You can just say you don't like it."

"I'm serious! Look, I've always thought you were great, and I can tell this is a big idea, and you've got beautiful composition, detail—"

"I'm not a child. You don't have to sugarcoat it for me," Adrian interjected. "If it's not any good, I need to hear that, not a load of bullshit." In the end, he hadn't been able to trust Nora for one single thing. If she'd been holding back on some major slide in his work because they lived together, he could understand that, but he hated it at the same time. He'd spent years running in the wrong direction.

Mike leaned forward. "I'm not here to say whether it's good or not. It might be very good. All I can say is it's not right for my gallery."

Adrian slapped the table. "If you could say it was good before, why won't you just tell me the opposite now?"

"Because I knew it was good before! You know that's what I thought because I bought that painting of the pretty women with the birch branches myself. It's still in my kitchen, you know? I sell art for a living and I bought your work. I buy what I like. Now, I don't know who this grim shit is for, but it's not for me."

Adrian sighed. "So that's it, then."

"No, that's not it. I'm trying to run a business, and I know what appeals to the guys who walk in here looking to buy something nice to hang over the mantel that they can pass down to their kids someday. I'm not an art critic, but I know what sells. I'm just saying I can't sell this. That's *all* I'm saying."

"You're saying it's not commercial enough?"

"You're not fucking listening to me. I'm not saying that

at all. Maybe there's someone else—hell, maybe in New York or somewhere with a hipper crowd, this is right for them. I sold your art when it was flowers and garden parties, and that was great. We both made plenty of money. But if that's not what you want to do anymore, there's no problem with that either. Find someone this stuff does speak to."

Mike clicked through the last few slides. Adrian's body ached at the thought of all the work that had gone into them. The research. The tiny details. The uniforms, the shadows of the broken trees over the battlefields. He wished he could disappear out of the room, to have never come to Mike's gallery in the first place.

Mike reached the last slide before Adrian could stop him; it was the portrait of Caroline cradling the goldenrod. Adrian had just added a final layer the previous day, mostly linseed oil and white highlights. He'd taken the picture to show her the next time he saw her. He'd thought about adding a few pops of cerulean here and there to buttress the violet shadows and capture more of the colors he thought of when he pictured Caroline, but he had not yet decided.

"Well, that's kind of interesting," Mike murmured, cocking his head appreciatively. "Is that new?"

"It's not finished," Adrian blurted, even if what he meant was that it wasn't for sale.

Before he could retrieve his phone, Mike clicked to the next picture, but that was just the selfie Caroline had sent him earlier that day. Mike flicked his eyes at Adrian, no doubt recognizing the subject of the previous painting, but he hit the power button on the projector without comment.

The room darkened, the silence becoming even more weighty in the absence of the hum of the projector's fan.

"You know, the critics hated the last show I did while I was at your gallery," Adrian said, teeth gritted. "They said my work hadn't progressed. That it was sentimental and juvenile."

"Yeah, I remember. I disagreed."

"I fixed that. I moved past that."

"Nobody could say your new work is sentimental, that's for sure," Mike said, but Adrian could tell the man was now humoring him, wrinkles forming in the corners around his mouth.

Adrian rubbed a hand over his face. "What do you think I should do now?"

"Don't you know?"

Adrian minutely shook his head, eyes closed.

"Apply for juried shows, competitions, find yourself a gallery you're a better fit for . . ."

It was what he'd planned to do ever since Nora cut him loose, but it all took money he didn't have.

"Do you want me to give you some names?" Mike offered hesitantly.

"No," Adrian said, chair legs loudly scraping the floor as he stood. "No, I've got it." A lie.

Mike's shoulders softened. "I'm sorry I didn't have a better answer for you. You know I'd love to see you succeed. I thought you were going to blaze a trail across the art world from the moment I saw your senior show."

"I appreciate that." Adrian was so dizzy with disappointment that he could barely lock his knees to stand.

He somehow managed to make his farewells and promises of continued correspondence, even if all he wanted was to be somewhere else. To be someone else, even. The only thing he'd ever wanted to be in his life was an artist, but now he was barely an artist, and during his tenure he hadn't managed to accumulate much in the way of either wealth or renown. Those might have served him better in this situation than a dozen paintings he wasn't sure he could sell to anyone, no matter what Mike said about them being too high-concept.

What was he supposed to say to Caroline? Was he supposed to ask her if she wouldn't mind putting the relationship on ice for a few months while he tried to pull himself together? That would hardly be fair to her; she was only twenty-three and looking to have more going on in her life, not less. Should he ask whether she minded having a boyfriend who tended bar or made Frappuccinos? She probably didn't, at least right now, but in a year and a half she'd be climbing the corporate ladder and associating with people who thought very poorly of men who worked 39.5 hours a week. And he could hardly ask her to take a step backward and keep him on the payroll—things couldn't go on as they had been now that their feelings were out in the open.

Late-afternoon snow was beginning to dust the sidewalks when he emerged, but he decided to walk home rather than catch the bus. The long walk across the city would give him the time he needed to come up with a way to break the news to her, regardless of which bad solution he decided upon.

"ELBOWS AND KNEES IN THE CAR? LET'S GO!" NATHAN shouted.

Caroline tried to remember what Tom had explained about cast parties before the run crew members bundled her into the back of someone's Camry, three girls hovering unsafely over the laps of two of the bigger members of the tech crew. She hadn't put a cast party on her calendar, just the tech dinner later in the evening, but everyone else seemed to take it for granted that they'd drink until then. The Sunday matinee had concluded the run of *The Iceman Cometh*, the cast had taken their final bows, and everyone was in a hurry to get very drunk as soon as possible. Caroline was tempted to get anxious about the whole thing, because she hadn't prepared; she'd intended to spend the free hours of the afternoon buying exciting underwear online and taking down some notes on sex positions she wanted to try.

"Should we wait for Rima?" Caroline asked Nathan's knees, which were all she could see from where she was uncomfortably wedged in the middle of the car.

The head of the run crew turned the ignition, and too-loud rock music filled the car. Caroline's head began to ache.

"She doesn't drink," Nathan cheerfully replied, failing to notice her discomfort. "She'll meet us for dinner."

They ended up at someone's little apartment, a fourth-floor walk-up in Brookline with standing room only. It was late in the afternoon, and the sun was already set, but it was earlier than Caroline expected people to be tossing back shots of flavored vodka and candy-colored schnapps.

She wasn't prepared for this party. It was crowded and noisy. She wasn't braced for it, and she didn't have a plan for what to do. At the lighting designer's insistence, she tried a swig of something that tasted like cinnamon candies, but it was terrible at room temperature; the drink nearly made a precipitous reappearance.

"It's really good for body shots with some lemon and cinnamon sugar," one of the follow spotters told her, lifting the hem of his T-shirt suggestively.

"Urk," Caroline said, waving him off with her palm over her mouth.

She edged away until her back hit the wall. It was cold outside, but the ancient, rusty radiators were running at full blast, and it was humid from the press of so many bodies in the small space. She would have worn something under her long-sleeved black T-shirt if she'd known there was going to be a party. She would have memorized something to sing if she'd realized there was going to be karaoke. She would have come up with something to talk about.

She made her way toward the kitchen, which was the hottest part of the apartment, but which at least offered the prospect of some escape from the closeness of the crowd and the blaring noise of the karaoke machine.

The counter was already cluttered with empty red Solo cups and desiccated lemon wedges, but Caroline was happy for a task she could narrow her focus on while she developed a strategy to handle the rest of the party. She cleared off the breakfast bar. Then she hopped onto the space she'd cleaned, glad to have obtained a seat where nobody could crowd into her.

"This the new props table?" Nathan asked, weaving out of the crowd with a handle of peach schnapps in one large fist. He surveyed Caroline where she sat amid all the cups and bottles.

"Sure, what would you like? Lemon wedge? No-name brandy? Moldovan liqueur?" Caroline asked, gesturing to the bottles and snacks around her. They'd probably make him go blind, but she hadn't been in charge of procurement.

"I'm good, but thank you," he said, hefting the schnapps. He pushed more debris into the sink and laboriously climbed up next to her. "Do you not sing?"

"I don't know any show tunes by heart," Caroline confessed.

"What?" Nathan asked, sounding shocked. "None at all?"

"No, I mean . . . maybe one or two from *Anastasia*?"

"*Anastasia*, of all shows?"

"What's wrong with *Anastasia*?" Caroline demanded, picking up on a note of judgment.

"Nothing! Nothing at all. . . . That's just . . . a choice." He cleared his throat. "How'd you end up here, then? Did you not do theater in college?"

Caroline clenched her jaw. "Not really."

Nathan blinked, blue eyes already a little bloodshot.

"Oh. Well, that's fine, I guess. Trying new things, right?"

"Yeah, that's the idea."

He appeared to struggle for a new line of conversation. Caroline decided to bail him out.

"Are you going to sing?" she asked him.

"Oh, I can act, but I found out in high school that my range is only three notes. Nonconsecutive ones. I might try out for one of the workshop plays next semester, but I'll be backstage again during the spring musical. You?"

"Spring musical? When are auditions?"

"Next week. Are you going to try out?"

"No, of course not," Caroline immediately replied.

She'd taken this gig only because of the deal with Adrian. But she pursed her lips, musing that Adrian might not agree to seeing her every night, and she'd want something else to do with her free time if he didn't.

"But I might ask to carry stuff on a volunteer basis again, if you think that'll be okay?" Caroline hedged.

"Fine by me," Nathan said. "It's been great working with you."

Caroline brightened. "Really?"

"Yeah, for sure. You've been a big help."

Caroline was staring at the ceiling, reviewing what she might have tangibly added to the production, when she realized Nathan was leaning in to kiss her. She only had enough time to pull her head back like a turtle to avoid it, and she banged the back of her head against the kitchen cabinet in the process.

The instinctive movement happened only because Caroline had never once considered kissing him, but she was glad she dodged as soon as she had a second to process it. As she'd learned the hard way in tennis, hooking up with a popular guy tended to make you *un*popular with the rest of the team.

"Oops," she blurted out, even if *ow* or *oh no* might have been more appropriate or definitive. It confused Nathan, for one.

"Are you okay?" he asked when she rubbed the back of her head.

"Sure, sure, I'm fine," she said, forcing a smile over the immediate chasm of awkwardness between them.

Nathan tilted his head in confusion. "Did you want to . . . ?"

"Uh, no," Caroline said, presuming that he meant the kissing. "Thank you. I'm good."

His face fell. "Right," he said.

He stared at her. Caroline tilted her head to look at the ceiling again, her heart rate picking up as she flailed for what she was supposed to do next. She didn't know. She hadn't thought about it. She didn't have a plan for this.

"Um, I'm going to go check on the bottles on the balcony," Nathan finally said.

He flexed his arms to lower himself off the counter.

"You don't have to go," Caroline exclaimed. Her stomach

lurched as she tried to imagine approaching any of the other groups at the party.

"I think I need to take a lap," Nathan said, face stiffening. "I'll catch you later."

He hurried off, soon enveloped by the crowd. Caroline remained on the counter alone. He'd been so nice since she started working with Rima backstage. Was it just because he was interested in her? She couldn't imagine kissing someone she didn't also want to talk to, but she seemed like a decided minority in that approach.

Caroline dumped out a few more abandoned cups in the sink and decided she'd just clean up until someone else came to talk to her. What would Adrian do in this situation? He'd probably just leave if he wasn't enjoying the party. She could just leave and meet everyone at dinner, like Rima. That's what she'd do as soon as she'd filled a trash bag. She opened the cabinets under the sink and rummaged through the debris until she found one.

"Thanks, Caroline," said the assistant stage manager, who lived in the apartment, coming into the kitchen with a big sack of ice. "You didn't have to do that!" Her eyes were squinty though, which tended to happen when people thought Caroline had done something weird. Caroline cringed.

"You know me," she weakly joked. "I see a table and I organize it."

"You can take the girl out of the props department but can't take the props department out of the girl, I guess? Anyway, no rush, but Sophia just said she wanted to talk to you."

Caroline hefted the full bag of bottles and empty cups. The stage manager hadn't spoken to her all week. Maybe she wanted to apologize for leaving her out of the program. "Okay, sure. If I don't see you again before dinner, thanks for hosting."

The other woman smiled through tight lips. "Thanks for coming."

ADRIAN EXPECTED THE APARTMENT TO BE EMPTY WHEN HE got back, because Tom normally worked Sunday nights, but his roommate was crashed out on the couch, *Drag Race* reruns blaring on the television. Empty bottles and dirty cups were stacked on the kitchen table and counter.

"What's going on?" Adrian warily asked as he hung his coat on the hook by the door.

Tom didn't verbally respond but instead lifted a wrinkled sheet of paper aloft over the back of the couch.

Adrian plucked it from his hand. It was addressed to the staff at the restaurant and informed them that the establishment was closing effective immediately. Final paychecks would be mailed, someone had added in ballpoint pen.

"Shit," Adrian said.

"Yeah," Tom said, voice blurry with drink. "That about covers it. I had some of the guys over to celebrate unemployment."

Adrian leaned against the rolled arm of the couch, because Tom's legs were taking up all the other space. "What are you going to do?"

"I'm going to some auditions in New York this week. If anything takes, I might try to couch surf over there."

"This week?" Adrian demanded, eyebrows shooting up.

"Well, yeah. I can't make rent next month. Couch surfing there is as reasonable as couch surfing here, right?"

"Shit," Adrian said again.

"There's still that St-Germain left in the cabinet," Tom helpfully informed him.

Adrian rubbed a palm over his face. He could sleep in his studio, he supposed. And shower at the gym. He was paid up through the end of the year there, and he had the studio space through May. He got up, considered the St-Germain, and decided he was still better than that. He returned to the couch. Tom pulled his legs back and made room for him.

"Sorry," Tom said when Adrian collapsed into the seat next to his roommate.

"Not your fault."

"Any luck with your old gallery?"

Adrian wordlessly shook his head.

Tom sighed. "Sorry," he said again. "Do you think you'll move in with Caroline?"

Adrian made an angry noise of rejection. "I've been dating her for *four days*. No."

"Pretty sure you've been dating her for, like, two months, but whatever. What are you going to do?"

"Get a job. Sleep in my studio. Maybe see if Tamsyn is looking for a roommate now that she's single."

"You'd rather do that than stay with Caroline? You know she'd let you."

"What if she only let me because I have nowhere to go?"

"Nora kicked you out anyway."

"Caroline's not Nora. I would worry Caroline didn't actually want me there."

"That sounds like a *you* problem, not a *her* problem."

Adrian put his hands in the air. "Sometimes things are just terrible. Sometimes there is no good solution."

Tom laughed scornfully. "And sometimes they're not! Are we not going to talk about that five-thousand-dollar check that's been sitting on the kitchen counter for weeks? I put it in the junk drawer, by the way."

Adrian glared at him. "I can't take Caroline's money. We're together now."

"You took Nora's money for years."

"And look how that turned out."

"It turned out that way because you wouldn't let her fuck around. She wanted to marry you! If you'd wanted to marry her, she'd be buying me a ticket to your obnoxious destination wedding in St. Barts right now."

"Didn't you tell me to stop letting Caroline pay me?" Adrian asked testily.

"I just wanted you to tell her you're her boyfriend. You have to work this money shit out *with* her."

"Don't worry," Adrian said, standing up to go take inventory of the food on hand. "I'll handle this. There's no reason I can't have a job during the day while I keep looking for another gallery. That's what I should have done already."

He'd begin a new series. Find some new inspiration. The winter landscape of New England made a good starting point, and he bet Caroline hadn't left the city much, if at all. If she really didn't have plans over winter break, there were places they could visit within a quick train ride's distance. It wasn't going to look much like things had been or would have been if he'd signed up with Mike, but he'd enjoyed the city during his college years on very little spending money. Maybe he could juggle a relationship, painting, a job, and the gallery search. He'd have to.

Tom snorted again. "Fine, your funeral."

Adrian's phone buzzed in his pocket. He fished it out and saw Caroline's selfie illuminating the screen.

He nearly let it go to voice mail. He was in no shape to be appropriately enthusiastic about the discussion she'd proposed, and he wanted to be happy when he talked with her about it—because he *was* happy about it; it was the single, solitary thing in his life he felt happy about at the moment—not reeling from the disintegration of his career.

But he forced himself to answer, readying excuses for why he couldn't see her until the next day.

The rough, wobbly quality of her voice had him ducking into his room instead.

"Hi," she said, with an audible sniffle. "I know I said tonight, but, um. Something came up."

"That's fine," Adrian said gently, waiting for relief to come. It didn't. "Are you home?"

"Yeah. Well, actually, I'm somewhere in Brookline, about to go home, but it looks like all the rideshare services have hour waits right now."

"The snow," Adrian said inanely.

"Yeah, the snow."

She sniffled again. Adrian's hand tightened on the phone.

"Do you know where Washington Square is?" he asked. "You can take the light rail to Park Street—"

"Is that the T? How do I get on?"

"The Green Line is the light rail. Take it toward Lechmere—"

Caroline swallowed audibly. "You're going to have to explain this to me like I'm from Mars," she said, voice tight with unhappiness. "I don't have . . . is it a card? An app? How do I pay?"

Adrian looked out the window. The sun had set, and the snow had really started to come down.

"Where are you, exactly?" Adrian asked. "I'll come get you."

There was a brief pause, and she read him an address.

Adrian walked back through the living room, ignoring Tom's quizzical look as he grabbed his jacket and started down the stairs two at a time.

"Are you safe where you are?" he asked, feet skidding a little on the new powder. "I'll be about twenty minutes."

"Yeah, I'm fine. I'm just on the steps outside someone's apartment. It's fine."

Adrian walked faster. When he reached a section of sidewalk that had been shoveled already, he ran. Good thing he'd been hitting the gym more often with all the painting he wasn't doing.

When he reached the address, he felt a surge of panic when he couldn't immediately find Caroline. It was dark, the nearest streetlight several big houses down the street. Then he saw her pink coat. She was huddled on the side of the stairs, barely sheltered from the drifting snow with her hood pulled up over her head and her hands tucked into her sleeves.

She didn't stand up when he jogged the last couple of steps on the approach, just looked up to check that it was him standing in front of her, then immediately ducked her head to wipe at her face.

When she began to struggle to her feet, Adrian sank down next to her and wrapped an arm around her shoulders. It was a ten-minute walk to the station, and he wanted to find out what had happened before they left.

She shook under his arm. He didn't think it was from the cold, but he unbuttoned his wool overcoat and wrapped the edge of the lapel around her to put another layer between her and the snow.

"Sweetheart, what's wrong?" he asked as softly as he was able to.

She pawed at her face with her palm. "Nothing. It's

really, really stupid. I'm sorry you had to come out to get me in the snow just because I'm too dumb to figure out public transportation on my own."

"You're not dumb, and I'm sure it's not stupid."

"It's just girl drama. You'll think it's—"

"Caroline. You can tell me."

She took a deep breath. "I just thought I was going to the crew dinner after this, and I'm not, actually. That's all it is."

"What was the problem with the dinner?"

"Nothing, really. The stage manager told me that the crew dinner was for crew, but you know, since I'm not in the arts and sciences program, I'm not crew. So they didn't have the budget for me."

"She said it was the budget?"

"Yeah. I said I could pay for my own dinner, you know, but she said that wasn't appropriate when nobody else would be . . ." Caroline gave a small choked laugh. "Okay, so that's just an excuse, right? She just said that because she didn't want me to go. And so now I'm snotting on this girl's front porch just because I didn't go to a dinner."

Adrian roughly rubbed Caroline's shoulder, wishing he could curse out someone he'd never met.

"Of course you wanted to go. You worked with these people for weeks."

Caroline's shoulders convulsed. "See, it's not even that I wanted to go so bad. I'm not good with big groups, or even, I guess, people at all. But I wanted them to want me to go with them, isn't that weird?"

"No," he said firmly. "It's not."

She turned her head to wipe her face against his shoulder. "I came all the way to Boston because I was tired of being this person who was just pretty good at tennis. You know? That's all there was to me. I told my grandmother I wanted to move away, so she changed her will to leave everything to me. My family didn't want me to take her money and move away when she died, but I did it anyway. This was supposed to change my life, but I'm the same person I was back home." She covered her face with her palms. "What's wrong with me?"

Adrian clutched her tighter against him. "Nothing," he said. "Nothing is wrong with you. Not a thing."

Caroline cried harder. "I thought it was that I was boring. And I thought I could fix that. I'd never been anywhere or done anything except tennis, so I was trying to spend more time with people, try new things, but that isn't going to help, is it? I'm the problem."

"No," Adrian said as firmly as he could. "You're not boring at all. You're funny and smart and brave, and the problem is with anyone who can't see that."

She shook her head in rejection.

"Caroline, sweetheart," he insisted, pulling away so that she had space to look at him.

She blinked at him, tears freezing on her eyelashes.

"I've met thousands of people, all over the world, people who made incredible art, people who've lived amazing lives. I've never met anyone like you. You don't need to change. Everyone else should."

He was desperate to wipe the expression of miserable resignation off her face.

"*I* love you," he said, leaning on the first word. When it came out of his mouth, it sounded too casual—like a reassurance, not a promise. So he repeated it. Then one more time, because he meant it.

Caroline didn't say anything. She didn't look at him either. Her next move, after a few stiff, silent seconds, was to duck her chin into her chest and scrunch her eyes tightly closed. He could feel her body vibrating with tension and hear the loud rasp of her breathing.

Well, what did he expect to get for dropping his unwise declaration in the middle of her unrelated emotional turmoil? He hadn't planned to tell her that day. It was probably not a good idea to tell her that at all before taking her temperature on his impending retail-worker lifestyle, but he'd wanted her to know there was one person, at least, who thought she was *perfect*.

Thinking he'd misstepped, he began to scoot away. But Caroline seized his lapel to keep him close and turned her face to press it against the bare skin of his throat. Her breath was hot and humid against his neck as she inhaled raggedly, but the tip of her nose was cold. Her hands flexed where she clutched the edge of his coat.

"Okay," she said without lifting her head. Her voice was thick and halting. "Okay. That's good."

Adrian choked on a laugh, not sure if he was about to cry too. "Good? Just good? You're going to break my heart, aren't you?"

Caroline swallowed audibly and wiped at her face with the insides of her wrists. She didn't meet his eyes, but she tilted her chin up to kiss him, lips pressed against his own as though she intended to keep them there for a long time. She hadn't said it back. But she hadn't rejected it either.

With his eyes still closed, Adrian tried to brush snow out of her hair, worried that she was only getting colder as they sat there.

"Okay," Caroline mumbled again, mouth against the corner of his own. "I mean, yes. *Thank you*. That's perfect. Will you please take me home?"

"Of course," he said, confused and uncertain of what

she was trying to convey, even though it was cold and snowing and they didn't need to be having this conversation on a stranger's porch. He got to his feet and reached down to pull her up as well.

"No, I didn't say that right," Caroline said more firmly once she was on her feet, seeming to settle with resolve. "What I was asking you . . ." She slid her hands inside his coat, resting them against his chest. Her breathing steadied. She leaned in to kiss him again, this time with more purpose.

He thought it would be brief, but it wasn't. Her lips lingered on his. She held on to him when he tried to move away. Her tongue slowly slid along his own as she nestled into him with unmistakable invitation. She broke the kiss only to lean her face against his jaw.

"I mean, I want you to *take me home*. Please?"

It took him a long aching moment to rule out any other possible meaning to that request. He couldn't think of any. Her thighs were pressed up against his body, stoking the desire he'd damped for weeks. His mind unwillingly began to riffle through all the images he'd composed of her body and put away for never: those long legs wrapped around him, her head tossed back, her lips parted.

Caroline pulled away only inches to give him space to reply, her big, shining sea-glass eyes filling his field of vision at last.

"Are you sure?" Adrian said gently, even as his heart started to pound in his chest and the blood to simmer in his veins. "You've had a day. So have I, actually."

"That's why I'm asking. I thought you'd come over after the play, and we'd talk, and then—I want one single thing to go the way I thought it would. I thought it was going to be a good day today. Please?"

He couldn't even breathe from the wide-eyed, nervous look of anticipation she gave him. He didn't know how he was supposed to make it to her apartment if he couldn't breathe on the way.

They probably ought to talk first, his marginal remaining executive function noted. Their relationship had changed so fast, would change even more in the next few days. And like Tom said, they had a lot to work out. *Shut up*, said his lizard brain. *Stop ruining everything for yourself.*

"All right," Adrian managed to work past his tight and swollen throat. "Anything you want."

Chapter Fifteen

ADRIAN HAD NEVER BEEN INSIDE CAROLINE'S APARTMENT before. The fact didn't occur to him until she unlocked the front door; his mind had been hung up on the fully absorbing prospect of seeing her naked. Like most new builds, the apartment had boring off-white walls, beige wall-to-wall carpeting, and anonymous brown countertops. It was the kind of place where people didn't stay for too long: three rooms on a one-year lease while the inhabitants waited for a transfer to a different city or saved up a down payment for a real home. But Caroline had been hard at work. There were colorful knit throws tossed over the backs of the couch and armchairs. There were ceramic jars shaped like mushrooms cluttering the counters. The entire place smelled like chocolate, a scent Adrian traced to the slightly lopsided torte in an ornate, cut-glass case. And on the walls . . .

Caroline had neatly cut his little oil studies of flowers out of his sketchbooks, pasted them onto thick artisan paper, and had them framed in big grids. Hundreds of them. They covered almost every square foot of the walls, blooming like a garden in the middle of May. It must have cost thousands of dollars; the ornate gold frames looked custom, and there were more than a dozen of them. It was easily the nicest thing anyone had ever said about his art without saying a single word. He sucked in a deep breath, his stuttering heart twisting to the left and right and suddenly too large for his chest.

Caroline slipped off her black ankle boots and thick black cotton socks, leaving both by the wall. Adrian stared at her long narrow feet with their chipped pink polish. He'd never seen her barefoot before either, and the sight felt unexpectedly intimate. He'd spent the entire ride to her apartment telling himself sternly that regardless of what she'd said, he shouldn't presume that anything would happen when he got her home. But looking at her toes curling into the carpet, Adrian couldn't deny he'd spent that time desperately hoping she meant what she'd said.

"Um," she said, gesturing vaguely at her couch. "Would you like to sit down? Or grab a couple of drinks from the fridge? I just need a minute."

"Of course," Adrian said, trying to summon the wisdom of his past self, a person who had struck the appropriate balance between nonchalant and attentive in situations like this. As he had not gone home to a woman's apartment in this decade, the role felt as awkward as new dress shoes.

Caroline vanished into what he marked as her bedroom while Adrian went to investigate the refrigerator. It was crowded with single bottles of a variety of different beverages, both alcoholic and not: everything from high-concept sodas to gritty-looking kombuchas. There was a half-empty bottle of gewürztraminer in front, but Adrian decided that *completely sober* was how he wanted to retrospectively characterize Caroline's decision to sleep with him, if she stuck with it. He found a large can of sparkling water, retrieved two glasses from the cabinet to serve it in, and sat on the couch to vibrate with uncertainty while he awaited Caroline's return. He turned on the television, which was set to a very specific kind of satellite channel devoted to shows about deadly wildlife, then hit mute before a gazelle could meet its grisly end in the jaws of a Nile crocodile.

Five minutes later, when he'd nearly convinced himself that he ought to make an excuse and allow Caroline a graceful way to cut the evening short, she reemerged. She'd changed out of the black jersey outfit she'd worn for her play's matinee and was now wearing the same little yellow knit dress from Tamsyn's opening, the hem short over her long bare legs. She favored him with a small, close-mouthed smile, her hands brushing the fabric down over her hips.

Adrian was often haunted by the ghost of the person he'd been, the last time he was really happy: a twenty-three-year-old art prodigy with a Back Bay loft and a frequently occupied bed. That man was happy to interpret this as a clear message: *Rail me in this sundress, please.*

And oh, Jesus, did he *hope* that was what she was saying, because he felt like he might die, could possibly die in a literal sense if he had to find his way home now that all the blood had rushed south out of his brain. He'd be hit by a MBTA bus in his disarray, covered with snow, and discovered only in the spring thaw.

Caroline sat down next to him on the couch, then immediately twisted to pull her feet underneath her, knees pointed in his direction. She put her hands on her thighs and looked at him expectantly.

"Do you . . . want to watch something?" Adrian croaked, gesturing at the television.

Caroline's blond eyebrows condensed on her forehead.

"Killer snake shows for bad days, right?"

He had to offer her the out, because what possible

reason did she have for propositioning him? He'd been careful, *so* careful not to transgress any of the boundaries she'd set. She had to have no idea of the hours he'd spent guiltily pondering what it would feel like to pin her down and make her gasp his name.

"No." Caroline drawled out the word like a drop of honey. She braced one hand on his shoulder and swung a knee across his lap, coming to straddle him. She settled comfortably on his thighs, tilting her head to the side. "I thought you were going to take me to bed?" Her expression was sweetly concerned: *No take-backs, right?*

Adrian let out the deep breath that had cluttered his chest, releasing some of his anxiety about the situation. Certainty wasn't all he wanted from her—wasn't even half—but it was a start. Her position put her cleavage at his eye level. He leaned in and ran his lower lip along the vee of her collarbone, inhaling the warm scent of her skin.

"All right," he agreed again.

He settled lower on the couch, letting her slide down his legs until her thighs were spread wide against him. Then he tipped his head back so that she could kiss him. Caroline tucked her hair behind her ears and leaned in, bracing her forearms against his chest. Her mouth tasted like toothpaste.

He smiled wide at the evidence of what she'd been doing back in her room, and she felt it.

"What?" she asked from a breath's distance away.

"Nothing," he said, putting his hands on her waist and finally allowing himself freedom to imagine the body beneath her clothes. "Just happy."

She hummed an agreement into his mouth and pressed herself further against him. He kissed her slowly, like he had no thought of anything else in his mind—although of course he did. His tongue stroked leisurely against hers as he savored the softness of her lips. Caroline made an impatient noise and let him feel her teeth against the inside of his lower lip. He grinned wider, keeping his hands chastely settled at her waist.

But then she adjusted her seat to roll her thigh directly over his hardening erection, and he had to give up the game when he groaned directly into her mouth. She yanked at his sweater until he obediently lifted his arms, letting her pull it off and toss it behind the couch.

"Sweet Jesus, how many layers are you wearing?" she complained, eyeing the long-sleeved T-shirt still covering his chest.

He shrugged instead of discussing his heating bill, going after a very important freckle located between her breasts as she attempted to divest him of the other two shirts he had on. Those small triangles of knit fabric that formed the top of her dress had taunted him with the possibility that they might just . . . slip . . . during Tamsyn's show. And now he tested that idea, finding that the straps slid easily down her round, tan shoulders to expose her teardrop-shaped breasts.

Indian yellow. He would have added the smallest dot of Indian yellow with the point of his paintbrush, a nearly imperceptible blush of warmth in the mix of alizarin crimson and titanium white that tinted the tips of her breasts. He wrapped his mouth around a nipple, tightening his fingers on her hips when he pulled hard enough to make her gasp.

Caroline spread her hands on his now-bare chest and looked down as though considering the logistics of the identical move from her position astride him. He didn't intend to give her space to try, turning his head and giving the same treatment to the other side of her body. Her hips bucked against him, more demanding this time. He didn't lift his head, enjoying the small, needy noises that escaped her throat as he teased and licked her breasts.

The buck of her hips grew insistent, and he slid a hand up the outside of her warm round thigh underneath her dress. His intention had been to hold on to her hips and slow things down for a few minutes, but as his hand slid higher and higher, unimpeded by anything like *underwear*, he realized that he was one zipper pull away from fucking Caroline on her living room couch, in full view of a dozen of the world's most dangerous reptiles. From the determined glint in Caroline's eye—and the way she was investigating southern territory after her success in removing articles of clothing at higher latitudes—she was perfectly capable of making that happen without any further effort on his part. He was really not covering himself in glory so far.

"Right," he said firmly, because he could at least do something more exciting than sit there with his mouth on her tits until one or both of them came from some light frottage. "Bedroom."

He slid his hands under her ass like a sling and stood in one rough movement. Caroline squealed and wrapped her legs around his waist but didn't fall, which he worried about after it was already too late to attempt a different move. It was a good thing she was mostly leg. He backed her up toward her bedroom, only slightly distracted by her teeth on his earlobe.

He staggered through the door, managing to drop Caroline on her big floral-print bed and not the floor. It was a good height. The perfect height, in fact, which was surprising if Caroline had picked it out, because he'd assumed she was—

He should have made some critical inquiries before this moment, before Caroline was scooting back to her bedframe—sturdy, that was good, not IKEA crap like the rest of her furniture—and looking up at him like the ten o'clock band had just come onstage early. He crawled onto the bed after her, dodging her grab for his waistband, then carefully propped himself over her, hands pressing her wrists to the mattress.

"Caroline, sweetheart, have you done this before?" he asked, trying not to sound terrified of the prospect that she had not.

Caroline looked up from her attempt to get his pants off, expression only slightly taken aback. "Why, do I suck?"

"*No*, no, not at all. I just, I need to know if—" He struggled for words.

Caroline snorted indelicately. She got her hands free and used her thumbs to stroke twin lines down his stomach. They came to rest in his belt loops with a decisive tug. "I spent four years basically living out of motels with the men's varsity tennis team. *No*, I'm not a virgin."

Adrian could barely absorb the relief of that disclosure under the weight of the most immediate, irrational prejudice he'd ever felt against a group of people—a tennis *team*? He framed her head between his arms and nipped at her lower lip to apologize for having asked, because of course it didn't matter, either way.

But Caroline squirmed out from under him, rolled to the MALM dresser next to her bed, and returned with a bright red condom, the kind of candy-colored freebie dispensed by sexual health groups on the street. Adrian wasn't in a place to be picky about it though; he possessed the same number of condoms in his wallet as firm thoughts on what he'd do next. Caroline clearly had her own plans, though she couldn't have had any longer to think about it than he had. She competently popped the button on his trousers, expression victorious.

It occurred to him that regardless of the number of varsity athletes she'd spent time with over the past four years, Adrian had still brought to bear very little of the finesse she might have expected him to accumulate over a far longer period of time. He probably wasn't impressing her very much. And he wanted to impress her. Very desperately so.

So he stuffed the condom in his pocket, grabbed her thighs, and pulled her back toward the edge of the bed. He shifted the hem of her dress up over her stomach when he had her arranged to his satisfaction.

"Where are you going—" she started.

Adrian just smiled and nipped her hip bone to shush her. If she didn't already know, figuring it out was half the fun. He knelt down in front of her, running the tip of his nose against the soft spread of skin below her navel before turning his attention farther down her body. Caroline propped herself up on her elbows and gave him wide, impressed eyes when he laid his cheek against her inner thigh and gently worked his shoulders between her knees.

"Oh," she said.

"Am I shocking you?" he asked against her skin, pressing his lips against the crease between her hip and soft mound.

Caroline audibly swallowed. "Not shocked. I mean, not offended. Surprised?"

Adrian chuckled, knowing she'd feel his exhale right against her heated intimate flesh. "The men's varsity tennis team doesn't do this?" he couldn't resist asking.

"Well," Caroline said, the quality of her voice slightly

strangled, because Adrian had run his wet lower lip up the entire length of her sex, "I don't know if the rest of them do or don't. Just that one didn't."

Adrian grinned at that, even though he ought to feel very bad for her sake, and got her heels arranged on his shoulder blades. She took a deep breath when he leaned in and ran the flat of his tongue across her. She let it out as her shoulders hit the mattress.

He pressed his advantage, laying an open-mouthed kiss over her clit. Her breath caught in her throat when he did it again. She was sweet and soft under his mouth, and his cock pulsed in near agony where it was compressed in his trousers. He readjusted for some temporary relief, then got his tongue further involved.

"Oh. Oh my God," she said after a few more minutes of very devoted work on his part, her tone revelatory. "You're . . . *really* good at this."

Adrian had privately *believed* that to be true, but it was nice to hear it anyway, and it did a lot to reassure him that he was meeting whatever expectations she had. He redoubled his efforts until Caroline made a feint as though to sit up.

"I mean, I'm ready," she squeaked out, collapsing back after a second when he didn't stop.

He looked up at her along the line of her body. She was already pink and flushed, her thighs trembling a little against his neck. *Close*, he thought.

"Do you want to come?" he asked.

Caroline hesitated. "Yes?" she said, like it was a trick question. He supposed that had not been a priority the last time she'd done this.

He shrugged, making her feet slide down his shoulder blades. "Well, then," he said, and leaned back in. He licked her open and wet, interlacing his fingers across her stomach when she squirmed and panted.

It felt very, very important that she know that he could make her come and that he *would* make her come with just his mouth against her body. He wanted her to know that this was a thing he would do for her whenever she wanted. He didn't want Caroline to think he was only doing this until she let him climb on top of her. Or under her. Or behind her. He wasn't going to be picky where he ended up. He was going to taste her orgasm on his tongue, he was going to kiss that fragile look off her face, and then he was going to count himself a lucky man if she still wanted his cock.

(He really, really hoped he was lucky.)

When she finally went rigid against his face and made a breathless little noise that he couldn't wait to hear directly in his ear, he smiled in triumph.

IT WAS A SHOCK, SOMEHOW, TO HAVE SOME PORTION OF him inside her. Conceptually difficult, even if she knew how things worked. Even if it was only the tip of Adrian's finger. Caroline had her arms looped around his neck, and she was trying to work herself up to doing something exciting and sexy, but the shimmery glow of her orgasm had made her entire body feel floaty. She couldn't do any more than pepper his wet face with loose kisses as one of his beautiful artist's hands stroked gently across her folds. Just that one fingertip dipping inside her and then back out to make a slick circuit of her clit.

God, he was probably going to make her come again. *Twice*, which was a thing she'd heard of but dismissed as fake news, like vaginas that naturally tasted like fruit, or twelve-inch dicks. (Adrian's wasn't twelve inches, thank

Christ. She observed that God had been feeling generous the day he made Adrian, based on the shape she'd rocked against while straddling his lap, but it was going to fit. Probably. Especially if he kept teasing her with just that single, maddening fingertip.)

Some portion of her brain was still amazed that this elegant, sophisticated man had his hand between her legs, had his eyes closed and swollen lower lip exposed as he concentrated on driving her wild. The ragged edge to his breathing—*she* did that. The pink spots on his cheeks. The hard press of him against her hip.

She felt a sudden resolve to make him feel even half as good as she did right now.

"What should I do?" she whispered as he slipped his finger inside her up to the knuckle. She let out an embarrassing whimper, and he hissed in satisfaction.

"Whatever you like."

"I mean . . . for you." She didn't have an extensive repertoire, but Adrian was obviously working off a longer menu that had a lot of very gourmet sex on it, and he might have some good ideas. More good ideas.

"You are doing perfectly," he said, which wasn't an answer.

He curled his finger, catching her gasp with his mouth. Caroline twisted her face into the smooth, shaving-cream-smelling side of his neck and bit him lightly on his Adam's apple, trying to gather her initiative. She wriggled free and got her dress all the way off, taking a moment to appreciate Adrian in his rumpled, shirtless glory. He already looked undone, with his dark copper hair mussed and his lips full and glossy. His eyes were dark and intent as he reached to pull her back to him.

She gave him a beseeching, impatient look, and he at

last began to unzip his trousers and pull himself free, still moving with less haste than she thought the situation deserved. She wanted him inside her right now. Ten minutes ago. No, two months ago. *Immediately*, in any event.

He held the condom in one hand and wrapped the other around the base of his cock, looking down at her with consideration that she could feel pressed against her bare skin.

"How do you want me?" Caroline asked, her voice catching in her dry throat.

He took a deep breath, like a man preparing to dive off a cliff. "Every way. Every single way."

She could have objected to that too, but she couldn't help the wide, silly grin that spread across her face. Yeah, every single way sounded good to her too. She opened her arms to him, and he bent over her after rolling on her ridiculous condom.

"We'll just start like this," he said, murmuring low into her ear as he braced his hand next to her head. "And you'll just hold on tight to me, sweetheart. As tight as you can. And then we'll do everything else."

"Okay." She kissed him again on his swollen mouth, hands cupped around his face. "Now?"

"Now," Adrian agreed against her lips.

She welcomed him with parted thighs and lips spread in a small, round O. He pressed his cock down to slowly sink inside her.

It had been so long since anything had been exactly what she'd expected. Since anything had gone exactly *right*. But the slow, effortless slide of his body into hers was everything she'd wanted. It was perfectly right. He tangled his hands in hers, and she felt everything else fly away, out of sight.

Chapter Sixteen

WHEN ADRIAN PULLED ON HIS PANTS AND STAGGERED OFF to the bathroom, Caroline decided that food was what they needed next. She had not eaten dinner, after all. Adrian had probably heard her stomach rumbling from close to the source.

There wasn't much in the way of leftovers, and she was hardly going to serve the first man she'd ever brought home to her own apartment a frozen microwave meal. Caroline glared at her pantry and closed its door. Then she grabbed a fistful of delivery menus off the fridge with one hand and her chocolate cake with the other.

When Adrian reemerged, still looking dazed, he caught her seated on the bed with her first forkful of cake halfway to her lips.

"I didn't have dinner," she said guiltily. "And I'll have to wash the sheets anyway, so . . ."

She wondered whether she ought to have put on some clothes, since she was still naked with the cake dish in her lap. She had a sudden image of herself in a frilly satin robe— what did people wear after sex, anyway, if they didn't have to put on clothes and go back to a motel room without waking up their teammates? Dinner, postcoital attire, underwear suitable for third-party review: these were among the sexual logistics she had not yet optimized.

Adrian didn't say anything but climbed into bed next to her, propping himself up on one elbow. He filched one of the decorative pecans from the top of the cake, then went back in with a finger for the puff of chocolate pastry cream the nut had rested on.

"You made this?" he asked, making a move to steal a second pecan before Caroline passed him a fork of his own.

"Well, sort of. I messed it up. The ganache was supposed to be shiny, but I don't think I tempered the chocolate right."

Adrian took an obnoxiously large bite, leaving chocolate icing smeared around his lips.

"I think it's perfect," he said. He leaned in and pressed a sucking kiss to the little wrinkle in her stomach where she was curled around the cake stand. "Delicious."

Caroline giggled as he licked off the chocolate crumbs he'd just left on her body.

"Best thing I've ever tasted."

She started to cackle.

He tossed one arm around her waist, and Caroline had to hurriedly slide the cake onto the nightstand to avoid knocking it on the floor. He pressed kisses to her stomach, the valley between her breasts, her collarbones, until he was holding himself over her again, cradled between her thighs. He smiled beneficently down at her, and his unusually sunny expression felt like daylight on bare shoulders.

Her stomach chose that moment to make another loud demand for food.

Adrian laughed, the movement shaking her where their bare chests were pressed together.

"I see where your priorities are," he teased her.

"I thought we could order something. Though delivery will probably take, um, *a while*, in this weather," Caroline said hopefully. "So, you know, we could order now and still have . . . time."

He smirked at her. "Is that a compliment? Or a request?"

She waggled her eyebrows suggestively, making him laugh again. He paused, holding himself above her on locked arms. His dusty-blue eyes were soft and lingering as he gazed down at her.

"What?" she asked.

"You're just the most beautiful woman I've ever seen," he easily replied.

Caroline squirmed and blushed. She didn't know how to respond to that, just like she hadn't known how to respond to him saying—what he'd said. Earlier. Out in the snow. She didn't know if she was supposed to say it back or just wink and nod or thank him, maybe? She supposed it was her prerogative to pretend that Adrian had actually picked her out of all the women in the world to be with and that he meant what he was saying.

Because she liked to hear it. She liked to *feel* it. It was everything she'd wanted to experience while watching the symphony or gazing at the most important new contemporary art. It was transporting—no, transformative. Lying there under his rapt regard, she was closer than she'd ever been to the person she had wanted to be when she left Templeton. It felt worth it, even if nothing else was working out as planned.

Caroline looped her arms around the back of Adrian's neck and pulled him down to her again, enjoying the solid anchor of his weight on her. He nibbled along her jaw, lips so warm they felt scorching against her face. Thoughts of dinner became less pressing as he kissed her, but her mind inevitably turned to other procurement failures on her part. She hadn't had time to go to the grocery store since Thursday because of all the performances. So she was not only out of real food but *also* out of condoms. She had only had the one that came in the welcome gift at the health insurance fair during her first week in Boston.

Well, there was a reasonable drop-in product she could substitute in this circumstance. She reached down to cup him through his jeans, and he automatically pressed his stiffening cock against her palm. Caroline grinned and began shifting down in the bed.

Adrian rolled to his side, making a half-hearted grab for her as she scooted to the level of his chest.

"I thought you wanted to order dinner?"

"I am rescheduling dinner," Caroline said, hands resting against his bare skin. Just to make herself clear, she wiggled farther down and laid the tip of her nose directly against the short line of fuzz below his navel.

Adrian sighed and tugged on a piece of her hair. "Come back up here. You should be on top next time. I want to look at you."

Caroline couldn't tell if he was being sincere or noble. Either way, it was sweet. Unfortunately, *on top* was one of those positions she'd wanted to research first, because she wasn't clear on what she was supposed to do, exactly. Caroline would probably default to waving her arms like Megan Rapinoe after a soccer goal if she didn't look up some technique videos in incognito mode first.

"I'm out of condoms," she said, putting a hand on his zipper.

That got a more determined exhale from him, and he began to sit up.

"Right. Well, how about I go out and pick up dinner, and I'll also buy more condoms?"

Caroline wrinkled her nose at him, looping a finger through his belt loop. She didn't want him to get out of her bed.

"My plan still works. Consider it a bonus," she said. "Or a fringe benefit." She pushed her hair behind her ears in a significant way as she propped her chin on his denim-clad thigh. "You've been doing all the work so far."

"Oh, I expect to do very little beyond stare at your breasts and count my blessings," he said lightly, but she could tell he was tempted by her offer.

Caroline pressed her offer, stroking him lightly through the thick material of his trousers. "We can do the up-top thing on Tuesday," she promised.

Adrian snorted even as he sucked in his stomach to give her better access to the button on his fly.

"Tuesday? I was already planning on round three when we wake up tomorrow, maybe round four in the shower. . . ."

Caroline guessed that meant he was staying over, which she hadn't been sure about. That would be lovely. Since she didn't have class until eleven on Mondays, Sunday nights would work through the end of the semester. And they had two days before Thanksgiving, when her parents arrived, if Adrian's schedule was clear too.

"Okay, that works for me," she said brightly.

Something about her phrasing seemed to catch his attention. Adrian tilted his head, expression tightening as his eyes flicked around her face. His lower lip twitched as he had a thought, caught it, and then had it again. "Did you say Tuesday . . . you meant Tuesday like the schedule we used to have?"

Caroline froze as his eyes narrowed and he shifted away to withdraw to the edge of the bed.

"I mean—it doesn't have to be Tuesday," Caroline said, feeling the chill in the air even if she couldn't identify its source. "It could be whatever day you wanted."

A flash of darkness crossed Adrian's face, condensing in a small, puzzled frown. Thoughts raced through his eyes. Unhappy ones.

"Am I on the clock right now?" Adrian demanded. "Is that what you think?"

Caroline sat up, trying to understand where she'd gone awry. She'd never kept track of his hours, exactly, because they never got close to forty hours a week, and he made a lot more than the minimum wage, however it was allocated. Her face must have been enough of an answer for his question though, because he scoffed and sprang up as though he needed to put feet of distance between them.

He turned away, palm swiping across the back of his neck in agitation. When he looked at her again, his eyes blazed with hurt.

"Christ, you really do think I'm a hooker, don't you?" he snapped.

"No!" Caroline protested. "No, I don't think that. I'm sorry I ever said that." She wished she'd never called him a name, because it was pejorative, mean, and she didn't think he'd done anything wrong at all. How could she look down on anyone for selling what she was buying?

She knew exactly why he'd created a profile on the sugar-baby site in the first place: it was an economically rational decision. She didn't judge him for that, even if she was acutely aware that he did.

Adrian gritted his jaw. "But you thought everything

was going to go on just like it had when we first met, except I was also going to fuck you sometimes?"

Caroline had pulled her knees up to her chest in unconscious defense, fists propped rigidly against the mattress. She still didn't know what she'd done wrong.

Adrian never swore at her. He never shouted. He had to be *very* angry.

"I thought—I thought you were going to tell me what you needed. That if you wanted me to act differently, you'd tell me," she said, wishing her voice didn't sound so high and reedy. Her sinuses burned like she'd just taken a tennis ball to the middle of the face. "I don't know—I didn't mean—"

Adrian blinked at the tone of her voice, expression softening. The tight muscles of his jaw worked. He exhaled and sat down heavily on the bed, making the mattress bounce beneath her. He put a palm on her bare shin even as he looked away and over to the wall where she'd hung one of his still lifes.

"I'm sorry I yelled," he said slowly. "This is my fault for assuming I was clear. I wanted—no, I *want* to be in a relationship with you. A real one."

"What does that mean?" Caroline asked, still confused.

Adrian took a deep breath, apparently still angry despite visible efforts to calm himself down. "It means we don't have a schedule anymore. It means you're not *paying me* for this. God, Caroline, you shouldn't ever pay for this."

That ignored the practical history of Caroline, in fact, *having* to pay for it, as nobody had previously expressed any willingness to be her boyfriend for free. Nevertheless, there was a bigger issue immediately apparent. If she wasn't paying him, who was?

"Did you sign with a gallery?"

Adrian winced. "No."

"Then are you going to the thing in Miami? Because my QuickBooks doesn't balance, which means you still haven't deposited my check, and even if you go, you don't really know—"

"No, Caroline, no." His tone didn't brook any dispute, but Caroline didn't see how anything could possibly be settled.

She pressed her lips together. "Are you going to start seeing someone else, then? Because I don't think I'd be okay with that . . . like, I know you'd be safe and everything, but . . ." Her empty stomach was forming a small, dense sphere that weighed her down. Her day had been so long, and she hadn't eaten since that morning, and hadn't she cried already? There ought to be a rule that nothing could happen to her more than once a day that would make her cry.

"I wouldn't expect you to be okay with me seeing someone else."

Adrian stood up and began to pace. He put a hand on the back of his head, knuckles white as he struggled for words.

"I'm . . . Here. Listen. I wish I had more of this figured out, but I'm going to find some kind of job. Any job. Probably retail at first, but I'll keep looking for a gallery that will take me. All right? Can you just bear with me for a while?"

"You'd rather do that than just deposit the check? That doesn't make any sense! When are you even going to have time to paint?"

Adrian gave her a stern look, as if she were a child protesting at bedtime. "I can't keep taking the money your grandmother left you for tuition. You know that's not what she would have wanted for you."

Caroline clenched her jaw. "That's not true. She wanted me to have a big life, to do everything I wanted, even if I didn't know what I wanted yet. All I needed to move away and go to school was the car."

If it had just been about school, she could have given the money to her father like he'd demanded.

Adrian came over and dropped a hand on top of hers as though to comfort her, but he didn't follow her point. Caroline made a difficult effort to look him in the face.

"I'm supposed to be doing *more*," she insisted. "Just like you are!"

Adrian looked at the ceiling.

"What would you say to one of your friends if she was dating some older, unemployed failure of a man and letting him sponge off her?"

"You're not a failure," Caroline immediately insisted. "But I wouldn't care, if he made her happy." And she didn't have any friends, anyway. She didn't know why they were dealing with hypotheticals rather than the very real financial problems that were standing between Adrian and what he wanted to be doing with his life.

She'd lived through this moment, where someone handed her money she hadn't asked for or earned. Her cheeks burned as she realized that Adrian probably wouldn't have taken it. Did he think she'd done the wrong thing?

They glared at each other in a sullen standoff.

"I could give you a loan," Caroline said. "Or—or contribute equity. To your business."

"No, Caroline! I don't know how many ways I can say

that. I don't want you worrying about me. I have a completely flexible schedule, and I can work forty hours on my feet. I'll just get a job waiting tables or making coffee."

"Have you ever had one of those jobs? They suck! I don't think you understand how much they suck. You have to stand up and smile for hours and hours, and at the end of the day, your feet hurt and you smell like french fries, and they still don't pay very much money at all, and . . . and I don't understand why you would take a job like that when you don't have to." She bet he hadn't even put together a budget. Could he even pay his rent on minimum wage? She bet he couldn't.

Adrian was staring at the floor. "I know. But, Caroline, I don't know what else to do. I love you. I want to be with you. This is how I can make it work."

"I don't understand how l-loving me means everything has to change." The floor was falling out from underneath her. It had been so good with him for the past few weeks. The best part of her life in Boston—the only part that had been even a little bit like what she'd hoped for. And hadn't he liked it too?

"Not everything. Not forever," he tried to convince her. "I need some time. Tom's probably moving to New York. I need to find a new place to live and a job. But other than that, I can be with you as much as you want—"

"Would you stay here, then?" Caroline promptly asked, gesturing at her room. "If you don't have a new apartment yet?"

Adrian scrubbed both hands across his face. "No, at least—not right now. I'll think about it. I'm not saying never."

"Would you—will you still come with me to Europe?" Caroline's chest felt like a glass bottle about to shatter. The thought might be selfish of her to voice, but she'd been looking forward to it so much, and she had already drafted the itinerary, and she'd ordered a book about the history of the *David*. . . .

"I can't, sweetheart," Adrian said, shoulders sinking. "Even if I weren't taking your money for that too, I won't have vacation time yet with any job I find."

Caroline stared at her hands where they were clasped white-knuckled across her knees. All of the happiness of ten minutes before had trickled out of her, and she felt sodden and soggy with disappointment. "And it's just . . . all of this is just because of me."

"It's *for* you. I don't want you ever to think I'm only with you for your money," he argued.

Her hands fluttered as her control frayed. "That's how we met! You can't change how we met. You know it doesn't bother me. Really, you're just saying that it bothers *you*."

Caroline could live with knowing that he'd started dating her because he was broke and out of options. She didn't think she could live with having taken any options away from him.

Adrian swallowed hard, trying to catch her eyes even as she ducked her chin to her chest to avoid it. "Caroline, I love you," he said as though that were some magical incantation that would fix everything else. That could substitute for everything else he'd ever wanted or she'd ever wanted.

She didn't want to be on the spot. She wanted to run away and think about it. She wanted to look at it on a calendar and a spreadsheet and a cash flow forecast until she felt the least bit of confidence and control over the outcome. She didn't have that opportunity though, because Adrian was waiting for her to agree to it.

"No. I don't want to. I don't want to do this," she said as evenly as she could.

"Do . . . do what?"

"I don't agree. And I can't—I can't talk about it right now. Please go," she sputtered, because her heart hurt too, and she wanted to cry and fall apart, and she *couldn't* while he was still there.

His mouth opened and closed. His cheeks reddened, but his lips paled. "Just because I won't take your money?"

"Because I think you're going to be miserable," she gritted out. "I think you're going to hate making coffee when you really want to paint. I think you're going to hate it if you never get to go to the symphony or the theater or your friends' openings because you're too tired from working a double or you can't afford to buy your own ticket. I"—Caroline gulped—"I think you're going to end up hating me too, if I'm the reason for it."

He didn't really love her if he wouldn't accept any of the things he wanted just because they came from her. And he didn't know her at all if he thought she'd ever regret doing something to make him happy.

Adrian stared at her in horror, but she could tell there was at least some part of him that she'd convinced, because he loved to argue, and he wasn't arguing back anymore.

Caroline brushed her knuckles across her cheekbones, trying to dash away tears without completely losing it. She had to be the one to say it. She couldn't jump out a window this time; she was naked and in her own bedroom. "Please just go."

Chapter Seventeen

CAROLINE WINCED WHEN HER FATHER ORDERED HIS STEAK well-done, with a side of ketchup. Their server was too skilled to so much as blink—in fact, she'd probably pegged Caroline's dad for a charred-steak-and-ketchup kind of a guy when he stomped over to her table. Nevertheless, Caroline mentally apologized to the cow that had worked hard for its whole life to become a good steak only to be consumed as gritty carbon and toddler sauce.

She wasn't sure whether it was useless yearning or spite that made her select the restaurant Adrian had planned for their first date, but neither was very productive of a nice dinner with her parents. She had probably made a mistake in picking this restaurant either way; the menu was heavy on seafood, and moules and langoustines were as foreign to her parents as ancient Greek. Her father had already complained about the prices and the menu options. She should have just taken them to the Olive Garden out on I-90, even though she was paying and he'd ordered steak with french fries instead of anything exotic.

She supposed she'd had some inchoate hope of impressing her parents with the restaurant choice. Her father didn't look impressed: he had his arms crossed on his broad chest, eyes narrowed amid his sunburned features as he surveyed the black-and-white photographs of Paris adorning the wall over their table.

Caroline had inherited her height and coloring from him, along with her athletic abilities. Raymond Sedlacek was a big, loud man, used to getting his way on and off the court. Caroline had always thought she'd gotten most of her personality from her mother, but then again, Nancy Sedlacek had never done a shocking thing in her life. Caroline might be more like her father than she'd thought.

"What are you going to order, sweetie?" her mother whispered to her as her father finished instructing their server on how to burn his meat.

"Sole meunière," Caroline told her.

"What's that?" her father demanded, overhearing them.

"Fish."

He sniffed disdainfully.

Caroline's big breakthrough on fish had come when she realized that, like vegetables, fish were edible if doused in butter and garlic before she put them in her mouth. She hadn't informed Adrian of that important scientific discovery yet, and now she didn't know if she ever would.

She was still thinking in terms of *yet*, despite no particular reason to think she'd ever speak to him again. She hadn't heard from him at all. Not the next day, not on Thanksgiving, not since her parents had arrived. It had been almost a week.

Not that she would have wanted him to meet her parents. She was grimly amused as she imagined him there at dinner: watching as Caroline's father ruined his steak and Caroline butchered the pronunciation of her fish, ordering escargot or something that would appall the rest of the table. *Yes, snails. They're excellent here. No, you probably wouldn't like them.*

Even so, when her mother had asked if she was still dating the man she'd met online, Caroline said "Sort of," which was sort of true. *Adrian* hadn't said anything definitive, after all. And maybe if Caroline rang him up and said, "Hey, I've thought about it, and it probably wouldn't be so bad for *me* if we saw each other after your shifts at TGI Fridays," he'd come back to her apartment, and they'd pretend like he wasn't trying to ruin his life on her account— while it lasted.

The inevitable failure of their relationship was what had stopped her, every time her hand inched for her phone. Because if she felt this wretched now, when she was reasonably certain she had done the right thing, how bad would she feel when it all blew up in a few months, if she hadn't?

"Is he a student too?" Caroline's mother followed up.

"No, he graduated a while ago," Caroline said.

"What's he do, then?" her father asked.

"He's a painter," Caroline said. Residual loyalty had her add, "He owns his own business."

Her father grunted, but with less judgment than he'd shown most of the other features of Caroline's life. He was probably imagining that Adrian painted houses, not portraits, but he'd approve of Caroline taking up with someone in a trade, especially a portable one. Her parents still thought she was coming home to Templeton at some point, preferably sooner rather than later. Caroline was closer to that than she'd been since she'd decided she was keeping her grandmother's money, all of it, since climbing out the bathroom window to escape her father's insistence that she sign the money back over to him and her uncle. But it was none of their money—it had been Gam's, and what Gam wanted should have meant something, shouldn't it?

Caroline hadn't thought it was right, that she would get all the money. But she also hadn't thought it was right that she would get none of it. Like everything else, she'd explained her plans poorly, and her family still didn't believe that Caroline would split the money with them as soon as she did what Gam had told her to do: go live a big life. And she was *trying*. She just wasn't succeeding yet.

Her apartment, her school, her recreational activities: none of these had passed muster under review. Her father wasted no opportunity to point out that she could have had a bigger apartment for half the price down in Texas. Her mother quietly mentioned that they'd missed her at her niece's birthday party. Her father mused that there wasn't a single employer in Templeton who cared if she finished her MBA. They were both very sadly unsurprised that when they asked if there was anyone she wanted to join them for dinner, she admitted that there was not.

It all had a subtext to it: *Account for yourself, Caroline.*

If her life were a ledger, she would credit all the money she'd spent on tuition, rent, and entertainment expense. What had she gained in exchange? Sitting there with her parents, she was hard-pressed to show any personal benefit. She did not have any of the assets she'd hoped to acquire. No boyfriend, no social life. No job offer. No veneer of sophistication or even normalcy.

"Do you think you'll make it home over winter break?" her mother asked once their lunches had arrived.

Caroline busied herself with deboning her fish as she considered the answer. Her gut reaction had always been, no, she wasn't going home, not now, not ever again. But how could she justify that, even to herself? What else was she going to do over the three-week break? Being alone over Thanksgiving had been hard enough. She'd cooked a turkey just to have something to do, but the smallest turkey she could buy was seven pounds, and even that was too much turkey for one person to consume over the relevant depreciation period. She'd texted Tom that night to see if he wanted some leftovers, but he'd written back to say that he was in New York meeting prospective room-mates. Caroline had spent way too much time trying to decode the number of emojis and exclamation points on his brief reply, ultimately deciding that he hadn't spoken to Adrian either. She didn't know where Adrian had spent Thanksgiving if Tom still assumed he was with her.

"I probably will," Caroline slowly said, and both her parents nodded and relaxed.

"That's great, honey," said her mother. "I haven't moved anything in your room."

Caroline gave her a bland smile and pictured the Holi-day Inn two miles from her house, where she'd lived for three weeks after the last time she saw her father. That would probably be safest. She didn't put it past her uncle to ambush her before she'd had her coffee and make an-other stab at convincing her to sign away Gam's money.

"How's your tennis game?" her father asked with a tone that suggested that they'd finally turned to serious questions.

"I haven't played much."

"Well, you still look like you're in decent shape," her father said, even though he couldn't possibly tell from the sweatshirt and joggers Caroline was wearing.

"The student gym is pretty good."

"I'd bet, for what they're charging for tuition."

"Yeah. You know. Indoor pool and everything."

Her father huffed dismissively. "Your coach keeps ask-ing about you."

Caroline scowled, because she hadn't changed her number, and he could have called her instead.

Raymond Sedlacek sliced the rest of his steak into small, brittle cubes and meditatively dunked one in his cup of ketchup. "He wondered if you might still think about going pro."

Caroline snorted. She'd barely touched a racket in six months.

"No, really," her father said. "You're still young enough. You just need access to some higher-level coaching. Your coach said he could give me some names, even up here."

Caroline almost replied that she didn't have enough time with classes, but that would have been a lie. Every minute she wasn't in class, she could have been playing tennis. It was no more or less productive than what she had been doing.

So she just gnawed on the side of her cheek and gave a noncommittal answer. Maybe she would feel better if she were playing tennis. At least she was pretty good at tennis.

Her father took that as a yes. "We can talk with him while you're home on break."

"Okay."

"You know, he's actually the one who told me about the old tennis center down off FM 8439 being up for sale," her father said with studied casualness.

"Yeah?" Caroline said without much interest. She'd practiced there for a few years in middle school while the high school's courts were under renovation.

"Yup. Your uncle and I went over to look at it a couple of months ago. They still haven't found a buyer."

"I see," Caroline said, even though she didn't.

"He thinks the bank's probably in a hurry to sell. It would probably drop the price a fair bit for a cash deal."

Caroline suddenly had the first inkling of where things were going.

"What?" she asked, sitting up further. "You're thinking of buying the tennis center?"

Her father shifted in the wooden bistro chair. "Jay and I looked at the accounts. It seems to do pretty well. It just needs some modernizing. New locker rooms, better lighting—"

"My uncle, who owns an HVAC business, thinks the tennis center is a good investment?" Caroline clarified, because she wasn't brave enough to point out that her father hadn't managed to expand the paving business he'd bought from his father.

Her father reached for the tennis bag he'd hauled along to dinner. He unzipped the top and retrieved a paper folder. He attempted to pass it across the table, but Caroline instinctively recoiled from being offered papers by her father.

"It's on sale for a million two," he said when she didn't accept the folder. "I can probably talk them down from that."

Caroline did not need financial advice from her father. She was almost a quarter of the way to a graduate business degree.

"I have almost everything in a brokerage account," Caroline said. "A conservative one. Index funds and municipal bonds. It's doing fine. I don't need to invest in a tennis business."

Her father scowled. "You don't understand. This is an opportunity for the whole family."

She looked at him helplessly. "Is there something wrong with the HVAC business?"

"No, Jay is doing fine, but—"

"And the paving company is okay too?"

Her father lightly bounced his fist on the table, making the silverware jump.

"That's not the point, Caroline! That's never been the point. You tried to make me out to be the bad guy, but we were always going to take care of you with your grand-mother's money. You acted like we were just going to leave you out on the street, but you had a full scholarship! You didn't need to touch a cent until you graduated."

Caroline scooted her chair away from the table, heart already racing.

"This is a good investment, because you can run the tennis center and earn a good living," her father insisted. "Jay and I can handle the renovation, and by the time you graduate, you'll be ready to manage it. You might even spend some time on the pro circuit first—that'll help bring in students."

"But I don't want to run a tennis center," she protested. Her ears were ringing. Her mother was staring at the black napkin in her lap, no help there. She must have known about this plan, just like she must have known about the last one.

"Seems to me you don't know what you want to do," her father growled. "You're just squandering my mother's money. You're not the kind of person who can be respon-sible for a small fortune."

Caroline jerked back, stung. She'd earned more in in-vestment income than she'd spent, and the market hadn't even been that great this year.

She hated her family's pity. She didn't want to be the person they thought she was anymore. Caroline, who never got invited to birthday parties. Caroline, who was sitting by herself at the barbecue. Maybe they'd thought they were doing a good thing for her by filling her life so full of tennis that she didn't have time to feel the lack of anything else, but even if she was terrible at most things, that didn't mean she couldn't be trusted with this.

"That's not true," she said, but her voice had gone wobbly and threadbare. "I'm keeping to a budget. I can show you. I have QuickBooks. After I graduate, we can talk again about what I do with the money—"

Her father exhaled through his nose. "I'm trying to help you," he said. "Because I can see where this is going already. I'm not going to let you flail when you graduate from this place. Caroline, you know there's no way you're getting hired against all the other kids who are graduating with you. You need to come home so your family can help you find a stable career."

Caroline took a deep breath, trying to gather enough of her wits to champion Boston College's career services office, its alumni network, her spreadsheet of potential internships . . . and noticed her hands trembling. She was so tired of defending herself and what she wanted. Maybe she'd fall on her ass when she graduated, but like Adrian had pointed out, she had two million dollars in the bank, and she could comfortably afford to study underwater basket-weaving as her vocation if nothing else worked out.

So why couldn't she just get a little time and grace to try things she might screw up at? To try things she might not like? Or might end up regretting? It was nobody else's job to save her from her own decisions but hers.

Caroline stood up, curling her hands into fists.

"I thought it was about wanting the money, you know," she said, and her father leaned back in surprise, because she was not allowed to raise her voice. "And I didn't blame you for that part. Because I wanted it too! It wasn't like I was more deserving than you or Uncle Jay. I thought you wanted to spend it on yourself. But that wasn't it, was it? You just can't stand me having it. You can't handle me having two million dollars' worth of choices, if I might make bad ones."

She didn't wait for his sputtering reply or finish her fish. She had five pounds of turkey in her fridge back home. She grabbed her purse and put a few large bills on the table.

"You know what?" she snapped at her father. "I think I'll be out of the country over the winter holidays. I'll send you a postcard."

IT TOOK ADRIAN A MOMENT TO UNDERSTAND WHAT WAS going on when his bedroom door crashed against the wall. He'd intended to just take a short nap after arriving home that Sunday morning, but judging by the light filtering in through the battered mini-blinds, it was midafternoon.

"What did you do?" Tom's voice demanded, and Adrian woke up further. He squinted blearily at his roommate's solidifying form. He must have returned from New York while Adrian was passed out.

Adrian had been sleeping at his studio ever since he'd left Caroline's apartment. He was testing that arrangement for permanency, since he needed to be out of Tom's apartment by the end of the next week unless he somehow came up with rent money. It was far from ideal, to put it mildly. The other artists kept wildly divergent work hours, and there was noise from the other spaces for all but a few of the small hours of the morning. And Adrian couldn't ask another artist to stop running a pottery wheel after midnight because he was trying to sleep.

So he'd drunk a lot of coffee and done his best to paint something commercial over the past week. His hands were aching, which meant he'd been careless about how long he'd worked, since he could hardly afford to injure himself at this point.

Six days of staring at a pile of produce and acclimating himself to his immediate future as a painter of attractive fruit. No need to worry what the critics would say; he wouldn't bother to publicize a lot of classical still lifes produced solely to refill his bank account. He imagined his artist's statement: *The glass bottle in the background is inspired by the eyes of the woman who broke my heart. The chipped bowl is evocative of sadness and loss. The fruit is depicted in a color that I think will match the sofas of most art collectors.*

"What?" he belatedly asked Tom. The man had his feet planted in Adrian's doorway. He was peeling a large navel orange and dropping the rind directly on the floor. His expression flickered between outrage and confusion.

Tom hooked a thumb in the direction of the front door.

"Caroline just came by, dumped a bunch of your paintings in the hall, and told me good luck in New York."

"Caroline's here?"

Adrian scrambled to get up, reaching for the sweater he'd dropped on the floor that morning. Then he realized that after seven days, it didn't smell great, and since he hadn't showered since going to the gym on Friday, he smelled even worse. He craned his head at the living room, heart pounding.

"No, she booked it out of here," Tom said grimly. "Which brings me back to my original question: What did you *do*?"

Adrian collapsed down in bed, head swimming like he had a fever. He pressed a palm to his forehead, which ached in a throbbing way. He hadn't had any coffee since finishing the painting late last night.

"Did she really dump my paintings in the hall?" he asked, feeling ill. He hadn't expected that. Of course, recent events had shown that he was bad, *very* bad at predicting how women would react to his relationship decisions, but he'd thought that Caroline was, at the most, disappointed that he couldn't be the partner she wanted. Not angry at him. He supposed he was wrong.

Tom snorted. "She looked like she wanted to put her foot through one!" He glared at Adrian before amending, "They're wrapped up. On a dolly. I brought them in."

"Did she say anything else?"

"No," Tom said, eyes still narrowed. He finished peeling the orange and chucked a section at Adrian. It hit him in his bare chest with a wet sound. "So?"

"So what?"

"What did you do?!"

Tom hefted the rest of the orange as though he'd hurl it next.

Adrian didn't bother to dissemble, since Tom was unlikely to believe that Caroline was at fault in any way. He simply stared at his oldest friend with flat, unhappy lips and let him draw his own conclusions. If Caroline wasn't willing to be in a relationship with him while his life was such a flaming mess, that was understandable, but neither did Adrian think that made him the bad guy here.

"You goddamn asshole," Tom said with less heat after a moment of studying Adrian's face. "You know, I felt really bad for you when Nora kicked you out and trashed your art, but now that it's happened twice this year, I think you need to examine your role as the common factor in beautiful women coming to hate your guts."

"Yeah, thanks," Adrian said with very little respect. "Do you have any other relationship advice for me? As an expert, I mean."

Tom did toss the rest of the fruit at him then. Adrian took an orange segment to the cheek and let it drip down his neck.

"Screw you," Tom snarled. "You should have told me straight up that you were never going to forgive me when you found me on your doorstep ten years ago. Maybe I would have gone back to Rosie and groveled if you hadn't let me mope around your apartment indefinitely."

"As you'll recall, I told you to do *just that.*"

"I was twenty-three, and I fucked up! What's your excuse?" Tom yelled.

Adrian jerked back at his volume and his furious expression. He swallowed his own anger.

"It's not a matter of groveling," he said. "Caroline said I was going to make us both miserable, and she didn't want to be with me."

Tom gestured around him. There were open cardboard boxes everywhere. He was already starting to pack up the place. A piece of orange slid down the wall to ooze on the floor.

"I can see you're getting right on fixing that." He sneered. "Making major strides in turning your life around. The ladies love the smell of self pity and BO. I'm sure she'll come around really quick."

Adrian clenched his jaw and got out of bed.

"It was never going to work out in the first place. Age difference aside, we don't have anything in common—"

"What are you *talking* about? She went to all that snobby shit you like, and as far as I could tell, you were having a good time."

"Well," Adrian said unconvincingly, "she wasn't." Or she wasn't going to have a good time once their recreational activities were restricted by the minimum wage and Adrian's food service schedule.

He found a clean shirt and put it on as Tom continued to scowl. Underneath it all, Adrian knew, was concern. Tom felt like he was abandoning him by heading back to New York. But Adrian was unwilling to be a drag on his best friend too.

"I'll be fine here," he said curtly. "I'm going to paint some still lifes to lure in a new gallery. I might even come stay with you in New York if I'm visiting galleries there."

Tom finally relented, tossing up his hands and returning to the kitchen to continue packing. He muttered under his breath in Polish for a minute and then louder, in English, that Adrian was the biggest drama queen he'd ever met. Adrian wasn't even sure that he was wrong. He finished dressing and went to look at the paintings Caroline had dropped off.

By their size and number, Adrian knew they were the paintings that had hung in his old house along with all the ones that Caroline had framed and hung in her own apartment. She'd also returned his portfolios. Everything was carefully wrapped. It must have taken her hours, assuming she'd done it all by herself. The jagged feeling in his chest sharpened as he imagined her stripping the walls of her apartment blank and bare, piece by piece.

Caroline would have left a note. An inventory, something. He flipped through the bundles, shaking them, until one sheet of paper slipped loose.

She'd typed up a bill of lading. Very professional, probably generated by top-of-the-line business software. He made a forlorn sound of amusement without meaning to. Most of the page was a list of the paintings she'd delivered, accompanied by very optimistic estimates of their individual values.

Thanks, Caroline. I am probably not going to achieve the same prices as Damien Hirst any time soon, but I appreciate the vote of confidence.

There wasn't any other note. Just a transfer of assets off her balance sheet and back onto his. His vision blurred. If it was Nora, he would have thought it was a final taunt about all his failures. But for all the times Caroline had jabbed him over his assumptions about her, he knew this was her honest goodbye. She still thought he'd sell these paintings and go on to some dazzling career.

She'd been wrong before. She'd also been painfully, heartbreakingly right. He wished he could tell the difference, especially when it came to him.

Adrian swallowed past the burn in his throat. He couldn't keep doing this. He couldn't even summon any pleasure from the idea that she might be right. He was numb to the mental image of himself at an opening, praised for capturing some complex thought about the history of his medium. He couldn't make himself want that anymore; what he wanted was Caroline's hand back in his.

He couldn't keep doing this.

"Tom?" he called. "Did you rent your moving truck yet? Can I borrow it?"

AN HOUR AND A HALF LATER, ADRIAN PULLED UP OUTSIDE of Mike's gallery, taking a moment to breathe as he sweated out the last of his adrenaline. Boston's drivers did not appreciate sharing the roads with moving trucks, and he'd taken his life into his hands by piloting the vehicle downtown on the Sunday after Thanksgiving, when everyone was rushing into the commercial district to start their holiday shopping.

The gallery was closing in a few minutes, but there were still some well-dressed patrons trickling out as Adrian loaded the paintings onto the dolly Caroline had gifted him. He hoped that he looked sufficiently like a working artist in his paint-splattered old jeans to avoid annoying Mike or the other gallery staff with his presence.

Adrian caught Mike coming out of his office, about to

start locking up. The potbellied man stiffened in surprise, because Adrian hadn't called ahead. It was really poor form. But Adrian had been rejected almost everywhere in Boston, and he couldn't become *more* of an object lesson in wasted potential, so he'd opted to just show up and plead his case.

"Do you have a few minutes?" Adrian pressed, trying not to look as desperate as he really was. "I brought some things to show you."

Mike hesitated. Looked down at his battered watch. After he made a concerned study of Adrian's face, he nodded at his office.

"Sure," Mike said, gesturing for Adrian to follow him with the dolly. "Always, for you. Whatcha got?"

He flicked the lights back on but didn't sit down at his desk, just leaned against it. His posture was of muted impatience. He was humoring Adrian. Fine.

Adrian had retrieved his two most recent paintings from his studio on the way to the gallery. The still life was barely dry, so he unwrapped it first. He leaned it up against the wall. The light wasn't fantastic inside the office, but Mike knew his work. He knew the colors would hold up in better conditions.

"I just finished this yesterday," Adrian said. It was a classic composition, slightly modernized by the shapes of the bottle and bowl and the choice of persimmons. There were probably three other works just like it hanging in the gallery, and they'd all turn over by the end of the month. It was commodity art.

"Okay," Mike said, face impassive. "What else?"

Adrian set his jaw, because that was hardly great praise, but it also wasn't the soft dismissal Mike would have given him if he knew he wasn't going to take it either.

Adrian got out his pocketknife and carefully cut away

the tape to expose one of the older works. Mike hopped off the edge of his desk and walked closer to take a look at the garden scene.

"This isn't new, is it?" Mike asked.

"No. I painted this series just before I left your gallery. But these paintings were never offered for sale before."

Mike's eyes flicked to his face again, but he nodded.

"There are three more of these larger ones. Twelve clusters of smaller studies, oil on paper. Already framed." Adrian gestured at paintings that had hung on Caroline's walls.

Mike nodded again, mind transparently calculating prices and gallery space. That gave Adrian enough hope to unwrap the last painting. His portrait of Caroline.

In the end, he'd just put a final coat of varnish over it to seal it. It was painfully evocative of the actual woman, from the little curve in the trailing lock of her hair where she'd tucked it behind her ear to the swell of her lower lip as she considered the flowers.

Mike tilted his head, then carefully reached out to pick up the painting by the edges. Adrian resisted the urge to snatch it out of his hands as Mike carried it closer to the window to catch the last fading rays of natural light.

Mike turned to survey the whole lot. The grouping was not tied together by much other than technique, but Adrian had seen shows of more disparate artworks together.

"You're really going to sell this?" Mike said, inclining his head at the portrait.

"Yes."

Adrian wasn't allowing himself to think about how he'd feel if he never spoke to Caroline again. He didn't know whether he'd curse himself for selling the painting or be grateful he didn't have to see it. It wasn't like he'd be able to forget her either way.

He strove to steady his voice. "You can call up Jan and Samantha Mayer. I bet they'll buy it." He was sure they would. They'd met Caroline. They knew a little piece of the story. They'd want to own it.

He'd really rather sell them a kidney, but after all the coffee he'd been drinking to finish the still life, those were probably shot. And Caroline would have dressed him down with everything she had if she thought he was holding back inventory out of sentimentality.

Mike sighed, obviously torn.

"What are you going to do about all those works you showed me last week?" he asked. "I wasn't kidding that I can't sell those."

"Sunk cost," Adrian deadpanned.

"Okay, but what about what comes next? This isn't enough for a show. You know it isn't. I can put these up in that room off to the front left—"

"That's fine," Adrian said.

"Not so fast. Listen to me. What comes next? I don't want to be telling you no every month. It's not good for either of us. I don't want to jerk you around."

Adrian pointed to the still life. "You can sell that. You know you can. I can paint things like that."

Mike set the portrait down and picked up the still life. "I don't know how you made a bowl of fruit so damn angry, but yeah. I can sell this."

"Fine, then," Adrian said, relief beginning to sweep down his back. "I am planning a series of still lifes. You can imbue them with as much emotional backstory as you want to."

"Are you sure though? You're done with the historical stuff?"

"I am done with being an artist who paints things that

nobody wants to look at, yes," Adrian said, fatigue making him punchy.

Mike screwed up his face, wrinkles bunching around his eyes. "Look, I know I'm just a sales guy, but I didn't get into this business because I wanted to tell artists what to paint. If you want to paint World War I battles, do that! There's enough fucking fruit bowls in the world already."

Adrian grunted and turned away, knitting his hands behind his neck. The only subject he'd really *wanted* to paint in the past year wasn't speaking to him.

"Mike, I am just—I am done. I am not going to suffer for art anymore. It's not worth it. You can file my reviews in the trash from now on. I spent seven years trying to make interesting art, and that's enough. I'd rather be an artist who pays the rent than an artist who says something important about the human condition. I'll paint the damn fruit. I'll paint the sentimental garden scenes. I'll—"

If Caroline ever spoke to him again, was still speaking to him by spring, he'd paint her dripping in peonies. She'd probably never seen them blooming before. He cleared his throat.

"I'll paint whatever you want."

Mike minutely shook his head, but after a few seconds of chewing on the corner of his mouth, he said, "All right."

Adrian's knees nearly sagged, but he kept himself together as Mike went to his desk and retrieved one of his form contracts.

"Deal hasn't changed since you were here before," Mike said, sliding the pages over to him. Adrian initialed, dated, and signed as Mike talked about the upcoming schedule of gallery events. He knew he ought to pay attention, but all he could think about was going home and sleeping for days. No, going home, calling Caroline, and telling her he might not be taking a McJob.

"I'll call those folks you mentioned tonight. I get the feeling you'd like me to move these."

"Thanks," Adrian managed. "I trust you to price the portrait."

Mike gave him a muted smile. He went back to the portrait and picked it up. He took it out to the hallway, and Adrian trailed after him. Mike carried the painting all the way to the front window, where the last late silver rays of the November sunset illuminated the piece. Adrian knew the brushwork was excellent and all the technique as good as he'd ever managed. Caroline was as soft and introspective in her regard for the flowers as a Titian Madonna. He could hardly blame Mike for just wanting to look at her too.

"It's good," Mike said softly. "But you know that, right?"

Adrian shook his head, unconvinced. "She's just beautiful. It's not any great skill on my part."

"Sure. You're obviously in love with the girl. That's going to come through even if you're not standing right here and glaring whenever I move the painting."

Adrian automatically scowled.

"Yeah, like that," Mike said. "But I'm saying it's a great piece. I'd buy it if I thought I could afford what I'm going to charge the Mayers."

Adrian took a deep breath. "I'm fortunate that there's still a decent market for paintings of beautiful women holding flowers, all trends in contemporary art aside."

Mike lifted a hand dismissively. "That's where contemporary art and I part ways. Who said that tragedy is more interesting than joy? I personally think joy is pretty damn important."

Adrian thought that had been at best a hypothetical

question, but the gallery owner turned to him and lifted his bushy, graying brows in demand.

"It's not that simple," Adrian said.

"Well, neither is your painting."

Adrian couldn't refute that. He gazed at the painting, memorizing the small details of the piece in case he didn't see it again in person.

Mike patted him on the back. "You know, I'm happy to sell as many fruit bowls as you like. I wanna convert the basement to a rumpus room this year, because my kid's turning fourteen. He's loud, stays up all night . . . And the fruit bowls sell, which is great. But I'd also like to see some more portraits, if you can manage it. From my perspective, there's a lot of people, a lot of artists, ready to tell you the world is hard and scary. And fine, that's important. We need to know that. But joy's important too. If I could paint, I'd want to make art about joy."

Adrian closed his eyes. That was what he ought to have offered Caroline. He'd never even told her that loving her made him *happy*.

"I'll try," he managed to tell Mike through his aching throat.

"You're a good kid," Mike said, thick palm thwacking him between the shoulder blades. "Now get out of my gallery. It's late. Go home and tell your girl you're going to sell some paintings."

"Yes," Adrian said, though that was the least of what he needed to tell her. He loved her, and that wasn't a tragedy. No matter what happened, it was a wonderful thing that he'd fallen in love with her. He regretted a lot of things in his life, but not a single moment that he'd known her.

Mike wrinkled his nose. "Just make sure you take a shower first."

Chapter Eighteen

CAROLINE ALMOST TRIPPED OVER ADRIAN ON HER WAY TO the lobby of her apartment. He was sitting next to the elevator, long legs stretched out across the hall. She yelped and windmilled back as she came around the corner. She'd been moving at a good speed because she was late, as per usual, and now she was flustered, also sadly usual.

Adrian scrambled to his feet, and Caroline had a brief moment of unworthy appreciation for how much of a wreck he looked. He was as dressed down as she'd ever seen him, in paint-splattered jeans and a faded T-shirt, a layer of fine copper stubble adorning the perfect line of his jaw. But it was the dark circles under his eyes that made her feel better about the twenty minutes she'd just spent determining which hoodie made her look most serenely composed.

She spread her arms in silent demand. She'd expected some kind of response after returning all his paintings, but not this one.

"You said, quote, around eight, at the Dunkin' Donuts by your apartment." His tone was careful.

Caroline frowned at him. The previous day he'd called four times before he finally left a message asking if she would meet him for coffee somewhere. He'd accurately described her single text back.

"Which is where I was going. And it's only—" Crap. Eight thirty, already. It had turned out that Caroline did not own athleticwear that appropriately communicated *I'm doing fine*, and she'd gone through a number of clothing changes. She scowled, which only made Adrian's expression turn very stoic.

"This is Boston. There are at least four Dunkin' Donuts within a quarter mile of your apartment."

"You could have asked which one."

"I didn't want to push my luck." He said it lightly, but his sad, worried eyes gave Caroline a pang of sympathy. She firmed the line of her mouth, summoning her willpower to quash the feeling. Putting her hands on her hips, she looked down the hall to her apartment.

"I guess you might as well come in since you're already here," she said, trying to feign annoyance. She was very reluctant to go back to the last place she'd seen him, and she'd already mentally prepared for talking to him in a busy coffee shop. She'd be able to escape from the coffee shop if things started going pear-shaped, but she worried that she didn't have the heart to throw him out of her apartment again.

What was she afraid of? That he might beg her to accept more free sex and declarations of love? That probably wasn't his agenda since it had taken him over a week to call.

Without waiting for his agreement, she walked back to her door and unlocked it, leaving it open behind her.

Her apartment wasn't as neat as the last time he'd seen it—the only time he'd seen it. She had a lot of shopping bags cluttering the living room floor, and her walls were now bare. Tamsyn's show would run for another two weeks before Caroline might expect to receive her bird painting.

Adrian shut the door behind him as Caroline rustled through her shopping bags.

"Here," she said when she found the box she wanted, thrusting it against Adrian's chest. "Do you know how to use this?"

He examined her new French press. One of the Food Network chefs had mentioned that it was the best way to brew coffee.

"I think I can figure it out," he said hesitantly.

"Good. The coffee is in the freezer."

Caroline spun on her heel, walked determinedly to her couch, and plopped herself down, wishing her heart wasn't beating so fast. She turned the TV on and pretended to be deeply invested in the perils of the annual wildebeest migration as Adrian opened cabinets and banged around her kitchen.

"Do you own a teakettle?"

"For coffee?"

"To heat the water."

Caroline scowled. "No."

There was more banging.

"I'm going to use a saucepan."

She grunted in agreement. After setting the water on the stove to boil, Adrian edged into her frame of vision. She wished he'd speak, but he just silently looked her over, gaze eventually landing on some of the previous day's purchases scattered in disarray near a stack of empty moving boxes.

The largest obstacle was a pink duffel bag with wheels and a tow handle. It was already unzipped with a few sweaters packed in the bottom.

"Are you going somewhere?" he asked.

"Paris," Caroline said curtly.

"Oh," he said quietly. Then, "What are you planning to do while you're there?"

"I'm going to take a class on choux pastry. At the Cordon Bleu."

"Isn't that the one that had the student loan scandal?"

"I. Don't. Care," Caroline growled, punctuating her words by slapping the sofa arm. She didn't care if the classes were severely overpriced. She was going to eat cream puffs thousands of miles away from everyone and everything that had disappointed her.

Adrian shifted on his feet. "Are you going to come back?" he asked even more quietly, eyes on the moving boxes.

"I don't know." If she liked it there, why would she? At this rate, she wasn't going to get a job with her business degree. And if she got one, she probably wouldn't even like it. She thought she might get better at choux pastry with sufficient instruction, and then she'd have done *something* right.

The water on the stove bubbled, and Adrian went to the kitchen to attend to that. The pot clattered as he packed the grounds and gingerly poured the water into the French press.

He took two mugs and the brewing pot of coffee out to the table and set them in front of her. He returned to her kitchen for the bottle of vanilla creamer in the fridge and brought that as well. Out of tasks, he looked away, at the front door.

"I hope you have a great time," he said, sounding defeated. "It'll be cold, but not worse than here, and the tourists won't be so bad this time of year. I could send you . . . I suppose there are a lot of guidebooks on what to do."

Caroline curled her lip, worried that she was going to cry, when her top, number one mission had been *do not cry*.

What reason did he have to look so sad about her trip? That was what he'd thought she'd do, after all. Go without him.

She swallowed hard. "I wanted to go with *you*," she nearly shouted, and that was true, but not a thing she'd planned on saying. It didn't sound like such a huge request, did it? Why was that such an ask?

Adrian crossed the room in two wide steps and dropped onto the couch next to her. He held up one hesitant hand, not sure where to put it. Eventually he placed it on her shoulder and lightly gripped the muscle there, thumb curling into the loose fabric of her hoodie.

"Oh, sweetheart. I did too." He swallowed hard, eyes fixed on her face. "It's not that I didn't want to go."

Caroline tucked her chin and tightened her shoulders, hands clenching in fists as she tried to get her voice under control.

Apparently giving her a moment to compose herself, Adrian reached for the coffeepot and depressed the plunger to fill the upper chamber with the filtered coffee. He poured two mugs and passed her one. She accepted it, grateful to have something to do with her hands, and blew on it to cool it.

"Would it really have been so bad? Just to let me handle the money?" she asked in a smaller voice. "I promise I wouldn't hold it against you, ever."

Adrian sighed. "You are always so generous, maybe you wouldn't, but—"

"I'm not that, really," she insisted. She was rational, that's what she was. She could understand why he needed more money, and she had it in excess.

"Caroline." His face was still tired, but the corner of his mouth tugged up. "You carried cardboard boxes of my stray socks and underwear out of my ex's house when you'd known me for a week. I know you must have given Tom the money to rent his moving truck, because he's been such a squirrel about it. I know how wonderfully generous you are. With your time, your money—everything."

"As a counterpoint, you were really good-looking, and I didn't have anything better to do that Saturday."

"Caroline," he scolded her again, voice finally sounding a little more like himself. "I don't think your motives for offering me money were somehow impure."

"It's about what I want," she insisted. "Isn't that selfish?"

Adrian looked like he wanted to argue with that, so she decided to tell him the entire story. Perhaps she could prove to him that he was as reasonable a recipient of her windfall as she was.

"Nobody ever talks about money, even when all their problems are because of money. It's not like I *need* two million dollars. Nobody does. My family doesn't think I need it, anyway. But they won't even work with me on what we all want to do. When they found out how much I was getting, my dad and my uncle had the estate executor make up a disclaimer—something to reject the inheritance from Gam. All of it. It would have gone to them instead, since they are my grandmother's two kids."

That was what everyone had agreed was fair. And maybe in a sense it was, since the money had come from the paving business her grandparents had built and her father had purchased—but then she wouldn't even have had the car she had *needed*. And she hadn't trusted her parents to give her that much, not when they'd never given her a say in her life before.

Caroline clenched her jaw. "They asked me to sign everything away, right then. So I said I needed to go to the bathroom, and then I climbed out the window and drove off. I never went home again. I haven't given them any of the money yet."

Adrian made a small, startled noise. "That's not selfish."

She didn't believe him. What else did you call it when you kept something for yourself instead of sharing it?

"I would have done the same thing. Well, no, probably not, because I'm not as brave as you are. But I would have wished I'd done what you did."

She shook her head at him, taking a first, small sip of the coffee. He would have refused the money and figured out some other way to get what he wanted.

"You weren't wrong," he pressed. "It wasn't their money. It was your grandmother's. And she wanted to give you more choices. You're not wrong for wanting to make them yourself."

The coffee was awful: bitter and *gritty*. She stared at the rainbow film of oil on top of the brew. There were a couple of grounds floating in it.

"Ugh," she exclaimed. "Is it supposed to taste like this?"

Adrian took a sip from his own mug. "I'm not an expert, but I think so?"

Caroline heavily set the mug down on the table. "It's not at all how I thought it would be. I feel like I'm doing it all wrong. Everything I want turns out to be the wrong thing or offends someone or just sucks, actually, like this coffee."

She pursed her lips, looking at him defiantly. What had she done with all that money and all those choices that had been good even just for her?

"Not all of it was wrong though, was it?" he asked, dusty-blue eyes focusing on her as though the question was very important.

Not absolutely everything, that was true. She liked *Anastasia*. And fish too, it turned out. And her bird painting. She even liked her classes, if she didn't worry about what she was going to do with them. Those were all just details around the edges though, not the subject of the work.

"I wanted you. That's not working out either." That was what she'd wanted the *most*.

His hand stilled on her shoulder. He ducked his head, as though he found this conversation as terrifying as she did. Caroline's pulse fizzed in her chest like carbonated water.

"If you still want me, you can have me," he said after a minute, voice halting. "Me and all my bullshit."

"Can I?" she asked, skeptical of that proposition. "I thought I wanted the wrong things from you too."

It had been so freeing to be asked for money at the start of their relationship. She knew she could give him exactly what he needed—no chance of screwing that up! She thought for sure he was going to be better off for having known her. She had no confidence that she could navigate anything more complicated, not when she transgressed everyone's expectations as easily as breathing.

"I don't think you wanted the wrong things from me. I think—I hope—you just wanted to be with me, the only way you could imagine it," he said. He lifted his face in a soft question.

Caroline nodded tightly, heart stuck in her throat.

"I didn't say that I was going to find some crappy job because I thought it would make me miserable. I thought I'd be happy—because you make me happy. I love being with you. That's what I thought I'd have. I didn't care whether it was getting pelted with tennis balls or going to the opening night of the opera. I didn't think past realizing that."

"The opera is not great either," Caroline put in stiffly. "Or rather, it's not very good if they don't stage it with costumes and props and things."

"I agree." He looked at her with tender amusement now hovering around his lips. "I'm sorry I didn't see that I was taking your choices away from you with mine. I knew you wanted to go to Europe with me. I should have just said yes. I have the rest of my life to work retail if I really have to."

"You weren't taking my choices away from me," she protested. "I know what that looks like, and you never have." She'd always been able to say no. They were at this standoff because she had.

"But I didn't tell you there wasn't anything wrong with what you wanted either." He smiled, and it was heartbreaking in its fragile hope. "You wanted good things for me. And Caroline . . . I want you too. I said I wanted to be with you. I'll do whatever I have to for that to work."

She was getting perilously close to violating her *don't cry, at all costs, no crying* mission statement.

"Yeah?" she asked, voice wobbling.

Adrian reached for her hand and carefully curled his fingers around it. He tucked it under his chin.

"Yeah," he said, and she could feel the vibrations of that single word all the way through her bones. She left her hand there, the back of it pressed against his throat. That small contact was grounding.

"I finished a still life this week," he said after another moment.

As that was perhaps the least objectionable thing he could have done with his time this past week without calling her, she tilted her head to encourage him to keep talking about it.

"And I sold a painting."

"That's good," she said honestly. "I'm so happy for you."

"I signed back up at my old gallery. The owner managed to get a decent price for the first work—"

There was no way he couldn't have expected her to focus on that detail, particularly the *decent* qualifier.

"Really? How do you know?" Caroline exclaimed. "What were the comps you looked at? Did you do any kind of price analysis?"

"I . . . did not," Adrian confessed. "I don't actually know how to do that."

Caroline sat up a little straighter. "I do, you know."

"I thought you might. Because you mentioned it, just now."

She looked at him suspiciously, but his gaze on her was soft and rueful.

"You should have called me," she said.

He took a deep breath. "I know. I will next time."

That was a simple statement, but in it were a lot of complex promises. He sat quietly as she unpacked and examined them. There would be a next time that he sold a painting. He'd call her. And he believed she could help.

It wasn't everything she'd asked for. It wasn't even an apology. But it fell into the *zone of possible agreement*, as her professors would have put it. Adrian painting again, optimistic about their future—that was in her bargaining range.

Caroline nodded, sniffed hard, and swept her hair back out of her face. She swung her legs around on the couch and draped them across his lap. Then she wrapped her hands around his bicep and leaned in so that her head was resting on his shoulder.

"Okay," she said. She felt him exhale in a shaky rush. Caroline rubbed her face into his shirt, breathing in his warm man-and-Lava-soap scent. She didn't know what things were going to look like now. But there was a slow, growing swell of relief suffusing her body because there was going to be *something* to look at.

"Do you want to learn how to make mille-feuille in Paris?" she asked, taking a shot in the dark. "Let's just go. You can tell me what the best school for cream puffs is."

Adrian chuckled, the sound a little pained. "Right now?"

"Do we have anything else we have to do?" she asked.

He turned his head and spoke with his lips against her hairline. "I told Tom I'd help him move this weekend. He possibly thinks I've been acting like a giant dick recently, and I think I need to correct that impression by helping him carry things into whatever godforsaken fifth-floor walk-up he's rented."

That wasn't exactly an invitation to go with them, but she'd only ever gotten this far by asking for what she wanted. And she wanted to hang on to every small piece of this life she'd managed to build over the past few months.

"I've never been to New York," Caroline said. "And I'm good at carrying heavy things."

Adrian finally shifted until he could wrap his arms around her torso and haul her all the way into his lap. Her body felt like a melting ice cube as he cuddled her against his chest so tightly she could hear his heart thudding in time with hers. Relief made her soft and dizzy, and she closed her eyes to tip her face against his neck. "Sweetheart, all I want to do is something I know will put a smile on your face," he said. "I'll take you to see the Rockettes."

ADRIAN DIDN'T GET A TURN BEHIND THE WHEEL UNTIL THEY had passed Providence on the ride back, and then only because Caroline had finished the entire collected works of Taylor Swift and was finally ready to yield control of the radio in her Tahoe. They swapped seats at a gas station off I-95.

The highway passed through a featureless gray forest for this last stretch of the drive from New York to Boston, but Caroline smiled at him as he slid the dial to Providence's classical music station.

"Is this okay?" he asked as he turned the Mendelssohn to a low rumble.

"Mm-hmm," she said contentedly, balling up his coat under her head and leaning against the window as though she might fall asleep. "At least until we can pick up Kiss 108."

He didn't know anything about negotiation, which was a situation he probably needed to remedy. Caroline had already studied *Getting to Yes*, *Getting Past No*, and *Getting More*, and probably a lot of other texts relevant to the kinds of negotiations they were likely to face unless his art career really exploded in the next few months.

He'd proposed that he cover the trip to New York if Caroline wanted to bring him with her to Europe after exams. She'd readily agreed, and he'd felt pretty good about that compromise until she turned around and accepted Tom's offer to let them stay in his new apartment over the weekend. Adrian had assumed he would spend his first night with her at a two-star hotel somewhere in Midtown, not on an air mattress on the floor of Tom's new bedroom in Hamilton Heights. It wasn't even private, let alone romantic.

Tom was moving in with an actor he'd met during his first sojourn in New York. Other people Adrian and Tom had known during college soon appeared with bottles of wine and six-packs of beer to welcome them back to the city, and it turned into a house party even before Adrian had finished carrying everything up from the rental truck and Caroline's Tahoe.

It wasn't how he'd expected to spend the evening. He'd planned to take Caroline to Rockefeller Center to see the lights and the tree, maybe eat dinner somewhere with a view of the city. Drinking cheap booze with the local bohemians was not what he'd promised Caroline, and he recalled that she was iffy on parties in general. But at one in the morning, he looked over at her and saw that she was happy. She sat cross-legged on a stack of broken-down cardboard boxes, one hand wrapped around her third watermelon White Claw of the evening and the other resting lightly on his knee where he sat next to her. Tom's friends were mostly in theater or adjacent; they had correctly identified Caroline as an appreciative audience for exaggerated stories about embarrassing things Adrian and Tom had done in college or soon afterward. Her smile was hesitantly optimistic, even as she kept one nervous hand on him the entire time.

She'd wanted things like this too, he realized. Things he could give her regardless of whether he could ever pay half the bills. She'd hired him not because she wanted to go to the theater or learn about art but because she wanted a big, full life, with color and joy and new people in it, and she didn't know how to do it alone. Giving that to her sounded like a thing he could do with the rest of his life, more important than any idea he'd ever tried to convey in paint.

So, the next morning, in a burst of inspiration, he snuck downstairs to call Tom's ex-wife while Caroline was fighting with Tom's aged Mr. Coffee and Tom was still sleeping off most of a bottle of Crema de Alba.

After Adrian was appropriately scolded for his delinquency with respect to months of missed texts and group emails, Rose was happy to meet him and Caroline for lunch all the way at the other end of the island of Manhattan.

It took some weaving and dodging to get Caroline dressed in business attire without letting Tom know where they were going, but it was worth it to see her face bloom as she realized they were headed into the thicket of skyscrapers in the Financial District. Adrian didn't know what Rose did, exactly, or more likely he didn't understand it, but years ago he'd pulled strings with Nora to get Rose her current job. Calling in that favor for Caroline felt like closing a loop. Rose was nothing if not responsible, and if he told Rose that Caroline needed someone to smuggle her into Spreadsheet City, she'd do it.

Rose was still as round, pretty, and polished as the day Adrian had held the rings and bouquet at her wedding, a vision of sleek professional confidence. While she gave Caroline the grand tour of the nonprofit art foundation where she worked, Adrian saw the wheels turn in Caroline's head as she calculated how badly Tom had screwed up ten years ago.

At least they were back in the same borough, he thought as Rose delicately interviewed Caroline about her professional aspirations without being obvious about it. If Tom possessed even a single functioning brain cell, he'd track Rose down and apologize, if for no better reason than to save Adrian from a second decade of alternating custody.

I like her, Rose texted under the table while Caroline peered down at the street from the thirty-first floor.

Good, because I'm keeping her, Adrian wrote back.

Adrian and Caroline walked out into Battery Park after

lunch. Caroline had Rose's business card and an invitation to apply for an internship. She squinted at the tops of the tall buildings like a tourist, but with an acquisitive gleam in her eye. She was already planning to come back; that was apparent. Adrian's stomach did a complicated maneuver as he acknowledged that he'd just encouraged his girlfriend to move to a city he didn't live in.

He hoped she'd take him with her then too.

Now they were nearly back to Tom's Boston apartment—Adrian's apartment, he supposed, because Tom was unlikely to be making any further payments on the lease—and Caroline seemed as unwilling to end the weekend as he was.

"Do you want to come up?" he asked when he parked her Tahoe at the curb. He got out and swung limbs that had gone stiff from the five-hour drive.

"Of course," she said, grabbing a cardboard box full of random things Tom hadn't found room for at his new apartment and carrying it up over Adrian's objections.

Her face fell when he unlocked the front door, and he cursed himself for not remembering the state of the place before asking her up. It was dirty, like all apartments were after most of the furniture was removed. The living room was mostly unfurnished, except for the small breakfast table Tom's new roommate hadn't wanted. Tom's bedroom was empty. The door was open to Adrian's bedroom, where his scattered bits of mismatched furniture stood sadly alone. There were no towels hanging in the bathroom; those had been Tom's.

Caroline didn't say anything as she kicked dust bunnies aside and moved to the center of the room, but her face was eloquent. After a minute, she went and investigated the refrigerator, which had no non-condiment food.

She shut the door to the refrigerator and spun to pin him with a glare, hands on her hips.

"It wouldn't have made sense to buy groceries *before* leaving for three days," Adrian began to argue with her.

"Then do you want me to take you to the store right now?" Caroline asked. "Or would you rather stay with me tonight?" Her tone presented it as a binary decision. The ultimatum made him stiffen his shoulders.

"I don't mind staying with you tonight," he said, pushing through. It would be nice to wake up next to Caroline without Tom five feet away and offering commentary on how he'd always assumed Adrian was the little spoon.

Caroline narrowed her eyes at his phrasing, which had been rather graceless.

"I would be *honored* to stay with you," he amended. It would be *really* nice not to spend his first few moments of wakefulness lying facedown on a mostly deflated air mattress until the morning wood caused by spooning his girlfriend's pert ass all night went away.

Caroline nodded, her small, tip-tilted nose stuck in the air as she marched back toward the front door. Then she stopped.

"What's the plan?" she demanded.

"The plan?"

She waved at the nearly vacant apartment. The empty kitchen. "The plan for this."

"I told you I sold a painting. I can pay the rent for a couple of months. I'm going to keep painting." It sounded plainly insufficient as he described it. "I could get a roommate," he added.

"Do you have a budget? A cash-flow forecast?"

"I expect I will soon," he said, as Caroline was unlikely to let this go.

Caroline pursed her lips, green eyes deadly serious. She tapped one of her big white sneakers on the scuffed wooden floor. "Okay, here's my proposal. If you don't have a roommate in two months, you will move in with me. I don't even have any furniture in my second bedroom—you can put all yours there."

The spike of irrational panic that idea sparked was in complete contrast to the actual image of sleeping in Caroline's clean floral sheets every night. Higher thought warred against not-yet-banished voices that warned that it was never that easy, Caroline was taking pity on him, and she'd come to resent him being there. The bitter experience of living with someone who didn't love him, of feeling trapped as they became desperately unhappy together, counseled against the risk.

"Why?" he temporized.

"Why? I mean, it doesn't make sense for both of us to pay for two bedrooms, and my place has the bigger kitchen—"

"No, why are you asking?"

She tilted her head in confusion.

"Because I want you to live with me."

And it really came down to that, didn't it? He had to trust that this was what she wanted, his brave girl who'd climbed out a window and driven across the country in pursuit of a bigger life. All he had to do was be as brave as her.

He crossed the floor and wrapped one arm around her. He used the other to cage her against the front door.

Adrian leaned in and kissed the frown off her mouth. Then the tip of her nose and the bunching corners of her lips. There hadn't been enough opportunities to kiss her that weekend. He hauled her tight against his body and rubbed his nose into her cheek.

"All right," he said to her proposal. He stole another kiss off her soft pink lips.

"All right?" she said, a little dazed.

"In two months, if you still want me to, I'll move in," he promised. "And I will make you breakfast every morning." He kissed her again. "And I'll frame Tamsyn's painting so that we can hang it over our bed."

Caroline leaned back to squint at him. "You're not very good at this. You're supposed to make a counteroffer that improves your own position. You can borrow one of my negotiation books."

"Do you want to make it three months?"

"Why would I ask you for something I didn't want? You really need to read that book." She shook her head in consternation.

That was a compelling philosophy when stated so plainly. Why had he done so many things he didn't really want to do? Why had he spent so much time with people he didn't even like? Why had he stopped painting flowers and started painting battlefields?

She'd offered him everything he'd ever wanted, and he just had to take it.

He gave Caroline another squeeze. "I know it's getting late, but do you mind if we stop by my studio before dinner? I want to show you something."

Chapter Nineteen

THE ACRID SCENTS OF TURPENTINE AND CLAY WERE AS EVOC-
ative as the first time Caroline had visited the studio
building. It was quiet and dark so late on a Sunday evening. The atmosphere was nearly religious, as far as Caroline was concerned.

Adrian unlocked his space and flicked on a solitary floor
lamp. There were blank canvases still stacked against the
walls, crates of bowls and bottles, and boxes of art supplies, but only one finished work wrapped in a corner.

"I put my last series in storage," Adrian said. He gave
her half a smile. "For my biographers."

"What's this, then?" Caroline asked, pointing at the
wrapped painting, even though she thought she knew.

Adrian turned and carefully unwrapped it, placing it
on the easel in the center of the room where the floor
lamp could illuminate the canvas.

Caroline stared at herself, made beautiful in luminous
paint. Her breath filled her entire chest, suffusing into the
corners and cracks in her heart until it felt overextended.

It wasn't just that he'd made her beautiful. He'd made
her radiant, soft, and adored by the light that cupped her
face in the painting. Adrian moved behind her and loosely
wrapped her with his arms. He rested his chin on her
shoulder and pressed his cheek against hers.

"Do you like it?" he asked when Caroline's dry throat could not produce words.

"Is that really me?" she whispered.

She didn't mean her nose, her hair, or her pointed chin. And if he'd made her beautiful, that was understandable, because he was trying to make beautiful art. But it was more than that. The woman in the painting was everything he'd said she was: kind, confident, *compelling*. If she'd worried that she was incomplete and boring, this painting was the most articulate counterargument she could imagine.

"That's what I see, at least." He turned his head to brush his lips against the side of her neck.

"It's the nicest thing anyone's ever said about me," she told him. "I'm glad you, at least—"

She bit her lip. Being rejected by the theater group and doubted by her family still stung. She wanted to believe that Adrian was right about her. But strategically, even if he was the only market for whatever her personal product was, that was still a viable launch.

"It's not just me," he insisted. "I can't tell you that everyone is going to like you. Because I know plenty of people I'd never want to spend another minute with. Not everyone is worth your time. But the people you care about, the people *you* want to know . . . they're going to love you. How could they not?"

Caroline didn't reply, but she cuddled back against his chest, hoping what he said was true.

"You know, I'm pretty sure Tom likes you more than me now," he said. "He threw fruit at me until I promised to fix things."

"You're saying Tom thinks I'm a catch?" she teased him.

"Not just him. Tamsyn's been blowing up my phone, trying to arrange what she *says* is a trip out to the Cape this spring but what I'm *afraid* is a request to have a four-some in a very small beach cabin."

Caroline made a strangled giggle. "A foursome? So she got back together with her girlfriend? The short one?"

"That has to be the case. I'm a little alarmed that the constituent members of that foursome were your major concern though. . . ."

"I bet it's a joke. We have an inside joke about it. I don't think she likes men."

"I'm fairly certain my role would be limited to providing towels and snacks in this scenario that you still have not conclusively ruled out," Adrian said, voice beginning to contain a note of alarm.

Caroline dropped her head back and laughed. "RSVP no with regrets. Can you suggest we all get dinner instead of beachside group sex? As a counteroffer?"

"Yes. I don't want to wait until the next time I have an art opening to see them. I let"—he took a deep breath—"I let a lot of good things in my life go. Because I was afraid they weren't as real as my problems. I'm not going to do that again."

"This looks pretty real," she said, nodding at the painting.

"It is. I'm glad you got a chance to see it. I'm going to hang it tomorrow."

"Good," Caroline said firmly. "Remember to leave some business cards."

Adrian's exhale ruffled her hair. "I'm sorry I had to sell it. When I started, I thought I'd give it to you."

Caroline opened her mouth to argue, but Adrian cut her off by squeezing her waist.

"I know," he said. "Besides, I'm going to paint more."

"More like this?"

"That's the idea. I realized I have a choice about what

kind of art I make. Like I have a choice about what my life is about. And I want them both to be about the things I love. The things that bring me joy." He turned his head and kissed her cheek. "Like you."

"That sounds like a good plan," Caroline said softly.

"This is what I want," he said. "This kind of life. This kind of joy. With you, Caroline. I didn't even know what I wanted until I met you."

She couldn't wait to see it. All of it. The next paintings, the next things he did with his life. With *their* lives.

His chest expanded against her back as he took a deep breath. "You always want to know what the plan is. Well, I have one now. On your final exams, you are going to make the best spreadsheets Boston College has ever seen. And I am going to buy some very expensive greenhouse peonies and begin working on my next series."

"I like this plan," Caroline said. "It seems very aligned with our strategic objectives."

"There's more. In two weeks, when you are done with exams, we are going to fly to Europe. You are going to drink coffee made by people who are to coffee as Michelangelo was to ceilings. We are going to look at paintings that have never left the countries where they were painted. We are going to"—he kissed the side of her neck again—"sleep in actual beds."

"It's getting better and better."

Adrian took another deep breath. "And when we come back from Europe, having had a really wonderful time, I will ask you, very genuinely and sincerely, if I can move in with you. Not because Tom's apartment is empty of everything except for lost socks, but because after three weeks of waking up next to you, I won't be able to imagine doing anything other than that ever again."

Caroline nodded, nearly too overwhelmed to speak.

"I'm going to say yes," she managed.

"I'm going to be overjoyed," he said. "Even if it means that I'm moving for a third time in six months. And it's a good thing you're very rich now, because after I repaint your walls, it's unlikely that you'll get your security deposit back."

Caroline squirmed in his arms until she faced him. She looped her arms around his neck and hung them there.

"I *love* this plan," she said, imagining Adrian painting flowers and trees and gardens directly onto her bare beige walls.

"Good," he said.

Caroline summoned a deep draw of courage. "I love *you*," she added.

His dusty-blue eyes crinkled up around the corners as his smile bloomed across his face. "Even better," he said as he leaned in to kiss her.

His lips were warm, despite the chill of the empty studio space. Caroline could tell he was trying to be delicate and romantic about it, but after three days of very PG-rated cuddling in very public rooms, her heart kicked in to action, fluttering hard inside her chest. She deepened the kiss, smiling as she felt him respond when she plastered herself against him.

She pulled away and took a step back. Adrian moved as though to follow her before catching himself. His brow wrinkled in confusion when she took off her big puffy coat and tossed it over a crate of empty wine bottles.

"What are you doing?" he asked.

Caroline glanced at the plywood door, which could be closed with the tumbler padlock, then over at his futon, which appeared battered but reasonably sturdy. She gave Adrian an innocent look.

"Don't you want to get started?" she asked.

His brain failed to load that formula. "Started . . . with the plan? Right now?"

Caroline managed not to roll her eyes as she pulled her fleece sweater off and tossed it with her coat.

"Don't you think you should? I thought you had ideas for more paintings?"

"Yes, but . . ." His gaze dipped as Caroline got down to her sports bra layer and wrestled herself out of it as well. "When I said I'd paint you, I didn't mean you had to take your clothes off."

"Seems like it would fit that romantic vibe in your old paintings," she said.

"It was the realists, not the romantics, who mostly depicted the female nude," he couldn't avoid lecturing, though he did not look away as Caroline kicked off her shoes and socks.

Caroline gave him a *same difference* lift of her eyebrows and nodded at his art supplies.

"I still think it would look nice with all those flowers," she offered as a bold artistic thesis. He gave that due consideration.

"I couldn't sell a nude painting where you were my model," he said decisively. He paused. "Well, of course I *could*, but I wouldn't."

Caroline stripped off her underwear and sat down on the futon.

"Maybe you could, you know, drape me. Strategically arrange the flowers." She sketched her hand vaguely across her chest.

"I suppose I could," Adrian said, the artistic image obviously warring with the more basic parts of his brain. He dragged his gaze off her bare breasts with obvious difficulty and turned to his art supplies. "There's no light right now, but I could just make a few gesture drawings. Think about the composition."

"That sounds good," Caroline said, flopping to her back on the futon. It was really cold in the room. This joke couldn't go on much longer before she was going to need the advantage of some shared body heat. Adrian clipped a swatch of butcher paper to his easel and sharpened a charcoal pencil as she watched him with great amusement.

"How do you want me?" Caroline asked, striking what she hoped was an alluring pose.

Adrian's face took on an expression of great and noble suffering as Caroline trailed her fingers down her side.

"I—perhaps a more classical position," he suggested. He still hadn't lifted pencil to paper.

"Maybe arch my back more?"

"No—"

"Or spread my knees a little?"

Adrian closed his eyes and put his charcoal pencil against a seemingly random spot on his easel, head tilted back as he muttered about impossible artistic conditions.

A strangled giggle escaped her, and he swiveled to stare at her with growing suspicion.

"You're fucking with me again, aren't you?" he said, outrage mixing with hope.

Caroline cackled, rolling to her back and howling with laughter even as she held her arms out to him. He dropped his pencil on the floor and crossed the room to her in two long steps.

"Oh God, it was taking you so long to figure that out,

and it's really cold in here," Caroline teased. "I was worried you were going to pass out, and then I was going to freeze to death here."

"Serves you right," Adrian said, bending his head to press his teeth against the top of her breast in a mock bite. "If you give me a heart attack, you *know* that Tom will make an age crack at my funeral."

"It'll basically write itself if we're both naked when that happens," Caroline agreed, cupping his jaw.

"Are we both getting naked? You'd be surprised what I can manage with most of my very warm clothing on."

Caroline made big eyes at him and slid her hands down his chest. "Can I have your sweater? I'm *very* cold, and it's only going to get worse if I'm on top."

His grin spread across his face as he pulled his sweater off.

"Whatever you want, sweetheart. Anything you want."

For that moment and onward, as far into the future as she could see, she really believed he'd give her anything.

Epilogue

Two months later

"CAROLINE!"

She heard someone calling her name as she crossed the business quad on the way from the parking lot to the auditorium. There was a guest speaker, the chief investment officer of the nation's largest charitable foundation, and Caroline was on her way to learn about grantmaking. As her summer internship involved making them, and Adrian's three-year business plan involved receiving them, she was hauling a lap desk, her laptop, and the speaker's most recent two books with her in her tennis bag to attend the speech.

Boston was bitterly cold in February. She'd skipped her morning workout in lieu of staying in her warm bed with her even warmer boyfriend to engage in some less-conventional cardio. That alone wouldn't have put her off schedule, but afterward he'd made coffee using the moka pot they'd brought home from Italy *and* crepes using the griddle they'd acquired in France, so now she was late, as usual.

But she halted in the middle of the slushy sidewalk, scanning the area around her. From the other side of the campus, a small figure in bright green wide-legged trousers and a long flapping white parka came splashing across the pavement.

"Rima," Caroline said with surprise. "Hi."

Rima made her way to Caroline's side, one hand pressed against her rib cage as she breathed heavily.

"Oh, you walk fast," she wheezed. "I thought that was you in the pink leggings, but I wasn't sure."

Caroline looked down at her neon palm-tree-print running pants with approval. They matched her coat *and* her socks.

Rima caught her breath and straightened, elegantly shaped eyebrows lifting as she addressed Caroline.

"I was worried about you!" she declared. "I haven't seen you at all, and you didn't respond to any of my emails."

Caroline leaned back in surprise. "I'm sorry. I thought your emails were just about, you know, taking down the set."

She hadn't even opened them. After being told off by Sophia, she hadn't wanted to show her face for the strike, and she'd been reeling from her argument with Adrian in any event. It was three disasters back.

"But you didn't show up. For that or dinner or anything. I was ready to send out a search party, but Nathan said he saw you on the way to the gym the next day," Rima said.

"I'm sorry if you expected me at strike, but I really didn't think I needed to go," Caroline said, wincing. "It wasn't like I was on the crew."

Now it was Rima's turn to look startled. "But of course you were. You were assistant props."

Caroline gave her a hard look. "No, I wasn't. I wasn't even in the program."

"But you were!" Rima said. "Nathan and I spent fifteen minutes printing and stuffing the substitutions every night. We put them in every program, you and the day's understudies."

"Really?" Caroline's shoulders softened. "I didn't know. Thank you. You didn't have to do that."

"Why did you think you weren't crew? You were there for the entire production," Rima pressed.

Caroline slowly gave an abbreviated description of her confrontation with Sophia at the tech party, watching Rima's pretty face grow horrified.

"Sophia! What an"—Rima visibly searched for an appropriately stern word that was not also a misogynistic slur—"*unpleasant* person."

Caroline snorted. "Really. A very unpleasant person."

"She just goes on and on about being in a preprofessional program! I don't know who she's kidding. I'm getting my PhD in music education, not theater. Is she going to kick *me* out?" Rima fumed.

"Well, I hope not," Caroline said. "If you're still having fun."

"Yes, but that's why I was chasing you. I thought—well, Nathan was actually worried that he was the one who'd chased you off. He feels really bad. He told me what happened."

"That's fine," Caroline said, turning pink as she imagined that awkward conversation. "I thought he might be upset."

"No, no, not at all. He had his tongue in someone else's mouth, like, six hours later." Rima rolled her eyes and cleared her throat. "He and I were talking about this semester though. We're both doing the spring musical, same capacities, but I'm also going to be stage manager for a one-act in April. *She Kills Monsters*."

"That's great," Caroline said, not sure where Rima was going with it.

"But . . . it's a very tech-intensive show. Lots of set, lots of costumes, lots of props." She turned a pleading expression on Caroline. "I thought I'd ask if you wanted to be props master?"

"Me? But . . . I've never even taken a theater class."

"But you were really good at it! I have this budget for so many swords and battle-axes and . . . and *dragon heads*, but so far I just stare at the balance and tremble." She pressed her lips together. "Would you like to do it? I promise Sophia is allowed nowhere near my production."

Caroline adjusted the strap of her tennis bag. She was going to have to sneak in the back of the speech this morning.

"When does rehearsal start?" she hedged. "I'm going to be in New York over Easter break. For the cherry blossom festival and my friend's premiere. He's in an off-Broadway play."

"Amazing! That's no problem though. The show is in the last week of April. You can start after spring break."

"Okay," Caroline decided, knowing Adrian would have urged her to say yes. "I'll do it."

Rima sighed, seeming very pleased. "You know, I'm from New York. I might be there over spring break too."

Caroline hesitated, because this sort of thing was still hard for her. It was easier when she had a script. Or when she knew what the other person wanted. Or if Adrian was there with a hand on her lower back for her to press against.

"Do you want to meet us for dinner some night? My boyfriend and me? We'll be there the whole week, and we don't have plans every night yet. . . ."

"I'd love to," Rima said delightedly. "I can meet you two anywhere in town. If you're there for the cherry blossom festival, you'll have to see the botanic garden in Brooklyn too. Maybe we could meet there earlier?"

"Yes," Caroline said, breaking out into an answering smile. She'd gotten this right. More and more things had been going right, clicking into place like a balance sheet moving into the black. "Let's plan on it."

Rima took her phone out and stored Caroline's number. "Got it. Is it okay to send you the script this week? So you can think about where we're going to rent half a dozen battle-axes?"

Caroline grinned at her. She had this. "Don't worry," she said, preparing to sprint for the auditorium, because she was *so* late. "You can buy *anything* over the Internet."

Acknowledgments

Dear reader,

I started writing this planned trilogy in early 2021, when I was spending most waking hours in my living room dreaming of art museums and concerts and farmers markets. Whether you started with Darcy and Teagan in *Bear with Me Now* or just joined me here, you probably caught the sense that *author wishes she was not in her living room right now*.

I think the essence of the romance genre is fantasy—I don't mean in the sense that it's unrealistic, since romance novels can do realism very well—because there's always a wish that gets fulfilled. Someone has really spectacular sex. Someone gets the family they wanted. Someone meets someone else who sees everything about them, all of it, the parts they like and the parts they don't, and loves them back.

In a way, this book was peak wish fulfillment. I gave Caroline two million bucks, a hot boyfriend, and the chance to do everything I couldn't do in lockdown. Lucky her! But while my family situation is very different, I also gave Caroline the biggest part of myself that I've given any character I've written, and that makes this release feel especially vulnerable.

As authors, we can't help but put bits of ourselves in

the characters we write: I gave Teagan my anxiety (he'd give it back if he could), Darcy my pragmatism, Adrian my philosophical arc on making art, and if you stick around for book three, you'll see my worst jokes in Tom and grandiose domestic aspirations in Rose. I gave Caroline the hurty bits. I hope you like her.

Thanks for this book go first to my Beaubeau, Ashley Mackie, and to Beth Gordon for holding my hand through every single chapter of writing it. I never would have written this book without your encouragement.

This manuscript only turned into a book due to the hard work of so many people at Berkley: my editors, Cindy Hwang and Angela Kim; Elisha Katz in marketing; publicist Chelsea Pascoe; art director and cover designer Vi-An Nguyen; production editor Liz Gluck; interior designer Shannon Plunkett; and the managing editorial team of Christine Legon, Catherine Degenaro, Dasia Payne, Sammy Rice, and Heather Haase. Thank you!

To my sweet husband, understanding children, patient cats, and supportive family members—you still can't read this book. Sorry.

Every smart thing Adrian says about art in this book came straight out of Anastacia Bersch's mouth, and every ignorant thing he says is because I didn't listen to her there. Thank you and/or I'm sorry!

I've never written a book without Celia's expert touch on the first draft, and I never want to. My books and I are so much better for having known you.

This book was nothing but a manuscript and a dream before Ali Hazelwood revised my query letter and sent it to my wonderful agent, Jess Watterson. Thank you Jess and Ali!

Jeeno, I finally wrote a story where the guy doesn't cry *at all*, not even after getting laid. Do you still love me?

Other pocket friends in All that [G]litters, Hyun Bin's Burner Phone, Getting Off on Wacker, and Berkletes: thank you for listening to me kvetch, panic, flail, and plot. This is a team sport, and every "win" owes so much to the other writers I've been fortunate enough to meet along the way.

Girlpool, you are such an awesome band. I choreographed the sex scene here to *American Beauty*. Stay horny.

Fen'Harem, this one's for you. The day after DA:D drops, I'll be back with the grossest, smuttiest, angstiest fic you've ever read, I promise.

♥ *Shep*

Keep reading for a preview from

No One Does
It Like You

ROSIE WOULD HAVE BEEN DELIGHTED WITH THE SOUTH-
ampton house party, Tom mused, leaning against the
twin bolsters of his seat belt and the cold windowpane.
She loved corny shit like lawn games and Cards Against
Humanity. This would have been her idea of a perfect vacation. She would have liked the big spread of imported
cheeses and fancy pickles he'd eaten, and she would have
been thrilled to be introduced to so many new and interesting theater people at the seated dinners, and she
wouldn't have told Tom to sit down and be quiet for the
whole drive back, because she'd liked his musical trivia
challenges too. Perhaps more important, she would also
have made sure they left the day before, by afternoon,
before traffic got bad, and certainly before the hurricane
arrived. But of course Rosie wasn't there, and now things
had gone to hell.

Three hours into their evacuation, the highway west
jammed with cars and the first bands of torrential rain
already tossing the branches of trees to the ground, Tom
was getting worried. He'd sobered up into regrets, both
for the delay and his drinking. He was from Florida. He
would never have messed around with a Category 3 hurricane on purpose; he just hadn't expected one on Long
Island in October.

The car came to a sudden halt. The rain was falling so thick and heavy that Tom could barely see out the passenger window of the back seat, where he was crowded with two other members of the cast. The windshield was little better, even with the wipers on their maximum setting, so Tom saw only the brake lights of the car in front of them illuminating the gray dark.

"Shit," said Ximena, the female lead and the car's driver. "Road's flooded ahead."

She rubbed her stomach nervously. Tom knew that Ximena was just a couple months pregnant, a fact that had presumably not come as a surprise to her or her wife but that she was not widely announcing until they were all sure their roles in the play were secure for the forthcoming transfer to Broadway, which they'd spent the weekend celebrating at a producer's vacation home.

Tom craned his head to look over the dashboard. The car in front of them, a plucky little Kia Sorento rented by the show's marquee actor, was stopped just in front of a rapidly moving brown stream where runoff from an overpass was flowing across the street and down the embankment to their left.

As he watched, the brake lights faded when Boyd put the car into park. There was no getting past the runoff, even for Boyd Kellagher.

Tom had been pleasantly surprised to land a big featured role in a well-funded off-Broadway debut even before he learned that the production had snagged Boyd for the lead. Tom was thirty-three, and his stage credits were mostly regional, mostly supporting, and mostly undistinguished. Boyd Kellagher had only this single stage credit to his name, but he *had* headlined several multibazillion-dollar superhero franchise spectacles since being plucked from Southern California car-washing obscurity on account of his extraordinary physique and darkly brooding good looks. Boyd's decision to pick up some more traditional acting chops by slumming it in the New York theater scene had catapulted their production into undeserved fame and success. Tom frequently reminded himself to be grateful; Rosie would have called his role a stepping stone. She would have been thinking about next steps already.

Tom peered out his window, squinting away from Boyd's car. He could see some dim lights through the trees, suggesting there were businesses or at least houses a few hundred feet away up the hill. They would need to ditch the cars before the main storm really hit.

Tom wiggled to get his battered denim jacket off, nearly knocking the actor sleeping to his left in the nose.

"Here," he said, offering the jacket to Ximena. "I'll get Boyd. You head out and start walking up the hill."

Boyd had sworn he was sober enough to drive, and Tom was sure two hundred pounds of muscle could efficiently metabolize a great deal of alcohol, but still nobody had wanted to ride with him. It wasn't that they *disliked* Boyd, but he was like a big exotic cat kept as a house pet: he looked majestic, but he was barely housebroken, he needed a lot of attention, and he always smelled kind of funny. So Tom and the other actors had crowded in with Ximena rather than ride with Boyd.

Tom sighed, imagining several more days trapped with Boyd in some emergency shelter or shitty motel. Boyd had decided that Tom was a *real actor* on the basis of his decade-old turn as Romeo, and he kept trying to corner him on their breaks to talk about Euripides when Tom just wanted to watch TikTok dances on his phone in peace.

Tom unlocked the car door and prepared to duck into the rain to fetch the feckless lead actor just as the brake lights in front of them flared back to red. He heard the engine turn over. Tom frowned. There was no place for Boyd to go. Ximena's car wasn't far behind him and there was very little shoulder. In front of Boyd's car, the road dipped; the water was at least a couple of feet deep and rising.

"Shit," Ximena said again, leaning forward over the steering wheel. She laid on the horn. "Don't do it. Don't do it, motherfucker."

Ximena was from Missouri, so she didn't know from hurricanes, but she surely knew about floods. She knew better than to drive through flowing water of any depth. Did Boyd?

"The water's too deep," Tom said, now really concerned. "It'll flood the engine." He fumbled for his cell phone, intending to call the big putz driving the car in front of them to tell him to desist, but he wasn't fast enough on the screen. Before he could connect, Boyd revved the engine and began to creep slowly through the water on the road.

"Boyd, stop!" Ximena yelled. Tom doubted Boyd could hear her through the storm though, and they all knew he didn't take direction well.

Tom hesitated with the door open and watched with morbid fascination, knowing what was coming.

Boyd made it no more than a dozen feet before the water rose above the level of the undercarriage, where it was sucked into the air intake and flooded the engine. The brake lights flared again, quickly followed by the cabin lights. The engine fell silent. Boyd's car was dead.

Rolling his eyes, Tom turned his attention back to his

phone, thumbing through his contacts for Boyd's number. Boyd needed to bail out and be careful about it as he went through the floodwaters, which could knock him over even at only ankle-deep. Tom didn't want to have to carry the guy up the hill to shelter.

"Oh *shit*," Ximena whispered again with additional feeling.

Tom jerked his eyes up, not understanding how the situation could be getting worse already.

The Kia, which was mostly plastic, was beginning to drift laterally as the water rose and carried it aloft.

Water had a stubborn tendency to flow downhill, which in this case was a large hill, an embankment dropping off a good ten feet into what had once been an empty drainage canal but was now a rapidly flowing stream.

"Get out now!" Tom immediately yelled, waving his arm, but Boyd either couldn't hear him or still wasn't listening. The car slowly, almost gently, drifted across the road and then began to slide down the hill. Ten feet over, it tipped sharply to the left, spun on one tire, and then disappeared from view.

The other people in Tom's car, drunk as they were, had finally cottoned on to what was happening, and they started to scream.

"Holy shit, holy shit," Tom yelped, hand reflexively caught in his hair before he remembered to move.

He jumped out of the car and ran to the edge of the embankment, looking down, full of horror as he peered to see what had happened to the Kia. He spotted it at the bottom of the hill.

It wasn't as bad as it could have been—the car had landed nose first on the concrete lip of the canal, the airbags had deployed, and Boyd's arms were moving in front of their billowing white shapes. He wouldn't have taken severe injury from the crash.

But the water was flowing around the vehicle, threatening to dislodge the car again and send it tumbling into the growing stream. The black floodwaters looked well over six feet deep, white-capped from their turbulence. They were halfway up the body of the car already.

Even if Boyd wasn't already injured, he'd drown if he was still in the car when it was pushed off the slope it precariously rested on.

Tom tested the hillside with one toe, and it promptly gave way. He scrambled back a step. It had been a dry summer, and the water was running off the ground rather than saturating it, making the earth treacherous and unsteady. It would probably send him tumbling into the ditch before he made it halfway to the Kia.

Don't die doing something that gets you described in the papers as "Florida man." That had been Rosie's number one rule, first whispered into his ear as she prevented him from stumbling in front of a Boston trolley on the night they met. Rosie would have made ten different plans to prevent this fuckup from ever occurring.

Ximena ran up next to Tom, cursing in a creative mix of Spanish and English.

"I told everyone else to call nine-one-one," she said, breath becoming ragged with alarm. "I told them we need a tow. Or a crane! How is a fire truck or anything going to get here though?"

"It won't," Tom said immediately. Emergency services wouldn't—usually couldn't—come in the middle of a hurricane. The roads were impassable, and nothing could fly in this.

"Shit. I guess we—we—we need to get down there and rescue him?" Ximena's voice stuttered with fear.

Tom found clarity in the sudden rush of adrenaline. He turned enough to meet Ximena's wide eyes for emphasis. "What do you mean *we*? You're pregnant! You have a wife and a kid on the way. Get out of here." He pointed up the hill.

Guilt flashed across her face.

"That doesn't—I mean—are *you* going to climb down there?" she demanded. She gestured at the car. Boyd still hadn't got his door open, even.

"Of course," Tom blurted out, looking at the smashed Kia. "I just—shit, I don't know."

How was he going to get out of this one?

He didn't want to die saving Boyd Kellagher, who'd gotten himself into this classic Florida-man situation all on his own. He didn't want to die at *all*.

That prime directive was only exceeded by the thought that it would be hard to live with himself if he stood by and watched a man die. Tom had managed to survive his lengthy litany of big mistakes, bad decisions, and colossal fuckups, but he didn't think there would be any coming back from this one if he didn't climb down to the drainage canal.

"Tom?" Ximena asked, shaking his arm urgently.

Tom glanced down at his phone, which was still illuminated in his hand, screen displaying his contact list. How odd, that the very next person in his contact list after Boyd was the one person Tom needed to call before doing something stupid and potentially deadly.

I can't die now, I was supposed to get Rosie back first, was the delirious thought that bubbled up to the surface of his mind, so fragile it was hard to examine. But it persisted even through the terror of the moment. How had he let it get to ten years since he'd last seen her, when he'd always thought he was supposed to get Rosie back?

Acting before he could think too hard about it, he pressed her name with his thumb and lifted the phone to his ear, leaning over to shield it from the wind and rain.

"Hey, Rosie?" Tom said when the call unsurprisingly went straight to voice mail. Who knew if this was still her number, or if she maybe had his blocked? "It's me. I'm, um. Well. I might be about to die. And in case I die, I just wanted to say I've always loved you. And if I happen to live . . . I'm sorry for everything. I really am. I wish I had the chance to make it up to you. Okay. Bye."

Tom hit the button to end the call and handed his phone to Ximena, ducking his face away from her shocked expression.

"Get inside!" he told her, even though his throat was closing up from panic, both that he might actually die and that he'd let it get to ten years somehow. "Don't wait for us."

She nodded shakily.

When he was sure she would comply, Tom rolled his shoulders back and focused on the slick ground ahead of him. He wiped all thoughts of the call he'd just made from his mind. He sent a small internal prayer to anyone listening in the sky.

And then he started sliding feetfirst down the hill.

Photo courtesy of author

Katie Shepard is, in no particular order, a fangirl, a gamer, a bankruptcy lawyer, and a romance author. Born and raised in Texas, she frequently escapes to Montana to commune with the trees and woodland creatures, resembling a Disney princess in all ways except age, appearance, and musical ability. When not writing or making white-collar criminals cry at their depositions, she enjoys playing video games in her soft pants and watching sci-fi shows with her husband, two children, and very devoted cats.

CONNECT ONLINE

KatieShepard.com

🐦 YTCShepard

📷 KatieShepardBooks

Ready to find
your next great read?

Let us help.

Visit prh.com/nextread

Penguin
Random
House